PRAISE FOR THE NOVELS
OF KENDRA LEIGH CASTLE

For the Longest Time

"A delightful story filled with endearing characters and laugh-out-loud humor."
— *USA Today* bestselling author Katie Lane

"Kendra Leigh Castle delivers a fresh and honest story guaranteed to make you smile, laugh out loud, and even shed a few tears. I can't wait to read more."
—bestselling author Candis Terry

"I enjoyed everything about this story and would say that Ms. Castle's jump from the paranormal genre to contemporary romance is a success." —Smexy Books

"[Castle's] writing is smooth and easy to follow, and she gives us a small-town romance in a place I can easily visualize. I'd recommend *For the Longest Time* to romance readers who like second-chance romance in a small town." —Harlequin Junkie

continued . . .

Also by Kendra Leigh Castle

The Harvest Cove Series

For the Longest Time
Every Little Kiss

One of
These Nights

The Harvest Cove Series

Kendra Leigh Castle

A SIGNET ECLIPSE BOOK

SIGNET ECLIPSE
Published by New American Library,
an imprint of Penguin Random House LLC
375 Hudson Street, New York, New York 10014

This book is an original publication of New American Library.

First Printing, September 2015

For more information about Penguin Random House, visit penguin.com.

ISBN 978-0-451-46760-7

Printed in the United States of America
10 9 8 7 6 5 4 3 2 1

Penguin
Random
House

To Fizgig and Daisy,
loving, lionhearted, smoosh-faced, and sorely missed

And to anyone who's ever loved a silly,
wonderful little dog

Chapter One

It was going to be one hell of a storm.

Jason Evans ducked his head, walking into a rising wind that made the leaves on the trees rattle and hiss. The air was sultry, loaded with humidity, and scented with the rain that was about to fall. He'd done plenty of work in the rain before, but today he was actually ahead of the game—there were no holes that needed digging, no trails that needed clearing, and, most important, no people who needed directions, saving, or a lecture on why they shouldn't do whatever they were doing. Most of the visitors had fled the oncoming storm, and Owens State Park was ninety-nine percent squared away, at least for the next hour or so. He'd have plenty to do once the wind had stopped throwing things around. For now, though, there was just one thing left on his list.

He was hoping the teenage kid with the awful sunburn was wrong about the noises he'd heard coming from deep in the trees along this part of the trail. The kid's flip-flops hadn't been suited to wading into the underbrush to investigate, but at least he'd been concerned enough to hunt down a park ranger.

Jason stopped near the trail marker he'd been headed for and waited, lifting his head and listening intently. At first he heard nothing but the wind in the trees and the stillness between gusts that was a sound all its own. He breathed deeply, beginning to relax. The kid had thought he'd heard a dog, and maybe he had. Could have been a camper's pet wandering where it shouldn't have been. Then again, it could have been a wild animal in the wrong place at the wrong time. The woods were full of creatures that preyed on one another. Those encounters weren't pleasant things to hear, but nature wasn't always pleasant.

Mostly, Jason just hoped that whatever the kid had heard out there was gone. He wanted to get back inside and enjoy the storm.

Encouraged by the silence, Jason gave a sharp whistle, then called, "Hey, doggie! You out there? Come here, pup!"

Almost immediately, he heard the whimper. Jason closed his eyes and cursed silently as thunder rolled overhead and rain began to patter to the ground around him, the first fat droplets wetting his face. This was going to be a soaking rain, and he was out in it. Again.

The fact that somebody's lost dog was also out in it got his feet moving. Jason left the trail and headed into the trees, his boots crunching through pine needles and twigs. He continued calling, and a stronger, sharper yelp had him shifting direction slightly. *Sounds like one of those yippy little mutts that bite everybody. Great. My favorite.* He rubbed his thumb over the old crescent-shaped scar between the thumb and forefinger on his right hand while he stepped over a fallen branch, then around a jagged old stump. When a twig snapped beneath his boot, the dog began to cry in earnest, howling for all it was worth. It definitely sounded small, Jason decided, and it sounded hurt. But the dog knew he was close, and it was strong enough to make a hell of a lot of noise. That was a good sign.

"Right here, boy," he said. "I'll get you." There was an answering bark, almost lost as the wind picked up and began to whip around him, strong enough to give Jason pause. They were under a severe thunderstorm warning, and out in the trees, with the ground already saturated from last night's heavy rain, wasn't the best place to be if this weather really got going. The sky opened up just as Jason stepped over another gnarled, moss-covered branch and saw it—a dirty tan-and-white ball tangled up in some sort of cord and an exposed root. Its dark eyes were bright and a little wild when they met his, but instead of continuing to bark, it just gave a high-pitched whimper that hit him like a gut punch.

He might not be much of a people person, but animals were his soft spot, yappy little mutts included. It was one of the reasons he'd become a park ranger. He got at least as much time with wildlife as he did with humans. Raccoons and Homo sapiens could both be assholes, but raccoons tended to be more entertaining about it.

Jason focused on the little dog, forgetting the rain soaking him. He made his way to it, then crouched down, mindful of the way wounded animals could react to well-meaning humans. "Hey, little guy," he said softly, and he saw its tail—a curled plume that it probably carried proudly under better circumstances—begin to flutter. The dog whined again and tried to come to him, its bowed front legs scrabbling at the ground without propelling the dog anywhere. Between the dog's fruitless struggle to get to him and the look on its odd, smooshed-in face, the sight melted him.

"Poor puppy," Jason said softly, gently reaching out. He half expected to soon find its sharp little teeth in his skin, right in the soft spot already scarred from Great-Aunt Tilly's Maltese. Instead, the dog quivered beneath his touch, then began licking furiously at his hand while Jason tried to figure out how it was caught. The sky above flickered with light, then crackled and boomed. The rain slapped his face when the wind gusted, plastering his hair against his head, but Jason barely noticed. Someone—someone not fit for animal ownership—had tied a thin cord around the little creature's neck so tightly that it was a wonder it hadn't strangled itself out here. That cord, which looked to be maybe four feet long, had snagged on the root, and the dog had wrapped itself around it good. Jason pulled a utility knife from his belt and cut the cord, finding his arms immediately full of ragged, wet, wriggling fur. A startled laugh escaped him.

"Okay, now. It's okay. Just chill out—I've got you." He liked big dogs, slobbery dogs that chased sticks and chewed giant bones and had big, shaggy heads. Fussy little pillow dogs just weren't his thing. So the rush of affection he felt for the animal he'd just freed surprised him. That intensified, and mingled with something darker, when a stroke of his hand made it yelp in pain.

Jason glowered at the blood on one of the dog's haunches. He'd seen this kind of thing before. Somebody had been having some fun with a BB gun.

"Hell," Jason muttered. He gathered the dog in his arms—all maybe ten pounds of it—and stood, holding tightly as another gust of wind tore at them. "Come on. My cousin Jake'll fix you up." There were perks to being related to the town veterinarian. Being able to get this sodden, wounded pup treated ASAP was one.

He began to clomp back through the trees, his boots sinking into soft and muddy ground. The next roll of thunder was so loud he could feel it reverberate all the way through him, and the wind pushed him so hard that he staggered to one side before bracing himself against it again. Unease unfurled in the pit of his stomach as the trees around him crackled and creaked, and a rushing sound filled his ears, blocking out everything else.

When the big old pine tree started to come down, time seemed to slow. Jason was incredibly aware of every tiny movement he made, from clutching the dog more closely to his chest to dodging out of the way and slamming his foot down into a shallow depression in the ground that had been concealed by leaves and debris. He felt a rush of air, scented with a whiff of pine, at the same instant his leg twisted oddly and then snapped. He felt it break, felt the searing pain shoot directly up his injured limb, so intense that it stole his breath. Jason landed hard on one hip, and the world went gray for a few long moments. When the woods, the storm, came back into focus even more sharply than before, he began to wish he'd blacked out. Shock became agony. When he could breathe again, he drew in a giant lungful of air and roared. The dog in his arms shivered, a dim reminder that he wasn't alone out there. Jason released it as gently as he could, then clutched at the leg now bent at a strange angle. Nausea roiled in the pit of his stomach.

When he could organize his thoughts into something coherent, he grabbed at the radio on his belt to call for help, then curled forward, hands over his face. Through waves of pain, he felt a gentle pawing at his thigh, then heard a soft sound of complaint just before a small, wet, injured dog clambered into his lap. Jason slid his hands down to look into a pair of dark and serious eyes focused intently on him. *You take care of me,* that look seemed to say, *and I'll take care of you.*

The idea of this particular dog being able to take care of anybody should have been laughable. Right now, however, it wasn't a sentiment he was in any position to argue with.

"Okay," Jason growled, putting one hand lightly on the dog's soaked back. He was surprised to find its warmth comforting. "Okay. We'll talk about it. Later."

That seemed to be good enough for the dog, which turned its head to look out into the woods. *Keeping watch,* Jason thought, and wasn't sure whether to laugh or cry. Still, a ten-pound guardian was better than none. Right now, he'd take what he could get.

The wind whipped around them, buffeting Jason and his small would-be protector. Then he heard a siren, distant but getting louder, and knew that Brent had been quick about calling in the emergency from the station. Lightning made the air around him flicker, and another violent burst of thunder echoed so loudly that he felt he must be at the center of it. He heard a sharp crack nearby as another tree gave way, not nearly so close this time, thankfully.

One hell of a storm, he thought. *It sure is.*

Jason breathed out on a moan of pain and focused on the steady breathing beneath his hand. He'd be fine, he told himself. A broken leg wasn't the end of the world, even if it felt like it right this second. He'd manage. He always did, especially when he had a job to do.

And as unlikely as it seemed, right now, he had a lap full of wet fur that said he was needed, and might be for quite some time . . . whether he had volunteered for it or not.

* * *

Zoe Watson adjusted the painting, took a step back, and eyed the grouping she'd just put together.

"What do you think of this?" she asked, tilting her head and narrowing her eyes. She could spend hours arranging and rearranging the work on display at her gallery, Two Roads. She found it soothing, even though it drove her assistant crazy. She knew this because Samantha Henry, now Samantha Smith in her day-to-day life, was more than just her right-hand woman and one of the gallery's top-selling artists. She was also her closest friend in Harvest Cove—close enough to have told Zoe on numerous occasions that she needed to find a better hobby before Sam lost it and stabbed her with a palette knife.

"It looks great."

Zoe turned her head to glare at the pretty blonde who sat at the antique desk they were currently using to handle purchases and some of the paperwork. Sam's head was down as she scrawled something on a Post-it, then stuck it on what looked to be a contract.

"You didn't even look!"

"Yes, I did," Sam said calmly, with a brief glance up. Zoe got a glimpse of striking blue-green eyes before Sam refocused on whatever she was doing. "It looks almost exactly the same as it did the last time you asked me to look. You know, ten whole minutes ago."

Zoe tapped a finger against her hip. "Part of your job is to indulge me, you know."

"Is it? Somehow, I don't remember signing anything that spelled that out."

"You're a terrible henchman, Sam," Zoe said with a sigh. "You're supposed to ooh and aah over everything I do, which in turn will give me the confidence I need to take over the world."

Sam looked up, propped her chin on her folded hands, and smiled innocently. "We prefer 'henchwomen.' And if you want me to look at a virtually unchanged grouping of paintings twenty times in the space of an hour while stroking your ego, we're talking overtime and extra perks."

Zoe wrinkled her nose. "Thanks a lot, henchwoman."

"You don't like it, take it up with the union."

Zoe gave a soft huff, but she was smiling when she turned to look at her handiwork again. It really *hadn't* changed much in the last hour. Enjoyable though fiddling had been, it was probably time to pack it in.

"Fine. You win. I'll leave it alone. For now."

"That 'for now' means I never really win." Sam sighed, rising to brace her hands on the small of her back and stretch.

"Come on, now. Every day with me is its own reward." That earned Zoe a grin.

"Of course it is, O Benevolent Ruler," Sam said, then glanced at the small silver watch on her wrist. "Any big plans for the evening? I heard a rumor that today is Friday."

"I heard the same rumor," Zoe replied. "I have plans."

That piqued Sam's interest, as Zoe knew it would. "Seriously? What kind of plans?"

Zoe had a brief, intense urge to make up something interesting—something involving a handsome stranger, a candlelit dinner, and the unspoken potential for the kind of date that was likely to continue through the following morning. Except Sam would know she was full of it, because ever since they'd known each other, Zoe hadn't been a spontaneous, wildly romantic date kind of person. She never really had been, much as she loved imagining such things.

Coming to Harvest Cove from Atlanta, Georgia, had been her choice. Starting a new life here, trying to plant some roots and make a go of her gallery: also a choice. The lack of attention she'd paid to her personal life had been less of a choice, more of a necessity while she'd been getting things off the ground, but lately, Zoe had started to wonder whether she'd been a little *too* determined to fly solo until she got settled in here. Because it didn't get much more settled—or much more single—than she was right now.

And her current dry spell, not counting a brief and ill-advised interlude with an egocentric orthodontist, was at three years and counting.

"It's true," Zoe finally said, trying not to let her sudden pang of melancholy creep into her voice. "My plans involve a comfy couch, some hot tea, my favorite blanket, some snuggling—"

"With the blanket, right?"

"Maybe."

Sam groaned and rolled her eyes. "Zo, we've talked about this. Binge watching recorded TV shows is not a substitute for actual human interaction. Why don't you come hang out with me and Jake? We were talking about going down to Beltane Blues and having a drink later."

"Just the two of you?"

"Emma and Seth might join us," Sam replied. "Maybe Shane and Fitz. So don't start with the third-wheel thing again, because you wouldn't be. You never are." Sam closed the distance between them and gave Zoe's arm a tug. "Come on . . . it's been a while since you let us drag you out. You're getting as bad as Emma used to be."

"Hey, you be nice about your sister," she said. Emma Henry was a little older than Sam and a lot more uptight, but she'd come a long way since her drunken dance at Sam's bachelorette party had given her a dose of unwanted local fame. Of course, the fact that her fiancé, Seth Andersen, was the laid-back, quiet type was probably just as much of a factor in her recent loosening up as her brief brush with notoriety.

That was how it should be with couples, Zoe thought. They should bring out each other's better natures. Lately she thought her better nature might have packed up and gone on permanent vacation, probably somewhere tropical with a lot of half-naked men. If it was smart, anyway. "Not all of us are born party animals, you know," she added, dismayed that her voice came out as a surly grumble.

"I know, because I'm not one, either," Sam replied, ignoring Zoe's tone. "But there's a lot of space between party animal and hermit. Even Aaron's been threatening to show up at your door, slap a sparkly bathrobe on you, and force-feed you Jell-O shots until you start having fun again. And I think he's serious."

"He usually is, underneath the sass." Aaron Maclean was a successful sculptor and one of her closest friends. He also took great pleasure in being a complete pain in her butt, though she loved him for it. Zoe rolled her shoulders uncomfortably, allowing herself a brief fantasy of having someone waiting at home to rub the knots out of them before banishing the images to the mental dustbin marked "Unnecessary Distractions." That thing was full to overflowing, Zoe thought with a wry smile. Kind of like the vacuum she kept in the closet in her office. Full of dust, dirt, sticks, the occasional rock . . .

"You're starting to sound just like Treebeard, you know that?"

Zoe wrinkled her nose at her nickname for Jason Evans, otherwise known as the Most Unnecessary Distraction of All. The big, surly park ranger darkened her doorstep at least once a week and seemed to take great pleasure in tracking in dirt, spending some time sparring with her, and buying something just often enough that she couldn't justify booting him out. Calling him Treebeard, after Tolkien's slow-moving and treelike Ent, made her feel a little better about the encounters. Especially because Jason didn't know she called him that.

It was as though she'd summoned him into the conversation just by thinking of the messes he left for her to clean up, courtesy of his giant boots.

"I do not."

"Do, too. You two ought to start a club for antisocial hot people. You'll be the only members, and I'll be the outside consultant who sets up your activities since neither of you likes to do things."

The thought of being alone with Jason was way more appealing than it should have been ... which would explain why she'd spent a fair amount of time pondering the scenario. Outwardly, Zoe brushed off the teasing.

"No way. I know enough about how your twisted little mind works. I don't need to see what you'd come up with for awkward seduction scenarios, which is all those so-called activities would be."

"By 'awkward' I'm going to assume you mean 'amazingly smooth.'"

"Amazingly *something*, anyway," Zoe replied. "Kind of like you, in fact."

Sam snorted. "You love me. Me and my schemes for

getting you and Jason together for an evening of hard liquor and strip poker."

"Setting aside the fact that I don't even know how to play poker . . . oh my God."

"Exactly." Sam's evil grin made her laugh, at least. And it was a good reminder that one thing she *did* have here in Harvest Cove was friendship. The important, tell-each-other-anything kind. The sort of friendship that stayed.

"There. You don't look quite as stabby now, at least. Remember that the next time you disparage my skills as a henchwoman."

Zoe laughed again and shook her head. "I'll try. And I'm not stabby. Just tired, I guess. Long week."

"Longer when you don't take days off," Sam admonished her, but her voice was full of affection. "Well, you've earned hanging out with your blanket and TV if that's what you want to do. But we'd love to have you along if you want to come tonight, okay?"

She was being let off the hook, Zoe knew. But that was Sam's way. Never a frontal assault, just a little smacking around with a velvet glove, followed by a hug. That was usually all that was needed, and this time was no different.

"I probably could stand to spend some time in civilization. Maybe I'll swing by. Okay?"

Sam's smile was immediate and full of delight. "Way more than okay. We should be there around eight."

Zoe bit back a groan, partly in complete disgust with herself. When eight o'clock sounded late, when the thought of being in her favorite pajamas at that hour on a Friday night was preferable to anything else she could think of, she worried she was turning into her grandmother. And at thirty-two, she was hardly grandmother material.

Whatever was wrong with her lately, she needed to break the cycle, Zoe decided. Maybe it was the fact that her friends all seemed to be moving into the coupled-up phase of their lives. Maybe she was still down from her brother Marcus heading back home after his visit. But she needed a change, and there was a cute little halter top with the tags still on it hanging in her closet at home that had *How* you *doin'?* written all over it. She'd been waiting to take it for a spin—knowing that the wait might wind up being forever—but really, there was no time like the present.

"All right," Zoe said lightly. "I'll see you there a little after eight."

Sam clapped her hands together, then did a small happy dance that shouldn't have been possible in heels. "Yes!"

"Don't get too excited. You know I'm only good for a couple of hours before I need to go curl up in a corner somewhere."

Sam waved her hand dismissively. "And you know I'm the same way. We can use each other as an excuse to bail and go watch some trash TV together when we've had it. And the people watching should be good in the meantime."

This, Zoe thought with a smile, was one of the many reasons she loved Sam. Though they operated at different levels of sociability, they were both homebodies at heart. She started to head back to her office, then paused, suddenly suspicious.

"You didn't find a way to drag Treebeard out of his forest to meet us tonight, did you?" she asked, turning back to narrow her eyes at Sam.

"Uh, that would require superpowers I don't possess, but I'm flattered you think I could manage it," Sam replied.

Zoe expected to feel relief, but there was some definite disappointment mingling with it. Sam was right. She really *did* need to get out more, especially if she was missing the sight of Jason Evans.

"I've seen you be formidable when you want to be," Zoe replied, then waved a hand. "Just making sure. You brought him up, so I thought maybe you'd cooked up some kind of crazy plan." She frowned. "You know, he hasn't been in to pester me in a couple of weeks. It's a little strange. I hope he wasn't eaten by bears or something."

Sam tilted her head, a puzzled smile playing at the corners of her mouth. "You mean you didn't hear?" The surprise in Sam's voice meant that she'd managed to miss out on some widespread local gossip, a subject Zoe prided herself on keeping up with. She might not be from the Cove, but this was her home now, and she liked to know what was going on. Things that escaped her notice irritated her, especially when they were things she tried so hard to pretend to ignore.

"Hear *what*?" she asked.

"Jason got caught out in those severe storms that came through last week. The ones that caused that nasty accident out on Juniper, with the hail? Some trees came down, and he broke his leg getting out of the way of one of them. Totally out of commission for the time being." Sam's look turned sheepish. "Sorry. I thought you knew."

"No." It was unexpected news, accompanied by an equally unexpected burst of concern that hit her like a punch to the gut. She spent a lot of time telling herself she didn't like Jason. Almost as much time as she spent wondering when he'd be in to bother her again. She felt her cheeks heating as Sam watched her, an involuntary reaction that was entirely unwelcome. She didn't fluster easily. And certainly not over men like *Treebeard*.

"Are you . . . blushing?" asked Sam, watching her with more interest—not to mention amusement—than she thought was warranted. Zoe gave her a warning look and turned on her bootheel to head for her office. Naturally, Sam followed.

"You *are* blushing! Aha!" she said, trailing her.

"Aha nothing," Zoe said without turning her head. She opened the door to her little office, which she thought of as Command Central. She kept it as neat as she could, but the paperwork was a constant battle. And if she let it go for a couple of days, the various cups she drank her tea out of began threatening a hostile takeover of her space. It hurt her neat freak's heart, but it seemed like the nerve center of her tidy little universe was destined to stay just a little messy. Zoe inhaled deeply, surveying the clutter, and tried to push the current conversation out of her mind. "I've been slacking. These cups have got to go."

"You know," Sam said in a tone that clearly indicated she was about to say something Zoe wouldn't like, "since you brought him up, Jason *is* a loyal customer. It might be nice to send, I don't know, a get-well card or something."

"*You* brought him up, remember? I just didn't know he'd busted his leg. I'm sure it's done wonders for his personality. Surprised he didn't bite the doctors who treated him." She stacked four cups one inside the other, straightened a stack of papers, and then braced her hands on the desk without turning around, dropping her head. "You're serious. You want us to send him a fruit basket."

"I know you don't like him all that much—well, you're good at pretending not to, anyway—but it'd be a nice gesture." Sam's voice was full of gentle, affectionate reproach.

"I don't dislike him. I don't *anything* him. Apart from his purchasing habits and his dirty footprints, Treebeard isn't even on my radar."

"Which is why he merits a special nickname, at least one daily mention, and those fire-engine red cheeks?"

Zoe turned to give Sam a pained look. "Really? We're going to go *there* again?"

"Nope," Sam replied. "Mostly because I value my life, and I really want you to come out tonight. I'm just saying that despite his more frustrating qualities, Jason has been supportive of the gallery in his own special way. He'd probably appreciate the well-wishes."

Zoe grabbed her big leather tote and slung it over her shoulder, heaving a loud sigh. "You may be right. I'm just finding the whole appreciative-Treebeard thing hard to picture. He doesn't respond to nice, that I've seen."

Sam's brows lifted. "You've tried nice?"

"In *my* own special way."

"Hmm." Sam waited as Zoe grabbed a few things she needed, slid them into her tote, and then walked out of her office.

"You're still following me, I see," Zoe said calmly as she checked the locks and switched off most of the lights. "Okay. Will it make you happy if I say I'll send a card? Maybe some flowers? Though he'd probably rather have a bundle of twigs. Seems like it'd be more his thing. He could light them on fire, poke people with them. . . ."

"Yes, it'll make me happy. Unless you really do send twigs." Sam laughed softly. "Some dog food and a few squeaky toys might be more useful."

Zoe turned, frowning. "Why? Is this some weird fetish of his I don't want to hear about, or did that man give up on humanity altogether and decide to inflict himself on some poor animal instead?"

Though it wasn't an expression she saw from her often, Zoe thought that Sam looked a little smug. It was rare that she knew something before Zoe heard about it, and she was obviously relishing the triumph.

"Neither. Well, maybe a little of the second thing, but not on purpose. Jason was out in the storm because he was saving a dog." When Zoe simply stared, unable to quite process that, Sam elaborated. "One of the park guests had heard it crying. Jason found it all wrapped up in a cord, caught on a root. And somebody had shot it with a BB gun."

Oh, hell no. I'm not going to feel mushy about this. I am not.

Zoe opened her mouth to say something dismissive, but all that came out was a soft, high-pitched sound: "Aww."

"I *know*, right?" Sam replied, eyes rounding. "Jake got her all fixed up, though. She's going to be okay. She also seems to be a stray, or at least nobody's looking for her. I think Seth would adopt her in a heartbeat—he said he had a dog just like that when he was a kid—but I don't think Jason's interested in giving her up. She's a sweetie."

"So, not just a dog, but a girl dog?"

"Yep."

Zoe shook her head. "Well, since that's probably as much female companionship as he gets . . . good for him, I guess. Dog probably minds the debris field less."

The idea of Jason Evans, Animal Savior and Softy, wasn't one Zoe could quite reconcile with her mental image of him. So she set it aside as best she could, squared her shoulders, and decided to end the conversation before she was confronted with any other information she didn't know how to handle. Like maybe that Big Al Piche, who was the Cove's bizarre, weirdly intelligent village idiot, was a James Bond–level international superspy.

Though all things considered, Big Al being a spy was easier to believe than Jason having a heart of gold.

"I'll make sure we get something over to him," Zoe said, then shifted gears. "So, are we doing food tonight, or just drinks? I'll wait to eat if this is a late dinner thing."

She caught the knowing look Sam gave her, but Zoe didn't care if she'd been smooth about changing the subject. She wasn't about to let Jason take up any more of her time than he already had.

Especially, she thought as she locked the gallery door, because he already took up a lot more time than anyone, even—*especially*—Jason himself, knew.

Chapter Two

"Mom, really, it's okay. No, no, I'm happy to have you come for a visit, but a week is more than enough. Yeah, I know I'm going to need help for a while."

Jason sat on the couch and glared at his bum leg, the lower half of which was immobilized in a clunky cast. His leg might be the issue, but this whole thing was a giant pain in his ass. He adjusted the phone between his shoulder and his ear and listened to another dozen reasons why his mother was coming to take care of him, possibly forever. Her voice, calm and deceptively patient, continued to gently pummel him. People thought she was sweet. She was . . . sort of . . . but they tended to miss the steel underneath. He didn't, and he knew when he was in for it. This was one of those times.

"Honey, I know you don't like anyone fussing over you, but I remember what it was like when your father broke his arm falling off that ladder a few years ago. He needed a lot of help, and I'm sure you do, too. Are you eating? You never did cook; you're probably just living on cereal. Do you have any clean clothes? I know you don't, Jason Patrick Evans, and don't even think about lying to me. You need help, and I'll be there on Sunday, just like we planned."

"Like *you* planned," Jason muttered, which earned him a sharp snort from the woman who he had once been convinced kept the entire planet from spinning off its orbit and out into space through sheer force of will. He'd gotten his stubbornness from her. That was one reason why occupying the same enclosed space with her for an extended period of time filled him with dread. He loved his mother dearly, but he gave it a matter of hours before she was after him about everything from his holey old boxer shorts to his lack of a social life. And right now, the state of his house wasn't going to help his cause.

Jason scanned the high-ceilinged great room, which encompassed most of the log home's living space, and winced. Dust swirled lazily in a sunbeam. Dishes sat haphazardly in the sink. Clothes were tossed over the furniture, left there because just getting them off was enough of a chore right now. The sight did nothing for his mood — he was a lot of things, but a slob wasn't one of them. Unfortunately, his plans of powering through this with sheer orneriness weren't working out that well so far.

"If I didn't do the planning, nothing would happen. You'd sit there and fester until your cousin called me out of desperation, and we'd be back at the same place." She sighed, and guilt mixed with his frustration. He didn't want to upset her. He just wanted to crawl in a hole somewhere until his leg was better.

"Sorry, Mom."

"Uh-huh. I'm used to it. You were never a treat when you were sick. Unlike your brother. You know he still asks me to come make him soup when he gets a cold."

Jason bit back a groan. This was one of the many reasons he had to find a way to give this impending visit a definite end point, and the sooner the better. He didn't want daily updates on the endless charms and delights of his baby brother, who had oozed perfection from his pores since birth. At least, according to the rest of the family. It wasn't that he didn't love Tommy. It was just that Tommy had never really seemed to need it . . . he got more than enough love from everybody else.

Story of his life.

"When your father gets back from this fishing trip they've got him going on for work—I don't think for a second it's not just an excuse for a bunch of them to escape onto the water and drink too much for a few days, but they're calling it work—he said he'd like to come out to stay for a bit, too, not just to get me and run. He has plenty of vacation time saved up. Maybe we can get your brother to come visit, too, at least for a weekend. What do you think? We haven't all been together since last Thanksgiving, and that was only for a couple of days. I miss the Cove this time of year. You know we love Florida, but it's hotter than hell right now and I don't want to learn to fish, even if your dad does keep after me about it. Oh, if we can get you up and around, maybe we can go to the field days! I told Tammy and Paul I was coming into town, and they said . . ."

Her words washed over him, but Jason stopped hearing them. It all sounded like a rushing, rising wave of pure panic to him. He had to do something. Anything. Otherwise, his small sanctuary in the woods was quickly going to become his idea of hell on earth. Unfortunately, in his current condition, running away until further notice wasn't a viable option.

It took a few seconds for the soft knocking at his door

to register, and even then he might not have noticed but for the way the bundle of tan-and-white fur that had been sleeping smashed up against his thigh suddenly burst into motion, barking furiously as she flew off the couch and scrambled toward the door.

Her injuries sure hadn't slowed her down any, Jason thought, ruefully amused. *That makes one of us.*

"Oh, somebody there?" his mother asked.

"Yeah, probably just Jake. He said he was going to swing by after work to check on me." He covered the receiver for a minute to call out, "Come in!" over the wild barking before returning his attention to the conversation at hand.

"Your cousin is sweet. I hope you appreciate what he's doing."

"Sure," Jason drawled. "He comes over, I verbally abuse him until I get tired, he plays with Rosie, and we both end the day happy. It works out."

"Jason."

He was in mid-smirk when he heard the light tap of a heel on his floor. A familiar—and very feminine—voice reached his ears and rippled all the way through him. Just the way it always did.

"Hello?"

He took a breath, pushed aside his immediate instinct to whip his head around and start snarling at her out of complete mortification at what she must be seeing, and managed a reasonably civil, "Hey," with a slight turn of his head. "I'll just be a . . . second."

Jason had to force the final word out, since his brain stalled the second he caught sight of her. He was used to seeing Zoe Watson in what he thought of as her work uniform: long, loose shirt, sometimes a sweater, usually with an incomprehensibly tied scarf, over leggings and a pair of boots from Zoe's wide and varied collection. The woman seemed to have some weird riding-boot fetish. Not that there was anything wrong with that. But this was after work—the first time he'd ever actually seen her outside the gallery, he realized—and either she was deliberately messing with his head or there was a lot he didn't know about Zoe.

Probably both.

She was wearing one of those shirts that looked like a silky handkerchief that had been cleverly tied to her in a couple of key spots, along with a pair of skinny white pants cut a few inches too short and some kind of strappy heels that made his mouth water despite the fact that they made no sense to him. Zoe was little, maybe five-two, and he knew she had a great figure, but this evening she was showcasing her hourglass curves in a way he'd only imagined. Every inch of her, from her long, shapely legs to the curve of her backside to the graceful neck she almost never showed off, was a feast for his eyes. Her mocha skin had a warm glow in the hazy light filtering in through the windows.

It took longer than it should have for him to realize she was watching him closely—curiously. However he'd been staring at her, she didn't seem to know quite what to do with it.

"Not a problem," Zoe said with a small smile. "I'll wait." Her big gray eyes regarded him with something like amusement before she shifted a potted plant she was carrying from one arm to the other and dropped into a crouch to fuss over Rosie. Jason tried to collect his thoughts, aware his mother was insistently repeating a few words. A question? Yeah, it was a question.

"Jason, *who is that*? Because if I didn't know any better, I'd say it was a woman."

Jesus, you'd think she just spotted a unicorn.

He readjusted the phone against his ear, listening to Zoe croon at his dog. He hadn't had her pegged as a dog person. He hadn't really pegged her as an anything person, actually. He was usually too busy trying not to drool on himself while he was arguing with her. The body might be heavenly, but her face, a perfect oval with a pert little nose and full lips she often painted some lickable shade of red, not to mention those *eyes*, was enough to knock any sane man on his ass. He'd been sure he was building up immunity thanks to their regular arguments.

So much for that.

"Jason, are you still there? Who—"

A thought occurred to him then, just a wisp of an idea stamped This Might Work. He grasped at it like a drowning man confronted with the bobbing remnants of a shattered ship. It might not be enough to save him, and Zoe would probably kill him anyway, but what choice did he have?

"That's Zoe, Mom." He saw her look up sharply from where she was petting Rosie.

"Oh?" It was a loaded question, and he knew it. He could hear all the other questions running just beneath the surface of that single, simple word. Zoe rose and came to stand before him, one hand on her hip in a stance he was well acquainted with by now. The arched eyebrow meant she was curious, but the hand on the hip? It didn't bode well for him.

Maybe she'd cut him some slack because he was injured. He was also desperate. And so while Zoe stared at him, he told Molly Evans the biggest lie since she'd been on the front porch at two a.m. asking his seventeen-year-old self whether he'd been drinking. "Yeah, well, she's been helping me out. That's why I'm not sure about all these plans you've got going. . . . I mean, I'd love to have everybody for the rest of the summer, but my place is pretty small and she's, you know"—he scrubbed a hand through his hair—"around a lot."

Zoe's mouth dropped open.

Yep, I'm dead.

To Zoe's credit, she didn't hurl the potted plant in her hands at his head. She looked like she wanted to, but she didn't. Instead, her storm gray eyes full of fire, she mouthed, *I will kill you.*

There was a moment of dead silence. Then his mother spoke: "Well, *finally!*"

Her laugh, her voice, held so much relief that any hope that his relationship status had ceased to be a topic of interest in the family evaporated. They still talked about him—poor, lonely, brokenhearted Jason—because of course they did. Because of Sara. When the divorce had been finalized, he'd assumed she was gone for good. He hadn't known that just the idea of her would continue to give him problems four years on. And as hard as she'd been at the end, he didn't think this was what Sara had intended, either. She'd just wanted to go. In the end, he'd let her.

He just wished everybody else would, too.

As Zoe's jaw tightened and the hand at her hip curled into a claw, Jason tried to tell himself that what he'd just done was no big deal. A girlfriend, even an imaginary one, would make his mother quit worrying and save him from weeks of having a social life forced on him when all he really wanted to do was convalesce and brood. It might keep Tommy Evans, Local Superstar, down in Miami where he belonged instead of up here showing off. Zoe didn't even have to be around. Hell, he'd invent a different Zoe if he had to, and then send her on an equally imaginary vacation or ... something. But no matter how he tried to sugarcoat it, he couldn't escape the fact that he'd just dragged the real Zoe into his life in a big way, without asking permission, and with a whole lot of potential ramifications that she seemed fully aware of. That was why she was going to kill him. He probably deserved it.

But that was still a more appealing thought than having his family pile in on him for a month.

Damn. This is a new low.

His mother's voice chirped happily in his ear, pulling him back into a conversation he had no idea how to participate in. Not with Zoe's death stare fixed on him. He held up one hand toward her, tried for an expression that he hoped was somewhere in the vicinity of too-pathetic-to-annihilate, and mouthed the words, *Wait. Please.*

"Hey, Mom, look, I've gotta go." Jason hoped he didn't sound as panicked as he felt. "Yep, see you Sunday." He was ready to hang up when she said the words that shoved a sliver of ice-cold fear directly through his heart.

"I can't wait to meet the mystery woman."

She was being perfectly sincere. But as it tended to do on the rare occasions he slipped into panic, the verbal tic Jason had worked so hard to rid himself of when he was a child returned to tie his tongue in knots. "I-I-I-I'm sure she'll be h-happy to meet you, too."

Nice. In front of Zoe, even. You're on a roll today, man.

Zoe's expression changed, ever so slightly, and Jason looked away. He had to. The last thing he needed was a dose of pity from a woman who was already way the hell out of his league. His mother clucked her tongue at him across the miles. "Oh, don't be nervous, honey. I'm sure I'll love her. It's about time you found somebody who appreciates you. After all Sara put you through, you deserve it."

"Uh." It was the only response he could muster, but she didn't seem to mind.

"Love you, see you Sunday!" she chirped. "I'll call once Moira picks me up and we're on our way!"

His aunt Moira, Jake's mother. A woman who knew damn well he wasn't dating anyone. His spur-of-the-moment plan was already in flames, and he hadn't even hung up the phone. Maybe he ought to be glad he now had an epic fail like this to hold up as the ultimate proof that he really just needed to give up on having a social life.

"Bye," Jason said, his voice barely a growl, and hung up. He tossed the phone to the side, where it landed between a couple of couch pillows, and shoved his face into his hands. He didn't need to look at Zoe's face to know what must be written all over it. There was a long moment of silence. And then finally, in a voice that would have been as rich as cream but for the violence vibrating through it, Zoe spoke. Carefully. Deliberately.

Homicidally.

"What. Did. You. Just. Do?"

Chapter Three

Zoe stared at the big scruffy idiot on the couch and tried to decide whether the man was some sort of cosmic punishment for a whole lot of wrongs committed in a former life. If he was, then his continuing torment of her might make some kind of sense. If he wasn't, well . . . somebody up there had a very twisted sense of humor.

Even now, laid up with one leg in a clunky cast and wearing a pair of ragged old cargo shorts and a T-shirt that had seen better days, Jason was too appealing for his own good. *Nasty, miserable, inappropriately attractive dirt farmer.* He lifted his face from his hands to look at her, and it was hard not to feel sorry for him. Well, a little sorry. The rest of her was too busy being furious with him right now.

"I can explain," he said, the low rumble of his voice rippling through her in ways that were just as inappropriate as the rest of him. His brown eyes were pleading, a new look for him. They were also flecked with gold when the light hit them, a fact Zoe had been determinedly ignoring ever since he'd first clomped into her gallery. Not that it was ever easy. And not that she ever really managed it anyway. His fault, obviously. Right now, she was happy to blame him for everything from his pretty eyes to the phases of the moon.

"Explain what?" she snapped. "Why you just told your mother I was your girlfriend? Good, because this is something I really have to hear."

"I didn't say that." Now he was getting defensive, and that was something she *was* used to. She stared at his guilty face—his annoying, ruggedly handsome, guilty face, with all its interesting angles and stubble and *Damn it, Zoe, focus*—and pressed her lips together, exhaling loudly.

"Jason," she said, "I am standing right here. Don't you lie to my face."

He screwed up his mouth and seemed to consider this, then winced as he shifted uncomfortably on the couch. His little dog jumped up beside him, panting happily as she settled herself against his side. Jason stroked her absently. Rosie, he'd called her. The fluffy little flat-faced dog, who'd done a happy dance while she'd petted her, was about the last kind of creature she would have expected to find Jason living with. Snakes, raccoons, maybe even a turtle, sure. Pampered lapdog, no. And Rosie was wearing a very sweet little pink collar. With rhinestones on it.

Zoe had no idea what to do with that, so she tried to stay focused on her anger. With Treebeard, that tended to be a good rule of thumb.

"Okay," Jason finally said. "I heavily implied it. I know."

She crossed her arms over her chest. "Yes. You do."

"I was kind of desperate."

"That's flattering."

He growled, sounding more like a bear than a human. "That's not what I mean. Zoe, look. I need help."

She kept her tone as cool and indifferent as she could. It was hard, since she'd never seen him looking this help-less or dejected before, and the way he was scratching Rosie behind her ears in a way she obviously loved was very sweet. Still, she managed.

"You do need help. All kinds of professional help." Zoe looked around at what would be a really great space minus the clutter and out of pure pique added, "You also need a maid service. Because *damn*."

His brow furrowed, and the familiarity of his glare was a weird sort of comfort. She knew where she stood if they were arguing. If they stopped doing that, then she might do something stupid, like be nice to him, and that would just lead to all kinds of trouble she didn't need. He was the furthest thing from her type possible, a leaf-covered hermit who probably thought that wearing a clean T-shirt was "dressing up." She liked men who were refined. Men who were cultured.

Well, she also fantasized about big, sexy alpha males who came from other worlds and could knock down buildings and fly and fight evil, but since Jason hadn't exhibited any superpowers except the ability to irritate her beyond all reason . . . no. Just no.

"It's usually clean, for your information. You try housekeeping with a busted leg."

"I wouldn't. I'd hire help."

He snorted and rolled his eyes. "Of course you would."

"Yes, of course I would," she shot back, letting him get to her. She always did, despite her best efforts. Some-thing about him just got her going. *Everything* about him. "Because I have a brain in my head and don't have a problem asking for help when I need it. Unlike other people who apparently have rocks in their heads and think they should just—"

She forced herself to stop and took a deep breath. If they headed down this path, she'd end up storming out of here without ever discovering why Jason had decided to make her his imaginary girlfriend. Really, really imaginary. *So* imaginary. Zoe held her hands in front of her, palms out.

"All right," she said slowly. "Let's just back it up. Forget about the clutter. What on earth possessed you to let your mother think you and I are together? And I mean, did I hear all that right? She'll be here in two days?" She searched his face for some clue as to what he'd been thinking, but he was as unreadable as ever. "What are you *doing*, Jason?"

He nodded slowly and seemed to be locking his own considerable temper away. His hand moved on Rosie's back, gentle, rhythmic, a sharp contrast to the venom that had been in his voice just a moment ago. When he locked eyes with her again, his had softened, full of a level of melancholy she wouldn't have thought him capable of.

"Okay," he finally said. He lifted his free hand to push back the wavy brown hair that was even shaggier than usual. "You want the short version or the shorter version?"

"Whichever one makes more sense."

There was a brief curve of his lips that had Zoe's breath catching, just for a beat. He wouldn't have noticed her pause . . . but she did, and she immediately wished she could kick her own butt to make it stop. If Sam ever found out just why she found Jason so frustrating, she'd never hear the end of it. Flustered, she schooled her features into polite interest and waited. Jason's flicker of humor vanished as quickly as it had appeared.

"All right, the short version. My mother is coming. She figures that me with a broken leg is a great opportunity to try and fix my life for the billionth time, mostly because I can't escape. I can handle that for a week or so, but this time it's going to be more like a month unless I've met her threshold for having my shit together. She was really winding up about her plans to include my father and little brother in the festivities, you walked in, I had a dumb idea to try and save myself, and here we are."

Zoe took a moment to process all that. It made a weird sort of sense. In a rude and unbelievably stupid way, yes, but she got it.

"What was the even shorter version?" she finally asked, curious.

This time his smile was more than a flicker, full of a boyish mischief that transformed his whole face for a brief instant. It was one of the first times she'd ever seen him look approachable. And maybe even . . . *fun*.

Dangerous stuff.

"Couple of grunts and a 'Get out,'" Jason said. "Kind of like you sound every time I walk in the gallery."

Her lips twitched with a smile she didn't want him to see. "I'm a lady. I don't grunt. And I don't tell you to get out when you remember to use that fancy doormat I bought just for you."

"I use it. You just don't think I do it right."

"Well, you *don't*." They looked at each other for a moment, and Zoe couldn't stop the soft laughter from bubbling up. This was their little routine, she guessed. Funny how comfortable it was by now. A low rumbling reached her ears, and Zoe was startled to realize that Jason was laughing with her. It made her feel uncomfortably warm and sort of mushy and strangely sweet, so she blew out a breath and looked at the ceiling. "Well. This is a new one on me—I'll give you that. I don't even know what to say."

He lifted one shoulder in a shrug. "It was a dumb idea. You don't have to say anything. I'll just . . . deal with it on Sunday. Forget about it." Then he looked away and mumbled, "My family makes me crazy."

That was something she could understand, at least. And not something she would have expected to have in common with Treebeard the Annoyingly Hot Park Ranger. Much against her better judgment, Zoe found herself intrigued. And sympathetic.

With a resigned sigh, she set the plant on an end table, then settled herself into one of the big chairs facing the couch. If she left now, she'd just spend the rest of the evening sitting at the blues bar wondering what kind of family could push big, quiet, grumpy Jason into what was definitely an act of desperation. Since denying her own natural curiosity had never been her thing, Zoe crossed her legs, folded her hands in her lap, leaned forward, and tilted her head. If he hadn't tried to kick her out already, she knew, it wasn't going to happen at all.

"That's it?" she asked.

He didn't seem to know what to do with the fact that she was still there. "What's it? I explained. I had a moment, okay? I'm not going to grovel. You can chuck that pot at my head if you want, but I'm pretty quick for a cripple, so you probably won't get a lot of satisfaction out of it."

"I may get to that later," Zoe replied. "Right now, I'm

more interested in knowing why, if you really need a way out of this visit, you didn't just *ask* for my help."

His eyebrows lifted so high she thought they might hit his hairline. "I remember saying 'I need help' and you telling me to go to the shrink, like, all of three or four minutes ago. Did I miss some kind of nuance in that?"

"Yes. For one, you didn't ask nicely," Zoe said. It was hard not to laugh at Jason's expression, which probably would have frightened small children.

"Jesus. If we're going to have a talk about saying the magic word now, I'm hobbling out the door and staying there until you find someone else to give a lecture on manners to."

"My mama was very big on manners," Zoe replied, offering a small smile. It was horrible, the fun she had poking at him. Especially when he couldn't get away from her. But if it was a vice, she figured it was a harmless enough one to indulge in, especially since Jason seemed to have the same one. "You also neglected to offer me an incentive. You didn't even try bargaining with me."

"You think this is hilarious, right? Of course you do. Your family probably thinks you walk on water. You probably had your own horse and played the violin and went to finishing school. A real southern belle, right?" His jaw tightened, and he looked as though he might like to kick her with that big cast of his. She didn't bother to correct him, but his impression of her upbringing startled her. So did the way he spat the words at her, as though a privileged background was something distasteful. Not that she would know. She'd been privileged . . . but not in the way he seemed to think.

"Yes, Jason. I drink mint juleps and have a fainting couch at home and everything. But I'm not the one dragging you into *my* business. Pretty sure I'm allowed to be curious."

He heaved a ragged sigh. "Zoe, my family's just . . . my family. You wouldn't understand unless you had to live with them. I was just trying to get her to back off a little. I don't think you want to hang out with me for a week pretending you like me. It's not like we're friends."

It was blunt, but he was right. "No," she agreed. "I guess we're more like antagonistic acquaintances. But I did bring you a present."

Jason turned his attention to the plant, which she'd repotted in a copper-colored, crackle-glazed pot she'd spent far too much time selecting at Mason's Garden Center on her way home from work. Another faint smile flickered across his face. "Yeah, I guess you did. What is that, oregano?"

"It's supposed to bring happiness," she said, surprised he'd known. "I figured you could use some."

His laugh was a low rumble that again put her in mind of a bear, though an amused one this time . . . if a bear could ever really be amused about anything.

"You got that right." He toyed absently with Rosie's fur. The little dog's eyes were half-closed, and as Zoe watched her, she gave a soft sigh, yawned, and dropped her nose onto her paws.

"Well, *she* looks happy, at least," Zoe said.

"She should. She got new digs, a vet who spoils her worse than I do, and my undivided attention. The value of that last thing is debatable, but I guess she likes it."

"Mmm," Zoe replied. Unable to resist, she added, "You pick out the collar?"

Jason looked at her balefully. "This is honestly a question?"

"Jake," Zoe guessed, and Jason nodded.

"He and Sam are helping me out with her, and every damn time she comes home it's with something new and pink. Food dishes, collar, toys." He closed his eyes and shook his head. "When I'm getting around better, she's getting new stuff. Dog looks like she belongs to either a teenage girl or a sixty-year-old socialite."

"I suppose you'll go for something leather? Studded?"

He snorted. "At this point, as long as it's not pink, pinklike, or in any way related to pink, I'm good." He looked down at Rosie, who had fallen asleep. "She's a sweet girl. I'd been thinking of getting a dog again. Granted, I was thinking of something, ah, different, but sometimes they just find you. I'd have let her go to a family or something, but she got all attached, so . . ."

He didn't finish the sentence, but the tenderness in his look when he glanced down at his sleeping companion put the lie to what he'd said. Zoe watched him, still trying to reconcile the differences between the guy who clomped into her gallery regularly looking for an argument and the one snuggling a little girly dog on his couch right now. It messed with her ideas about him in ways she wasn't entirely comfortable with. This whole situation did.

"What kind of dog did you used to have?" she asked. Immediately his gaze flicked back to her, shuttered as though she'd just asked him something far more personal.

"Golden retriever," he replied, then changed the subject back to the matter at hand. "Look, Zoe, if it makes you feel better, I'll buy something next time I'm in Two Roads, okay? Sorry for dragging you into my family crap.

I'll tell Mom I was full of it. Or if you'd rather, I'll tell her you dumped me because I was a complete asshole. Your choice."

"Gallery purchases. See? There's that incentive. You *are* teachable." She considered him for a moment. "Is it really that bad to have your family come take care of you for a month while you're down?"

His laugh was short, sharp, and humorless. "The last time she was here, my mother put me on an online dating service without asking, had the television on from six in the morning until ten at night, hid my PlayStation because she said it was making me antisocial, and spent at least an hour every day trying to get me to buy insurance from my brother."

Zoe blinked. "She did not."

"Swear to God. Week from hell. It almost broke me."

She studied his face closely for any sign that he was joking, but Jason looked deadly serious. It made her feel a lot better about her own parents, who drove her crazy only in garden-variety ways and whom she wished *would* visit her. The problem was, she was beginning to feel sorry for him. That wave of sympathy was making her question things. Maybe there were good reasons why he was quiet and surly. Maybe she'd seen only one small facet of the man. And there was the matter of that brief but unmistakable stutter when he was on the phone. . . .

Suddenly, he seemed less like the world's most irritating fantasy and more like a real person. It might— *might*—be worth checking into. After all, he was closely connected to people who were her friends. They liked him. Could be he was worth helping. Could also be that he just needed to be smacked upside the head with one of his crutches. Regardless, just like she'd told him, Jason seemed to need all kinds of help. And she needed ... something. A change. A challenge. Maybe just something to take her mind off her own boring problems. Maybe this was it.

It's just like Mama and Daddy told me when I packed up to move here. I have lost my damn mind.

Zoe sighed. Her mental state notwithstanding, she'd come to a decision. "All right," she said, and stood. She tried not to notice the way his eyes immediately skimmed down her body, or her own body's reaction to his attention. That had nothing to do with this, she told herself. And she almost believed it.

"All right what?" he asked.

"You agree to purchase an item of my choosing from the gallery—maybe another of Zeke's rockers for your porch, since I know he could use a sale—and I'll play along. There are going to be ground rules, and if things get too crazy I will fake dump you so fast your head will spin, but if a week of my time helps Zeke keep working and saves you from a new profile on scarysingles.com and insurance you don't need, I suppose I can spare it."

Jason stared at her. "You're not serious."

"You're welcome. I'll come back tomorrow and we can figure this out, but I have someplace I need to be, and frankly, I need a glass of wine."

She started for the door and immediately heard a commotion behind her as Jason struggled to get up. "Zoe ... hang on. Wait just a damn minu—" Something toppled over and hit the floor, followed by a barrage of cursing. Zoe hesitated, then turned around, walked back to the couch where Jason was now sitting with both feet on the floor, and stooped to hand him the crutches he'd managed to knock halfway under the coffee table. She almost offered to help him up, but the expression on his face made it easier to bite her tongue. Instead, she watched silently as he got up, then closed the small distance between them to tower over her the way he always did.

As usual, Zoe couldn't decide whether having all six foot four inches of him close enough to touch was a good idea or not. Because close enough to touch was close enough to smack . . . but it was also close enough to drag him down for a long, lingering—

Oh my God, I really do need a drink.

Tea was her beverage of choice for most occasions, but that just wasn't going to cut it tonight. Especially not when she was going to have to try to explain to her friends why she was about to go to a lot of trouble covering for a man she complained to them about on a regular basis.

With barely a foot between them, his presence was overwhelming. She always kept a certain amount of distance between them at the gallery, aware that getting too close would shift the power balance between them in his favor just due to his sheer physical size. She'd been right. Zoe started to bristle, but the warmth radiating from him, not to mention the scent he wore, a faint hint of woods and musk, kept distracting her.

He looked a mess, she thought, balancing there on his crutches in his ratty clothes and frowning down at her. The man needed a keeper. No sane woman would want the job, Zoe thought, and she prided herself on being very sane. But oh, did she want her hands on him, sliding under that old T-shirt over bare skin. The lust muddled her thought processes. It was the only excuse she had for not being out the door already.

She swallowed hard and wished there was a way to

back up without looking as though she was intimidated by him. Intimidated had nothing to do with it. Though she guessed that was what he was trying for.

"What the hell?" he asked.

"Is that a rhetorical question?"

"Don't be a smartass. What's this about? Is business that bad?"

She looked up at him, wondering if she'd give herself neck strain trying to maintain eye contact. "No, business is good. How did we go from 'please help me' to 'how dare you help me'? I can't keep up." She squinted into his eyes. "What kind of drugs do they have you on, anyway?"

"I'm not on anything. I should be asking you that. How is this supposed to work?" he asked. "We just irritate each other. We have ever since you showed up in the Cove, what, three years ago?"

"You mean ever since you poked your nose into Two Roads right after it opened and kept coming back. Which was three years ago, yes. You might be local, Jason, but I'm still not sure more than two words would have passed between us at this point if you didn't arrive in my presence in a cloud of dust on a regular basis." She frowned, asking the eternally puzzling question. "Why *do* you do that, anyway?"

His eyes shifted away, ever so briefly. "I like art."

Zoe shrugged. Something about the explanation didn't ring true, but pressing him on it would get her nowhere. Besides, it wasn't really relevant. "Well, this was your bright idea. As for getting along, I can manage, at least. Jake likes you, so you've got to be worth something."

"He's my cousin. He has to like me."

"I have a lot of cousins, Jason, and no, he does not. Look . . . do you want my help or not?"

He stared at her, his look turning curiously searching. Zoe didn't know what he was looking for, but after a few seconds, she felt heat creeping into her cheeks. Maybe she should have run before she'd waded into this mess. Of course, if he'd changed his mind already, it was a moot point. And since she didn't like to be told "no" once she'd made a decision, Zoe found herself in the awkward position of wanting him to let her follow through.

"Yeah," Jason finally said, and he looked so deflated that Zoe had a hard time feeling very triumphant about it. Not that there was likely to be a whole lot of win involved in lying to someone's mother in order to get her to go away. "Yeah, it's worth a shot. I can't have another visit like last time." His brows drew together, and he looked genuinely concerned. "What are you going to make me buy?"

Zoe waved her hand, too relieved to even think about messing with him. "You'll have some wiggle room on that. For now, why don't we just consider this a bonus opportunity for some mutually aggravating entertainment outside of our regularly scheduled arguing and go from there, okay?"

He still looked as though he expected her to change her mind and make a run for it. "You sure about this? You might decide it's not worth the trouble. And I'm not talking about me. What I said about my family . . . I'm not exaggerating, Zoe." He seemed serious, so she decided to answer in kind.

"They can't hold a candle to some of the customers I've dealt with. Look, we have friends, close friends, in common. It's probably about time we tried for friendly, too."

She decided his answering grunt was as good as an agreement. He needed to stop looking at her this way—

any way, in fact—for a while so she could get her head back on straight and really think about what she'd just gotten herself into. She had a feeling it wasn't going to look any saner after a couple of glasses of wine and a rehash with Sam, but hope sprang eternal. She took a step away, making sure it looked casual and not as skittish as she suddenly felt, and turned with what she hoped was confident grace.

At the very least, she didn't fall over, so that was something, because her legs weren't sure they wanted to work properly.

"Fine, then. I'll be by tomorrow around dinnertime so we can work out the details."

"I don't have food."

He was back to sounding like a disgruntled grizzly again, and Zoe was relieved. She looked back at him, one brow arched. "Of course you don't. You probably share Rosie's food. But I'll take care of it."

"I don't need taking care of."

She had to stifle a laugh, only because she thought he might actually come after her with the crutches if she let it out. The smile, though, was impossible to suppress completely. She very deliberately looked around the house, and the clutter that seemed to cling to every available surface, then looked him dead in the eye.

"Oh yes. I can see that. Still, I'll bring dinner. Have a nice night, Jason. You're welcome, by the way."

She wondered, for a brief instant, whether he would tell her to forget it. If he was miserable enough about it, she decided, she would. But a final glance at him as she turned to shut the door behind her told her that as much as he'd protested, there was no way he was going to turn her help down.

Jason hulked over his crutches while his little dog hopped back up on the couch she'd been forced to vacate, shooting her benefactor an unmistakably dirty look for disturbing her. Zoe almost smiled, but she was struck all at once by just how alone the man looked. She felt a little twist in her chest—he might have the personality of a honey badger, but why would a man so physically appealing choose to be so solitary? The state of his house just reconfirmed what Zoe had always assumed about him. He liked to keep to himself. And since she knew he had people who cared about him, he was obviously as stubborn as hell about keeping them out.

But not her. Not this time.

It might just worry her when she got around to thinking straight again.

"Zoe?"

"Hmm?"

He stared at her for a long moment, and she could see a muscle in his jaw twitch. He seemed to be struggling with something but unable to get it out, until Zoe was ready to just dismiss it and leave. Before she could, though, he ground out four words that were like music to her ears.

"Thanks. I owe you."

"I know," she said with a smile, and shut the door.

Chapter Four

"**Y**ou're going to *what*?"

Zoe paused for a moment to appreciate the looks of pure amazement on the faces of her friends before lifting her glass the rest of the way to her lips. The Cabernet she'd ordered was like velvet on her tongue, the jammy currant flavor of the wine soothing even though she hadn't had enough to do anything about the knots in her shoulders. Yet. She suspected it might be one of those rare nights she'd need a ride home.

She set the glass back on the coaster primly, folded her hands in front of her, and tried to look as unconcerned as she wished she felt.

"I'm going to help Jason convince his mother to go home," she said, hoping her voice didn't carry to any of the other tables. "He needs a girlfriend to do it, and I'm available, so . . . just play along and consider it free local theater." The band was between sets, so she didn't have to shout, at least. Still, it looked like she might have to start shouting for the people now staring at her from around the table to believe her.

Shane Sullivan, a big, handsome redhead whose mouth

was something of a local legend, was the first to react with something other than confusion. Unfortunately, that reaction was an evil grin worthy of an over-the-top B-grade horror movie, with an appropriately ominous chuckle to go with it.

"You have fun with that."

"And just what is that supposed to mean?" Zoe demanded. "You look like you'd be twirling your mustache if you had one."

His friend Fitz, who'd been quietly nursing a beer beside him, was the one who answered. "He would be. He was the villain in every play our high school put on when we were there."

Zoe blinked and stared at Shane, who'd stopped looking smug and started glaring at his friend. "You were into theater? I thought you were some big obnoxious jock."

Shane's voice lowered to a growl. "I *was*."

"He pretended he was just doing it for the girls," Fitz replied, relaxing back in his chair. "Of course, no one knew that he went to see *Phantom of the Opera* twice with his mom in New York. And *Les Mis* when it was on tour . . ."

"Damn it, Fitz!"

Zoe laughed along with the rest of their small group as Shane hunched over his drink and turned a shade of red close to the color of his hair. It wasn't often she got to see the man taken down a peg, but Fitz, though relatively quiet, was usually the one to do it. She shook her head as Jake needled him a little more, looking around at the group crowded around one of the bar's bigger round tables. It was a motley crew—the infamous Henry sisters, Sam and Emma; Jake, the local vet; Shane, who was improbably a lawyer at his father's firm; Fitz . . . she still wasn't clear on what Fitz did for a living, though he seemed to have money to burn; and Seth, a cop who was an even more recent transplant than she was. One of these days they might stop surprising her, but she doubted it would be anytime soon.

So, Shane was a theater rat.... I'll just file that away to bother him with at my leisure. Zoe smiled at him, and even in the dim light he seemed to pale. She was tempted to give an evil laugh of her own.

"Hilarious," Shane said flatly, turning back to Fitz. "But we're not talking about me. We're talking about the infamous Molly Evans. You won't think it's so funny if she brings Tommy with her, like she usually does. You'll get almost as much of a two-for-one pain in the ass as Jason will."

Fitz shrugged, his expression mild even though his dark eyes glittered with what looked to Zoe like slightly malicious humor. "That was forever ago. Like I told him last time he was here, some of us got over being sixteen." He paused, then shot Zoe a smirk. "And some of us make a lot more money than the guy whose mommy made sure he took our spot as a starter on the soccer team."

Zoe laughed softly. "That definitely helps heal old wounds." She looked around at her friends. "You all are not giving me confidence in my decision."

Jake shoved a hand through his hair, making it even more unruly than usual, and offered her a sympathetic smile. "Speaking as Jason's cousin, you're actually doing a really nice thing helping him out, Zoe. He was born into the wrong branch of the family. Mom always says that Aunt Molly must have been some kind of genetic fluke, and then she went and made a family that's just as, you know ... fluky. Except Jason. He's pretty normal, really."

Zoe huffed out a laugh and took a sip of wine. "I don't know if I'd go *that* far."

"He's quiet," Jake said with a shrug. "So?"

"He's grumpy," Zoe shot back. "And difficult. And antisocial. And—"

"And that's a front, which you're going to understand pretty quickly if you go through with this. It hasn't been easy for him. Not his family, and not . . ." He trailed off cryptically, then shook his head. "Don't tell him I told you that, okay? He'd kick my ass."

She rolled her eyes. "Evidence of true sweetness, right there." Inwardly, though, she was intrigued by Jake's reaction. And she'd gotten yet another hint that there was much more to Jason than she'd seen in her three years in the Cove. Her intense interest in digging deeper on that was worrisome. It had gotten her in enough trouble already.

Jason's family sounded *special*. Of course, not all of her brothers were peaches, either, she supposed. Not like her . . . as she'd told them on many, many occasions.

Sam put a hand to Zoe's forehead, pulling her from her thoughts. "I just want to know what made you agree to this. Purposely spending time with Treebeard? Are you feeling okay?" she asked, and though her tone was playful, the puzzlement in her eyes was real enough. "This *is* Jason Evans we're talking about, right?"

Zoe swatted her hand away. "Yes, and don't pretend you're not secretly gloating. I took him a present. Your idea, remember? I walked in at just the wrong time, and he asked for my help. So I said yes." "Asking" was maybe stretching it a little, but something stopped her from elaborating. Maybe it was that she'd stopped being mad that he'd boxed her in about two minutes after he'd done it. Or maybe she just felt wrong blaming him when he'd so quickly and sincerely offered her a way out. She'd been the one to insist.

It wasn't a decision she felt like explaining. She was already tired of the subject.

"Just like that?" Emma asked, her big blue eyes wide where she sat on Zoe's other side. "I guess I missed something. I thought all you two did was fight." Sam's older sister had seen at least one of her and Jason's altercations in the gallery, Zoe knew. And unlike Sam, Emma had never teased about there being some kind of hot-and-heavy undercurrents there, taking Zoe's dislike at face value.

She'd been wrong, of course, but Zoe chalked that up to Emma dating about as much as she did, which was to say, barely ever. Well, until she'd met the man who currently had his arm across the back of Emma's chair, hand resting on her shoulder. Seth Andersen was a cop who'd moved here because of family and, according to him, fallen for Emma almost immediately. It had just taken the older Henry sister a while to notice, considering she was . . . well, Emma called it "focused." And since Zoe was prone to some of that sort of focus herself, she was apt to defend it as a good quality when people tried to call it something else.

Regardless, Emma and Seth gave Zoe hope. If someone as tightly wound and relationship shy as Emma could find a man to share her life with, there had to be somebody around for her, too. Somewhere. Unless he'd been run over by a truck or something.

Or busted his leg out in the woods . . .

"Yes, just like that," Zoe replied, knowing she sounded peevish. "I'm not coldhearted." She glared morosely into her wine and took another sip. "He's friends with half the people at this table, unless I missed something. Maybe one of you could at least reassure me that this is going to be something other than painfully awkward? He does date, right? Sometimes? Maybe?"

Jake's eyes were a pretty green-hazel even in the dim light of the bar, and suddenly full of sympathy. "Well, ah . . . Jason is a good guy, but he was never a Casanova. We used to joke about the stuff he'd be more likely to do than ask somebody out. Chew glass. Staple his hand to a board."

"Take a bungee jump in a loaded porta-john," Fitz said.

"Wrestle a bear while wearing nothing but raw fish," Shane chimed in.

Sam groaned and held up a hand. "Maybe stop there. That's enough visuals for me."

"And me," Zoe said. "I got the idea. He's bad with women. Thank you for making my misery complete, and pass those hush puppies in this direction before I bite you, Shane."

"Now who's grumpy and difficult?" he asked, but he shoved the basket toward her.

She plucked one out and bit in, sighing a little over the warm, sweet, fried corn bread. It was as improbable a thing to find in Harvest Cove as a blues bar that looked like Steven Tyler's boudoir, but she was grateful to have both tonight.

"So, is this woman going to stab me on sight?" she finally asked.

"Oh no. That's not the way Molly operates. She's very, ah, enthusiastic," Emma said.

"About *everything*," Sam added. "And she's always

working an angle. I've seen her be nice, but you can never take it at face value."

"She's also really competitive," Fitz said, his mouth tightening as he circled the rim of his glass with the tip of his finger. "*Really* competitive. But maybe you'll have it easier since you're not with the golden boy."

"Tommy the insurance salesman?"

Fitz chuckled. "Yeah."

"I didn't get the impression he and Jason were very close," Zoe said.

Fitz shook his head. "Nope."

"Tommy's a year younger than me. Jason's a year older," Jake said.

"Tommy was in my class," Sam said. "Actually, he was at my wedding. Drunk blond guy? Loud, bad dancer, kept hitting on Larkin?"

"Until he found out she was there with me," Shane said, looking pleased with himself. "He's not a complete idiot."

Zoe sifted through her memories of that day—it had been a good one, with nothing to spoil it, but she guessed there had been a few antics at the reception. Finally, it came to her. "The guy who took his shirt off during the Macarena?"

"One and the same," Sam said. "He passed out at his table shortly thereafter and ceased to be a problem, thanks to the magic of having an open bar."

"Wow," Zoe said. "I would never have pegged him as Treebeard's brother."

"A thing that would please both of them, I'm sure," Jake said. "I told you, in that crew, Jason's the oddball. And he's fine with that."

"No wonder." She mulled the new information over.

Maybe it wouldn't be so bad. She was only getting the mother, and she had some experience with controlling, passive-aggressive women. In the past, she'd simply sliced and diced that type with her tongue. That wouldn't be an option here.

"I guess this explains why Jason is so charming," she finally said. She tried to imagine what he might be doing right now, and immediately pictured him on his couch, Rosie at his side, watching TV. Maybe he'd have a beer on the coffee table, and some popcorn, or some chips and salsa. It was a surprisingly cozy image. Zoe had a fleeting moment of wishing herself a part of it before pushing the thought aside. Good friends, good food, good music . . . Everything she needed tonight was right here.

"So, how are you going to convince Molly you're crazy about her son?" Seth asked. "I know you two argue pretty regularly, but I don't think that's going to cut it." He'd been sitting with his arm around Emma and listening with the quiet intensity Zoe had come to associate with him. *Leave it to the cop to ask the toughest question.* Her eyes darted to Emma for help, but she only nodded, silently seconding the question. She scrambled for an answer. It wasn't something she'd put a lot of thought into yet, but she didn't want to seem like she didn't have a plan.

"Well . . ."

"What kind of rules are you going to have," Shane asked, waggling his eyebrows, "for, say, touching?"

"We didn't . . . what do you mean *rules*? Jason doesn't touch people."

"You're not people. You're his girlfriend," Shane replied.

"Fake girlfriend."

"Not to his mom, you're not. Or to anybody around here not in on the plan, which is almost everybody. What are you planning to do, some kind of creepy platonic thing where you keep about five feet between you at all times? Nobody's going to buy that. People in new relationships are always gross." His eyes went far off for a moment, and his small smile looked almost wistful. "You know. People yelling at you to get a room. That kind of gross."

"If that's so appealing to you, then you go be his girlfriend," Zoe said, hoping her voice was steadier than her nerves. She'd stopped herself from thinking about that particular subject several dozen times today, because what level of physical affection constituted a believable relationship? Should she hold his hand? Hard when he was on the crutches, but possible when he was sitting. Kiss him on the cheek? On the mouth? The possibilities were endless. Terrifying.

And really kind of tantalizing, if she was being honest. Which she refused to do about this, at least out loud.

Shane wrinkled his nose at her. "Uh, no, you can have him. He'd make a really ugly woman."

Zoe tried to picture it. "You have a point."

"I always have a point. I'd rather have another beer." He waved down their waitress while the chatter at the table surrounded Zoe, enveloping her in friendly warmth as the band returned to the stage and launched into a soulful rendition of "The Sky Is Crying." All the noise spared her further questions, allowing her to finally relax a little in her chair and try to enjoy the evening. At least, until Sam leaned over to speak softly in her ear.

"If you start feeling like you might Hulk out and start smashing, you call me. If I can't come help, Em will. Okay? We're good distractions, and we've got your back."

"Thanks," Zoe replied, mustering a smile for her friend. "I'm sure it'll be fine." After all, this was Jason they were talking about, a country boy laid up in a log cabin. She could handle him when he was walking around, so this should be less trouble. Even with the addition of his mother, how hard could this really be?

She didn't know, Zoe realized. She was no longer sure she wanted to. But right now, there was nothing for it but to enjoy the night as best she could and take some solace in the fact that if nothing else, this would be an experience neither of them would forget . . . even if they wanted to.

Chapter Five

Saturday evening, Zoe stood on the front porch of the cute little log cabin in the woods with two plastic bags full of food and her "I mean business" boots on. Because Zoe Watson was a woman of her word. Her thickheaded, hastily given word. And they'd made a deal.

Damn it.

She squared her shoulders, took a deep breath, and knocked at the door. *It's just Treebeard,* she told herself firmly, even as a flurry of butterflies began to flop mindlessly around in her stomach. Something—some*one*—thumped around inside, and a volley of sharp, high-pitched barks started up.

"Hang on!" Jason's gruff voice carried through the door. He sounded thrilled, as usual. Must be his mother hadn't passed on any of that frightening enthusiasm she was said to possess. A bang, followed by a muttered series of curses that would have made a sailor blush, only reinforced her opinion.

"Take your time," she drawled, turning her head and letting her eyes drift over the riot of flowers that bloomed, lush and full, across the front of the house. And around the base of the wrought-iron lamppost in the front yard, like something out of Narnia. It was an ocean of color. Some part of her had expected to find that Jason lived in a dilapidated little shack in the woods, equipped with nothing but a hot pot, an outhouse, and an old black-and-white TV with rabbit ears on top. Instead, he lived in a cozy cabin that, from the outside at least, was completely charming. He obviously took a lot of care with it, and with the neatly trimmed, thick green lawn that rolled back behind the wooden split-rail fence surrounding a yard that backed up to the trees.

There had been a brief, disconcerting instant upon pulling into the driveway yesterday when she'd been hit with a wave of homesickness, brief but strong and bittersweet. There was something about this spot—not so much the look of the house, but the feel of it—that put her in mind of the long, lazy summer days of her childhood, of the time before she'd lugged her adult worries around like a sack of bricks. This had the look of a warm place, a *safe* place. And because it belonged to a man who had never struck her as either thing, she'd walked up onto the wide, low-slung front porch with more apprehension than she'd expected to feel. All her ideas about yesterday's visit had scattered the moment she'd walked onto his territory.

In retrospect, she should have taken it as a sign and hightailed it out of there while the getting was good.

Rosie was barking for all she was worth right on the other side of the door now. Zoe shifted her weight from one foot to the other and tried not to think about how hungry she was. She had a sneaking suspicion that the sound of Rosie's scrabbling paws against the wood was more about the smell of dinner than about the human carrying it. She still found it strange—the Treebeard she knew might want to plant himself in the earth and hang out in nature, but it was weird to think of him being bothered with any one small creature in it. Especially when that creature was of a sort known for needing attention and affection. Between this and the hints of vulnerability she'd seen yesterday, Zoe thought, maybe she'd been wrong about him.

"Jesus, Rosie, knock it off before you give yourself an aneurysm!"

Or not.

The door opened suddenly, and she found herself staring through the screen into a pair of wary brown eyes that should have been far too familiar to be causing the punch of pure, liquid heat she felt at the sight of them. Especially because he looked as though he'd just caught her in the act of leaving a flaming bag of poo in front of the door.

She'd had moments where that idea did hold some appeal.

"Hi," she said brightly, hoping that being friendly from the get-go would set the tone. For once, she was in no mood to argue with him. She was also anxious to see what kind of a job her friend Alex Hoult had done earlier. Jason's house had desperately needed a thorough decluttering, and Alex had been able to work him in this morning. Not that he'd bothered to pick up his phone when Zoe had called to let him know. And not that she'd let that stop her from scheduling it anyway. Alex had reported 'surprise and satisfaction . . . I think.'"

Zoe decided his current expression fell more into the "I think" category.

"We need to talk about boundaries," he said.

"I know what they are. I'm standing in front of one," Zoe replied. "Can we talk about boundaries later?"

"You paid to have my house cleaned," he said. "Without asking if I *wanted* my house cleaned."

"I tried to ask. You don't pick up your phone."

"You didn't leave a message, and I don't know your number," he pointed out.

"Well . . ." He had a point, but Zoe quickly brushed it aside. He could have picked up the phone. She had a local number, not 1-800-BUY-STUF. "You said yourself the house looked like hell. You haven't been able to clean it, and your mother is coming tomorrow. Do you really think I'm going to make a good first impression if she sees I've been letting you fester in your little hovel here, slowly sinking into the paper plates and soda cans?"

She had him there, and it hadn't even been hard. He stared at her, looking silently annoyed. Zoe flexed the fingers that gripped the handles of her plastic bags, tired of standing there with them.

"Jason, I'm hungry. I brought food, which I'm going to eat even if I have to go back out to my car to do it." She looked down at Rosie, who was staring up at her wagging her glorious plume of a tail for all she was worth. "Your dog can join me. She looks like she's ready to be good company."

"Of course she is. She was just as excited about finding and eating a dead spider earlier. It took me three tries to find a dog food she wouldn't turn her nose up at, but spiders are some kind of delicacy." He frowned at his dog, who looked completely unfazed.

"Then I guess she'll like Chinese just fine."

"Probably. Whether or not it agrees with her is a different issue. One I have a personal stake in." His eyes moved down to the bags of takeout. "House of Gee?"

"Only the best for my fake boyfriend. Unless you're fake breaking up with me, in which case I'll be taking my gourmet takeout elsewhere."

Jason's lips twitched. "That a hint to let you in?"

Honestly. "Do I look like I want to carry all this crap back to my car?"

"I thought you said it was gourmet." He lowered his head a little to examine what she carried, and she couldn't help but notice that he really did need a haircut. Though she would never say so, she could appreciate the fact that he always left it long enough to show off the loose curl it had—but he was letting it turn into a mop. She bit her tongue, though, and tabled the discussion for later. The house was clean. That was one step toward getting his life back in order.

The pleasure she felt at the thought worried her. She loved projects, but she was pretty sure Jason would be the kind of project that was both thankless and never ending.

His eyes lifted back up to hers, missing their glimmer of humor. "I would have bought dinner."

"It was on my way. I came straight here from work, and once again, I am *hungry*. It's not a big deal, Jason. Though if you want to cook out of a sense of honor or something, be my guest. I'll just drag home all these leftovers. These piping-hot, amazing-smelling leftovers." She rattled the bags a little for effect, hoping the scent that wafted from them would push him to end his teasing. And that's what this was, too—*teasing*. Rusty, maybe, but effective.

She might celebrate its normalcy if her stomach would quit growling.

"Well . . . I'm paying you for the maid service," he finally said. Zoe tipped her head to the side and widened her eyes to stare at him.

"Fine. Write me a check. I only hired them because I knew you wouldn't, and I don't do clutter. I bet your mother doesn't, either. Now, are you going to open this door or what?"

"Oh." He looked so surprised at the realization that there was still a screen door between them that Zoe couldn't suppress a laugh. She wondered how many other people got the screen-door treatment and never got inside. Most, probably. "Yeah. Sorry. Come on in."

Relieved, she opened the door, cooed a hello to Rosie because her hands were full, and marched right past Jason toward the kitchen. Rosie padded along at her ankles, tail flying like a furry flag.

Alex and her crew had done a fine job, she decided, glancing around as she walked. Jason had a home that was as appealing on the inside as it was on the outside now that it had been cleaned and decluttered. Most of the log cabin was one large, open space, with the exception of an area off in the back that she assumed concealed an office or a bedroom. There was a big family room with a stone fireplace as its focal point to her right, open to a spacious kitchen in the back of the house. A cozy dining area was to the left, with a nice rustic table she hadn't been able to see yesterday. Stairs climbed into a loft overhead, its contents hidden but presumably more organized now. The honeyed color of the wood lent a feeling of warmth everywhere she looked. It was a good layout, Zoe thought, her habit of mentally sizing up spaces for decoration taking over for a moment. He'd even done a decent job of placing the furniture . . . and the pieces he'd been buying from Two Roads. Those made her smile.

Not bad, Treebeard. Not bad at all.

Zoe deposited her two bags of food on the counter, marveling that the kitchen, post-excavation, was one she liked almost as well as her own. Everything was just so . . . put together. Was that his doing? she wondered. Even if he hadn't chosen all the materials, he'd picked the house. Then he'd made it a home, somewhere she'd be inclined to settle into and be comfortable. Well, if Jason weren't in it.

How a guy like him had managed to create such an inviting space was something she knew she'd be mulling over later. It would require at least one cup of tea. Probably more like a whole kettle, though.

An odd noise pulled her out of the impromptu home inspection. Zoe looked down, frowning, then burst into laughter.

"What's funny?" Jason asked, making his way over. Zoe didn't look at him, but the *creak-thump* of his movement on the crutches was unmistakable. She wouldn't have thought there would be a way to make his clomping footsteps even louder, but he'd found one.

"This dog," she said, pointing downward. "You sure she isn't actually a groundhog?"

"Oh, that," he replied with a low, rumbling chuckle. "That's one of her signature moves."

The Pekingese sat very steadily on her butt, perfectly balanced, paws drawn up in front of her. Every time she caught Zoe's eye, Rosie waved her paws insistently and made some sort of strange, cartoonish sound.

"She sounds like an alien. Or a Muppet."

"Well, she also looks like she's been chasing parked cars, so I don't know what you expect," Jason said.

"Oh, now, that's mean. She's beautiful." Zoe reached down to ruffle Rosie's ears, surprised when the little dog ducked her head sideways and gave her what was an unmistakably dirty look.

Jason laughed again, low and warm. "One of the many things I've learned about Pekingese in the past two weeks. If they're begging, you don't interrupt them. Even if you're the one they're begging from. It's a personal space thing."

"Pekingese have a personal space thing?"

He snorted. "You have no idea. She's educating me on that. Seems to think I'm kind of a slow learner, though." The way he looked at Rosie, who'd gone back to waving her paws and looking between them expectantly, was so unguardedly affectionate that warmth bloomed deep in Zoe's chest, flooding her with a lot of completely unwanted affection of her own. *Knock it off, girl. You don't even really know him. And what you do know isn't all sparkly rainbows.*

Of course, all of that begged the question: *So then why are you here?*

She knew very well why. Embarrassingly, it had nothing to do with either kindness or charity, and it barely qualified as mercenary. It did, however, have a lot to do with how his butt looked in his old, faded jeans every time he stomped out of her gallery.

"I'm sure you pick up just fine when it's a subject that interests you," Zoe said, trying to shake off the nerves that seemed to go hand in hand with her attraction. Jason looked down at her, and Zoe realized she'd never been quite this close to him before. Heat seemed to radiate off of him . . . or maybe that was just the effect he had on her. She had to fight the urge to fan herself. *Stupid.* He probably had enough women tripping over themselves around him, even with that attitude of his.

The thought left a bad taste in her mouth.

"Now, there's a backhanded compliment," he said. "I bet you've got a long list of things you think don't interest me." He seemed more entertained than offended, and she couldn't resist taking the bait.

"I do. At the top of that list are manners and dirt removal. As evidence, I have a special doormat at the gallery that looks almost as new as the day I bought it despite *someone's* assurances that they'd make an effort."

"Maybe that *someone* just has cleaner shoes now and doesn't need fancy doormats."

"I'm afraid my vacuum cleaner says otherwise."

"You should never trust machinery when it starts talking to you. Don't you read any science fiction?" They were toe-to-toe now, and Zoe realized too late that she'd moved as she was talking, drawn to him without even realizing it. He was looking down at her with the oddest expression. There wasn't a bit of hostility in it. Instead, his gaze skimmed her face, long, dark lashes dropping as he focused on . . . her mouth? Oh God, was he looking at her mouth?

Without thinking, she drew her lower lip into her mouth to wet it and his eyes went dark, hot. Her heart skipped in her chest.

"You need a shave," she blurted, desperate to banish the sudden sense of intimacy. She immediately wanted to kick herself. *Yes, Zoe, too smooth. Let him know you're staring at that nice square jawline of his. That will definitely make things less awkward.* Jason's brows lifted a little, but he still didn't seem annoyed. Just thoughtful. And he didn't move away.

"I guess I do. I'll get to it by tomorrow," he said, lifting one hand to rub at his chin for a brief moment. "So, are we going to talk about my hygiene next, or can we eat? Because that smells great."

"Yes!" Zoe said, inwardly cringing a little at the forced brightness of her voice. That, and the fact she'd nearly shouted the word. "Let's, ah, eat." She took quick steps back and turned toward the counter, tucking a few curls behind her ear. "I didn't know what you'd like, so I got a bunch of things—lo mein, egg rolls, dumplings, some sesame chicken, General Tso's, hot-and-sour soup. Um, sweet-and-sour . . . something. I think. What is this?" She removed cartons from the plastic bags and put them on the counter one by one, examining several before she remembered exactly what she'd bought. Jason said nothing while she worked. When she finally turned her head, he was staring at the cartons incredulously.

"Wow. That's . . . that's some food." He looked down at his stomach, then back up at her. "You trying to tell me something?"

She felt her cheeks heat. "No. I just figured you could use some leftovers in the fridge, since you can't drive and that has to be a pain."

"It is."

"Then don't complain."

"I'm not." A long pause, then, "Thank you."

She looked up from opening the cartons, startled to find him wearing an expression that suggested she'd just challenged him with a particularly hard riddle. If she wasn't careful, she'd end up flustered all over again, and that was *not* how this evening was going to go. Jason would get the help he needed, she would get to work him out of her system from a position of power, and they'd both go away happy. Well, in Jason's case, as happy as he got. That was the deal.

Just because he wasn't in on it didn't make it any less valid.

"You're welcome. Now tell me where the plates and forks are and go sit down. You're no good to me in here."

She saw the mulish glint in his eyes, but then he glanced at the steaming food. Hunger won out. "Corner cupboard for the plates. Drawer to your left for silverware." He hesitated, as though about to say something else. After a moment, though, he shook his head and creak-thumped his way out of the kitchen and toward the table. Rosie stayed put without looking a bit conflicted about it.

"Where is your loyalty?" Zoe asked her as she got out a couple of plates.

"It's not in her stomach," Jason called over his shoulder.

It wasn't, either. Rosie followed her back and forth between the dining area and the kitchen several times as she got their dinner together. By the time she slid into the chair across from Jason, his dog heaved a sigh that sounded distinctly annoyed before resuming her groundhog pose, this time at Jason's side. Zoe eyed her.

"I suppose you're going to tell me you don't feed her table scraps."

"I don't. I feed her high-quality, nutritional food," Jason replied, stabbing into some pork lo mein with his fork. "Some of it just happens to come off of my plate."

"And what does Jake have to say about that?"

"Not sure. He has this weird affliction where sometimes he opens his mouth and the only thing that comes out is a *blah-blah-blah* sound."

Zoe opened the top of one of the containers of hot-and-sour soup and dipped into it with her spoon. "Sounds like you may have a hearing problem."

"No, I'm just surrounded by people with the same disorder. There's a high concentration in the Cove, seems like." Only his cheeky grin saved him from having some noodles flung at him. She put the spoonful of soup into her mouth, closed her eyes, and swallowed. *Bliss.*

When she opened her eyes, she was staring into his. The heat in them was back, pulsing between them like a living thing. Why hadn't she ever felt this from him when he was in the gallery? Maybe she just hadn't noticed because it was her place. It was safe.

Or maybe she'd just wanted to think so.

"So," she said, trying to break the spell. "Let's get down to business. I can work while we eat." She slid a slim notebook out of the purse sitting beside her chair, unclipped a pen from it, and opened to a fresh page. "Your mother is Molly, right?"

Jason looked at the notebook as though it were a foreign object. "You're taking notes? What do you think she's going to do, give you a quiz?"

"I'm thorough. If we've been dating a few weeks, I should know more about you than where you live and what you do for a living."

He shrugged. "She knows I'm not big on small talk."

"Then what would she think we've been doing all this time?" She knew the instant the words left her mouth what the answer was, and Jason's smirk was anything but innocent. "Oh, come on!" she said, picking up a wad of paper napkins and throwing them at him. "She has a dirty mind on top of all the other things I'm supposed to deal with?"

Now he wrinkled his nose. "If she does, I don't want to know. Okay, maybe write down to avoid that subject with her completely."

"I don't even need to write that down." She sketched

a small doodle, took another bite of soup, and tried to reorganize her thoughts to start again. "Let's start with basics. Molly Evans."

Jason nodded while he chewed. "Yeah. Molly. Married to Dan. I have one brother, Tommy. He's two years younger than me."

"Do you get along? I got the impression that you don't."

"What's that got to do with anything?"

"And I was right. I'll keep that in mind." She wrote the names down.

His voice quickly dropped into his usual surly grumble. "We don't *not* get along. He's busy. I'm busy."

"Selling insurance. Sometimes to you," she added, and his smile was rueful.

"No, not to me. Not for lack of trying. But if it wasn't insurance, it'd be something else. He's a born salesman, according to everybody."

The tone in his voice struck her as a little off, and Zoe watched him curiously as he stabbed at his food with a little more gusto than before. "And what are *you*, according to everybody?"

"Stubborn."

She had the feeling there was a lot more to it than that, but the look on his face told her to leave that one alone. For now.

"That sounds about right," she said. He was quiet as she helped herself to some of the sweet-and-sour chicken, and the tension that rose in the silence was almost like having an extra guest at the table. The man frowning at his food across from her looked to be deep in some unhappy thoughts, but those thoughts were as inaccessible to her as they'd ever been.

Maybe if she understood him, she'd find him less interesting.

One could only hope.

He startled her when he spoke, since she'd already resigned herself to having to prod him for information all evening. "There's one thing you probably should know. I'm divorced."

Zoe went completely still, staring at him as though he'd just spoken something in a foreign language. "Ah ... okay?" Some important part of the pathway from her brain to her mouth seemed to have short-circuited. Divorced? Her hermit—*not mine, the hermit,* she corrected herself—had been married?

Her shock must have shown. Jason exhaled loudly and looked out the window before his gaze found her again. "It was about four years ago. We were married for a couple years before that."

She had no idea what the appropriate thing to say in this situation was, which flustered her since she was generally good with words. "I'm sorry," was the only thing that sprang to mind, so that was what she went with. He shrugged.

"It's old news. I'm only telling you because it'll come up. It always does."

That didn't sound promising. But it was another piece of the puzzle. A sudden question occurred to her, and its implications were less than pleasant. It was a struggle to keep her voice neutral. "Is she still around here somewhere?" Did she know this person? Had she met her, sold art to her? Had she accidentally been *nice* to her? Not that there was any reason she shouldn't have been, of course. Not at all.

Zoe's hand clenched around the handle of her spoon.

One side of Jason's mouth curved in a halfhearted smile. "Nope. Believe it or not, she didn't think Harvest Cove was the end all, be all."

An unpleasant mixture of curiosity and jealousy coiled together in the pit of her stomach, no matter how much she tried to banish both. This woman, whoever she was, was gone. And considering Jason's sparkling personality, it wasn't like his marital status mattered much anyway. But the guarded expression in his eyes before he looked down at his plate tugged at her, and her competitive nature reared its head before she could stop it.

"What's her name so I can execute a lip curl if your mother brings her up?"

"Sara." A hint of humor softened his expression. "Lip curl. That'll win you points."

"Was she awful?" The words were out of her mouth before she could stop them, though she instantly regretted it. Jason's faint smile vanished as though it had never been, replaced by the hard lines she was used to seeing.

"No. She's just gone." The finality in his statement meant that this line of questioning was now over with, Zoe knew. And truth be told, she'd just as soon find something else to talk about. She wracked her brain, which was suddenly full of nothing but images of Jason and this mysterious, unexpected ex-wife. Was she gorgeous? Probably. In her head he spun a skinny blonde around, the two of them looking like they'd stepped out of a Hallmark Channel movie. He'd shaved and cut his hair. The woman wore a sundress and fabulous shoes. And they looked at each other like they were completely, madly in love.

She didn't know if the image was right—close enough, she decided, even if the real Sara had been a brunette who'd favored coveralls—but the way it made her feel was completely unacceptable. For once in his life, Jason was right. This person was gone. She, however, was here. And she was completely, one hundred percent in control of the situation.

"Well, good to know," Zoe said, keeping her voice smooth. "Now, I think it would be a good idea for you to tell me what kinds of things you like. Movies, TV, food, sports, anything you can think of. Then I'll give you a short list of mine, and we can compare."

"What is this?" he asked, looking slightly horrified. "It sounds like homework."

"That's because it is," she replied, beginning to get exasperated again. The mention of his ex-wife had dampened his mood, and naturally, she was going to bear the brunt of the shift. Joy. "Apart from my knowing your tastes in art, Jason, and where you work, I don't know a damn thing about you. Somewhere, somehow, we've got to have at least a few things in common. Otherwise, your mother isn't going to buy this at all, and I don't know why I'm sitting here."

"I can already tell you we don't," he said.

"Excuse me?"

"Have anything in common," he said. "We're nothing alike, you and me. And she'll buy it for exactly that reason."

She dropped her spoon onto the table with an irritable little *smack* and steepled her fingers beneath her chin. *Serenity,* she commanded herself. "This is the part where I remind you that you don't know a thing about me, either. Nowhere near enough to make a judgment like that. But I do have to ask why, if you think we're such a horrible match, you asked me for help in the first place."

He looked as though he wanted to shout, but he refrained. Instead, Jason spoke in a low voice that fairly thrummed with his annoyance. "Two reasons. You're what she'll want, and right now, you're all I've got."

Her own temper rose to match his, and Zoe could feel them slipping into their regular pattern. It was different this time, though. It was, Zoe realized through the haze of her own anger, the first time he'd managed to find a chink in her armor and hurt the feelings beneath. That was unacceptable.

"That's right," she said, her voice going as cold as ice. "I am all you've got. So, it'd be nice if you tried to remember that instead of working on making me head right out that door. I don't need a sale that badly." She heard her accent thickening up, the way it always did when her emotions got the better of her, until it was sweet, syrupy fury. She knew she was an outsider here. She'd been "Zoe, that nice black girl from Atlanta" for three years now, and for all the progress she'd made, her status wasn't fixing to change anytime soon. She was from a small town. She knew how it worked.

But having Jason classify her as some kind of incompatible stranger carried a different kind of sting. They might not be friends, but their lives had plenty of shared threads. It would be surprising—to her, at least—if they didn't find a few more.

He seemed, finally, to have realized that he'd overstepped. The look on his face was somewhere between embarrassed and stricken. "Zo—"

The sound of her nickname on his lips was too much right now. "Mmm-mmm," she corrected him, index finger raised. "You don't get to call me that. Not right now, and maybe not ever. That's for my friends."

"Zoe," he began again. He looked as though he wanted to say something, but no words came. Finally he dropped his fork beside his plate, dug his hands into his hair, and squeezed his eyes shut. "Shit."

"That about sums it up, yes." She tapped one nail on the table as she regarded him. He was, she decided, a hot mess. One she felt sympathy for despite his attitude, his mouth, and her own better judgment. She wasn't exactly sure why, except that he seemed to be as much of an outsider here as she was in some ways, despite having lived in the Cove all his life. And he was so bad at socializing that she felt sorry for him. That was, when she wasn't infuriated.

When he opened his eyes again to focus on her, she was struck by those pretty gold flecks she wished she could stop noticing. But they were impossible to ignore, just like the solemn intensity he regarded her with. "Look," he finally said. "I'm terrible at this. It probably isn't going to get any better, so maybe we should just give it up. I'll deal with tomorrow. She'll get over it."

Zoe watched him slump into his chair. He'd quit bristling and instead just looked about as forlorn as a person could look. She couldn't stay angry, either, between his acknowledgment of his own horrible people skills and the way his big shoulders slouched as though a heavy weight bore down on them.

"So you want me to go," she said.

Jason shrugged. "You'd be better off. It's not like I'm going to quit buying stuff from the gallery if you bail."

"That's not an answer." She exhaled loudly. "Tell me something. Are you this bad at women all the time, or is it just me?"

His mouth softened, and she caught the faintest trace

of a startled smile. "It's an all-the-time thing. You're just one of the only women I talk to on a regular basis."

"Argue with, you mean."

He shrugged again. "That counts."

"Not really." She watched him, wishing she could see what was going on in his head. "Just tell me one thing." His brows lifted a little, which she took as close enough to agreement to push ahead. "Putting aside the desperation, your crap attitude, and what you think would make your mother happy, there's one thing I'm not clear on at all." She took a deep breath, then asked the question she should have asked before anything else—the question that meant the difference between staying and leaving. And though she'd taken the answer for granted before now, it suddenly occurred to her that she might have made a rare and very big mistake.

"Jason, do you even *like* me?"

He blinked, looking startled. "Do I—what kind of a question is that?"

"A simple one," Zoe replied. "I don't care how much I match up with whatever you think your mother would like, or whether I'm just the only female who'll talk to you for longer than sixty seconds. I already knew you were a pain in the butt when I said I'd help you out, and I know we don't really know each other, but I assumed we were at least starting from a place where there was some kind of—"

"Of course I like you." His answer was rushed and exasperated and sounded perfectly sincere. Zoe took a moment to try to will her heart rate to slow down, frustrated with herself for the relief coursing through her system. *Why didn't I just pass him a note that said, "Do you like me? Check yes or no." I could take it to work and file it for future reference.* "You think I'd be sitting here eating Chinese with you if I didn't like you?"

"Well," she said calmly, "I don't know. You might be. You're a captive audience, and Jake says you'd rather eat than talk."

At that, Jason actually rolled his eyes, and then she couldn't help a smile. "General rule of thumb: Jake's full of it. Don't listen to him. Especially about me." He shook his shaggy head. "Do I even like you . . . That's such a *girl* question."

"I am one, if you haven't noticed."

"I noticed." This time, the growl in his voice hinted at a very different sort of frustration, and Zoe's toes curled inside her boots. He thought they had nothing in common. Maybe he was right. But that didn't seem to dampen the heat in his eyes before they dropped to her open notebook.

"Okay," he said, as though she'd asked him a question. An annoying question, but one he supposed he'd deign to answer. "Let's see. I'm thirty-one. My birthday's November second. I went to college in—" He broke off and looked up at her abruptly. "Are you going to write this down or what?"

She could sense the shift in him as strongly as if he'd announced it. He'd decided to cooperate. He wanted her here after all. In fact, he *liked* her. Treebeard of the bad attitude and improbably fluffy dog liked her. It was a tiny admission that shouldn't have done much but make her a little more comfortable, since no one really wanted to sit around with a guy who hated one's guts. Instead, Zoe felt herself relax into her chair as she picked the pen back up, a frisson of what was either nerves or excitement—or both—raising goose bumps on her arms and threatening to make her shiver.

I like you, too, she thought. *God knows why, but maybe I'll figure it out one of these days.*

Tomorrow might be a disaster, Zoe knew. But for tonight, watching Jason slip Rosie a piece of chicken so she could devour it like a very small great white shark, Zoe couldn't shake the certainty that she was exactly where she needed to be.

"I'm writing if you're talking," she said. "Let's do this."

Chapter Six

Nerves.

Jason woke up to their jangling like an alarm clock in the back of his mind. Even the air seemed heavier as he dragged himself out of bed. No matter how many times he told himself it was ridiculous, that he was a grown man who managed a hell of a lot of responsibility with, if not ease, then extreme competence, it was always like this right before a family visit. Probably because he'd gotten so used the relative lightness of the atmosphere without them around. If they hadn't moved, Jason knew, he likely would have. Not because he didn't love the Cove, though. Leaving this place would have meant he'd spend the rest of his life looking for somewhere just like it, and he knew that for him, it probably didn't exist.

A soft sigh distracted him, and Jason registered the warm weight curled into his side. He untucked his arm from behind his head and reached down to give Rosie's fur a ruffle. She stretched at his touch, as groggy as he was but no doubt in a better mood. That was something he'd come to count on since she'd arrived in his life. Some things pissed her off—the mailman, most notably—but his company seemed to be her favorite thing. She didn't expect him to be anything but a good owner, and that was his pleasure.

Jason hauled himself out of bed, picked up the hated crutches, and made his way out of his not-bedroom to try to drown his resentment in some morning coffee. Rosie hurried after him, going from sleepy to alert in the blink of an eye once she figured out where he was headed. He still wasn't sure whether he occupied the number one spot in Rosie's heart or breakfast did.

Had to be a close contest.

He started his morning routine, letting Rosie out, letting Rosie in, letting Rosie out *again*, making himself a cup of coffee while he told Rosie to hold her horses, and finally distracting her with her breakfast. It wasn't until he opened the fridge to find something for himself, however, that he found his first real smile of the day. What had previously been a relative wasteland of unrelated food items and bare space was now filled with takeout cartons.

He might have imagined Zoe whipping up classic French cuisine using locally sourced ingredients for dinner every night, but if last night was any indication, they at least shared a love of carbs and MSG. And she'd gotten enough to keep him in leftovers for a couple of days. He had a sneaking suspicion his mother was going to keep that from being necessary, but eating egg rolls for breakfast was always more pleasure than necessity. Remembering Zoe and her notebook, Jason smiled as he pulled out a couple of those egg rolls, along with some of the fried rice, and set about dumping it on a paper plate to heat up in the microwave. Maybe Zoe was out of his league, but she wasn't as unapproachable as he'd figured.

He'd expected to spend the evening bickering and wondering what the hell he'd been thinking when he'd enlisted her help.

He'd been wrong.

The smile faded as he got the plate out, maneuvered both it and himself over to the kitchen island, and sat on one of the stools to eat. Jason looked at the clock: eight a.m. He had about five hours of freedom left. Acting had never been his thing, and now he'd need to put on one hell of a performance to get what he wanted. There was a part of him that felt guilty that what he wanted was for his family to leave him alone. He just didn't feel guilty enough to call Zoe and tell her to forget it.

At least Tommy's not coming. Waving a new girlfriend in front of his brother would be like pouring gasoline on a fire. He wasn't supposed to have anything Tommy didn't . . . and his brother would never, ever have a Zoe.

Of course, he probably wouldn't, either . . . but Tommy wouldn't make it five minutes with her before one of those stylish riding boots was planted where the sun didn't shine. The thought made him smile.

She'd promised to be here for lunch so they could go over things one last time. So she could be here smiling brightly for his mother, who'd be thrilled for maybe half an hour, if they were lucky, before she started competing. Jason rubbed a hand over his face, sighed, and began to munch on his egg roll. Zoe didn't know what she'd gotten herself into. And because he was both selfish and desperate, he hadn't told her. Not really. He figured she'd probably gotten some sort of warning from her friends, but there was no way Zoe would run from a challenge. It was one of the things he liked about her.

"Do you even like me?" He snorted at the memory of

the question and shook his head. Of course she'd miss the fact that he did. Just reinforced that she didn't think of him that way. And all things considered . . . that was probably just as well.

"You sure you have a handle on everything?"

"Yes."

"Because I can stay."

"No."

"I don't mind."

Zoe watched as Sam heaved an exasperated sigh and turned from the door to look at her. She'd just ushered out a very happy couple with their new painting, a thrill that never got old for either of them. Sam was looking less than pleased at the moment, however.

"Stop stalling. You got yourself into this thing, and I know you won't back out, because you're you. So just go do it." She paused, one corner of her mouth curving up. "I see that look, you pervert. That's not what I meant. *Or is it?*"

"I didn't say anything!" Zoe cried, throwing up her hands. She was torn between laughter and the intense urge to run and hide under her desk. She was glad she had Sam to lighten the moment, but nothing changed the fact that she was headed out of here and headlong into the unknown. With Treebeard. Her new fake boyfriend.

"Maybe I should just call him and tell him I'll be late," Zoe said. "We're busy."

"Obviously," Sam said, arching one eyebrow and sweeping her hand around the empty gallery. "Swamped."

"That's what I'm *saying*."

Sam sighed. "Zo, I love you, but if I'd known you got this freaked-out about men I wouldn't have bugged you so much about needing to find one. Why don't you just pretend he's one of your superheroes? Like an under-cover Thor or something."

"No. Trust me, that way lies madness and a pile of shredded spandex." She raised her hand and hooked her fingers into claws for emphasis. "I mean it. Shredded."

"Ooo-kay, maybe not, then. But you've got to go. Didn't you tell him noon? Seriously."

"I'm going," Zoe told her, then proceeded to find a painting to adjust. She clearly heard Sam's disgusted groan. "That's not very nice."

"Do you want me to fight you? I can try to kung fu you toward the door. Then you can take some comfort in the fact that you didn't go voluntarily."

"I . . . you want to . . . you don't even know kung fu," Zoe replied, caught momentarily off guard and amused despite herself. Sam was good like that.

"I've watched *The Matrix* enough times to fake it convincingly," Sam said. "Wanna see?"

Zoe stared at her friend, who looked back without cracking a smile, and finally burst out laughing. "Kind of, actually. But not today, though I appreciate the thought."

Now Sam did smile, and it lit up her entire face. Zoe took some comfort in that. However this craziness panned out, things would stay the same here at Two Roads. This place was her refuge, much like she supposed Jason's cabin was his. That thought was what finally got her moving. The man had always struck her as being rather private, but until this weekend, she'd never found it all that endearing. Now, thinking of him waiting for her, probably attempting to pace on his crutches while Rosie sat wondering what on earth was wrong with her human, she couldn't help but want to keep her word to him.

He wasn't what she'd thought. Not entirely, at least. And from the way he'd looked at her last night, she didn't seem to be quite what he was expecting, either. Maybe that was to be expected when most of your interactions revolved around telling each other, in an endless variety of ways, to piss off. Entertaining? Sure. Informative? Not so much.

"All right, I really am going now," Zoe said. "Without you pretending to beat me up in slo-mo, though. We'll save that for when we really need the publicity."

"You got it," Sam said with a nod. "Until then, I'll just hold down the fort. I like your 'meeting the mom' outfit, by the way."

"You think?" Zoe brushed a hand down the simple shift in a royal blue and black print she'd pulled from the closet after a few minutes—okay, maybe it had been more like an hour—of contemplation that morning. It was loose and breezy, with three-quarter-length sleeves and a hemline that showed off her legs without making her feel like sitting down would give the world a show. She wasn't much of a dress girl, but this one was comfortable, and it went great with her favorite flats. She'd looped a long string of beads around her neck, pinned the top section of her hair back, and hoped she looked like somebody Jason's mother wouldn't want to immediately annihilate. She needed some time to figure out a strategy before engaging in battle.

Not that she wanted a battle . . . but given what everyone had said—and what they hadn't—it was best to be prepared.

"Definitely," Sam said. "I don't think I've ever seen that dress. Snazzy."

"Well, you know I try to stay fabulous," Zoe replied.

She pulled on a long sweater that was functioning as her jacket for the day, slung her bag over her shoulder, and took a deep breath. "Wish me luck."

"You don't need luck," Sam said. "You're already well armed for any battle of wits. Just, you know, watch your back. And Jason's." Her eyes sparkled with mischief. "Not that I think you'll have a problem with that last part."

"Do you want me to beat you with my purse? This isn't real. I'm not sleeping with Treebeard!"

"Doesn't mean you can't appreciate the view," Sam pointed out. "And don't even pretend you haven't noticed it's a nice one. I've seen you looking after he's stomped out of here."

Zoe rolled her eyes. "I'm not *blind*. Hey, call me if Marlis Pritchard comes in, will you? I had a talk with Aaron about doing a commission for her, and he had some questions."

"You want me to just have her call him directly?"

"No, not until she figures out he doesn't bite."

Sam laughed softly. "Oh, you want me to lie to her, then."

"Yes, please. He's domesticated now, remember? He hardly ever bites at all anymore." Which reminded her, she was going to owe him a phone call tonight as well. Aaron and Sam were about the only people she went out of her way to sit down and gossip with on a regular basis, and they all checked up on one another. Not that he was needing to be checked on quite as much lately, since he'd gotten awfully cozy with Ryan Weston, one of Jake's friends.

She was happy for him and just a little sad for herself. She'd aspired to be many things in Harvest Cove, but "third wheel" wasn't one of them. And the two men were, as Aaron loved to point out when they were all together, disgustingly adorable. Though Ryan was as apt to roll his eyes over that description as she was.

"Hardly ever isn't never," Sam said. "And he and Marlis are like oil and water."

"Just have her call me," Zoe said. "I'm sure I can take time out from . . . whatever."

"I want a full report on the whatever." Sam's smile was more than a little evil.

"Maybe there won't be anything to report."

"Maybe. She might have mellowed," Sam agreed. She didn't look any more convinced than Zoe felt, however, and Zoe wondered, not for the first time, whether she'd finally managed to bite off more than she could chew. Only time would tell.

Sam struck a reasonable facsimile of a kung-fu fighting stance, and Zoe knew that was her cue to get going. "Okay, okay. I'm leaving." She walked out into a September day just shy of being crisp, with the sun just breaking through the clouds. It was beginning to feel like fall in earnest now. The wild storm they'd had, the one that Jason had been caught in, seemed to have been summer's last hurrah. Temps had been on a downward swing ever since, and it looked like there would be a definite nip in the air by the end of the coming week.

Zoe welcomed it, just as she did every year since she'd come to Harvest Cove. She was into her fourth year here, having chased a dream all the way from a little town in Georgia. Her parents still doubted her sanity, but this was the time of year, every year, when she was sure she'd made the right decision.

She took a deep breath, loving the way the air was

scented with cooling earth, turning leaves, and ocean—here, you could always smell the ocean. Then she headed down the short path that led through a knee-high wrought-iron fence to the sidewalk, hanging a right to where her car was waiting. As Zoe pulled out her key chain to unlock the navy blue and white Mini crossover she'd bought herself as a present last year, she turned her head to look down Hawthorne toward where it became the Cove's historic square. She'd opened the gallery on a day a lot like this, she realized. That day, the world had seemed full of possibility, her future like a flower with petals only just beginning to unfurl.

That was when she realized why she was thinking of that first day. The feeling of possibility, or life just waiting to happen, was in the air again. And this time, instead of savoring it, Zoe could only give it a suspicious side-eye before getting into her car and driving away, uncertain of whether what she felt was the echo of a memory, a tantalizing hint of the future, or the promise of impending doom.

Chapter Seven

Over the past week, Jason had envisioned dozens of nightmare scenarios involving his mother's visit. Some part of him insisted that in imagining something awful happening, he was actually inoculating himself against it. If he could dream it up, it couldn't happen. So naturally, the one thing he hadn't considered was the thing lying in wait for him just as he hobbled out of the downstairs bedroom, freshly dressed with his hair still damp.

"Rosie," he complained as his dog continued the spate of operatic barking she'd launched into while he'd been dressing. "One of these days your head's going to explode if you keep that up." He figured she was probably losing it over a squirrel or something. Her intense hatred of squirrels was matched only by her loathing of the mailman, and she kept watch for both of them from her favorite perch—the back of his comfy reading chair, which backed up to one of the front windows.

He might even have adjusted it a little just so she could see better, though he regretted it often enough that he would never admit to having done it.

As soon as Jason moved into the great room, he could

see that Rosie wasn't on the chair. She was standing in front of the door, barking with such ferocity that she bounced every few seconds, her tail wagging furiously. She turned her head once to look at him with an expression that clearly said, *Come on, slowpoke, can't you see I'm trying to tell you something?* That was when the doorbell rang.

"Christ," Jason muttered, heading for the door. It had to be Zoe, even though she wasn't due for another hour. His heart lifted at the thought, which he immediately tried to mitigate by finding something irritating about it. He couldn't, though—which he guessed was irritating enough all on its own. If he ever let on that he was actually glad to see her, who knew what sort of hell would be unleashed.

Still, he found himself smiling like an idiot as he unlocked the door, murmuring at Rosie to cool it while she continued to try to bark their unseen visitor into submission. "Hey," he said as he pulled the door open. "You're—"

His smile went tight, frozen in place when two pairs of eyes stared back at him, neither the color of a stormy sky.

"Surprise!" his mother cried, throwing her arms wide before glancing down uneasily at Rosie, who was very close to clawing a hole in the screen of the storm door. Her eyes flicked back up quickly, but he caught the glance, and his stomach sank. *Great. She still hates dogs. One more thing to look forward to.*

"You're early," he blurted out. He could tell immediately that he'd said the wrong thing. Her smile turned biting, and he sighed inwardly. "I'm glad you're here, Mom. Come on in."

It wasn't enough to please her, but it seemed to be good enough for now.

"I'm so glad to be out of that car. Between the bumpy plane ride and Moira's driving, I was tempted to kiss the ground right here in your front yard." She opened the door, his aunt Moira trailing in her wake carrying a pair of large suitcases and looking deeply annoyed. When she caught his eye, though, she rolled hers and offered a small smile, which he returned. His aunt had always been a sweetheart, though one unfortunately prone to be dominated by stronger personalities. She'd finally found someone worthy of her, though, since her loser ex-husband had taken off, and Jason had enjoyed seeing her finally relax into the kind of life he'd always wished for her.

It was why his temper quickly turned to a low boil when he saw that his mother, true to form, had opted to drag her little rolling carry-on and let her little sister do the heavy lifting. Since he was in no shape to be able to help, all he could do was try to shame his mother into helping, and she didn't shame easily. Actually, he wasn't sure she could be shamed at all.

"Wow, Aunt Moira, I thought Mom was the one who just ran an obstacle course race and a half marathon last month. You been working out?"

"Nope. Just naturally buff, obviously," she replied, and he was glad to see the humor light pretty eyes the same green-hazel as her son's. His mother turned, looking exasperated, and let go of her carry-on's handle to put her hand on her hip, taking a swig from her ubiquitous water bottle before commenting.

"Oh, stop it, both of you. I've had a long day already. The guy in front of me on the plane reclined his seat the whole time, and the woman next to me was wearing enough perfume to gag a maggot."

Since his nose was already full of whatever floral bomb she was currently favoring, he didn't think she had a lot of room to complain. He also made a mental note to pop a couple of aspirin before the headache set in.

"Well, you're here now," Jason said, hoping he sounded happier about that than he was.

"Yes, I am! Here to take care of my poor baby boy." She made a show of embracing him then, though he could feel the nervous tension running through her wiry frame. She wasn't a hugger, not really, but sometimes she tried when she felt the situation warranted it. Her touch filled him with the same uncomfortable mixture of love and bitterness that had come with her presence for at least as long as he'd been able to identify the feelings, and probably a lot longer.

He patted her back awkwardly, with one hand, and wished the two of them enjoyed each other as much as she and Tommy seemed to. But he wasn't Tommy, as he'd been continually reminded for most of his life.

His mother drew back, smiling at him, but her eyes were assessing, the way they always were. "So," she began, and he knew where things were headed. For once, he'd done something that interested her. "When do I get to meet her?"

"Soon," Jason said, glancing at the clock on the far wall. "She planned to be here when you got here."

"Oh, that's sweet! I like her already!" Somehow, he doubted that, but a guy could hope. It was no charming surprise that she'd arrived earlier than planned, with no word. This, he knew, was about gaining the upper hand early. His stomach began to knot, and he tried to regulate his breathing, pushing back the anxiety that might tangle his tongue and provoke unwanted commentary from the woman who'd only reluctantly gotten him help for his childhood stuttering in the first place. He thought of Zoe with more than a hint of remorse and knew he was going to owe her big . . . if she ever spoke to him again after this.

She's tough. She can probably out-snob her, Jason tried to tell himself. But all he could think of was the Chinese food, and the piece of chicken she didn't know he'd seen her slip to Rosie. And her smile—so new to him, and surprisingly open.

He stopped himself before his thoughts wandered any further in that direction. There was nothing that way but trouble, and he had enough of that on his hands already.

"Ah, do you want to stay for lunch, Aunt Moira?" he asked. She'd dumped the suitcases by the base of the stairs and stood looking around. Jake had filled her in on everything, he knew. And from the small smile playing on her lips, that "everything" included the thorough cleaning the house had gotten yesterday.

"No, that's okay, honey. I've got some things to do, and we'll all have dinner sometime this week, I'm sure." She moved to give her sister a quick, perfunctory hug, and Jason had a stark reminder of the contrast between the two sisters. Moira was small and dark, with a quiet, classical prettiness that made her look years younger than she was. Molly was her opposite, tall and artificially blond, with a sturdier frame she took pains to keep whittled and a brashness that came through in every move she made. One had been an athlete, one a theater rat, and from the time they were young, newcomers to town rarely picked up on the fact that they were sisters until they were told, despite the matching last names. If they noticed Moira at all, that was.

Molly had been the star, Moira the shadow. That dynamic, Jason knew, was probably why he'd always felt an affinity for his aunt. His mother had done her damnedest to re-create that dynamic with him and his brother. He couldn't say it had been completely unsuccessful, but he also knew that one of the reasons he continued to frustrate her so much was that he'd simply refused to be put in the box she'd designated for him.

"Thanks, Aunt Moira," he called after her as she left. She stooped briefly to ruffle the fur on Rosie's head, but where she normally would have lingered to fuss over her, she vanished out the front door with impressive speed. He couldn't blame her. Having escorted some of the company out, Rosie trotted back over to where Jason and his mother stood by the couch.

"Good girl," Jason told her. She wagged her tail at him, panting happily.

"I don't know why you got such a little dog. They bite."

"She doesn't bite," Jason said firmly. "She just barks. And you see where the fur's just starting to grow back on one of her haunches? That's where somebody got her with a BB gun."

"Oh. That's too bad," she replied, turning and heading for the kitchen without so much as a glance at his dog. "Why didn't you get another golden retriever? You loved Max."

He watched her fill up her water bottle, already tired of the conversation. For someone who professed to hate his ex, she sure talked about her a lot. Her, and the trappings of his former life. Poor Max. Taking him was the one thing Sara had done that Jason had found truly vindictive. The dog had always been more his than hers.

"I did, yeah. I just like dogs, Mom. Rosie qualifies."

"Hmm. Well, I hope she behaves. I like goldens better."

His eyes narrowed as she opened the fridge. "You didn't like them in the house." One of his great pleasures as a kid had been letting Pongo and Perdy inside when she wasn't around, putting their paws on all the furniture that she wanted to keep immaculate. They'd seemed okay with their doghouses, and with the garage on the truly frigid days, but he'd always wanted them in where it was warm, where maybe one of them could have slept at the foot of his bed.

Well, now he had Rosie, who slept wherever she wanted on the bed and snored like a freight train. The thought of the sound carrying tonight made him happier than it should have.

"Oh, stop," she said, waving her hand while she dug around. "Those dogs had good lives outside. Can you imagine what a mess the house would have been if we let them run around the indoors? We'd have had so much dirt, not to mention the ticks and fleas . . . did you get me my lemons? And what is all this Chinese food? Is this what your girlfriend is feeding you?"

"I haven't been doing a lot of running to the store," he said flatly. "We can go out later. I'll have Zoe drive." *Hopefully. If she hasn't run screaming out of here by then.* "We did takeout last night."

"Well, you'll be eating better while I'm here," she informed him, shutting the fridge. "I thought I'd take the three of us into town for lunch today. She and I can get acquainted, you can get some air . . . it'll be fun!"

She had the wild look in her eyes that brooked no argument, so Jason moved around to the front of the couch and sat. He barely had to pat the cushion beside him before Rosie appeared there, circling once before flopping down with a sigh as heavy as the one he wanted to heave. His mother chattered away at him while she got situated, moving her suitcases up into the loft bedroom he couldn't use right now, turning on the TV so she could keep half an eye on her daytime talk shows, and offering running commentary and critique on everything from the state of his house (acceptable, still too small) to his shorts (didn't he have something better than that to go out in?).

But to his surprise, he didn't feel like the rest of the day was completely hopeless. It was still weird to think of Zoe Watson as an ally, but it was true. She was probably headed this way by now. And given how he felt about that, Jason guessed the old adage must be true.

Misery really did love company.

Zoe was nothing if not punctual.

She pulled in at noon on the dot, silently patting herself on the back for getting there exactly when she'd meant to. "Like Gandalf," she said quietly, and grinned. She felt a little ridiculous for the way her stomach began to flutter immediately at the sight of the house, which was still as quiet and cozy as a cabin in the woods ought to be. The trees surrounding it, just beginning to turn, were going to be gorgeous in fairly short order. This whole scene would be as pretty as a painting.

And she would be busy elsewhere, she told herself firmly. By then, Jason ought to be back to whatever kind of routine he had—yelling at clouds, frightening small children, whatever he did for fun—and she'd be busy with the gallery's fall schedule. Which was good, because they would have run out of things to talk about long before she was done here—she was sure of it. Even if last night had been sort of . . . surprising. The man could actually talk. Without saying anything antagonistic, even.

Maybe it had just seemed all right because his dog was so cute. The way things were going, she was a long while from being able to have a dog of her own, but Rosie was certainly selling her on the Pekingese breed. She was pampered and pretty, but she had some sass. It was a winning combination.

And she wasn't going to get to fuss over her if she just stayed in the car imagining the beings currently in the house instead of actually interacting with them.

Zoe stepped out of the car, smoothed her dress, and headed up onto the porch. Rosie's immediate barking made her smile. Jason had told her to just let herself in today. He sure didn't like getting around on those crutches, even if he seemed to be doing just fine on them.

She felt a little strange about just walking in like she owned the place, but knocking and waiting just to annoy him was, for once, the less appealing option. They had to function as some kind of unit today. Better to start off on the right foot. It wasn't like they wouldn't have plenty of opportunities to poke at each other later.

"Hey, Rosie girl," she cooed as she opened the screen door and then turned the knob, actually looking forward to getting a little puppy time in. Two conflicting scents hit her at once—strong perfume mixed with cooking meat. Startled, she stepped inside and then stopped, barely hearing the door shut behind her. Jason looked up from where he was sprawled in a chair, his broken leg resting on the ottoman. Rosie bounced around her feet, growling in her funny way that made her sound kind of like a purring alien, and Zoe absently reached down to pet her when a woman's sharp voice carried from the kitchen.

"Jason, call off that dog! She's going to bite somebody!"

Zoe looked at Rosie's hopeful little face and without much thought reached down to scoop her into her arms. She was a surprisingly solid little thing, but willing enough to be held, fortunately. Zoe wasn't sure why she'd done it, apart from a strong burst of irritation that anybody would find Jason's dog anything but harmless. For her trouble, Rosie tried to wiggle herself around to face her, tongue working furiously. Zoe let her get a couple of kisses in on her chin before readjusting her.

"It's fine," Zoe called to whoever had spoken. She took a few more steps in, curious, when Jason caught her eye. His expression wasn't one she'd seen on him before. He looked . . . relieved? Grateful? And there was something more she couldn't quite put her finger on. It had warmth curling through her, heating both her blood and her cheeks. Suddenly off-balance, she offered him a small smile. To her amazement, he returned it, though his expression grew shaded again when that voice piped up from the kitchen.

"Well, you just put her right out if she's bothering you. That dog is mouthy. Come on in! I'm just prepping some dinner for later. I think he was planning to feed me nasty leftover takeout tonight. Can you believe he ate that for breakfast?"

"Um." Rosie started to wiggle again, so Zoe dropped a kiss on top of her head and lowered her to the floor. Another look at Jason's face as he started to maneuver himself out of his chair and Zoe put the pieces together. Somehow, the schedule had changed. His mother had arrived early . . . and no one had bothered to let her know. She'd dealt with worse last-minute changes of plans, but she still felt panic welling in her throat, forcing her to swallow it down. There was supposed to be some time. She and Jason were supposed to go over a few last-minute things. For God's sake, could the man not have *called*?

"Zo," he said, and somehow hearing her nickname on his lips when he'd just let her walk into an ambush annoyed her beyond all reason. She gave him a look that she hoped promised doom, even while slapping a big fake smile on her face.

"Hey, baby," she said, and the way his eyebrows shot up toward his hairline *was* sort of funny. If he thought she couldn't lay it on thick when the situation called for it, he was sorely mistaken. Besides, the sooner they got his mother out of town, the sooner she could drop the act and annihilate him. "You didn't tell me your mother was going to be here already. What a nice surprise!"

She walked over to where he was now upright and hulking over his crutches, his hair falling over his forehead in loose brown waves. His clothes looked clean, at least, though she suspected she was going to get tired of his baggy shorts and seemingly endless selection of slightly ragged T-shirts by the time they were through.

"Ooh, are you Zoe? I should have known! Not like he has so many girls visiting him. Just let me wash off my hands . . ."

Zoe looked into the kitchen, where a tall, attractive blonde was waving at her. She returned the wave, noted that the woman was still watching her and Jason expectantly, and bit back a sigh.

Well, here we go. Hope I'm not too out of practice.

Steeling herself, Zoe moved to stand directly in front of Jason, only inches separating them. He looked down at her like she might bite him, and the familiarity of that was weirdly comforting. She arched an eyebrow at him, hoping he got the message behind it: *It's only me, you idiot. Just go with it.* She wondered briefly how long it had been since he'd had any practice at this, whether it might be as sad as her own dry spell, and then pushed that thought aside. Looked like they were both getting a crash refresher course in Relationships 101. She supposed she should be grateful that he smelled good, kind of fresh and piney. Kind of . . . yummy.

That cologne is making me want to nibble on you, and I don't even know if that's helpful or not. She rose on her tiptoes, heard him inhale softly, even as his eyes lowered to fix on her mouth. Whether it was with anticipation or horror, she had no idea.

"Sorry," he whispered, his lips barely moving, the word a puff of air against her skin.

"You will be," she whispered back, then pressed her mouth to his for a quick, friendly, appropriate-for-in-front-of-moms kiss. At least, it was meant to be quick. Zoe had calculated that maybe three or four seconds was the right length. Not a peck, not awkwardly long, but clearly demonstrative. She'd worked it all out. Written it in the notebook, even. Except Jason's lips were soft. Really soft. And warm.

He lowered his head just a little before she could move away, those sinfully long lashes twining together when he closed his eyes. Zoe's slipped shut as well, every well-organized, perfectly reasonable thought she had in her head vanishing at once. Instead, there was nothing but Jason's warmth, drawing her in. Her hand found his shoulder, reassuringly solid, and she could feel his response to that simple touch ripple all the way through him. He tipped his head just slightly, changing the angle of the kiss, and moved his lips against hers to take a taste of her bottom lip.

The delicious shock of it was the only thing that brought her back to herself. But instead of heeding her body's sudden, shrieking insistence that she wrap herself around him, she pulled away with a sharp intake of breath. They locked eyes as Zoe lowered her heels to the ground. It had lasted only seconds, she reassured herself. A few seconds too long, maybe, but not as many as it had felt like. It was okay. It had been smooth enough for a casual observer to think nothing of it. Up close, though, there was no way Jason could miss the effect the kiss had had on her. That hot little nip at her lips—what was he *thinking*?

You did that on purpose, she wanted to hiss at him. But she couldn't seem to do more than stare into brown eyes that looked both hazy and confused, as though she'd been the one to catch him off guard.

"Aren't you two cute? It's so nice to finally meet you! Well, I say finally . . . I didn't even know about you until two days ago."

Zoe started to move away from Jason as Molly Evans approached, then remembered that right now she was actually *supposed* to stay close to him. She shot him a quick, awkward glance before positioning herself beside him, close enough to touch but not touching. Definitely not touching. Or even thinking about it—much.

Flustered, Zoe tried to focus her attention on the woman coming at her with her arms open wide. She didn't look scary. She looked ... tall. Of course, being five-two, she thought a lot of people looked tall.

She quickly found herself enveloped in a heavily perfumed embrace. Zoe tried to relax into a quick, tight hug that felt stiffer than she'd expected. His mother pulled back quickly, holding Zoe at arm's length to examine her. She felt a little like she was dangling from a pair of hooks, being sized up for dinner. It was a fleeting impression, but one she couldn't shake.

After hearing the stories, Zoe had pictured Molly Evans as a frumpy sort of woman, with flyaway hair, mom jeans, maybe some ugly glasses. And of course, a permanently sour expression. This person, however, had the fit, tanned look of a woman who'd always been an athlete. Strong featured, with sharp brown eyes and blond hair cut into intricate, jaw-length layers, she wasn't soft enough to be called pretty. Attractive, though, definitely. Her tall frame was clad in yoga pants and color-coordinated athletic gear—her tee, hoodie, and sneakers all strongly featured the same bright shade of magenta—and several very large diamonds glittered on her fingers. Another solitaire glittered on a chain around her neck.

Lady of leisure, Zoe thought, and then kicked herself for it. She didn't know this woman, and that was unkind. Just because she'd dealt with that type plenty back when she was at the gallery in Atlanta didn't mean Jason's mother was like them. It just meant that some people really liked to wear a lot of jewelry with their workout clothes ... which they wore for a lot of things that weren't working out. They also tended to drive a specific type of crossover SUV in a couple of specific colors and *Oh God, I have to stop—I'm being awful already and she's done nothing.*

"Well," Molly said, "it's nice to see Jason still has some taste. Very pretty. I'm Molly Evans, Jason's mother. But I think you knew that." She smiled, but despite the creases it produced at their corners, the expression didn't quite reach her eyes. Zoe hoped she was just being cautious. After all, they'd only just met. And Jason did have some kind of hated ex-wife.

"I'm Zoe," Zoe said, hoping her own smile looked more genuine. "But I guess you knew that, too." She was released, though Molly didn't move away.

"The kiss was a big clue, unless a whole lot of things have changed since the last time I was here. Jason never dated much. Not that I understand why he's still so bad at attracting women. I mean, isn't big and rugged and hairy kind of a thing right now? Or is that just in those books everybody's reading? With the restraints and riding crops." Her laugh was loud, echoing to the high ceiling. "I might have a few of those at home," she added in a stage whisper. "Kinky billionaire heroes. Love 'em." Jason groaned.

"Mom."

Zoe was amused despite herself. She'd never seen Jason turn that particular shade of red before. "I don't know about any of that, but I like Jason just fine. Broken leg and all," she added, remembering why she was here in the first place.

"It shows," Molly said, widening her eyes along with her smile, which Zoe had begun to feel was unnaturally sunny. "Not everybody would come out here and try to keep things running out of the goodness of their hearts! I expected a mess, but it isn't nearly that bad."

The half compliment, half insult hit Zoe like a cold slap of water, and she knew right away what she was dealing with. She also knew that whatever Jason might purchase from the gallery to repay the favor, he was the one getting a bargain here. She glanced up at him, saw a jaw in his muscle twitch, and realized he was more irritated than she was. Of course, she hadn't had to grow up with this.

"You don't like it, you can take it up with my cleaning service," he said flatly. "Are we going to go to lunch or what?"

"We are?" Zoe asked.

"You need a cleaning service for a log cabin?" asked Molly.

He looked between them. "Merry Meet works for me. I'll get my shoe."

Molly shook her head as she watched him head for the sandals by the back slider. "Well, *some* things haven't changed."

Zoe eyed her before returning her attention to Jason and the impressive way he managed to stalk even with crutches. Maybe that wasn't surprising, but as for everything else? She couldn't disagree with Molly more.

Everything had changed. In a matter of minutes, Jason's goal—to get his mother the heck out of Dodge—had become her own.

From here on out, they were a team.

Chapter Eight

Merry Meet sat at the bottom of the square, a squat, curious little building of aging brick that tended to put people in mind of a ramshackle witch's house—an association the owners had unabashedly played up. There was a peaked roof, and just beneath it a circular window where the silhouette of an arching black cat could be seen, especially in the evening when a light came on behind it. The curtains in the windows were cheerfully mismatched, and a carved wooden sign, adorned with both the name of the restaurant and the outline of a cauldron for good measure, moved gently in the breeze.

Zoe found a parking spot not far away, in front of Jasper's Used Books, and pulled in. Jason sat in the passenger seat, and she wasn't sure it would ever be adjusted correctly again considering how far back he'd pushed it. Molly had insisted upon driving Jason's SUV, since she "had some errands to run" after lunch. She appeared to have also taken a detour on the way to the square, since the truck was nowhere to be seen.

They'd spent the ten-minute drive over in silence, and when Zoe killed the engine, the complete absence of conversation filled the car. She made no move to get out, simply sitting with her hands on the wheel. After a moment, Jason sighed.

"So, my mother."

"Mmmhmm," Zoe replied. She tapped her fingers on the wheel. She actually kind of liked the silence. The entire process of deciding who was taking which car where, and with whom in it, had been the opposite of silent.

"She's got some issues," he said.

Zoe widened her eyes and looked ahead of her, through the windshield, where there was a couple browsing Jasper's shelves with smiles on their faces. She bet it was quiet and sane in there, too. "Yes," she finally replied, since it seemed like Jason was waiting for some sort of acknowledgment. Jasper Reed, a tall, lanky Brit in his late fifties whose short little ponytail and hoop earring made him look like an aging pirate—which worked on him, everyone agreed—moved to help the male half of the couple, looked through the glass, and spotted Zoe. He waved and gave her a cheeky grin, and she was glad to raise a hand and return the greeting before he went about his business.

Life went on normally in the Cove today, it seemed. *Almost* everywhere.

"So, are you going to wait for me to get out and then take off like a bat out of hell?"

Now she turned her head to look at him. He was, it pained her to note, adorable even in his misery.

"Ye of little faith," she said. "You think I'm afraid of a woman who takes twenty minutes to decide how she can get her own car to drive so she can keep everybody waiting on her?"

"Not afraid, exactly," Jason replied. "More like annoyed beyond all reason."

Zoe watched him steadily. "Jason Evans. I have been dealing with people professionally for my entire adult life. I have been screamed at, called ugly names, had things thrown at me, my boss called, and once had the meanest toy poodle in existence sicced on me because I wasn't offering its owner enough of a special-person discount."

His mouth curved up ever so faintly in that almost-smile he had that made her brain fuzzy. "So you don't think she's annoying?"

"I didn't say that. And stop making puppy-dog eyes at me. I'm not going anywhere."

Jason wrinkled his nose and frowned. "I don't make puppy-dog eyes."

"Uh-huh. Come on, let's get moving. You're so slow it'll take us an hour to get where we're going. Maybe by then she will have shown up."

Zoe got out of the car, catching a few choice words from her passenger that made her grin as she did. Rather than wait for him, she rounded the car and opened Jason's door. He looked up at her balefully.

"I could have done that."

"No kidding. I don't have a year, though."

"Keep calling me slow," he warned her. "You'll be walking along and one of these crutches will take your feet out from under you before you even know what happened."

"Am I wearing earplugs in this scenario? Or are you going to hire a ninja to do your dirty work for you while you watch from a bench somewhere? I'm not sure how this works, otherwise. Nice fantasy, though."

He handed her his crutches to hold while he got up, then took them back while she shut the door and locked the car. They walked together up onto the sidewalk, and he *was* slow, but Zoe found she didn't much mind. It was too much fun teasing him about it. They were only a block from the Cove's small harbor here, where various boats bobbed in the choppy waves. The sound of the ever-present gulls looking for fish or whatever else they might manage to stuff into their gullets had come to sound like home to Zoe. She listened to their cries and debated about wandering down here by herself later to have a walk on the short stretch of sandy beach that was always covered with people during the summer. This time of year it was far more peaceful, the tourists sticking to the town itself. Harvest Cove was a treasure in any season, but fall was when she came into her own. Supposedly founded by witches, the Cove had proven irresistible to people seeking a historic New England town with a bit of spooky charm. They even had a magic tree.

Well, that was the story, anyway . . . that the founding witches had planted the tree, and that as long as it grew strong so would the town, its families rooted here in a way that tended to bring even the most prodigal locals back eventually. Zoe didn't buy the magic part, but the gorgeous old oak in the park that sat at the center of the square, its branches numerous and gnarled, stretching to shelter whoever chose to spend some time with it, was a beautiful symbol for the town. And she supposed Sam, who had loved to sketch beneath it as a girl before she'd run as far as she could from here, would argue that there had to have been *some* magic in the Cove to have brought her back permanently.

Zoe was of the opinion that Sam's current living situation had more to do with a sexy smile and a nice butt than a tree, but what did she know?

"What are you smiling about?"

She turned her head, startled out of her thoughts by Jason's deep voice. He was watching her curiously, his brown eyes warmer and more open than she was used to. It was a nice change, even if it left her feeling at a bit of a loss. They hadn't had much in the way of normal conversation yet. But they were in her place now—she thought of the square as one of her places, at least—and all of the familiar sounds and smells put her more at ease than she might have been otherwise. She was just a girl talking to a guy on their way to lunch. No crazy mothers, no fighting, no weirdness. Just a normal date.

That makes it pretty abnormal for me, actually, but I'll try to go with it.

"Just thinking about Sam and her Witch Tree," Zoe replied, and the look on Jason's face told her that wasn't the answer he'd expected. "She likes to go sketch under it on her lunch breaks when the days are nice. I'm sure she'd be there right now if I hadn't left her in charge for the rest of the day." She arched an eyebrow. "Why, what did you think I was smiling about?"

"The thought of tripping me, maybe."

She laughed and shook her head. "You have an inflated opinion of my meanness, Jason. I can't decide whether I should encourage that or not."

"You're pretty mean when I come into the gallery."

"Well, you're pretty annoying when you come into the gallery, so . . . you might want to consider that there's a cause-and-effect thing going on there." They crossed a narrow street, moving past buildings of brick and stone, all the storefronts decked out in autumn finery. Little flags on the wrought-iron lampposts were bright orange, bearing a silhouette of the Witch Tree and the words "Welcome Home to Harvest Cove."

"Those are so cute," she said, indicating a flag with a wave of her hand. "Makes me excited for the Jack o'Lighting."

"Really?" he asked. They stopped just in front of Merry Meet, which Zoe thought smelled like heaven itself. She was hungry. Much to her chagrin, she was her father's daughter that way. She liked her meals on time, and thanks to Molly's machinations, her stomach was complaining about the delay. She only hoped that Jason wouldn't hear it growling. That or just be nice enough not to mention it, which was a long shot.

"You don't like the flags? How can you not like the flags?" she asked. "And don't even think about hating on the Jack o'Lighting. If you do that, I *will* trip you."

Jason shrugged. "I like all of that fine. I just didn't know you went in for that sort of thing."

"Meaning . . ."

"You know, the cutesy cornball townie thing." When she just leveled a blank look at him, he continued. "You just, you know, you own an art gallery. You get written up in the *Globe* and host private artsy cocktail parties. You're carrying a giant purse with a designer name on it even I recognize, and trust me, that's saying something. And Jake said you have some kind of tea . . . thing."

She paused to digest all of that before shaking her head. "I'm going to be honest with you, Jason. I need to order some food before I even get started on all of that. So let's go get a table, okay?"

"As you wish," he said. When she stopped and stared at him, he asked, "What?"

She hesitated, thinking that she was just imagining things, but there was a sly humor in his expression that insisted otherwise. After a moment, Zoe decided to test him. "Nothing, farm boy. I just didn't realize I was walk-ing into a battle of wits."

"I don't know what you're talking about," Jason re-plied, and Zoe rolled her eyes to cover her embarrass-ment. Of course he didn't know. He'd probably grown up on movies about manly men who liked to shoot things and smash up fast cars in realistically gritty settings. Or maybe he just watched a lot of Discovery Channel or something. *When Wildlife with Sharp, Pointy Teeth At-tack.* One of the hostesses opened the door for them, and just as Zoe started in, she heard Jason mutter, "Should have brought the iocane powder for my mother."

She burst into delighted laughter. "Treebeard quoting *The Princess Bride*? I would never have . . . um . . ." Her eyes widened as she realized what she'd done. She'd taken care never to let him know her nickname for him, and that had been easy enough when all of their interac-tions had been short. Now, though, she'd relaxed too much and slipped. The confusion on his face would have been a lot more entertaining if she didn't think she was going to catch hell once he figured it out.

"Treebeard?"

"Let's go get a table." She hurried past the hostess, who held the door for Jason and then led them to a table beside a large painting of a coven of traditional-looking witches kicking up their skirts (to reveal striped stock-ings, of course) beneath a full moon. It was cute and kitschy, much like the restaurant itself, with its warm and rustic interior decorated with all manner of witch-themed memorabilia. Each table had a candle situated inside a glass pumpkin, making the tables glow in the dim light. Zoe settled herself in the seat closest to the wall and looked around, trying not to notice the look Jason was giving her. The place was busy, as it usually was. She ordered things to go from here sometimes, but rarely came in to sit down and eat.

Now if she could just manage to enjoy it.

"We're waiting on a third before we do appetizers," Zoe told the server who came to take their drink order. She ordered a cream soda, while Jason got a root beer. He was silent when the server walked away, and Zoe continued looking around, pretending she couldn't feel his eyes boring into her skull.

"*Where* is your mother?" she asked.

"Treebeard? Seriously?"

She made eye contact then, and discovered something new—the face Jason made when he was trying to figure out whether he was mad or not. His nose was slightly scrunched up, his dark brows drawn together, and he looked as though he'd just been told there was nothing to drink here but toilet water.

"I don't know why you're all bothered," Zoe said, unfolding her silverware from her napkin and setting the linen on her lap. "I'm not the one who accused you of being a snob."

"I didn't say you were a snob. And what the hell are you doing? We're not eating yet."

"I'm exhibiting a strange behavior called manners," Zoe replied. "My mama always made us put the napkin on our laps right away, and since she is a lady with class, that's what I do."

"Well, I'm not doing that until the food gets here."

"Fine."

"And I didn't say you were a snob."

"You implied I think I'm too good for the cute little traditions the Cove does. That I walk around with my designer purse judging things."

"No, I didn't. And why am I named after a big, stupid talking tree?"

"Maybe because you drag half the forest around with you on your shoes, at least when I see you."

His eyes narrowed. "Yeah, I'm sure the big and stupid part has nothing to do with it."

She realized he'd decided to get offended about it, which was going to ruin lunch if she didn't do something to stop it. The problem was, she was still smarting from having been called a snob. It was a barb slung at her often enough when she was home, seeing people who'd never ventured outside of the little world that was small-town Georgia. It didn't sting from those people as much as it once had, but getting it from Jason was less expected and decidedly more painful. She silently counted to ten, breathed deeply, and looked directly at Jason.

"If I thought you were big and stupid, I wouldn't be sitting here. And if I were a snob, I wouldn't be living in the Cove. I like small towns. I grew up in one. So maybe give me a little credit before you make a bunch of assumptions about me."

He watched her for a long moment, and she could tell there was a lot going on in his mind, even if he didn't say anything. When he finally spoke, it was with careful deliberation.

"Come up with a different nickname," he said, "and I'll work on the assumptions."

"Cool. Start with the assumption that I mean anything bad by the nickname. I love Tolkien. Ents are cool.

They're also trees, which I have sometimes suspected you are, considering what you track into my gallery."

Jason grunted, which she supposed she could take as either positive or negative. Or possibly something between the two. Thinking about it, maybe? That she'd managed to get under his skin so easily surprised her, considering how long they'd been doing battle. Big and stupid? Was that really what he thought she'd meant? Zoe felt as though he'd cast aspersions on her honor. She also felt an unexpected pang of sympathy for the man sitting across from her. She'd thought him big, gorgeous, and fairly well impervious to everything life might throw at him—failures, insults, the elements, large rocks—but here he was with a busted leg and hurt feelings.

The thought that he might have gotten the "big and dumb" thing from other people provoked a flash of protective anger that flared white-hot before vanishing as quickly as it had appeared. It might have worried her, if she'd had time to think about it, but a voice carried to them from the front of the restaurant in a sharp singsong.

"Hey, you two! Sorry I'm late!"

"Oh God," muttered Zoe. When Jason snorted with laughter she realized she'd said it out loud. Apparently, this was not her day for discretion. She blamed him. Him and his puppy-dog eyes and his damned yummy cologne. She touched her forehead with her hand, then allowed herself a brief face palm before peeking up at him. On the upside, he didn't look upset anymore. Actually, he looked pretty entertained. At her expense.

"Sorry," she said quietly. Out of the corner of her eye, she saw Molly making a beeline for them.

"Don't be," Jason replied. "I'd be more worried if you didn't have that reaction."

"Well. But it's still your mother."

"She sure is. Which makes me an expert on the subject."

Molly arrived at the table in a rush of perfumed air, tossing herself into the chair next to her son with a dramatic flourish. "You wouldn't believe," she said, "who I ran into at the gas station!"

"The tank was full, Mom."

"Never hurts to top it off," she admonished him. "And I wanted to run into the mini-mart. Anyway, who should be pumping gas next to me but Janie Fredericks! You remember, Tommy used to go out with her daughter, Kristin." She waved her hand dismissively. "Nice girl, but he didn't need to be tied down back then. You could just tell she was always going to be a local, and he was on his way to bigger things."

"Nothing wrong with staying local," Jason said, and though his voice was cool, Zoe could see the tension in the way he held his head, in the set of his jaw.

"I know that," Molly replied. "You know I loved living here. But small towns are so limiting. Your father had a hellish commute for years because he wanted more. And look where we are! Sun all year, amazing shopping, friends who've *lived* . . . There's just so much more opportunity. And money. It doesn't buy happiness, but it sure as hell helps."

"It helps, but it isn't everything. I wouldn't like the city, Mom."

"As if you ever tried it," she shot back, an edge creeping into her voice. "You never pushed yourself."

"Sure. That's why I was a straight-A student."

"There are other ways to push yourself. Out of your

comfort zone, for instance. The football coach wanted you—"

Jason groaned, cutting her off. "Jesus Christ. I'm thirty-one. Could we not have this discussion again? I liked running, not football. So I ran. I'm not outgoing. Oh well. I love the outdoors, so I got a degree I could roll into a job that let me be outside. And stay here. Because I like it here." Each word was enunciated perfectly, his speech slowing. Zoe picked up on it immediately. So far, it was the prime indicator he was agitated or upset.

Oddly enough, she'd never noticed it when he came into the gallery. Apparently he really *did* enjoy coming in to argue with her.

"Well, Tommy—"

"I'm not Tommy."

"Of course you're not. I swear to God, Jason, you're not even *listening*."

Zoe looked between them and noted that Molly seemed pretty oblivious to the emotions she was inspiring in her son, focused instead on her own frustration with what felt like a well-worn argument. Jason's hands rested on the table in front if him, and Zoe watched his fingers flex, as though he was trying to keep from simply balling them up. She felt herself tensing in response, a natural reaction that was difficult to stop. She'd always been good at picking up on other people's emotions, a boon where her business was concerned. But in uncomfortable situations, it sometimes made her want to crawl out of her skin. She'd trained herself, over the years, to tune some of it out, at least enough to get through the day. Then she'd curl up and decompress. She was well aware that people not built the same as she was didn't understand, that she sometimes looked antisocial. Or snobby.

The flicker of annoyance that thought provoked was quickly banished when Jason caught her eye. In that single look was frustration, weariness, and apology. She might have imagined him apologizing for mucking up her floors from time to time, but this was one thing he didn't need to be sorry about.

"Oh, look, here's our server," Zoe said, giving the waitress who'd been hovering hesitantly a couple of tables over a warm smile. The girl looked relieved at the signal to approach, and Zoe knew she'd been listening to the escalating argument. It was nothing she'd want to get in the middle of, either, but here she sat. And because she wanted to try to enjoy the food she was about to order, it behooved her to find a way past this ugly little spat as soon as possible.

Long experience told her exactly what was needed.

"So, Molly," Zoe said, turning all of her attention to the woman whose mouth was pressed into a thin line as she fiddled absently with her rolled silverware. "Jason tells me you used to sit on the Harvest Cove Arts Council. I guess I have you to thank for some of the things I enjoy so much about our little downtown. Are you an artist yourself?"

It was the right call. Molly blushed with pleasure. "Oh! Well, no, not exactly. I mean, I've always gotten compliments on my decorating. My friends say I have a good eye for what works in a space. They're the ones who insisted I should be on the council, really, and it did turn out to be fun. Bringing some beauty and culture to the Cove, you know. I was more of an athlete, of course . . . Jason probably told you that, too. Basketball. I still play in a league, actually. Have to keep in shape somehow, and it's fun to smoke some of the younger ones who don't think old ladies can play. Not that they think I'm old," she added quickly, eyes rounding. "They can never believe it when I tell them I'm in my late fifties. I've gotten to be such good friends with some of them, and they're *so* fun . . ."

"Sorry to interrupt, but are you ready to order?"

Molly barely took a breath to order her food before resuming her monologue, and Zoe listened with half an ear, smiling and nodding in what she knew was a reasonable facsimile of rapt attention while quietly keeping an eye on Jason. He ordered a sandwich and fries in a low voice, probably so as not to disrupt the flow of words coming out of his mother's mouth lest she return her attention to him. His hands still rested on the table, though the fingers had relaxed and gone still.

It was silly, Zoe thought, to want to reassure him. The man was obviously used to this, and he didn't seem to have a problem fighting back. Still, that look he'd given her refused to let her be. So because it was in character, and because she had no other way of telling him it was okay, she slid her hand over to cover one of his, giving it a gentle squeeze. It was all she could think to do. And if she was being honest with herself, it was what she wanted to do.

His hand was warm, and Zoe felt her heart stutter just the way it had the first time a boy had ever held her hand. Silly, maybe, but no one had to know. She started to pull her hand away, since holding hands at lunch seemed like it might be overkill after they'd already shared that strange, slightly amazing kiss earlier to show off their "relationship." At the first hint of movement, though, Jason turned his hand over to thread his fingers through hers, capturing her hand and holding it in place. Keeping them connected.

Zoe risked breaking eye contact with Molly just once, unable to resist a look at Jason, unable to shake the feeling that he *wanted* her to look. He seemed focused on his mother—probably as concerned as she was that things be kept as pleasant as possible—but he must have sensed her gaze. His eyes met hers, sending an electric little thrill of awareness through her. Molly's voice faded to a background drone, completely secondary to the overwhelming awareness of Jason's warm skin against hers, of the faint but unmistakable pulse of his heart. His eyes seemed to darken, full of their own heat, before he looked away as though nothing had passed between them.

Zoe forced her gaze back to Molly and immediately set about trying to convince herself that she'd imagined what she'd seen in Jason's expression in that brief moment. That her neglected libido was playing some nasty tricks on her, making her acting job a little too method for comfort. It was hard when her hand was still captured by his. It became impossible when his thumb moved in a single, gentle stroke against her finger, up and then down. Such a tiny motion—and Zoe knew that if she'd been standing, her knees would have buckled.

This isn't real, she told herself, even as her heart began to pound. *He's just playing a part.* Except she hadn't seen any acting ability from the man yet, and that tiny thumb stroke, the small but delicious twist to his kiss, wouldn't have registered to any audience but one.

Her.

Which meant that at some point very soon, she might need to rethink just how imaginary this whole thing was . . . for both of them.

Chapter Nine

Just had to bust my driving leg.

It was a thought that occurred to him multiple times a day, varying depending on how badly things were going. By Wednesday afternoon, the idea had occurred to him several hundred times. He could limp screaming into the forest, he guessed, but poor Rosie was not a woodsy dog, and if she stayed home she'd probably end up locked out and relegated to the doghouse his mother had helpfully shown him on her tablet. So affordable! So warm!

So completely unacceptable yet totally predictable!

He wanted to go to work, but he wasn't cleared for it yet. It was raining, so he couldn't hide out in the yard. He wanted the TV off, but that wasn't going to happen, and besides, it kept his mother busy. Sort of. She'd baked him cookies earlier, and he'd felt like an ass for being grumpy beforehand. The guilt lasted only about twenty minutes or so, though. Then she'd started in on the doghouse thing, absolving him of any ugly feelings he might have toward her for the rest of the day.

By two, she was just about vibrating.

"Let's go out to Withrow's Farm!"

"Why?" Jason asked. He looked up from where he was doing bills on his laptop at the table. It was boring, but at least it was keeping him busy.

"Maybe they have apples or something. Or pumpkins. Or a wreath for your door. You could use a wreath!"

"Not really," he replied. "I don't do wreaths."

"That's a great attitude," she complained, rolling her eyes. "This place needs a woman's touch. I've been saying it for years. If you're going to insist upon living in the woods, you could at least decorate. Your house in town—"

"I didn't decorate that. As you know." He looked down and kept working, with a silent wish that she'd find a different subject to distract her soon. The little house on Moonstone, an old Craftsman that had the kind of charm that meant a lot of repair work, had been decorated well according to everybody. Everybody but him. He hadn't hated it, but it had never felt comfortable, maybe because he'd had no part in it. The décor, in fact, had been one of the only things his mother and Sara had agreed on. They'd had a lot of stuff. A lot of *fussy* stuff. Even he had been afraid to touch it, and with good reason. Sara had just about had a nervous breakdown over a crystal saltshaker he'd bumped onto the floor. Plus she'd ignored every hint he'd dropped about wanting a comfortable recliner to flop in at the end of the day. But yeah, he supposed the place had looked nice.

So did museums. But he didn't want to hang out in them.

"Why doesn't Zoe do something with it?" his mother continued. "She works in art. This house must make her crazy!"

So much for wishing she'd let this drop. He couldn't quite keep the faint smile from his lips, though. On the list of things that made Zoe crazy, his house was probably way down right now.

"Zoe isn't going to redecorate my house, Mom. We haven't been together that long, and I wouldn't let her anyway."

"Then she won't stick around," she warned him. "Girls like her need to have nice things."

He bristled, even though he knew he shouldn't let it bother him. Taking the bait was always a pointless exercise. Didn't mean he could always help himself, though. "Guess she thinks I'm nice enough or she wouldn't be around."

"She left pretty quickly last night."

"She came for dinner. She was tired." That she'd shown up at all had been a pleasant surprise. After Sunday, he'd been positive she'd run while she could. Instead, she'd worked, called, kept tabs on him . . . and yesterday, at his mother's invitation, come by after work to eat. His only complaint was that she hadn't tried to hold his hand again, and the only kisses he'd gotten were quick pecks when she knew he wouldn't see them coming.

She was avoiding him without actually avoiding him. Zoe was the only woman he knew who could be capable of such a thing, and she was good at it. His only consolation was that it had to mean she'd felt something. Whether the something was good or completely repulsive was the question, and he hadn't been alone with her to ask. Not that he probably would. He'd rather just take action.

What that might be—at least if he didn't want any chance of her punching him in the face—was still a work in progress.

"Are you even listening to me? I know she was tired. That's not the problem."

Jason eyed her, wondering what kind of scenario she'd conjured up to get dramatic over.

Better to defuse it now than let it fester all day.

"I don't think she likes me. She didn't say anything about the pork chops."

"Only if you don't count when she said thank you, and that dinner was good," he replied. This was what he'd been hoping to put off. The competition. His mother had an intense need for immediate adoration, and if she didn't get it, things got weird very quickly. Zoe had a natural reserve about her that he actually kind of liked—it gave her an air of "don't mess with me" he could appreciate. But she was unfailingly polite, on top of being beautiful, both of which he'd thought his mother would respond well to. Apparently that wasn't going to be enough.

"She was just saying that to be nice. I can tell." She leaned against the wall and tapped her fingers on her hip. "Why do you always end up with the ones who don't like me?"

Jason had to swallow a groan. "That's crap, Mom. You haven't even given her a chance." Guilt tried to twist itself into a knot in his stomach, but he wouldn't let it. So what if it had taken him a while to figure out that Zoe wasn't exactly the cold snob he'd thought? He was busy. Things took time.

Yeah. Years, even. Genius.

"Maybe." She affected a long face. "Tommy's girlfriends always like me right away. Angela and I go shopping all the time."

"Oh, is that the flavor of the month's name? I lost track."

That earned him a glare. "Not everyone is ready to settle down at his age. He has a career to think about."

"Uh-huh." He decided to drop the subject, since he didn't want to talk about his brother, or the latest in the long string of silicone-enhanced wonders he was dating, or why he was supposed to be the one who settled down and stayed that way because obviously he had nothing better to do. There was also the danger she'd start talking about shopping, and he didn't want to do that, either. There were a few blissful moments of silence, but they didn't last.

"Let's go somewhere," she insisted again. "Why don't we drive out to Mel and Pete's? We can go to lunch!"

"We went to lunch yesterday, and I already ate." That was the one thing he could always count on—the eating. For her it was more about seeing people and being seen, he knew. For him, it was just about food. He was going to have to watch it. Without being able to run, he would blow up like a balloon eating this way. In some twisted way, it might make her happy. She'd have another thing to needle him about, anyway.

"Maybe the Tavern? Do they still have a good lunch?"

In that moment, he missed his grandmother with a strength that still carried with it the painful echo of his feelings when he'd lost her. Nanny had been fiercely protective of him, her house his refuge. He knew she was the reason why he wasn't far more screwed up than he was. Unfortunately, she never could spare him from everything, and he'd known since before he could remember that nothing he did, no one he chose, would ever be quite right for his mother. Worse, while she was criticizing him, she would never be able to sit still.

"Yes. And no, I'm not going anywhere."

She clucked her tongue in disgust. "Nice, Jason. Did they give you grumpy pills when you broke your leg? No wonder we've barely seen your girlfriend."

Maybe he could send her to the store for something, Jason thought, if he could come up with an item he needed. She'd gone crazy at Fresh Pride yesterday, though. It would be years before he ran out of either olive oil or tissue. Now she was just bored, and that was a problem. Her compulsions, her weird mix of love and disapproval, and her fixation on what everyone else thought of her had pushed Jason right back into the tangle of love and complete exasperation he felt whenever they spent time together. It was as exhausting as it always was, and it had only been three days.

Zoe would lighten things up when she came by tonight. That was what he had all his hopes pinned on, and what made wading through the day so excruciating. She'd made yesterday better. She would make today better. He didn't want to depend on that, but he didn't see where he had much choice. It was that or implement his half-assed running-away idea, and frankly, he wasn't feeling all that motivated.

"Well, we're going somewhere," his mother announced. "It's not good for you to be cooped up in here. You need to move around and get some fresh air, see some people. I came here to take care of you, and that's what I'm going to do. Get your shoes on. We can at least go down to the harbor."

Jason briefly considered refusing. After a few moments, though, he blew out a breath and closed up his laptop. She was right—it wouldn't hurt him to get out. Besides, it looked like a decent day outside. Maybe the fresh air would make his bones knit faster. At the very least he wouldn't have to listen to this stupid talk show. He glanced at the television, where someone was very involved in making something out of pipe cleaners and a gourd.

"Fine," he said. "There's some new stuff on the square since the last time you were here. I can park it on a bench somewhere if you want to check it out."

She clapped her hands together. "Perfect! We can stop into Zoe's gallery, too! I really want to see it."

"Uh, sure." He knew he should have seen that coming. A trip to the gallery to investigate had probably been her aim from the start. It wasn't something he could really get upset about, though, considering that it actually sounded better than just waiting around here. "Just don't get weird, okay?"

She stopped in the middle of putting her jacket on. "And what is that supposed to mean?"

"Nothing. Just be friendly. She likes you fine."

"I'm always friendly," she sniffed. "I was friendly yesterday."

"And you're already inventing stories about how she doesn't like you. Maybe just take it down a notch or ten and try to relax. She's nice," Jason said, and was surprised to find that he meant it. He'd considered her tough, beautiful, and difficult. Genuinely nice had been pretty far down on his list of expectations, and yet it seemed to be one of her defining characteristics.

Not that she was any less tough, beautiful, and difficult in her own special way. The thought, rather than irritating him, made Jason smile.

"I'm nice, too," his mother retorted. "Are we going? You should put the dog out back so she doesn't pee on anything."

Rosie, who had been sound asleep on the chair, opened one eye to regard Molly warily. Jason hobbled over to get his shoe, ignoring the suggestion.

"Are you really wearing that?"

"Yep."

"But your sweatpants have *paint* on them."

"Probably because I painted in them once." He wouldn't normally have worn them out, but he refused to buy an entire wardrobe full of clothes featuring elastic waistbands. Besides, a part of him enjoyed her irritation about it.

Jason sat on the bench by the front door, often a repository for shoes, coats, and whatever he might have an armload of at any given time, and shoved his foot into a beat-up old sneaker. He looked longingly at the other sneaker, wiggled the toes poking out of his cast, and sighed. Just about four weeks left of this, as long as he continued to heal right. At least he'd be out of the cast before the snow fell, but it pissed him off to lose the fall to his injury. This was his favorite season in the Cove.

If his rotten luck held, though, he might have to revise his opinion.

Jason didn't miss the way his mother eyed his sweats one last time before they headed outside. It was the same old story—in his family, he was the big one, the awkward one, the quiet one. The one who was always, for reasons he'd never completely understood, just a little bit embarrassing to his parents. He'd gotten used to it. He could even joke about it. But on days like today, when he was already worn down, it still managed to sting the way it used to.

Zoe, at least, would expect him to look like this, even if she didn't like it. But her stink-eye would be subtle, and whatever sort of welcome he got would be genuine. It wasn't much, but he didn't need much. Just a friendly face. And maybe a stingy kiss he could obsess about later.

Clinging to the thought that his day had nowhere to go but up, Jason jammed his crutches beneath his arms and headed out the door.

Two Roads gallery was quiet when they arrived, but for a couple of browsers who looked a little too dressed up to be local. Jason sized them up as he clomped in, announced as much by his noisy crutches as by the silvery tinkle of the bell above the door. He was so accustomed to dealing with out-of-towners by now that he could almost smell the difference on them. These two were daytrippers who'd probably taken the day off to escape the sprawl of suburbia and soak up a bunch of small-town charm. Tourism was the lifeblood of the Cove, so it was hard to complain much about visitors.

"This is gorgeous," the woman was saying to the man she was with, waving her hand at one of Sam's recent paintings that hung on the wall. Jason angled his head to see which one it was—he was in here often enough to have more than a passing acquaintance with the work on display—and smiled. It was a summer dreamscape, an impression of a garden in surreally vivid bloom, soaked in what might have been a passing silvery rain and lit by the glow from a single, tall lamppost. There was something otherworldly about all of Sam's work, and Jason had wondered more than once what sort of filter she saw the world through to create images like this one.

None of it would go with his stuff, but he found it fascinating to look at nonetheless. The one he really liked was the big one of the Witch Tree in its full October glory, with Loki, Sam's black cat, just visible in the tall grass nearby. Maybe he'd commission something one day, after he snagged a couple more of Zeke's rockers for the porch. He was by no means rich, but he was low maintenance . . . and he saved for what he liked.

"I mean to come in here every time I'm home," his mother said, craning her neck to look around. "I didn't think it would be this nice!"

Jason slid a look at her, but she was as oblivious to it as she always was. She ignored him, instead heading for a display of Andie Whitman's pottery. He had a couple of pieces at home, though he suspected she hadn't noticed and would continue not to unless he said something. Which he wouldn't.

There was a soft creak above him, and Jason turned his head to watch first Zoe's brown riding boots, then the rest of her, descend the stairs that led up to a number of studios used for both classes and rentable artist space. He felt the way he did every time he spotted her—a sudden tightness in the chest, a rush of heat. She looked as perfectly put together as she always did, the picture of casual elegance from head to toe. He wasn't sure how she managed it, since he usually saw her in some kind of stretchy leggings and big, loose sweaters and scarves this time of year. He thought of the leggings as, like, sweats for women. Socially acceptable pajamas. Except Zoe always looked like she was about to have tea with the queen.

Her curly black hair was up in a loose bun, the caramel highlights in it set off by the butterscotch color of her sweater. She was carrying a disposable cup that had steam rising from it, and from here he could see the faint imprint her lipstick had made on the rim. It took him a few long seconds to tear his eyes away. There was no earthly good reason why he should be so fixated on Zoe's mouth and whatever it had touched, but it was a hard habit to break.

When he managed to lift his gaze, his eyes met hers immediately. She looked . . . surprised. Pleased? He wanted to think there'd been a flash of that, but it was too quick to be sure and he wasn't into fooling himself. She looked quickly around the room to find his mother, and there was definitely no pleasure in her expression then. More like resignation.

"Hey," she said, smiling. "Welcome to Two Roads."

It seemed more like a general welcome than one just for him, so Jason offered only a small smile while the out-of-towners peppered Zoe with questions immediately. Was this her only gallery? Did she carry any more of Samantha Henry's work? How long would she hold a piece for with deposit?

The exchange had drawn Molly's rapt attention, but Jason had seen Zoe work her magic on customers often enough. She was tough not to buy from. That was part of the reason it was so entertaining to make several visits to look at a single piece before finally giving her the sale.

While the couple tried to decide between two of Sam's smaller paintings, Zoe excused herself for a moment to head for him. Her big gray eyes were both curious and wary, but her smile seemed real enough.

"Look at you, out in the real world," she said. She looked down, and for a second he thought she was going to give him a rough time about his clothing choices, but instead she simply said, "You haven't been hiking or anything, have you?"

He chuckled. "I think you're getting paranoid. Do I look like I could hike?"

"I put nothing past you. How's the leg today?"

The concern, so quickly and casually given, surprised him. He shrugged. "Fine. Itchy. A big pain in the ass."

"I bet." She glanced past him, to where his mother was momentarily distracted by a glass case full of handmade silver and gemstone jewelry. "Everything okay?" She said it quietly, barely moving her lips.

"Hell if I know."

That earned him a real smile, a flash of dazzling white as her eyes crinkled up at the corners. He found himself returning it without a thought. It was easy, too damn easy, to pretend she was really his.

It was some small consolation that her cheeks flushed prettily before she looked away, as though she was thinking the same thing. It felt a little like an awkward first date, friendly but flustered. You'd never know she'd kissed him just the other day. Not that it had meant anything. Probably. Even if she'd tasted like heaven and looked at him like maybe, just maybe, she would consider letting him take her clothes off with his teeth.

Careful, genius. You've gotten yourself into enough trouble here already.

"Molly," Zoe said, "have you been in before?"

"Never," his mother replied, moving to join them. "Love what you've done with the place. I always thought they'd tear it down eventually. It was such an eyesore, and we used to scare each other walking past it with a bunch of made-up crap about seeing people in the windows, stuff like that. But this is *amazing*. What a cute little gallery! It's just right for Harvest Cove!"

Jason winced, since he knew damn well Zoe didn't

consider the physical representation of her life's work either "cute" or "little," but she didn't miss a beat, even if the light in her eyes cooled considerably.

"Thank you," she said smoothly. "It was a lot of work to get this place in shape, but I knew right away it was perfect. The artists here are really something special, too."

"I wouldn't have thought," Molly said, looking around. "But I'd even buy some of this."

Zoe glanced up at Jason, and he was relieved to see she was more amused than angry. "Well, while I help these lovely people make their decision, you'll have to have Jason give you the grand tour if there are specific pieces you're interested in."

Molly laughed. "Right. I love my son, but you've seen his house. I think I'll give myself the tour instead."

Zoe's brows rose. "But haven't you seen—"

"Forget it," Jason interjected. "No big deal. You go ahead and do what you need to, Zo. I'll just hang around while Mom looks."

She blinked, but though she looked between them with enough confusion that he could see, she didn't argue. "Okay. I'll, ah . . . just be a few minutes. Enjoy." With one more searching look at him, she turned and walked back over to her customers. He heard her turn on the charm immediately, and wondered how anybody could work around people all the time without going insane, much less without just scaring everyone off in complete frustration.

Molly was still smiling, apparently tickled by the idea of her older son hanging around an art gallery. "You really come in here? I'm trying to picture that."

"Why wouldn't I come in here?" he asked. "It would've been hard to get her to go out with me if I hadn't."

"Good point. Ooh, what's that?" Molly walked past him, suddenly interested in Grace Levrett's photography. Obviously she hadn't noticed he had some of that on his walls, either. Jason shifted his weight uncomfortably and looked around the large room, with its gleaming wood floors and eye-catching arrangements of art—paintings and sculptures, pottery and jewelry, glimmers of light and beauty everywhere encouraging people to look further, closer. When he breathed in deeply, he could smell the light potpourri Zoe had planted somewhere, making the whole place smell like apples and spice. The first time he'd come into the gallery, it had been on a whim. He'd wanted a look inside for just the reasons his mother had given Zoe, with one addition. He'd also wanted a closer look at the small, curvy dynamo he'd seen only from a distance at that point.

Both the woman and the gallery had been far more compelling than he'd expected.

"What are you doing?" Her voice was a soft, irritable buzz by his shoulder. He turned his head as Zoe reappeared. "Why don't you want her to know that you actually know what you're looking at? She think *I* bought all that stuff in your house?"

"She hasn't noticed it," he muttered, hoping his mother didn't hear him. He needn't have worried, he realized, when he saw her join the couple still agonizing over which painting to buy. Lending her expertise, he was sure. Hopefully they wouldn't bolt.

"Hasn't noticed?" She tipped her chin down and looked up at him, arms crossed. "Did you hide everything? It was all there last night."

"No. She just doesn't see it. She only sees what she feels like seeing. It's some kind of superpower. Trust me."

"You could point it out," Zoe replied. "I know I will."

"No," he said quickly. "It's not worth it."

Her expression was incredulous. "Because . . . ?"

"It just isn't," he said flatly. Even if he felt like going into it, which he didn't, this wasn't the place to get into the reasons he no longer pushed back against his family's perception of him. He was happy. Happy enough, anyway, and they weren't around ninety-nine percent of the time, so there was very little struggle about it anymore. Visits were frustrating, but with any luck, this one would be over soon.

Zoe's eyes flashed a warning. "Jason," she began, and then closed her eyes. "Oh Lord. Is she really trying to talk them out of those paintings?"

He listened a moment. "Yes. Yes, she is. And she's got her phone out to show them something that they'd like better. Must be she's been redecorating her house again if she's got ideas about stuff to hang on the walls."

Her nostrils flared and her chin went up. "I'll be right back." Then Zoe turned on one heel and walked over to the small group, her voice as warm as melted butter as she soothed the ruffled feathers of her would-be customers. "That *is* nice, Mrs. Evans. But the style is completely different, and I believe these people were interested in one of Sam Henry's originals as opposed to buying a framed giclée." Her voice turned gently questioning. "Unless you'd prefer to look at something more traditional here? I can show you Mara Prince's work. She paints some beautiful local scenes."

Jason turned away, amused at how deftly Zoe defused the situation. The couple were adamant that they wanted one of Sam's paintings—the summer scene, as it turned out—and his mother was smart enough not to try to argue them out of it again. He didn't know what got into her sometimes. He never really had. But there were reasons she had as many enemies as friends in the Cove.

He glanced back over at Zoe, considering. Maybe he could make a little of this up to her. Stupid idea, probably, but once the idea materialized he found it impossible to banish completely. She steered the couple over to the antique desk she used for business, politely dismissing Molly with barely a word. His mother was left looking disgruntled in front of a very fine grouping of Sam's work. Stifling a sigh, Jason made his way back over to her.

"Nice, Mom."

"I was just trying to help," she hissed. Somehow, she managed to look wounded.

"Yeah, well, driving away business doesn't qualify. Come on, let's go down to the square. You can look in the shops and I can sit in the park. I'm already tired of lugging my cast around."

She shook her head. "I don't know how you can be so antisocial. You need to get out more. Your father and I have friends, your brother has tons of friends. . . . It's not that hard, Jason. You grew up here!"

"I have friends. I'm as social as I want to be. Not everybody's built the same. You raised me. You should know."

She looked up at him, her expression intense in the way it always got when she was mulling over his multiple shortcomings and various ways to fix them. The latter part was the one that worried him. This was the look that happened before she *did something*. It was the look she'd worn the day she'd driven him to football tryouts without telling him. And the day she'd had the basketball coach come to the house to assess him while he shot hoops in the driveway. And the time she'd set him up with a friend's daughter for homecoming, announcing it only on the day of the dance when she handed him a newly bought suit.

It was also the look she'd worn the day she'd signed him up for online dating.

Jason had the sudden and overwhelming urge to go lock himself in Zoe's office.

"It's my fault," Molly said. "I didn't push you hard enough because of your stutter. I should have made you interact more. Got you involved."

Jason bristled instantly. This was a subject he didn't want to canvass with her anywhere, much less here. "Not now, Mom."

She waved him away like she always did. "No, really, I—"

"Not now." He growled the words forcefully enough that he could feel Zoe's eyes on him, questioning. All at once, he'd had it with the day, this stupid outing, his damn leg, and most of all, family time. If that made him a terrible person, so be it.

"You and I have very different memories of my childhood, and I don't want to talk about it," he said slowly. "You're bored, so go ahead. Find something to do. Take the truck. I'll get a ride."

Molly's eyes rounded, and she looked as exasperated as he felt. "Jason Patrick Evans, don't you get miserable on me already. I've only been here since Sunday. You can just come on outside and lighten up. We'll go see—"

"No," he interjected firmly, trying to keep his voice low so that the other customers, who sounded like they were happily engaged in conversation with Zoe, didn't hear. They'd caused enough of a headache for her today. "I'm not interested in limping all over downtown. I'm tired and I'm done. Go see your friends."

Her nostrils flared. "Fine. I'll get out of your hair. But you're not going to hide forever. I won't let you. And if she does," Molly snapped softly, jerking her chin toward Zoe, "then you might as well still be single for all the good she'll do you. At least Sara made you push yourself."

She turned around and stalked out the door without so much as a look at Zoe. Though the conversation behind him never faltered, he could feel the curiosity radiating off of the customers, and it further darkened his mood. He hated making a scene. Dealing with park guests when they got unruly never bothered him this way—that was cleaning up a situation, not causing one. But drawing attention out in public for this kind of thing? No. And of course, the parting shot was classic. He was so tired of the insinuation that his marriage had fallen apart because of his own personality defects.

That was one thing he'd hand to Sara. She hadn't stuck around to trash him. When she'd taken off, people had drawn their own conclusions. Some were funny. A few were sad. Most, surprisingly, were somewhere in the vicinity of correct, not that he'd say so. Sara was as much a local as he was. That so many people had been shocked about their marriage in the first place should have been a warning, he guessed.

And the only time he really thought about it much anymore was when his mother arrived to remind him.

Damn it.

Jason tried to look casual as he headed over to look at Aaron Maclean's newest sculpture. He didn't know what the hell it was, but it was at least interesting. Something to stare at while he waited for Zoe to finish up.

It was hard to concentrate while he was seething, so while his eyes traced the fluid lines of the pale stone figure, his mind wandered. Zoe's rich voice, friendly and warm, was the only soothing thing he found, so he listened to her.

"Sam is actually teaching a class out at Bellamy Farm this October. Just one night. Wine, hors d'oeuvres, and painting. If you're interested, you should come check it out. She's not just a gifted artist, she's a lot of fun, and we've enjoyed putting this together. We'll probably do it more often if it goes well, since I have a few artists here who are interested in rotating on the schedule. And Zack Bellamy—he inherited the farm when his father passed away just recently—is excited about trying some new things apart from the weddings they host. Have you been out there? Absolutely gorgeous."

There were interested murmurs and questions as Zoe chatted with the couple, and Jason decided she'd probably hooked two more people into this painting-and-drinking class, or whatever it was. He didn't think he'd be signing up for that. His artistic ability was sparse enough when he was sober. Still, her enthusiasm for her new venture was apparent.

Her bootheels clicked against the hardwood as she moved from the desk to the wall where the chosen painting hung, and then back. "I'll just get this wrapped up for you, if you don't mind waiting a minute." Jason looked up in time to see her head toward the back of the gallery, giving him a meaningful look that clearly demanded he follow. Right now, he couldn't find a good reason not to comply.

Jason headed back into an area of the gallery he hadn't been in before, making his way to a small room that looked to have been added onto the back of the house at some point well after its original construction. The little enclosed porch had been converted into a wrapping and shipping station, with a large table against one wall and a variety of boxes folded flat and stacked on shelves and against the wall. A small space heater was tucked into one corner, currently unplugged, and the windows looked out onto a tiny yard. The floor back here was still scuffed, showing its age, but an oriental rug covered most of it. The air had a chill to it, and Jason was glad he'd worn a jacket. He imagined this room was an oven in summer, an icebox in winter. Fixable, but probably low priority since it wasn't an area anyone but Zoe or her employees would see.

Zoe pulled thick brown paper from a roll beside the table and cut it with an expert swipe as he walked in, then set to work wrapping the painting she'd set on the table.

"Something wrong?" he asked.

She turned her head, just for a moment, to let him see her incredulous expression. "You're asking *me* that? I'm just minding my own business, working, making a sale. I'm fine."

"So am I."

"Oh, obviously." She leveled a hard look at him before folding the paper around one edge of the painting and then securing it with several pieces of tape. "You usually come in here to fight with *me*. I'm a little offended."

Jason snorted. "Sorry."

"No, you're not." She snapped off more tape, leaving

it stuck to her thumb while she got to work on the other side of the painting. Jason watched her fingers move deftly over the paper, folding and taping, quickly turning Sam's painting into a well-wrapped brown rectangle. Her hands were small, like the rest of her, but her fingers were long and elegant, moving with grace.

"Do you paint?" he asked suddenly, feeling stupid at once. He was usually better about not blurting out the first thing that popped into his head. Zoe looked at him quizzically.

"A little. Not well. Nothing special, anyway. Why?"

He shrugged. "I don't know. You own a gallery. Just a question." There was no way in hell he'd tell her he thought her hands were graceful. Who said things like that? Maybe it worked in movies, but he'd only come off as creepy.

Zoe didn't look perturbed. "Oh. Well, loving art isn't necessarily tied to the ability to create it." She offered him a small half smile. "Just being around it makes me happy. Probably like you and your park." Her smile turned wry. "Though maybe you just don't do happy."

"I'm happy sometimes," he grumbled, and she laughed softly, warm and low in a way that wrapped itself around him.

"Not today you're not." She regarded him a moment, tilting her head, the gray of her eyes as inscrutable as fog. "Hang on a minute," she said. "I'll be right back."

Again he found himself following orders, which wasn't a compulsion he experienced much. It was simple curiosity, he told himself. Zoe being nice to him, not to mention interacting with her without any intent to antagonize, was still new. So he watched her march purposefully out of the room with the painting in her hands, unable to keep from noticing the sway of her hips when she walked. He moved to the windows while he listened to her hand off the painting, looking out on a small yard that had been turned into a garden. It looked like it was still a work in progress. There was an old brick path that bisected the flower beds, some of which looked like bare, recently weeded earth and the rest of which teemed with mums and the remains of late summer flowers. A small wooden bench sat at the end of the path against the iron fence that surrounded the yard. It looked peaceful, if unfinished. The kind of thing it might be fun to get his hands on and dig into in his spare time. Well, his *normal* spare time, when his leg was healed.

And he really was desperate for entertainment if he was considering doing free gardening for Zoe.

The silver bell above the door rang, but Zoe didn't return right away even as silence descended over the gallery. He heard her boots, the sound of water. Then surprisingly, soft humming while she typed, muffled clicks on the keyboard. Jason thought he recognized the tune, though he couldn't quite place it. Broadway show? The idea made him uneasy, provoking a flash of unwanted memory.

"Sara? Babe? You home?" The door had been unlocked, her car was in the driveway, but she didn't answer. The house seemed strangely still, apart from the melancholy song winding through the air. She'd put on Phantom, *never a good sign. He'd gotten so he could gauge her moods by her musical selections, and the sweet, seductive melancholy of "Music of the Night," far from meaning she was waiting for him wearing little but a smile, was a warning. She was unhappy. She was always unhappy lately, and hell if he knew what to do about it anymore.*

He heard Max whining and scratching at the back door, relegated to the yard while his mistress hid inside. "Sara?" He frowned, beginning to worry. He'd been looking forward to getting home, hoping to surprise her with the trip out of town he'd planned. They'd fly to New York, stay in a nice hotel. He'd chosen a couple of restaurants based on Shane's recommendations, places that required a jacket and tie. And he'd gotten tickets to a show that was supposed to be some big deal right now. It might not be his idea of fun, but he was glad to do it for her. If she loved it, he would, too, simply because it would make her smile. He missed her smile.

Ignoring Max for a moment, he headed upstairs, finally hearing movement, the creak of a bedspring. He rounded the corner, stepped through their doorway, and saw her sitting on the end of their bed, her face in her hands. A suitcase was on the bed, mostly full, the clothes dumped in haphazardly. He frowned. Had someone wrecked the surprise? It was all he could think, all he could imagine. Until she lifted her head to look at him, her blue eyes flooded, tears running down her cheeks.

"What's wrong?" he asked, wanting nothing but to make it better.

"Everything. I can't do this anymore. I want a divorce."

"Looking at my work in progress? I'm not much of a gardener, but I'm not above bribing people to help me out back there, which is why it's coming along."

Jason blinked, glad to be pulled into the present instead of wandering back through a bunch of unpleasant memories that didn't matter anymore. He turned his head to see Zoe, as physically unlike Sara as she could be, holding a steaming mug. Something on his face made her frown. He could only imagine.

"You're having a rough day, huh?"

He considered denying it, then decided it was pointless. "Something like that."

"Well, here," Zoe said, walking toward him. "It isn't much, but a cup of tea always makes me feel better. It would be better if I were making it at home, but I make do with teabags and a hot-water dispenser in my office." She stopped only inches from him, and the way she looked up at him was, for the first time he could remember, almost shy. A small, hopeful smile played about her lips. Jason breathed in, scenting the surprisingly comforting aroma of the tea along with the warm, simple vanilla of her perfume.

She was trying to make him feel better. It was a simple thing, and not even the first time she'd done it, if he counted her willingly getting into this mess in the first place . . . but it was incredibly sweet. People didn't surprise him often, but Zoe kept on doing it.

"I wasn't sure how you'd like it, but I noticed you took some sugar in your coffee the other day so I thought you'd want it sweet—"

Yes, I do. He wasn't smooth, not with the crutches, but he had the element of surprise on his side. Jason balanced himself, let one crutch go, and used his newly free arm to pull Zoe close. She didn't resist, but her gray eyes were wide and her words trailed off to nothing as he lowered his head for a kiss.

Chapter Ten

The man had no business being able to move like this. It took Zoe precious seconds to register Jason's intentions, and by the time she had, it no longer mattered. One of his big, strong hands pressed into the small of her back, and then his mouth was on hers without even a hint of uncertainty. He seemed to know just what he was doing, which made exactly one of them. The first time, she'd initiated. For an audience.

Today, they were alone, and all she could do was react.

Lord, the man tasted good.

Zoe's hand tightened around the warm mug in her hand, right before she forgot about it entirely. Jason pulled her close, surrounded her, overwhelmed her in a way she'd often imagined but never experienced. She let him pull her in without a thought. Maybe it was because he'd surprised her. Or maybe she'd wanted this too long to bother trying to convince herself she should be resisting. Either way, Zoe slid against him, instinctively rising on her toes to get better access to the lips currently wreaking havoc with her decision-making processes.

His mouth was firm, warm as he teased at her lower

lip, tasting it as he had before but far more thoroughly. She opened for him, unable to help the soft sigh that escaped her when he changed the angle of the kiss. She moved with him, meeting the first testing flicker of his tongue with her own and then inviting him deeper. She felt his hand slide all the way around her waist, holding her, though she was far more interested in what his mouth was doing to her. As she'd long suspected, beneath the gruff facade lurked one incredible kisser.

There was a slow-burning intensity to the way he tasted her, a barely restrained hunger that rippled through her body with every long, languid stroke of his tongue. Zoe reached up to slip her fingers into the silken curls at the nape of his neck, tangling them there. She felt his breath hitch as her nails lightly scraped his skin, and the kiss turned harder, deeper, until Zoe was clinging to him so tightly she was quivering. His body against hers was better than she could have imagined. Jason was big, solid, so deliciously real . . . she hadn't realized just how long it had been since she'd given in to pure pleasure until now, when having his body against hers felt like nothing less than heaven itself. His heart was hammering as hard as her own, the beat of it wild against her chest, and each of them was taking air in shallow little sips.

Zoe could hear nothing but the rush of blood in her head, Jason's ragged breathing, and the soft rustle of their clothes as they tried desperately to get closer to each other. There was a clatter and a splash, sounds that barely registered as Zoe slid her other hand up Jason's chest and over his shoulder. Another clatter, the briefest impression of a hand sliding over her hip, and then . . .

Everything began to give way.

Zoe yelped as they toppled over, trying and failing to

stay upright as Jason's full weight took her down with him. He landed with a pained grunt, and Zoe came down hard on her hip right beside him into a puddle of warm liquid.

"Ow! What the—" *The tea. You dumped the tea, wild woman.*

She was draped halfway over him, and it took some effort to push herself up into a position where she could get a look at the man underneath her. Jason had one arm over his eyes, his expression hidden. She didn't know whether to laugh or crawl away in embarrassment. Pretending this had never happened was pretty much out of the question, and there was a not inconsiderable part of her mind still consumed with coming up with ways to get his clothes off right here and now.

Somehow, she managed words.

"Are you okay? Your leg . . ."

A low rumble vibrated through her, jostling her for a few seconds before she realized that Jason was laughing. Really laughing. He lifted up his elbow, peeked at her with one eye, and then dropped it again in favor of laughing even harder. Zoe grinned, putting aside her embarrassment and allowing the humor of the situation to sink in.

"Smooth," she said. "New heights of smooth."

"I forgot about my leg," Jason told her, moving his arm aside to look at her. His usual dark intensity had lit up with a boyish mischief that stole Zoe's breath all over again. She'd never seen his eyes sparkle quite like that. Of course, she realized, she'd never seen him in a moment of simple happiness. The sight left her with a strange ache deep in her chest, not unpleasant, but certainly not normal. It was just a smile.

A beautiful, honest smile.

"What am I lying in?" he asked her.

"Your tea," she replied. "You're not the only one who forgot what he was doing."

His smile stayed, but it softened, and there was something in the way he looked at her that Zoe knew would stay with her for the rest of the day. Something new. The kind of thing that could push a girl into some rash decisions if she wasn't careful.

Except she'd made enough rash decisions where he was concerned already, and right this second, it was awfully hard to worry about consequences.

"Is your leg really okay?" she asked. She couldn't quite bring herself to get up and break the connection, even if the warm tea beneath her wasn't the most comfortable thing in the world as it soaked into her clothes. Jason was reassuringly solid, and she wasn't sure when she'd get him in this sort of position again, if ever. It was . . . nice. Better than nice. Even if it was slightly soggy.

"It's okay," he said. "I didn't break anything this time. Maybe I'm only in danger when there's a small dog involved."

"Well, we're clear there." She looked at him for a long moment, felt her cheeks heating, and dropped her eyes to study his shirt. "Ah, I guess I can help you up."

"I'll manage. You'll just end up back in the puddle."

She huffed out a laugh. "I think my leggings and shirt have absorbed most of the puddle."

"Not true. I feel like I got at least half of it." He paused, chuckled. "Hey, I think I finally found a downside to wearing sweatpants."

"Oh, if you're looking for more I'm sure I can help you with a list," Zoe said. She pushed up onto her knees and winced. Immediately, Jason was sitting up, one big, reassuring hand on her waist.

"Hey. Don't tell me *you* broke something."

"No, short people are tough. It's just a bruise." She gave him a wry smile. "You sure it was the storm that made you fall and break your leg?"

"Yes. Probably. Natural grace isn't a job requirement, you know." His eyebrow quirked just a little. "Ents are kind of clunky, but we're resilient."

Guess that means he forgives me for Treebeard after all. Zoe dropped her head and laughed, her voice blending with his. They stayed where they were, her on her knees, him up on one hip, his hand lingering on her waist. Zoe could feel the connection between them, new and humming like a high-voltage wire. She was loath to break it, and he seemed to feel the same. One of them had to, though, unless she wanted to spend the rest of the day hanging out on the packing-room floor instead of working. The idea had merit, but there was the matter of the puddle to deal with.

With a wistful sigh, she got her feet under her and rose. Jason seemed reluctant to let his hand fall away, and when he did, Zoe could still feel her skin tingling where he'd touched her. He stayed on the floor, looking up at her. His gaze was so direct that Zoe felt her embarrassment return, and she reached up to tuck a stray curl behind her ear, suddenly unsure of herself, and of what came next.

She'd thought she understood the rules, but Jason had just changed them.

"You sure you don't need help up?" she asked.

"Do you want to do something?" It was so out of the blue that it took Zoe a moment to figure out what he was asking, and even then, she wasn't positive she had it right. She could think of a number of somethings she wanted to do right now, none of which were a good idea at work.

"Ah," she said, cringingly inwardly that the best she could manage was a sound. Frustrated that she was so susceptible to Jason's questionable charms and complete lack of coordination, she forced herself to focus. "You're going to have to be a little more specific if you want an honest answer."

She wasn't sure whether to be glad or mortified when his cheeks reddened. *At least I'm not the only one whose mind goes right in the gutter.*

"I don't know. Dinner. A movie."

Zoe pressed her lips together while she regarded him. "With your mother?"

"Hell no." Jason looked horrified enough that she knew it was the truth. She laughed, though it sounded nervous to her own ears. It wasn't like she had any reason to be nervous with him, she chided herself. She was used to Jason. And to her fantasies about taking his clothes off. Which had just made a whole lot of progress toward becoming reality.

Zoe swallowed hard and then cleared her throat, trying to get it together. "So, you mean like a date."

"Yeah. I mean, you know. Yes. Pretty much."

Her brows arched up. "Pretty much or yes? Which is it?"

The slightly sheepish way he looked up at her, lifting one hand to rub the back of his neck, was unnervingly cute.

This is Treebeard. He's either grumpy or irritating or hot or all three at once. This cute thing is bad news. You're too susceptible to cute.

Lecturing herself did about as much good as it always did, which was exactly none.

"Yes," he said.

"A real date," she said, hoping that saying it out loud would help it sink in for her.

"Do you want me to submit a formal request or something? I didn't know this was going to require paperwork."

"There's an online request form," Zoe replied. "And then you've got to give me seven to ten business days for processing."

He exhaled, an almost-laugh, and began to get to his feet. "You're more of a smartass than I thought you were."

"I have layers. It's all part of my mystique." She watched him try not to put weight on his broken leg and sighed. "Honestly." She grabbed his arm and helped him up, throwing her weight back so that he didn't simply topple her over, appealing though the thought was. Jason grunted, but after a brief hesitation he used her to steady himself. She scooped up the one crutch he hadn't been able to manage and handed it to him, and when he took it from her his hand brushed hers, then covered it.

If she'd had any questions about him being serious, they vanished at that simple connection, his touch singing through her like electricity from a live wire.

"Well?" he asked. "What do you think?"

"Okay." She said it before she meant to say anything, but once it was out there she didn't feel any particular urge to take it back. That was different. Everything was different from what she'd expected. She still didn't think they had a single thing in common. The weird thing was, she was no longer sure that was a problem.

"Good," he said. The look on his face, one of grim

determination, wasn't the most romantic thing she'd ever encountered. Then again, neither was he. She still wanted to climb him like a tree. It was endlessly puzzling, but undeniable.

"When is this real date happening?" she asked. "I like schedules."

"No kidding," Jason replied. His voice was gruff, but his touch remained gentle, and Zoe found it hard to keep her mind on his words when she could feel his skin against hers. "What about this Friday?"

"That's doable, since I figured I'd be seeing you anyway. Just not alone." She frowned. "This is alone, right?"

"Unless she follows us and I don't know about it, yes, that's the idea." He exhaled loudly. "I'd say let's do something tonight, but that won't fly. She's already pissed off at me."

"I noticed. What *was* that, exactly?"

"Typical." He looked, for a brief moment, both younger and wearier than she was used to before pulling his hand away and moving back. He'd barely opened up the space between them, but Zoe felt it like a sudden gulf. She wished she understood the dynamics better, but even if she did, she doubted she could fix it. There was a whole lot of history at work here that she could only guess at. She'd started to try to put the pieces together, and it wasn't a pretty picture.

Zoe found herself scrambling to lighten the mood, preferring him playful. Well, what passed for playful where he was concerned. "So what are you thinking? Fancy dress-up dinner, maybe an art-house film?"

It surprised her when he didn't even crack a smile. There was only that wariness, stronger now. "Uh. Is that what you wanted to do?"

"Jason." Zoe shook her head. Was he ever not exasperating? It worried her that she might like it. "You know what? I keep forgetting that even though I'm used to seeing you, we don't really know each other at all."

His expression cleared a little, and his brown eyes warmed. "You ought to know me. You have that notebook of information going, right? Isn't that thing filled by now?"

"In four days? No. You're not that easy to study, and I'm not psychic." One hand settled on her hip. "Seriously, though. You think I'm that kind of high maintenance, don't you? And don't lie—I saw the look on your face. You didn't know I was kidding."

He shrugged uncomfortably. "I . . . wasn't sure. I mean, you own an art gallery."

"Yeah, and?"

His expression began to settle into its usual glower. "And I assume you've got the fancy taste to go with the fancy job. Maybe that's the kind of date you like. How am I supposed to know?"

She had to fight the urge to massage her temples, which were beginning to prickle a warning at her. It had been a weird few days, and often enough the tension that went with that kind of weirdness manifested itself in a nice, blinding migraine. She'd been careful with herself, knowing it wouldn't take much to push her over that edge. Of course it would be Jason who arrived to just pick her up and toss her over.

"You have a lot of assumptions about me," she said. "A lot of what appear to be dead-ass wrong assumptions. What?" she asked, narrowing her eyes when he snorted.

"Nothing. I just don't think I've ever heard you swear."

"It happens occasionally, when I'm at the end of my patience. Like now, for instance. You just kissed me."

He looked at her, and after a moment said, "Yeah."

"You kissed me despite the fact that you've told me we have nothing in common and after insinuating repeatedly that I am, to put it nicely, a lot of work."

Jason still looked as though he wasn't sure what she was getting at, since all of this was obvious. "Yeah."

Her free hand went to rest on her other hip and Zoe glared up at him, getting a strong sense of déjà vu. This position was an awfully familiar one. It seemed to be where they were always destined to end up.

"Then why did you kiss the sense out of me and ask me out?"

When he had to think about that, Zoe considered punching him. Just as her fingers were balling into a fist, though, he answered.

"Because I wanted to. And anyway, you kissed me first."

"That was so we looked like we were *together*!" she shot back. "You know that! It doesn't count!"

"Felt like it counted," Jason replied.

"Well . . ." She didn't have a good response to that, since he was right. The best she could muster was a lame, irritable, "That was your fault."

"How was it my fault?"

"You did that thing. With your mouth," she said, making a pointless gesture somewhere in the vicinity of her lips to try to illustrate the thing. It accomplished nothing except making Jason look like he was trying not to laugh. At *her*. "This isn't funny."

"It is, actually."

Zoe gave a hopelessly exasperated growl, throwing

her hands up. "I don't even know why I bother arguing with you."

"Same reason I kissed you and asked you out."

Now she did lift a hand to rub one of her temples. "Which is?"

"You like me."

He had her there. She looked up at him, sighed. "Yes. For some reason, I do."

"Well, it's as good a place to start as any, right?" Jason replied. He lifted a hand, hesitated, and then stroked his knuckles down her jawline. The touch made her shiver, and she knew he felt it when his eyes darkened. He was wrong, she decided, about them having nothing in common. They had this. And after all this time, their slow burn was finally ready to combust. The thought of it pooled like liquid heat deep in her belly, suffusing her with tingling warmth.

I'm going to sleep with him. The thought rose unbidden, shocking her with its sudden, blunt appearance. But she couldn't deny it, and Zoe repeated the words to herself, feeling the truth of them. *I'm going to sleep with him. And soon.*

The little bell above the door rang out just as Zoe was sliding back into him, ready to throw caution to the wind and steal another taste before the day was over. She stopped short, then cursed softly under her breath. Jason's laugh rumbled against her chest.

"Twice in one day."

"Shut up. This is your fault, too." She tried to glare at him, but it was impossible when he was grinning like the Cheshire cat.

"I'll take credit for that," he said.

"You would."

"Hello? Zoe? Is Jason still here? He isn't picking up his cell. Hello?"

Now it was Jason's turn to mutter an expletive, and Zoe laughed, briefly dropping her forehead against his chest before stepping away from him. She needed a little distance, *now*, before Molly came back here and found them all tangled up together. The thought of his mother seeing them like that shouldn't have bothered her, except that this wasn't for show. It was private, and she suddenly wanted to keep it that way. She'd never been one to parade her personal life, and she didn't think Jason was, either.

It was different when it wasn't real. She slid a look at him, big and solid and glaring through the doorway. He really was a hot mess with his broken leg and his ancient sweatpants and his battered old jacket. His hair had fallen into his eyes again, and as usual he needed a shave.

Mine. She tried the thought on for size, rolling it around like a foreign word she was trying to learn. He was more Wolverine than Bruce Wayne, bad attitude in-cluded. But . . . he might do. She'd have to wait and see.

Chapter Eleven

"I need a cupcake."

Larkin O'Neill regarded Zoe from behind the counter of Petite Treats, her bakery on the square, with striking green eyes that normally sparkled with mirth. Right now, though, they were focused and serious, and after a moment she gave a short nod.

"Go sit. I'll hook you up."

Zoe obediently went to one of the pink-and-white tables, too tired to do much but follow simple instructions. She dumped her purse on the floor, propped her chin on her hands, and closed her eyes until Larkin's voice pulled her out of what had almost turned into an impromptu nap.

"Wake up, sleepyhead. Have some sugar."

Zoe could smell the chocolate even before her eyes fluttered open to see what Larkin had brought her. "Oh my God. Chocolate cherry cheesecake."

"For my friends, I bring out the big guns." Larkin sat down across from her, nudged the cheerful turquoise plate toward her, and smiled encouragingly. "Go on. Stuff your face and tell me everything. It's been a slow day."

"You don't have slow days," Zoe replied, picking up the fork and diving in. When the cheesecake hit her tongue her eyes rolled back in her head. "I think I'm in a relationship with your baked goods, Larkin. It's not natural."

"Oh, it was busy workwise. But nobody came in and told me anything fun, and no eye candy wandered in. So I occupied myself with sinful thoughts and made food to go with. Are you chewing? This is going to be the shortest relationship on record."

Zoe swallowed her bite, held up her fork, and said, "Turns out it's more of a hot fling. Anyway, thanks. I'll pay Aimee when I'm done." Hearing her name, Larkin's teenage protégée looked up from behind the long glass display case and smiled.

"On the house," Larkin said, waving her objections off. "So, what's up? Tell me something good. Or juicy. Or . . . well, anything really." She grinned, and Zoe could only shake her head. Larkin was a transplant herself, from California instead of Georgia, and she gave off a carefree supermodel-surfer-girl vibe that would have been off-putting if it hadn't been so genuine. Her blond hair was piled on top of her head in a messy bun, showing off her big green eyes, pert little nose, and generous mouth. She had a double strand of painted beads around her throat, and her apron was still snowy white, though dusted with flour across the Petite Treats logo. She was five-ten, long and lean, and prone to tripping over imaginary objects that most of her friends thought were probably just her feet. Zoe liked her, not least because she'd been instrumental in drawing Emma Henry out of her shell this summer. Besides, the Harvest Cove misfits needed to stick together, and Zoe knew that no matter how long she stayed, she'd always have a bit of that about her.

"You want gossip? Let me see," Zoe said. She shoveled in another bite, chewed thoughtfully, and swallowed before continuing. "I've got a big show for Aaron coming up. Like, 'people coming here who would not normally deign to notice me and my little gallery' big. I'm excited for him, but I'm stressing. I've got less than four weeks. If my brain caves in before then, we're all in trouble."

"It won't. You'll wait until afterward, then crash, sleep for twenty-four hours, binge on a bunch of your fancy tea and maybe some Cheetos in front of your TV, and then return to normal life."

Zoe laughed. "Probably. Maybe not the Cheetos, though. I'll just beg you to make me one of these cakes. Then I'll set it on my coffee table with a fork and I'll be good to go."

"I like this plan. I'll make it so." Larkin looked at her curiously, with a tilt of her head. "What else is new? How's your man holding up?"

The fork paused halfway to her mouth. "Um."

"Yeah, I heard about that from Emma. It's cool," Larkin said, lowering her voice. "I heard you were holding hands at lunch last weekend. And somebody saw you give him a smooch before he got in his car with Psycho Mom. Kimmie from Brewbaker's thinks it's adorable, and Troy and Lindy from Merry Meet were like, 'It's about time!' Oh, and none of us buys that this is fake, since you two have been trying to have a night of anger-fueled passion for what, like, two years now? He's hot, by the way. Nice job."

She still hadn't gotten the fork to her mouth. "What is this place? Are you bugging the cupcake wrappers? How do you hear all this stuff?"

"People talk to me," Larkin said, nodding sagely. "I know things."

"Petite Treats, sponsored by the CIA."

Larkin's grin was infectious. "If I told you, I'd have to kill you, standard disclaimers, etcetera. Seriously, though. How's your man holding up? Shane and Fitz were in here, and Fitz had kind of a moment when Shane brought her up. Something about soccer a bunch of years ago. I guess he played with Jason's brother?"

"I don't know," Zoe replied. "I think so. I haven't gotten a lot of backstory. As you might expect, we're not exactly alone. *Ever.*"

Larkin wrinkled her nose. "I feel you. She sounds like a pain. Actually, I think she was in here yesterday. Only got a glimpse, though, since I was in the back getting my groove on and Aimee had to throw a pen at my head to get my attention. She has good aim."

"That would make sense," Zoe said. "I had a text message yesterday afternoon. Well, a picture of an open beer on his patio table, next to Rosie."

"Who's Rosie?"

"His dog. She gets herself up on that patio table sometimes and then doesn't know how to get off. Looked like she was taking a nap up there while he had a beer. I assumed he was getting a break."

"Aw. He has a little dog."

"Yes. She's very cute."

"Nothing like a big, sexy man with a little foofy dog. Plus he has a nice smile." Larkin looked slightly dreamy, and Zoe pursed her lips.

"I didn't think he *could* smile until last weekend. When did you see him do that?" She wasn't jealous, Zoe told herself. Not even a tiny bit. Just . . . surprised, was all.

"He comes in once in a while," Larkin said with a shrug. "Sometimes with this other park ranger he works with. Jason is always very polite, and he always orders the same thing."

"Which is?"

"Lemon meringue pie. I don't always have it once the weather gets cold, but to be honest, I make it once in a while in the winter just in case he stops by. Not," she added hurriedly, "that you should take that as me in any way hitting on him. But you know, he's pretty adorable. I think he's shy."

"We're both talking about the same guy, right? Jason Evans, tall, needs a shave, probably yells at clouds when he doesn't like the weather?"

Larkin laughed. "Okay, he looks intimidating, but you're forgetting that I give people food. There's a lot of instant gratification going on in here, and I swear the smell improves people's moods. So all I see is the shy. He's quiet, polite, and he always smiles when I hand him his pie."

"Oh." All right, maybe she *was* jealous. "That's . . . nice."

"Stop. I know when guys are interested, and he wasn't. He's just into my kick-ass baking skills."

"Who isn't, though, really?" Zoe asked, and popped the last bite in her mouth. "Mmm."

"I did hear he gets a little feistier with you," Larkin said, waggling her eyebrows. "Thus I assumed his affections lay elsewhere, and I continue my vigil for Chris Evans so that I might seduce him with my sexy food."

"I wish you all the luck in the world with that," Zoe said. "Just as long as you promise to make him go for shirtless runs a few times a week so we can all admire him."

"But of course." Larkin poked at the empty plate. "Feel better?"

"Yes. It'll be fleeting, but yes."

"Why fleeting? I thought you and Treebeard would be all domestically blissed out by now. Oh. But you said you're never alone. So you can't—"

"We're not even really dating. I mean, we weren't, but we are, I suppose . . . sort of. Soon? Possibly. I think this weekend. But it's not official. At least, I don't think so." Zoe rushed out the words, knowing they sounded ridiculous even as they tumbled from her lips. Larkin watched her quietly, looking like the cat that got the canary. "Don't repeat that."

"I wouldn't know what to repeat. Was there information in there?" Larkin smiled, and this time it was full of understanding. "I won't, anyways. I think it's cute. So, when do you get to be"—she fluttered her lashes— "alone?"

"It was supposed to be tomorrow, which then became Saturday because *someone* invited a bunch of people over for a bonfire. I am eagerly awaiting what she comes up with to keep him there Saturday night."

Larkin winced. "Ugh."

"You're not kidding." Zoe poked at the empty paper plate with her fork. "You know, this all started because Jason thought I'd be just what that woman likes. She'd be charmed, satisfied, and go in peace."

"Uh-oh. She's *that woman* now."

"She's certainly something. But anyway, if she likes me she's got a funny way of showing it. I drove him to a doctor appointment this week, I've stopped by to make nice, and she smiles, but I get the feeling it's more because she's thinking about taking a bite out of me. Just hypercompetitive. I can see why she makes him crazy. She competes with him, too. It is," she finished, "deeply messed up. And I don't think she's going anywhere until she's good and ready."

"If it gets really bad you can fight her."

"Sure. I may be short, but I can punch her in the kidneys." Zoe smirked and stretched out her legs. "I need to head home. Thanks for the cheesecake. It was exactly what I needed."

Larkin held up a hand. "Say no more. Happy to be of assistance." She stood, drawing herself up to her full height. Zoe noted that her sneakers were neon blue, and smiled. There was something ever so slightly goofy about Larkin that made her endearing, and there were hints of it all over her not-quite-tacky pink-and-white-and-turquoise bakery. The sparkly unicorn by the cash register, for instance. Or the Care Bear drawn on the Daily Specials board. Sam joked that hanging out with Larkin was a little like being with a kid who'd just eaten an entire bag of Pixy Stix. That wasn't entirely accurate. But it wasn't entirely inaccurate, either.

"Have a good one," Zoe said. Larkin grinned, waved, and tripped on her way through the door to the kitchen. Zoe picked up her purse, slung it over her shoulder, and was still smiling when she headed back out into the day.

Jason plotted his escape carefully.

Not that carefully, because he was panicked and his house was full of his mother's friends and they were talking about the housing market and some actor they all thought was hot and *oh God shoes*, and desperation moved things along a little more quickly than usual. But he needed to get out, he and poor Rosie, who was probably about as tired of his mother's attempts to lure her outside as he was. The dog narrowed his options a little, but that was okay. He wasn't flush with options on the best of days.

Jason peered around the corner, having spent enough time hiding in the bathroom that it was probably beginning to look odd. He looked longingly at the TV, which was turned to a rerun of a sitcom he didn't watch, and at his PlayStation, which he could no longer play on one of his many sleepless nights because it would keep his mother up. There was a nice spread of snacks on the coffee table, wine chilling in a bucket on the counter, and nowhere for him to sit even if he'd wanted to. Which he didn't.

It wasn't a big house. Right now, it was even smaller. And he was trapped in it.

The cell phone in his pocket buzzed, and Jason pulled it out to read the text. Jake was in the driveway. It was go time, and he didn't exactly have stealth on his side. He texted back quickly, then shoved the phone back in his pocket and headed as quickly as he could to the closed door of his bedroom. Poor Rosie had been shut in there for a couple of hours now, which in his opinion was a much better deal than sitting at the dining room table with his leg propped on another chair, ignored, uncomfortable, and without a feasible way to leave. That was, until Jake got off work.

He'd almost called Zoe, then stopped himself. She was probably tired. She'd been a trouper this week, but he knew she needed a night away from the crazy, so he'd do her a favor.

That was the explanation he was comfortable with, anyway. He'd been honest—he liked her. Too much, for a fake relationship that wasn't even a week old. So letting it turn into something real needed to be slow. Glacial.

Kind of like him on these stupid crutches.

"Rosie," Jason half whispered when he opened the door. She was curled into a little ball in the middle of the bed, and he heard her snort when he called her. She didn't move, though, instead regarding him blearily from where she lay. He'd interrupted her nap.

"Oh, come on," he said quietly. "You take a dozen naps a day. You can move your furry butt this once. We're breaking out."

He tried to pretend she looked more interested at that, but no. She closed her eyes, licked her muzzle, and heaved a long-suffering sigh. She'd already suffered the indignity of being shooed away from the pretzels and wrapped cocktail weenies. Rosie was apparently done being pushed around . . . which was why he'd smuggled a couple of weenies into a napkin and stuck them in the pocket of his flannel shirt.

"Want to go for walkies, girl? Go for a walk?" *Thank God the guys at work can't hear this.*

Nope. No movement. She loved her walks, but there were too many people here she felt robbed of barking at, Jason guessed. Hence the drama. He went to the side of the bed and dangled the treat he'd brought her. There was nothing wrong with her nose—it twitched while her dark brown eyes popped open and stared.

"Yeah, now I have your attention. Come on, Rosie girl. We're going out."

She stood, took her time stretching, and then happily panted her way to the side of the bed, where she bounced from paw to paw, dancing for the food. He wished he could just scoop her up and carry her, but that would have to wait. He braced himself, clipped her leash onto her collar, and fed her half the cocktail weenie. She ate it like a tiny shark, and he checked his fingers afterward, just to be sure.

"Come on," he said, and she toddled down the stairs he'd bought to allow her to get on and off the bed more easily. He held on to the loop along with his crutches, and the two of them slowly made their way back into the noisy great room. He heard Rosie's purring growl and knew their chances of going unnoticed had just slipped from *Yeah, right* to utterly nonexistent.

"Aw, look at the cute little doggie!"

Jason hobbled out, Rosie prancing ahead with her tail flying. She barked happily at anyone who looked at her, delighted to be able to announce herself and defend her territory. His mother, sitting in his chair, looked up and pursed her lips.

"Where are you going? Aren't you supposed to be resting?"

"I'm taking Rosie out," he said.

"You can't walk her with those crutches," she said. "Just put her out back and come sit down. We're going to watch *Magic Mike*."

"Jesus, Mom. I'm not going to sit here and watch a movie about strippers."

He was fourteen again, and red-faced because she'd done another embarrassing thing in her long career of embarrassing things. Her reaction hadn't changed, either.

"Jason Patrick. Language."

He arched an eyebrow and gave her a look. "I'm going out."

He didn't bother with his jacket, hobbling as quickly

as he could toward the door and ignoring her admonition that he was going to freeze. Rosie, thankfully, seemed more interested in vacating the premises than she was in trying to go beg for more snacks, and she padded along ahead of him happily enough. He got the door open and headed onto the porch, relieved when there was nothing but unconcerned chatter and cackling behind him. The last thing he needed right now was another obstacle to leaving. It was enough of a pain in the ass just maneuvering himself and his dog out the door.

Jake had pulled onto the grass, bypassing the line of cars in his driveway. He hopped out of the SUV and headed toward him, looking a lot more entertained by the subterfuge than Jason was.

"Hey, man. She know you're leaving?"

"She knows I'm walking the dog."

"Going to be a long walk. Hey, Rosie!" She gave a sharp bark and then began making odd little Muppet noises, as pleased to see Jake as she always was. She started to tug at the end of the leash, but Jake picked her up, let her cover his face in kisses, and then situated her in his arms. "You planning on coming back tonight?"

"Maybe."

"Well, the spare room's all yours if you want it." He looked at the row of cars and shook his head, a wry smile on his lips. "Typical Aunt Molly. Every visit is a hostile takeover."

"No shit. They're going to watch *Magic Mike*."

Jake winced. "Yeah, you definitely need to get out. Come on."

Jason boosted himself into the truck and shoved his crutches into the back, then accepted Rosie onto his lap. The front door opened just as they were pulling out, and his mother's confusion quickly turned angry. Even in the fading light, he could clearly see her lips form the words, "What the hell?"

Jake rolled down the window as he backed up to turn around. "Hi, Aunt Molly! Just stealing Jason for a few hours. Don't worry. Have fun, see you tomorrow night!"

They drove off, and Jason heard the squawk. "Well, that pissed her off," he said.

"Not much of an achievement where you're concerned," Jake replied, then smacked him in the shoulder. "So, what do you think? Wild night out at the bars? We can bring Rosie; she needs to cut loose."

Jason snorted. "She'd probably just get disgusted with the noise and then fall asleep on the bar." He looked at his cousin, who looked tired and a little mussed after what had probably been a long day at work, and felt guilty. "Sorry to drag you out here. I know it's a pain in the ass."

"Oh, come on," Jake said, wrinkling his nose. "Don't start that. I know how it is with her. You hid out at my house often enough when we were kids. It's like a tradition."

"I didn't think it would still be one when I was thirty. At this rate we'll still be doing this when I'm sixty."

"You could tell her off," Jake said, glanced at him, and then sighed. "I know, not an option."

"It would be different if she were just evil," Jason grumbled. "She tries. Sometimes. She cooks, and she cleaned even though the place was already clean. But she gets bored in about five minutes, and she'd rather have an audience for the stuff she does so she can play Mother of the Year. I've never been the best audience. And she still doesn't listen to a word I say. I'm like a prop. Or furniture."

"How's she doing with Zoe?" Jake asked, his voice full of sympathy. "They getting along, at least?"

Jason made a noncommittal noise, and Jake groaned. "She decided to do the thing. The weirdly off-putting competitive thing. Didn't she?"

"You got it.

"How does Aunt Molly have friends? I'm serious. She thinks the world revolves around her. It drives my mother nuts. You know this."

"She can be pretty magnetic when she wants to," Jason said. "I've been watching it my whole life. She's got one of those big personalities that a lot of people are drawn to. She keeps friends who don't question her, let her run everything, and kiss her butt. The ones who push back at all get blacklisted. It's why Dad is the way he is."

"Uncle Dan is cool sometimes."

"Sure, when she's not around to tell him what to do." Jason sighed and tipped his head back against the headrest. "Whatever. I just want her to go home. I thought having Zoe around would help, but I think she just took it as a challenge. And you know Zoe's not going to kiss her butt."

Jake laughed. "No way. Zoe takes no crap."

"She's put up with enough of it this week." *She's not going to want to put up with this forever, either.* "I'm going to have to talk to Mom. After I buy her a return ticket and explain that she's going home next week." He rubbed a hand over his face. "I knew I was setting that money aside for something. I thought it was a new couch, but it looks like I was wrong."

"Well, look at it this way. Having her gone will be even more comfortable than a new couch."

Jason had to chuckle. "True."

They rode in companionable silence most of the rest of the way to Jake's house, a remodeled Craftsman not far from the square. He and Sam lived on a quiet street lined with mature trees and older, well-kept homes. The streetlights had come on, and one of the neighbors jogged down the sidewalk, lifting a hand in greeting as they passed. Jake turned into his driveway, pulling up to the small detached garage in the back. The lights were on in the house, blazing with cheery warmth. It was a place Jason liked coming to, and often did, though ever since Jake and Sam had gotten together he tried to be better about just dropping in out of the blue.

They headed inside, Jake helping him up the front steps while Rosie bounded ahead. No doubt she was anxious to harass Loki, Sam's cat, Jason thought. It was one of her favorite activities, and the two of them had developed a weird love-hate relationship in the short time they'd known each other. Though apart from Sam, that was the only sort of relationship Loki tended to develop with anyone.

"Tucker, don't even think about it!" Jake called before he even opened the door. Rosie gave a short, sharp warning bark at the horrible groaning and whimpering coming from inside. She and Tucker had established some ground rules, which seemed to be very simple: Harassing the cat together was A-OK, but any of his forays into her personal space merited a good hard nip or three. And sure enough, as soon as the door opened, the dogs' usual greeting played out. Tucker pounced, Rosie snapped, and the big, silly cattle dog mix turned his attentions to greeting the men while shooting the little Peke longing glances as she trotted inside like she owned the place.

Jason felt his tension ease as soon as he stepped inside, taking a moment to rub the wiry fur on Tucker's head while the dog wiggled in pleasure before dashing after his master. He could smell whatever they'd had for dinner—must be Sam had cooked, since Jake was less than talented in the kitchen. Music played softly up ahead, in the family room, and he could hear the soft murmur of women's voices. It was warm and quiet, and part of him wanted to just undertake the task of getting upstairs now so he could flop facedown on the bed.

"That you, babe? Did you extract the prisoner?" Sam called.

"Mission accomplished," Jake said, peeling off his jacket. "Come on in. Did you eat? Sam made some kind of vegetable soup in the crockpot. House smelled so good when I got home I just about dove in headfirst."

"I'd love some," Jason confessed. "It was just finger food tonight, and I didn't get into it because I knew I'd eat all of it."

"Rosie!" That was the other voice, clearer now, and he recognized it instantly. Jason froze, his eyes darting to Jake. His cousin was trying too hard to look innocent.

"What?"

"You didn't tell me Zoe was here."

"Didn't think it mattered. Unless you're hiding from her, too, and forgot to mention it." He shrugged, one corner of his mouth curving in a half smile. "She and Sam are friends, remember? They do this kind of thing."

Jason managed some sort of grunt before Jake strolled on ahead of him to the back of the house, hanging a left into the kitchen and leaving Jason to follow slowly. He didn't understand why his nerves would pick now to kick in, of all the times to do it. He could blame the long day—that would be easy enough. But he was pretty sure this particular feeling was coming from a different place. The one where he got to test the waters with Zoe on his own terms, in his own comfort zone. This was elsewhere, unplanned. Different. Just two couples hanging around his cousin's house . . . except he wasn't quite there with the whole "couple" thing yet. He didn't know what he and Zoe were.

All he could see before him were endless possibilities to screw this up just because he no longer knew how to act with her on their own, and that was a problem. They could fight, he guessed. That was at least familiar. He just didn't seem to have a lot of appetite for it lately.

His appetite for her mouth, on the other hand, was a different story.

Jason followed Jake, cursing himself silently the entire time for being so wound up. Not to mention, he was pretty sure he looked like death warmed over. A few hours of his mother and her posse would do that.

Why the hell do you care how you look? It shouldn't matter.

Except it did. What Zoe thought of him absolutely did.

He hated how loud he was as he moved, the crutches thumping and creaking against the wood floor. He could hear Rosie's tags jingling, Zoe's soft laughter. Then he was past the corner, looking into Jake and Sam's cozy family room, with its fireplace and big furniture and giant television that had once been almost the only thing in here. Sam had made it homey, with art and a rug and small touches that made it more than just a room. She and Zoe sat on the floor in front of the darkened television facing each other, Rosie rolling around on her back in between them and getting her belly rubbed. A sleek black cat brushed by Jason's foot, tail up and in high dudgeon.

"Hey, Loki." The cat shot him a reproachful look before vanishing down the hall. He knew where Rosie had come from.

Sam grinned at him. "Jason! You made it out alive!" She had her platinum hair in a ponytail, and her unusual blue-green eyes seemed to dance with light. He took in the ratty sweatshirt and Rainbow Buddies pajama pants and no longer felt quite as bad about his own current state. She and Zoe both had cotton balls wedged between their painted toes.

"Yeah, by the skin of my teeth." He shifted his gaze to Zoe and found himself looking into eyes like storm clouds. She looked . . . cautious. And just a little reproachful. But even as his defensive instincts kicked in, he couldn't escape that she also looked as beautiful as he'd ever seen her.

"Hey," he said, and wished he didn't always feel like he was saying the dumbest possible thing at any given moment where she was concerned.

"Hey yourself," Zoe replied. "Trouble on the home front?" She had on a pair of gray plaid flannel pants, a plain white camisole, and a gray hoodie with the sleeves pushed up. Her curls were tied back at the nape of her neck, revealing the only evidence of her work attire — small, glinting diamonds. It was the most relaxed he thought he'd ever seen her.

Funny, since he was as uptight as he'd ever been right this second. Longing so sudden and strong it knocked the wind out of him formed a knot deep in his chest, pulsing there and refusing to dissipate. He remembered what it was like to come home to somebody like this. To somebody who could take your breath away with nothing but a lift of her eyebrow.

I don't know if I can do this again.

The thought rose unbidden, but ringing with truth. He really didn't know. Just like he didn't know if he was going to be able to help himself. Because whatever came next, one thing was certain: He had it bad for Zoe Watson. And far from being a new thing, it had been going on for a very long time.

"Jason?" Concern creased her brow, and Jason shook himself out of it. Standing here gaping at her wasn't going to do either of them any good.

"Yeah, sorry. Mind drifted. It's been a long day."

"So I hear." She gave Rosie's belly a pat, then rose. He was expecting her usual purposeful stride, but she waddled over to him on her heels, and he felt the foolish grin on his face before he could stop it. She tipped her chin down and gave him a look. "My toes are still wet. Don't."

"I don't know what you're talking about."

"Sure," she drawled. But when she got closer, her expression turned serious and her voice dropped while Sam continued to fuss over Rosie. "If it was that bad, why didn't you just call me? I would have come out."

"Didn't want to bother you."

She looked at him incredulously, and he knew he'd said the wrong thing. Again. "Wasn't having me available to bother kind of the point?"

"It's been a long week." He shrugged. "You don't have to be on the clock all the time."

Her eyes narrowed, and he watched her jaw tighten. "On the . . . Oh, is that still where we are? That's good to know. Thanks."

"Zo." But she turned around and tottered back to Sam, who looked between them like she wasn't sure whether to laugh or slink away quietly. Zoe sat down, picked up a can of ginger ale from the coffee table, and held out a hand in his direction.

"Nope. Go eat your soup. I'm *off* the clock right now."

He opened his mouth to try to defend himself, decided that would do nothing but make things worse, and managed nothing but a low growl. Sam winced and made a shooing motion with one hand while Zoe looked elsewhere. *Go eat,* she mouthed. He couldn't blame her for not wanting to be caught in the cross fire, but he also refused to just go silently.

"That's not what I meant, Zoe, and you know it."

She turned her head to look at him. He expected the anger. The surprise was when a little of the hurt feelings showed through. "Jason, I don't know anything right now, and that's the truth."

He sighed, considered his options, and decided that he was too tired for any more exercises in futility today. She could think what she wanted. That was all anybody seemed to do anyway. "I'm not that complicated. I'll be in the kitchen if you want to talk."

And with all the dignity he could muster, he hobbled away, Rosie trailing in his wake.

Chapter Twelve

"Well?"

"*Well* what?" Zoe took a break from quietly brooding to look at Sam, with whom she'd been having a very nice evening up until a few minutes ago. *Don't have to be on the clock all the time. Is that what he thinks this is? I guess crawling all over each other in the back room was just overtime, if we're using his jacked-up logic.*

"You should probably go talk to him."

"Hmm."

Sam's eyes rounded. "Zoe. If you two decide to have one of your arguments in my house, I will personally kill both of you. This is a bicker-free zone. I come here to escape these things."

"You and Jake fight," Zoe pointed out, but it did nothing to assuage her own rapidly developing guilt. Sam was right. Fighting might come naturally to her and Jason, but that didn't mean anybody else wanted ringside seats.

"My house, my husband, my stupid fights," Sam replied. "You and Jason need to find your own arena to wreck each other in."

Zoe hung her head and blew out a breath. "Sorry. The man just has a knack for getting my back up. Did you hear what he said? I don't *work* for him. And after the other day, which you're not supposed to know about—"

"I know, I know," Sam soothed her, patting her arm. "Just try and remember that Jason has some, ah, baggage."

"Everybody has baggage."

"Well, a whole bunch of his is currently parked in his house having a party. So, you know . . . bend a little, Zo."

She rolled her eyes back in her head, but Zoe stood up. Sam was right. She hated it when someone else was right, but it happened occasionally. Besides, this time she didn't actually want to stay mad at Jason. Not that she was interested in admitting it to him, but it was more hurt than anything. Why hadn't he just called her if he'd needed somebody? Even before they'd gotten all tangled up with each other, she'd committed to helping him. True to form, he still looked elsewhere.

Sometimes she wondered if he'd been put on this earth solely to drive her crazy.

"I'm not bendy," Zoe informed her. Sam had the audacity to smirk.

"I know. But you are *especially* not bendy with him. So go save him from melancholy solo soup eating and then come back so we can do our fingernails."

"Fine." She started away, muttering, "And he thinks *I'm* high maintenance," hearing Sam's soft laughter behind her. It was funny, she supposed. Especially if you were standing on the outside of it. From where she stood, it was way less amusing. She was as twisted up as she had been about anyone in years, and it wasn't something she liked to feel. Because her business was constantly shifting and changing, she placed a high value on peace and stability where she could find it.

Jason had intruded onto formerly peaceful territory and was making a damn mess. And it was worse because she'd let him do it. She'd invited him in, and booting him back out didn't feel like any kind of option. She just wished he'd let his guard down with her as much as she had with him. His kiss had told her more than he ever had in words, but there was so much more she wanted to know beyond simple attraction.

Reserve was one thing. She understood that. But he had walls up that she wasn't sure he was going to let her past. Though right now she'd settle for not being treated like she already had one foot out the door, ready to bolt as soon as things settled down and it was just the two of them.

Resigned, frustrated, Zoe walked into the kitchen, trying not to waddle quite so badly since that was not the way she wanted to make any kind of entrance. She just hoped her toes were almost dry. So much for her relaxing evening.

Jason sat at the small table against the wall, hunched over a bowl of soup while Jake chattered at him. When Jake saw her, there was no mistaking the relief on his face. *Must be I put Treebeard in a mood. As usual.* Rosie didn't spare her a glance, completely focused on the biscuit that sat on a napkin beside Jason's bowl.

"Hey, Zoe. You want to hang out for a minute? I need to ask Sam something."

"Sure. I might steal another one of those biscuits while I'm at it. You're lucky one of you can cook," she said, hoping her voice, at least, was calm. Jake gave her a cheeky grin.

"I know it. I'm spoiled forever. She saved me from ramen. Help yourself. The bowl's still on the counter."

He was gone in a flash. Zoe walked to where the bright blue bowl containing the remaining biscuits was set by the sink, picked one of the bottom ones that was still slightly warm, and then set about buttering it while Jason sat in stony silence behind her. His discomfort was a palpable thing, and Zoe couldn't help but remember what Larkin had said about him being shy. He'd always been willing enough to engage with her, though the *way* they'd engaged didn't really require him to open up.

It made her wonder again if she'd been wrong all this time about what sort of man he was. There seemed to be an endless number of things she didn't know. It wasn't the kind of revelation that she enjoyed having, but in Jason's case, "still waters run deep" definitely seemed to apply.

She steeled herself, turned, and leaned back against the counter to eat her biscuit, pulling off a piece with her fingers. *Relax, or he'll just shut down on you. Be cool, because he sure isn't.*

"So, what happened?" she asked, deciding not to start throwing elbows immediately. Jason looked up, and she could see the surprise on his face. He looked almost wolfish tonight, she thought. Half-feral, at least, big and dark and dangerous. He would have been at home in any one of her favorite fantasies . . . and in fact, he had been. There was something about him that was compelling in a way that no other man had been for her. And rather than working its way out of her system over the past couple of years, it only seemed to get worse.

His voice, which had dropped into that low growl of his, rippled over her skin and made the little hairs on her arms and the back of her neck stand at attention. "Nothing major. My house was full of people I didn't invite over, my mother was holding court, and I needed to be someplace where I didn't want to crawl out of my skin."

"This is where you come for that, I guess."

"Usually." She didn't miss the subtle dig, and she wouldn't let it pass.

"You know, you're not the only person who came here tonight trying to relax a little. I was having a perfectly good time."

"Nobody said you had to stop. You're the one who got all huffy."

"And you got huffy right back." She exhaled through her nose. "We really need to work on the way we react to each other if we're going to keep spending time together. I don't know how I feel about being Harvest Cove's odd couple, mismatched and walking around bickering."

She saw him stiffen, the way his shoulders tensed, and wondered what she'd said.

"I told you we didn't have anything in common," Jason said. "We *are* mismatched, if you haven't noticed."

"Oh, bull," she shot back with more snap in her voice than she'd meant to put there. "Why? Because you're Mr. Shy Moody Sweatpants Man and I get dressed up every day and talk to people? Because I'm black and southern and you're white and northern? Because I'm into grooming and you need a damn haircut? Which part of this is bothering you? Last time I checked, the whole opposites-attract thing was about differences keeping things interesting, not making people want to kill each other. It doesn't have to be like this with us. It's just going to take some effort. On *both* our parts. I'll tell you that I'm willing, since I actually enjoy you when you're not trying so hard to drive me crazy. What about you? Because if you're not, there's really no point in taking this past our weird little arrangement."

And here she was, getting all worked up when she'd promised herself she wouldn't. To make herself stop talking, Zoe popped the piece of biscuit in her mouth and glared at Jason, daring him to give her an honest answer. He didn't look angry, for once. In fact, he looked slightly awed.

It took everything she had not to stomp her foot before she demanded, "What?"

"You sound really southern when you're angry," he said. "I've just never heard your accent get that strong before."

She stared at him. "I take back the part where I said I enjoy you. I may have to kill you after all."

"You're not going to finish with 'bless your heart'?"

"Where are the knives?" She turned to scan the countertops for sharp objects while Jason laughed, a low rumble that made her slightly less inclined to cause him bodily harm. She turned her head to give him the stinkeye, but she couldn't maintain it when she saw the way he was smiling at her. He still looked tired, but good humor looked incredible on him. Of course, this was a man who could make her overheated when he was wearing paint-spattered sweatpants. He obviously had some kind of dark magic going on. Her parents would not approve.

The thought struck her oddly. She hadn't really considered what her parents would think of him, because up until recently, there was about zero possibility they'd ever meet him. They refused to come here, and Jason wasn't hers to introduce even if she'd thought he might attempt to make a good impression on people who weren't her. Which she wasn't at all sure about.

"Where'd your mind go just now?" he asked, watching her closely. "You disappeared on me for a second."

"Oh," Zoe said. "I, ah, well, my parents. I was thinking about my parents."

"Okay," he drawled. "That's . . . weird."

She shook her head. "I was just wondering what they'd think of you. That's all." She had a feeling he'd get funny about that, and he didn't disappoint her. Jason returned his eyes to his bowl of soup, and the tension between them returned as though it had never really left. Zoe sighed.

"Was she that bad?"

"Who?" he asked.

"Your ex-wife. I'm starting to think she must have been as bad as your mother if you're this screwed up about relationships." Manners would normally have prevented her from asking something so personal, but with Jason, she was quickly discovering that if she didn't hit him with a direct question, she'd probably never get an answer.

"Cautious and screwed up aren't the same thing," he said, lifting his head to meet her gaze directly. "I like to take things slow. That's all."

"Obviously. I mean, we've been doing this dance for, what, two years and some change now? You've certainly accomplished slow."

"I didn't know we were dancing," he said, but there was a hint of mischief in his expression. "It felt more like a really long argument."

"It was. One that continues today. We're headed for the Guinness book of world records, you and me. So are you going to answer my question?" She popped another bite of the biscuit in her mouth and waited for an answer. Jason was silent for so long that she thought he'd simply decided to ignore the question, but just as she was about to prod him, he spoke.

"She wasn't bad. It just didn't work. I own half the blame for that. She was . . ." He trailed off, seeming to search for the words before finding a way to continue. "She was looking for something else."

"And what were you looking for?" she asked, curious. This was the most he'd said about the mysterious ex. She couldn't imagine this woman who'd walked away from Jason and left town. There were no details, no one ever mentioned her . . . it was as though she had never existed. She supposed she could ask around, but it felt wrong, like snooping. She wanted *him* to tell her.

"I was just looking for her. Any way I could get her," Jason replied. He seemed surprised, though whether it was at the question or his own inclination to answer, Zoe wasn't sure. But what he said, the simple honesty of it, hit her with unexpected force. It made her hurt for him. It made her angry at the woman who'd rejected him. And it filled her with a sudden, painful longing to be wanted that way, that much. Jason had been burned, badly. What if he just never wanted to open himself up that way again? It was a distinct possibility.

One of his brows arched. "What, not the answer you were looking for?"

"No, no," Zoe rushed out. She really needed to watch herself around him. Over the years, she'd gotten pretty good at not wearing her emotions all over her face, but all that training seemed to fly right out the window whenever she spent any time with him. "I just . . . didn't know."

He shrugged and fed Rosie a piece of his own biscuit. "Nothing to know, really. I tried to be somebody else for a while. It didn't work out. She left. Neither one of us was as honest as we should have been, so we ended up about where you'd expect. Anyway, it doesn't matter. I got on with my life, and she found a guy who was what she wanted. Older. Sophisticated. Rich."

"Boring."

That made him smile. "I'm sure he and I would find each other very boring, yeah. You might like him. I hear he's a big art collector." He paused, seemed to assess the implications of what he'd just said, and then added, "I didn't mean that in a shitty way. Sara was into art, too."

She could see he hadn't meant it as an insult, but Zoe wasn't thrilled with having something so important to her in common with his ex-wife. Still, it explained a few things, even if she didn't like all of those explanations.

"I guess that's where you get your own interest, right? She helped you figure out what you liked."

"What I like isn't what she liked, but yeah. You watch your house get redecorated enough times, you develop an opinion whether you want to have one or not."

"What did she like, out of curiosity? I'm assuming you know what it's called."

The corners of his mouth curved up, but there wasn't much humor in it. "She called it French country. I called it fussy."

Zoe was silent a moment. "She was into toile, wasn't she?"

He closed his eyes. "If I never hear that word again, it will be too soon."

"A little goes a long way," Zoe agreed. She'd seen people go crazy with the pastoral French prints before, which was a shame because done well, French country could be beautiful. "And here you are, with your whole rustic-log-cabin aesthetic going on. Did she let you have a room, at least?"

He leaned back, stretched, and she could tell they'd reached the end of this particular subject. "No. So I got a whole house instead."

"Fair enough." It was more information than she'd expected, and Zoe didn't feel right pushing for more. How had he ended up with a toile-addicted control freak for a wife? she wondered. *Probably had a bunch of ugly botanical prints all over the place, too. And white furniture nobody was supposed to actually sit on.* It was unkind, especially since she didn't know this woman from Adam. But she couldn't feel all that charitable toward someone who'd obviously messed Jason up good before walking away. She shifted her weight, repositioning herself against the counter.

"So . . . are you still coming to the stupid bonfire tomorrow night?" he asked.

She nodded. "It's on my calendar. Stupid Bonfire written in big red letters. Unless—"

"No. I want you to come." He interjected it so quickly and forcefully that Zoe completely forgot the rest of what she'd been about to say.

"Oh. Well, then, I'll be there." Their eyes locked, and she felt herself flush. She'd gotten used to his particular brand of intimidating, though, and long experience let her hold his gaze instead of looking awkwardly elsewhere.

His smile was slow and easy now, though it lasted barely any time at all before Jason dropped his shaggy head forward, shoved a hand through his hair, and then peered up at her with a pair of puppy-dog eyes every bit as effective as Rosie's. She was glad she had the counter behind her to prop her up; otherwise, she thought she might wind up nothing but a puddle on the floor.

"Listen, I didn't call you tonight because I didn't want you to have to deal with any more of this than you already are. When I said you needed a night off, I meant it. My family is no picnic. Every time one of them visits I want to sleep for a week once they leave. And I'm *used* to them. That's all I meant, Zo. Jake's family, so he gets it. I just needed a break."

"I'm sorry it's like that." What else could she say? She wasn't sure it was the right thing, but at least it wasn't the wrong thing.

"You and me both." He reached down to ruffle the fur on Rosie's head. Zoe smiled when the little dog ducked and gave him what appeared to be a dirty look, probably because she was still trying to beg and he was ignoring it. Jason must be used to it. He didn't seem to notice. "She'll leave eventually. Might be later than sooner at this point."

"Hmm. I need to step up my efforts, then."

One of his eyebrows quirked up. "I didn't know you were slacking."

"I'm not. I just don't think me hanging around is going to be enough. Maybe it would be different if she were really here to help you, but that's not exactly the impression I'm getting."

"She's . . . kind of helping." He lifted one shoulder. "When she feels like it. Mostly I'm just sorry for dragging you into it. Now you're stuck for no good reason."

He was, hands down, the most exasperating man she'd ever come across. And as she had brothers, that was saying something. Zoe exhaled loudly. "Let's get something straight. I don't get stuck anywhere I don't want to be. Okay?"

"Oh yeah? You *want* to be stuck with me now?" His voice was laced with humor, but there was something in his eyes that demanded an honest answer to the question. Zoe considered her options—calling him an idiot, smacking him upside the head—and quickly settled on the one she would normally have avoided. Her mama had raised her to be a lady, damn it, with manners and a decided preference for being pursued over giving chase when it came to men. But given that Jason was determinedly thickheaded when it came to her, and since she hadn't been able to shake the memory of what his mouth had felt like on hers, just this once she chose the direct route.

Zoe approached him slowly, her eyes locked with his. She saw the way his gaze slid down to her feet and then all the way back up to her head, saw the heat that kindled there. It was like being caressed by invisible hands, and when she spoke, her voice came out in something like a purr.

"I'm right where I want to be," she said, putting one hand on the table and leaning down so that her face was inches from his. His breath fanned her face, his long, dark lashes lowering, and she wished she could simply climb into his lap and wrap herself around him. That would traumatize Sam and Jake, though, and she really wanted to be allowed back. Not only that; she didn't think going to bed with him now, when he was still acting like this strange thing of theirs had an expiration date, was a great idea.

He didn't seem to know what he wanted from this. That

made two of them. The only certainty was the heat that rose between them, such that the air seemed to crackle and snap with the intensity of it. It was a start. But it couldn't be everything, and she suspected that Jason knew it as well as she did.

"I wonder," he murmured, and then stopped himself. He couldn't seem to take his eyes off her mouth, and she used it to her advantage, drawing her lower lip in to wet it. She could actually *feel* him tighten, though no part of her touched him.

"What do you wonder?" she asked.

"What you do want." His voice was soft, breathless. The power in having pushed him so far made her bold.

"One of these nights," she said, "you might just find out." Then, before she lost what fragile grip she still had on her self-control, Zoe stepped back and walked away.

Chapter Thirteen

Jason woke up late Friday morning to the sound of the television blaring and the vacuum cleaner being run.

"Oh my God," he groaned to no one in particular. "Why?"

No answer was forthcoming. Probably, he decided, because there wasn't one, other than "because you were stupid enough to come home last night." He was just lucky. His little island of sanity had been turned into a funhouse, he had no current viable way of escape, and he'd spent the night tossing and turning while he imagined Zoe leaning over him, her voice full of dark promise: *One of these nights . . .*

Yeah, well, it hadn't been last night. She'd gone back to Sam and painted her fingernails like nothing had happened, and he was left to watch TV in the half-finished basement with Jake and Tucker the wonder mutt, nursing a beer and trying to keep his mind on the conversation. By the time he'd come up, there was nothing left of her but an empty teacup and the faint scent of vanilla.

At this rate, he'd be hard every time he walked by a bakery. He'd never be able to go into Petite Treats again.

He'd been so flustered, having Jake bring him back so he could think about Zoe naked somewhere he wouldn't feel pretty awkward about it had been the only real option. So here he was. The sexual frustration added a new dimension to his post-broken-leg funk.

Miraculously, it was making him even more miserable.

After lying there with the noise pounding at him for a few minutes, he hauled himself out of bed and stood. Rosie looked less interested in getting up, but she did with a little prodding and the promise of breakfast. Jason pulled some old athletic shorts on over his boxers, braced himself, and then opened the door to head out into the kitchen.

His mother was vacuuming, wearing athletic gear that told him she'd already been for a run. He had to tamp down the ugly twinge of jealousy he felt at that. It would take him a while to get back to running, he knew, even after the cast came off. But he'd get there. By then, he'd have his space back. And maybe—

Don't even go there. He shut down all thoughts of Zoe before his imagination could run anywhere with her. She'd be around in some capacity. He'd learned not to count on more, and this should be no different.

"Morning," he said, but of course she didn't hear him. With a sigh, he went to let Rosie out, then started to get her breakfast together. When the vacuum shut off, he knew she'd finally noticed him. He found himself tensing and tried to stop it. It was an old reaction—and oddly, the thing that helped him relax was imagining Zoe calling him Treebeard. Drawing his mother's attention *had* always been a little like finding the Eye of Sauron upon him.

"You look happy this morning," she said. "Excited for the bonfire tonight?"

"Sure. Hey, can you turn the TV down? I don't really need to know how to make a decorative fruit bowl, and it's like they're shouting it at me."

She rolled her eyes but obliged him. The volume went lower than he'd expected, actually, which meant she wanted to talk. *Great.*

"So, what was last night about? The way you left was pretty rude, son of mine."

He looked around, nodding slowly. "Yes. Yes, it was. Know what else was rude?"

"What?" Her chin went up, arms crossing over her chest. Defensive in an instant, because she knew exactly what else was rude. She just didn't give a damn.

"Throwing a girls' night in my house without asking me. You know, the son you supposedly came out to help and spend time with? In the house you always complain is too small? It was either leave or lose my mind."

"You could have said something," she said flatly.

"I tried. When the doorbell rang. You ignored me."

"You know," she said stiffly, "I never get back here. Not ever. Your father works, I have a lot of commitments, and your brother—"

"You could come if you felt like it, and Tommy is twenty-nine years old. He doesn't need a babysitter."

"Not like you'd know. You never even talk to him," she said. *Ah, here comes the guilt trip.*

"I used to, actually," Jason said, setting Rosie's food down. "He never called me back, so I finally gave up. But you can rest easy, because he does call of his own free will once in a while. Just to keep me caught up on how much better his life is than mine. I also love the texts of his girlfriends in bikinis." He tried to keep his tone conversational, and was able to mainly because this was just another variation on a very old conversation. Why didn't he do things like his brother, why didn't he go with Tommy and his friends (because hey, he didn't have that many, and the ones he had weren't flashy), why didn't he study something more useful like Tommy had? And on and on and on . . .

He was more interested in how much better his balance had gotten from having to do so much one-legged. "Did you see that? I got her breakfast together and put it on the floor without wobbling once! I'm awesome."

"You're . . . Jason, don't try to blame this all on Tommy! He's busy!"

"So am I, when I don't have a broken leg." He glanced at her and saw the wild gleam she got in her eye whenever she thought she was being challenged. Inwardly, he sighed. She was more on edge than usual since she'd gotten here. It was nothing he could put his finger on, but she was thrumming like a live wire all the time. It made him nervous. Maybe he'd call his father about it, if he could catch him. And if he could get him to dig into a topic a little deeper than, say, how the weather was in the Cove, which was tough.

With considerable horror, he heard himself asking the question that never brought forth anything good. "Mom, are you okay?"

"I'm fine. *Fine,*" she repeated, drawing out the *f* almost like a hiss. "I'd just like to feel like you actually want me here. I mean, it's not like I spent every waking moment on you when you were a kid. It's not like you don't ever come visit, right?" Her voice was watery, but her eyes were as hard and bright as sapphires. "You know, I get tired of this passive-aggressive crap you pull with me. I raised you to be strong and say what you think. You know

I don't have any respect for people who don't stand up for themselves. If you have a problem, say so."

He was well aware that this was so much bullshit, since she respected only people who agreed with her in all things, but he still had to take a moment to decide which undesirable path to go down. There were two. On the one hand, he could tell her exactly how he felt and then ask her to leave, which would lead to anger, hate, suffering, and eventually the Dark Side. This would end with him lying about wanting her to stay. On the other hand, he could skip the theatrics, pretend he'd wanted her to stay from the get-go, and then seethe quietly until he got over it. He'd spent his youth doing the latter, and he was damn tired of it.

But this was a small house, and she'd be leaving eventually, hopefully not to be seen for another year. He wished it were different. He just understood that it wasn't going to be. And whatever her underlying problem was, she wouldn't be sharing it with him.

This sucks. Just like always.

He didn't know how Tommy dealt with it. But then, his little brother had a whole life he knew almost nothing about, apart from the jazzed-up, so-much-better-than-yours version of it Tommy occasionally dispensed to him. He was mostly past guilt on that one and had settled into a faint ache that he recognized as loss. As long as only one of them was interested in fixing it, it just wasn't a fixable thing.

That seemed to be a recurring theme with him. It was almost enough to make a guy leery of his relationship choices, he thought with a small, rueful smile. Then, because he supposed he could handle this for one more day so that the bonfire wasn't a complete disaster, he gave in to the inevitable.

"Nothing's wrong, Mom. Just please ask next time you have a bunch of people invade my house, okay?"

"You need more fun in your life," she said, sidestepping any sort of apology. "Don't you and Zoe go out? Does she entertain? She must, in her business."

He really had no idea. "I . . . sometimes."

His mother walked into the kitchen and opened up the fridge, which was now stocked with random things he didn't eat. There were vast quantities of yogurt. She pulled out a couple of packages of hamburger meat and set them on the counter, then went to the pantry and started to pull out what he recognized as the ingredients for barbecued meatballs.

He'd always loved those things. And her remembering that brought on all the guilt he'd successfully avoided before. While that came in for a landing, she chattered.

"She's not as friendly as I was hoping, you know. I mean, she's on-the-surface friendly, but I just find her cool. Not that she doesn't seem to treat you well. She's certainly underfoot enough, and I can see she's been helping you. I just—I don't know. A *gallery owner*."

He'd been hobbling over with the idea of giving her an awkward hug—most of her hugs fell into that category—but that drew him up short. She finished mashing up the hamburger with a few seasonings and started rolling meatballs, oblivious.

"Yes, she is. Is something wrong with that? I thought you'd find it interesting."

"Oh, I do. You know, my friends are always saying I should get into that sort of business. Small scale, but I have a great eye, according to them. I'd love to pick artists and pieces to showcase. Not," she added, turning her head to regard him for a second before returning her attention to the meatballs, "that I'd do anything like what Zoe has. The old Hamilton House has been transformed for sure, but the selection . . ." She pulled a face. "It's very Harvest Cove—I'll give it that."

"It definitely is," Jason agreed. That was one of the reasons he'd walked in there the first time. The other was Zoe. "They're all local artists, Mom. There are plenty of different styles in there. Anyway, you *like* Harvest Cove. You're always saying that, and you're from here."

"Oh, honey. Of course I do. But there's a great big world out there. Now, where did Zoe move from?"

"Georgia." If he was going to be quizzed, he wished he'd asked Zoe for a spare notebook to fill out. It occurred to him all at once that Zoe knew a lot more about him than he did about her. He'd been too busy deflecting her questions to ask any of his own.

"Huh. Well, why did she come here, of all places?" She shook her head before he had to try to scrounge up some sort of answer and came up with one herself. "She'll get tired of it. Out-of-towners always do." She turned her head to give him a meaningful look. "You're going to want to be careful of that. I thought maybe you'd found some nice local girl. Somebody more . . ." She waved her hand as though she might catch the appropriate word out of thin air, but there was nothing, and Jason was pretty sure he didn't want to know what she meant. *More your speed,* maybe?

"You know, I could see if the Fiores' daughter is still in town, Chessa. They could bring her. I mean, it's not like you're serious yet, right? She was always a beautiful girl, very stable, good family . . ."

He didn't have the energy to be angry with this sort of thing anymore. It was an unpleasant realization, but true nonetheless. This was just par for the course. Whatever he did, it was never going to be quite right, never going to be good enough. He couldn't do what Tommy had done, couldn't follow her blueprint for his life so exactly. He should have known that rather than see Zoe as a catch, she'd just feel threatened by her. It had been that way with Sara, to some extent, though he couldn't blame his mother for destroying that. She hadn't had to try. It had been a mess all on its own.

Zoe's different. But he wasn't. And that was what worried him.

"I'm with Zoe," he heard himself saying, calmly, with only a hint of the weariness he felt. "I don't want to be with anybody else, so it would be nice if you tried to get to know her instead of making a bunch of assumptions."

The irony wasn't lost on him. It was advice he hadn't followed himself where she was concerned. Maybe he should start.

"Oh," Molly said, and for once, she didn't appear to have anything to add when she turned her head and gave him a curious look before continuing to make the meatballs. He didn't know what about his statement had silenced her, but the fact that it had was good enough for now. He was beginning to hobble away when she piped up once more. "It's only because I care about you, you know."

She sounded almost tentative, wholly unlike her usual brash statements. He even believed her. She did care, in her way. So he turned, made his way back to the counter, and with a sigh dropped his chin on top of her head. "I know," he said. She stiffened, then relaxed as much as she ever did when he touched her. She'd never known what to do with him . . . but there was still a part of him that wished she would figure it out. He didn't want much.

"Well, go on and shower. We've got a busy day ahead, and I've got some things I have to go get in a bit. You don't have to come," she said quickly, "but you should get dressed. It's good for you to have a routine even though you can't work."

He knew her well enough to be suspicious, but also well enough to understand that he wouldn't know what she was up to until she sprang it on him . . . whatever fresh horror it happened to be.

Before he got in the shower, he picked up his phone on a whim and texted the only person he had much interest in having a conversation with this morning.

I miss tracking dirt into your gallery. Just saying.

He thought about it for a moment, then decided to sign it in a way that would make her smile.

-Treebeard

Chapter Fourteen

Zoe made sure to get all her ducks in a row before leaving Sam and her new part-time hire with the gallery. She still wasn't sure the new guy would behave himself, mostly because he never did. But anyone who came in would be entertained, at least.

"Don't make me regret this," she warned Aaron Maclean as she grabbed her purse. "When you told me you needed human interaction, I sympathized, but remember why I'm paying you."

"To bring in business with my stunning good looks, of course," Aaron said with a wicked grin. He was tall and lean and handsome, with blond hair carefully styled into a perfect quiff and shot through with a streak of ebony right in front. The streak never stayed the same color from month to month, varying with his mood. She'd asked whether the black meant he was in mourning, but his explanation had been decidedly dirtier.

He was wonderful at making her sorry she'd asked various questions. He was also one of her best friends in the Cove. Aaron and Sam together were going to be either an amazing combination or just plain trouble. Zoe hoped it was some kind of balance between the two.

"Well, just remember who's in charge of making your big show amazing," Zoe warned him, though she couldn't keep her lips from curving. He was a brat, but a lovable one, and his sculptures were incredible. He certainly brought in enough money these days not to have to be here, but she knew he thrived on company, so when he'd asked if he could pick up some part-time work just to get out of the house, she'd relented. She'd been through a few employees who hadn't worked out very well. Sam was the only constant. It would be nice to have another artist in here, one she knew she could trust.

Make that *hoped* she could trust.

"We'll be good, Mom," Sam said. Aaron grabbed her from behind and hugged her tightly, making her squeal.

"Don't lie," he whispered to her loudly. "She'll be even more disappointed when she comes back to find confetti all over the floor, a disco ball hanging from the ceiling, and Big Al passed out in the corner with his head through a painting."

"I love the smell of impending doom in the morning," Zoe said. Just imagining Big Al Piche, whose antics in the Cove were legendary and whom she had told at various times, in some very strong language, never to darken her doorstep again—despite the fact that he always returned, sometimes without pants—gave her the willies. "How about this: Try to behave, okay? Just make a good-faith effort? Please? Or sell a few things, which will go a long way toward making me forgive you for whatever you get up to while I'm gone."

Aaron released Sam and saluted. "Aye, aye, Captain."

Zoe pointed at him. "That's right." She turned and walked out, passing Ryan Weston as he hurried in, slightly wild-eyed, with a metal lunch box in his hand. She paused with her hand on the door to watch him head right for Aaron, who suddenly looked sheepish.

"Uh, oops?"

"I've got better things to do with my lunch period than play delivery boy because you'd forget your head if it wasn't screwed on," Ryan complained. "Why the hell did you ask me to make you a sandwich if you were just going to leave it on the counter?"

"Because you make amazing sandwiches. And because you love me enough not to hurt me when I forget things."

Zoe caught the long-suffering look Ryan gave his boyfriend as he shoved the lunch box into Aaron's hands. "You're lucky you're cute. Jackass."

Zoe grinned and shook her head as Ryan lightly cuffed Aaron upside the head before accepting a quick kiss, which she knew he was still shy about. The young, athletic high school teacher hadn't been out for very long, but Aaron had pushed him to be more open. Probably because Aaron was kind of like a big puppy dog around Ryan. It was funny to see her friend so smitten, but she was happy for both of them.

See, Treebeard? Opposites attracting can work just fine. She waved good-bye and headed to her car, her mind as occupied by Jason as it had been all week. If he only knew just how he affected her . . . but then, it was probably better he didn't. It had taken her a good half hour to calm down after she'd walked away from him last night, and even then she'd decided to hightail it out of there

before he emerged from the basement in case her re-
solve broke.

It was no longer a matter of if she would take him to
her bed; it was when. She knew it, and that knowledge
gave her butterflies every time she let herself think about
it. Still, she wanted to know that afterward, he wasn't
going to just go skulk off somewhere and find reasons
they shouldn't have done it. She had hope, though. He
could be surprisingly sweet when he forgot to be unhappy about his leg, his mother, and whatever else wasn't
currently right in his universe. The man needed to get
out. It was time for Jason to rejoin the world, and lucky
him, she was just the woman to help him do it.

She pulled out her phone to glance at it and was surprised to see a text from Jason waiting for her. She
opened it up and smiled. Maybe he wasn't doing so badly
getting his mind off of things after all. She wasn't about
to complain about his area of interest. After a moment
of thought, she texted him back.

> Some guys miss my ravishing beauty. You miss
> my floor. You're lucky I like you, Treebeard. On
> my way. -Z

She pulled up to the house to find Molly just getting into
Jason's truck. Zoe pulled in beside her, hoping that the
woman would just go, but she watched Molly look, think
about it, and then wait.

Wonderful. Well, this was the reason she was here to
begin with. Might as well try to make nice. Again.

Zoe stepped out of the car. "Hi, Molly. Is Jason inside?"

"Yes. Showered and everything, if you can believe it."

"He really hates that cast," Zoe said, and that, at least, seemed to be something the two of them could agree on. Molly nodded vigorously.

"Don't I know it. He clomps around like an angry bear. Used to do that when he was a kid, too. Never said much. Just clomped."

"I can picture that," Zoe said. The image made her smile. Small, grumpy Jason, a miniature Treebeard. "I'm sure he was cute, though."

"He was, in a quieter way. Both my boys were cute kids. It was hard for Jason, I think, when Tommy came along. Jason was skinny and shy, and he had that awful stutter . . . you did know about the stutter."

Zoe looked uneasily toward the house, hoping Jason couldn't hear this conversation. She doubted he would appreciate it. "I did, yes. I've only heard it once. But you can tell he slows down when he gets upset."

"Using his strategies," Molly said with a satisfied smile. "That's what his speech therapist was big on, strategies. Seemed to work. She helped him a lot, but he stayed shy, for the most part. Had a few friends, liked to run—he was a good runner—but a tough nut to crack. Tommy, now, my younger one, he could never help but shine. He had everything going for him, really. Everything." She fumbled her phone out of her purse, an odd note in her voice. "Do you want to see a picture?"

"Ah," Zoe said, knowing her answer didn't much matter. She was going to get to see the famous Tommy Evans. When Molly handed her the phone, Zoe wasn't sure what to expect. She blinked, frowned, and then raised her eyebrows. "Oh. Well, he's . . . he's a very good-looking man, Molly. I'm sure you're very proud. Of *both* your boys."

She handed back the phone, with its picture of a blond who was indeed good-looking, and bore some resemblance to Jason although he was much cleaner-cut. Actually, Tommy looked like he spent a lot of the time at the gym and getting tan. The clothes were very casual and very expensive. He was on a patio somewhere, martini in hand, grinning at the camera. She wasn't impressed. He did make for a stark contrast to his brother, though. Jason might be a tall, striking guy, but he acted like somebody who was used to being overlooked. Sometimes she thought he actually preferred it that way.

"Oh, I am. I am proud. I just worry. About Jason, you know. Always did. He's just got problems Tommy never had."

One of Zoe's brows rose. "Jason doesn't seem like he has any big problems to me. No more than the average person."

Molly looked toward the house. "He's just so stubborn. He didn't want to leave here and try to make something more of himself. He has a degree. Could have gone to work on the administrative side of things, maybe even in DC, but no. Just wants to hug the trees on the Cove and find some woman who wants to marry Paul Bunyan. I wasn't a big fan of Sara, but she had her priorities together. She knew he could be more than he is. I wish he did, too."

It never seemed to take any time for Molly Evans to irritate her. "Jason's job is very important," she pointed out. "Tourism is what keeps this place going. The park is a big part of that in the summer and fall. Not to mention the fact that he saves small animals."

Molly grunted. "That is *not* a dog." She relented a little, though, even if Zoe got the impression it was more to take pity on her than anything else. "I guess he likes his job, so that's something. It's just not . . . what I was hoping for."

"Well, he's exactly what I like," Zoe said coolly. This was some messed-up family Jason came from, where his mother played favorites and his brother ignored him. And who knew where the father was? Apparently he was about as meaningful as wallpaper. "I liked him from the first day he walked in to buy something at the gallery."

Molly looked back at her, incredulous. "Buy what? A coffee mug? There was some nice pottery—"

"He has a nice little collection going, actually," Zoe said, cutting her off. Whether or not Jason was okay with his mother being aware of his hobby, she couldn't handle the misconceptions about him, the insinuations that Jason being here in the Cove was some kind of failure. If this was what he'd grown up with, no wonder he was standoffish.

It made her sad and filled her with gratitude that her own family, for all its faults, had been warm and loving. She was suddenly, unexpectedly homesick. One day she'd get them to come up and visit. Until then, maybe it was time to start planning another trip back home. She wondered again what her parents and brothers would think of Jason, but brushed the thought aside. It wouldn't do her any good to imagine things that were probably never going to happen, and him meeting her family was about as likely as Thor showing up on her doorstep and begging for her hand in marriage. Though she actually *did* enjoy imagining that . . .

Molly was watching her, confusion writ plain across her face. "He collects . . . art?"

"Yes," Zoe replied, knowing some of her impatience finally showed through. "The pieces he has didn't get there by themselves, and I sure didn't put them there. Didn't you notice? You've been here a week."

"I—"

"His taste might not match up with yours, but it's still good," she said. "In *fact*, he has a very good eye. He also, in case you missed it, is a good guy who works hard and loves his job and saves wounded animals and is polite to people who are waiting on him, unless those people are me, which is fine because he and I have an understanding about that." Her voice was rising along with her temperature, but the half-astounded, half-stupidly blank expression on Molly's face encountered her last nerve and began trying to destroy it. "I'm sorry you find him so disappointing. So is he, I'm sure, because there's no way he's missed it. But if you think cutting him down is going to change him, you're wrong. And if that's your idea of helping him when the man has a busted leg on account of *doing his job well and being a decent human being*, then you might want to find a different patient. Because you are *not helping*."

Molly stood frozen, staring at her. Zoe waited a few seconds for a response, but when she got none she put her hands up and turned toward the house. "Good talk. Forget it, I'm out."

Behind her, she finally heard an enraged rasp. "How dare you?"

Zoe barely turned her head to answer as she headed up the steps and onto the porch. "Oh, I don't know. Ask Tommy. He's brilliant. Maybe he'll have an answer for you." She didn't feel guilty. Even her brief burst of fury was gone, vaporized in the flash of her anger the way it always was. That was the nature of her temper. But her protectiveness lingered, the fierce need to stand in front of Jason and fight. Not like he probably needed or wanted it, but she'd always been this way with the people she cared about. The people who mattered. And like it or not, he did.

The door opened just as she hit the top step. Jason filled the doorway, looking both rumpled and concerned. His hair was still damp, curling at the nape of his neck, and he smelled good even from where Zoe stood. But the sight of his ancient sweatpants was nearly enough to give her apoplexy. Her patience with this week was at an end.

"Zoe?" he asked. A car door slammed behind her, and gravel kicked up as Molly slammed the SUV into reverse and pulled out. "What the hell is going on out here?" Beside him, Rosie barked. As much as she loved the little dog, Zoe felt every sharp yelp like a nail in the temple. She winced. The headache she'd been holding at bay all week felt like it was finally going to come in for a landing.

"I yelled at your mother," Zoe said.

Something in the way she looked must have given him pause, because Jason sounded uncharacteristically cautious when he spoke again. "I heard that." She wondered if he'd also heard what she'd said, her unqualified praise of him, and whether he knew it was sincere. She hadn't, not exactly, until it had all come pouring out of her mouth. And now she'd engaged his mother in battle, and her eye was starting to ache with warning, and Jason was watching her as though she might have a psychotic break at any moment.

Her happy plans for the day evaporated like so much

smoke. All she wanted was a dark room, the absence of Molly Evans, and for Jason to buy some new sweatpants. And not necessarily in that order.

"Are you okay?" he asked.

"No, actually," Zoe said. "I was going to drag you out for some shopping and a haircut and maybe an early dinner before this bonfire tonight. But you know what? I think I'm going to go home and lie down."

"Maybe you should come in instead," Jason said. "You don't look so good."

She glared up at him. "Thanks, but I think I'll just—"

"Come in," he said, his expression hardening. He opened the door, and Rosie bounced out to dance around her feet. "I mean it."

"Jason, I just told your mother that I think she is, in essence, a complete asshole. You really want me in your house right now?"

He seemed unfazed. "Zoe, I love her, but I know what she is. Now, come inside before I try to throw you over my shoulder and break the other leg."

She hesitated, torn between retreating into her own comfort zone and giving in to the concern she heard in Jason's gruff voice. The bright pain beginning to radiate through her eye, however, made the decision for her. She didn't want to drive like this.

"Fine," she said, and skulked past him, dropping her purse on the dining room table and then digging through it to find the Ziploc baggie containing two pills she'd been carrying all week, just in case. She jumped when Jason deposited a water bottle on the table next to her.

"For the meds," he said.

"Thanks," Zoe replied, reminded of how fast he could be when he wanted to, even when impeded by crutches.

She unscrewed the cap, popped one pill in her mouth, and took a swig.

"You didn't mention you had migraines," he said.

She looked at him wearily. "Yeah, well, you didn't ask. I'm going to need to lie down for a few."

He nodded, and his concern penetrated the thickening fog of pain enough that she could manage a small, strained smile for him.

"Back there." He pointed. "The downstairs bedroom. I've been sleeping in it so I don't have to do too many stairs with this stupid cast, but it's neat enough. Get comfortable, okay? I'll be out here if you need me."

She nodded, knowing she needed to lie down ASAP and close her eyes so the medicine could work. "Thanks." There was nothing else to say. She meant it, though, and he seemed to understand.

"Anytime."

She headed for the bedroom, feeling his eyes on her as she left. The house was full of competing smells. Under other circumstances, her mouth would probably have been watering, but at the moment all it produced in her was a slow roll of nausea. Zoe stumbled into the bedroom to find a neatly arranged bed with the covers turned down, the dresser and nightstand each with a scatter of things that belonged to Jason. She shut the door behind her and then hurried to close the curtains before kicking off her shoes and crawling into the bed.

There was no sound but the quiet whir of the ceiling fan, and she found herself enveloped by his scent. It was pine and rain, clean and subtle, and far from making her nausea worse, it soothed her. She breathed it in, curling into herself and closing her eyes. Somewhere in the distance, the phone rang. She heard him answer it, his deep voice making for comforting background noise while she began to drift. It was strange not being on her own to nurse herself through a bad headache, but here, with Jason, she liked knowing she wasn't alone. He made her feel safe.

The realization would have had more impact if she'd felt better, but all she managed was a small frown before she escaped into sleep, hoping that when she woke up, the meds would have worked and she'd be ready to deal with the aftermath of what she'd done. There would be trouble, she knew. But what form it would take was a mystery to her. And then there was the bonfire. Would Molly still be coming? How could she navigate that without a scene?

Worried but exhausted, Zoe gave up thinking and just listened to the pleasant buzz of Jason's voice down the hall, depending on its slow and steady rhythm to center her until her body relented and let her slide into sleep.

Chapter Fifteen

S he opened her eyes in the dark.

Zoe awoke slowly, her mind fuzzy in the way only her migraine meds could produce. The bed beneath her was soft and comfortable, and there was a wonderful warmth curled like a ball against her stomach. For a few seconds, she thought she was home. But the door was in the wrong place, a gold rectangle of light in the dark, and the soft sounds coming from beyond the door weren't home sounds. They weren't *bad* sounds, just different. Where was she, again?

She caught a faint and lovely whiff of pine and blinked, disoriented. After a moment, though, it came back to her. For a few brief and wonderful seconds, she relaxed into the bed, content. Then she remembered the rest of it, and the contentment vanished.

She breathed in deeply, pausing when she heard a soft snore. Zoe frowned, then realized that the warmth curled against her stomach was coming from a small, sleeping ball of fur. Rosie had joined her while she slept. Jason must have let her in, she thought, and smiled. There really was nothing like a sweet, soft dog when you didn't feel well. The vise grip at her temples, however, had vanished, leaving her with the tired, slightly wrung-out feeling she always had after a migraine. At least she'd caught it early. She probably wouldn't need that second pill, though if the evening went south, all bets were off. Laying low for the rest of the day, or night—whatever time it might be outside—was a must if she didn't want to head right back down Stab Me in the Face Trail.

Zoe lay there a few minutes longer, allowing herself to wake up fully, and then eased herself away from Rosie to slide off the other side of the bed. She couldn't stay in here forever, and hiding from problems wasn't her style. She and Jason were going to have to sort some things out, whether or not he'd decided to be angry with her after all. All she hoped was that they got to do it on their own. Molly would have to come back eventually . . . if she hadn't already.

Her head gave a painful twinge at the thought, and she decided it might not be a bad idea to take the second pill anyway, just in case.

She stood slowly, waited to make sure the headache was going to stay gone, and then went to the door. There was nothing but a soft snort behind her, indicating that Rosie had decided it was perfectly comfortable right where she was. Zoe couldn't disagree. And later on she would no doubt spend plenty of time thinking about the fact that she'd just spent at least a couple of hours in Jason's bed. For now, though, she needed to keep moving before she thought *too* much.

Zoe opened the door, hearing the soft sounds of the television. She could finally appreciate the way the house smelled, though she didn't have much of an appetite right now. There was both savory and sweet in the air, a homey smell, and layered beneath it the faint scent of Jason's cologne—or maybe it wasn't cologne. Maybe it was just him. Either way, she liked it. She was cautious when she stepped out into the great room, uncertain about who might be waiting for her. But the only one she saw was Jason, sprawled on the couch, his foot propped up on a pillow on the coffee table. He looked perfectly content with a PlayStation controller in his hand, staring at the screen and talking softly to himself. Zoe stopped, letting herself enjoy the view before he noticed her. Despite everything, he actually looked relaxed and happy.

"Just a little closer . . . just a little closer . . . *yessss!*" He bit his lip, lifted the controller, and pressed buttons furiously while leaning quickly to the side, as though that would have some sort of effect on whatever was happening on-screen. He gave a convincingly evil laugh. "Suck it, you f— Oh, hey, Zoe."

His eyes widened a little when he spotted her. Then he leaned back slowly, trying, Zoe suspected, to look like he'd only been mildly interested in his game. He was too cute for his own good sometimes, she thought. Even though nobody seemed to see it but her.

"Hey," she replied, walking toward him. She glanced at the TV and at the game he'd paused. "What are you playing? *Deep Space 4*?"

"Yeah." He looked between the screen and her with a small, puzzled smile. "How'd you know?"

"I have five brothers," she replied. "When we talk, which is fairly often, I get to hear about what they're doing. Right now, three of them are obsessed with this game. I know more about the continuing saga of Commander Aegis than I ever wanted to. The space guns. The scantily clad alien warriors who love him. The upcoming DLC maps for multiplayer. I could write a manual."

His brows lifted. "Maybe you should."

"Nah. I think my inherent dislike of shooters would bleed through. Sam's the shooter queen. If I can't be a warrior woman with pointy ears and a big sword, it's probably not for me."

That seemed to take him aback, which she'd known it would. "You like RPGs?"

"Sometimes," she replied.

"Why didn't I know that?"

"Because you didn't ask. I feel like I give you this answer a lot for some reason." She stopped when she was next to the couch and looked around, eyes lingering on the loft above. It was still and silent, but she knew that was no guarantee.

"She's gone," Jason said, saving his game and turning off the system. "Staying at a friend's."

"Ah." Zoe winced, putting her hands on her hips and looking around the room. Anywhere but at Jason. "Her idea?"

"Mine, actually," he said, and she felt the first twinges of guilt after all. Some amazing fake girlfriend she'd turned out to be. She was supposed to *wow* his mother into leaving, not yell at her until she took off. "You don't have to look so worried, Zoe. A week is about all we ever manage before she and I get into it. We were almost there."

"Oh? She usually take off and sleep elsewhere when that happens?"

"No. I usually start spending a lot of time at work until she's ready to go. She's easily bored. Never takes long. I just couldn't vanish this time."

"Which is where I was supposed to come in," Zoe said, and then sighed, exasperated with herself. "I'm sorry, Jason. I should have kept my cool with her. She just started *talking*, and there were pictures of Tommy and all this garbage about you and your brother, how different you are."

"It's nothing I haven't heard before," he said. "I'm the older brother, but she locked in our roles pretty early on. I was always kind of quiet, I guess. Tommy wasn't." He shrugged. "Little late to do anything about it now."

She wrinkled her nose at him. "I guess. Don't you get bitter?" He sounded preternaturally calm. She'd be on the ceiling somewhere, shrieking.

"Sometimes," he admitted. "Doesn't change much. I have Aunt Moira, though, and when my grandparents were around I had them. Mom was so busy trying to be involved in everything—town committees, team mom for every sport Tommy played. She wasn't actually around much. Not for me, anyway. I was with Nanny and Pops a lot. Her parents. They didn't understand her, either. I think they finally just decided to do what they could with damage control."

"Oh," Zoe said.

One corner of his mouth quirked up. "Don't look so sad about it. It wasn't all bad. They love me. They're just not that interested." He paused, tilting his head a little. "You want to sit for a while? You don't have to leave. Going to be a quiet night."

It suddenly dawned on her that it was still Friday. "Oh God! The bonfire!"

"I made some phone calls. I have a sick girlfriend who needs somebody to take care of her. People tend to understand that."

His voice gave away no hint of whether he was teasing her or not, and there was something in the way he watched her—steadily, carefully, as though he was gauging her reaction—that left her feeling off-balance. She wasn't quite sure how to respond.

"Well . . . I'm glad the whole girlfriend thing was useful once, at least," she finally said.

"Useful or not, I liked saying it," Jason replied. "The girlfriend part. Not the sick part." Then he smiled, and it was sweet and just a little bashful and Zoe knew she was in trouble. How he'd gone from the surly Treebeard who stomped in and out of her life at random times to the rumpled sex god flopped on his couch smiling at her was one of her life's great mysteries. It was hard to complain, even if he'd amped the drama in her life up to eleven. She hated drama. But she really, really liked him. And the way his eyes crinkled at the corners when he smiled. And how he'd—

"You shaved!" she exclaimed. "When did that happen?" The man almost always had some kind of five-o'clock shadow going on, but right now his jaw was smooth and clean, without a bit of stubble to mar it. The angular lines of his jaw were even sharper this way, the hard, inviting line of his mouth even more tempting.

"While you were out cold," he said. "I thought you might appreciate the effort." He swept a hand across his legs, now clad in a reasonably new-looking pair of cargo shorts. "You didn't even notice the rest of it. I'm hurt. I'll just go get my sweats back on."

"No!" Zoe yelped, and when he grinned at her again, that bright and mischievous smile, she knew he was playing with her. Jason Evans, playing. She wouldn't have believed it unless she'd seen it herself. And in the back of her mind, she continued turning over what he'd said about enjoying calling her his girlfriend. Despite the sudden flurry of butterflies in her stomach, she couldn't say it bothered her, either. What that meant going forward remained to be seen ... because they were still the same people who'd spent the last two years arguing over dirt, and she needed to remember that.

His smile faded into concern. "How are you feeling, anyways? Better? My friend Rich at work gets them. He pukes, but you didn't seem to have that problem, unless there's a surprise in my room I don't want to know about."

"Sometimes nausea, rarely puking, definite excruciating pain, but I caught this one before it went nuclear. And I'm doing better, thanks." The concern in his eyes was doing things to her, making her want things she hadn't allowed herself in a very long time. Being vulnerable wasn't something she enjoyed, but when she wasn't feeling quite right, the only thing she wanted was a pair of strong arms around her. She knew she could be okay on her own. She always was. But that didn't mean she always wanted to be.

"You still look tired," Jason said. She gave a soft laugh and rolled her eyes. *Typical Jason.*

"Thanks," she said.

"Oh, come on. You know you're beautiful, Zoe."

She blushed at the compliment, given so matter-of-factly. She took care of herself, but as far as being beautiful, she knew no such thing. "I'm all right," she said. "I'm sure I do look tired. I *am*."

"You're a lot better than all right. And what I meant was, you don't need to take off. Stay awhile. It's just me." *Just him.* He had no idea how not "just" anything that was. But looking at him sitting there like an overgrown teenager, alone with his video game and waiting with an expression that couldn't be mistaken for anything but hopeful, Zoe couldn't think of a good reason to say no. He was different tonight. More open, she realized. Less combative. And he'd had a rough day, too. Her natural inclination to retreat to the safety of home receded surprisingly fast.

Maybe she wasn't the only one who needed somebody tonight.

"Okay. But if you think we're going to watch sports and grunt and drink beer while making manly noises, I'm going to have to draw the line," she informed him, walking to the couch.

"Can we negotiate on the beer and manly noises?"

"Maybe."

He scooted over a little to make room for her, and she sat down, giving up any sort of decorum after the first few seconds. There was no way to arrange herself in a ladylike manner on this big, soft couch that felt like it already had a Jason-sized divot in the middle, whether or not he was physically present. She sank back into the cushions, put her feet on the coffee table, and heaved a sigh. There was no way to avoid being smashed up against his side, so she didn't bother trying, though the feel of him next to her was the only thing about her position that *wasn't* comfortable. Nice, but not comfortable. He was big and wonderfully warm, and the urge to snuggle in closer was tough to ignore.

Jason turned his head to study her, one eyebrow raised. "I'd tell you to make yourself at home but I guess I don't need to."

"I've been paying attention. This is how one sits in the House of Treebeard."

He chuckled. "I'm never getting a new nickname, am I?"

She tipped her head back and forth, pretending to consider before giving up the pretense. "If it really bothers you, I'll stop."

"Actually, I rewatched his parts on YouTube the other night. I still don't see the resemblance, but he did kick a wizard's ass, so I guess I'll accept it."

Zoe laughed. "You researched it? No, you know what, don't even answer. I'm sure you did. Glad it meets with your approval."

"*Acceptance.* You started calling me that because I reminded you of a tree. That means it takes a little longer to get to actual approval."

"As the woman whose place of business has been the recipient of your traveling deposits of earth more times than I can count, I assure you, I know the feeling."

They grinned at each other, and Zoe could feel the remaining barriers between them shift and give way, crumbling into dust. She couldn't keep any kind of emotional distance when they were this close physically, his heat keeping her warm, his breathing keeping time with hers. For all that she'd prided herself on staying rational about this, her defenses were low right now.

He wanted her here. She wanted to be here. Those two simple facts were enough to have her temperature rising. The longer he looked at her, the less she knew what to say. Zoe cast around for something to break the intimate, awkward silence.

"This doesn't count as our date, by the way," she told him. "If that's what you're thinking, I do expect something that requires leaving your house."

"I'll take that under advisement," he said. "So . . . what do you want to do? Watch a movie?"

The way his gaze moved over her face, as though he was much more interested in simply watching *her*, left her wanting to melt into the couch. Zoe's heart skipped in her chest as she smiled for no reason she could discern. She just felt kind of . . . good. *Stop it, he'll know you want to crawl all over him,* she told herself. But she couldn't seem to help it. Slowly, she shook her head.

"No, I don't really want to watch a movie. I guess we could play a video game or something."

It was his turn to shake his head. He was so close to her she could see the little gold flecks in his eyes, the tiny scar on his forehead. "No," he said, "I don't really want to play anymore."

"No," Zoe agreed. "Neither do I."

He started to lean in, and Zoe tipped her chin up, lashes lowering, when his warm breath fanned her face with a whisper. "Does this mean you like my new shorts?"

She wasn't sure whether to slap him or kiss him, which was a problem she expected to continue to have. Tonight, at least, it was easy to choose the latter.

"It means I plan on liking you right out of your new shorts."

Jason's groan rippled right through her. Every muscle tightened in response, a knot of pleasure forming in her lower belly that she could think of dozens of ways for him to untangle. It had been a long time. Too long, maybe. But she could think of no one she wanted to be with more than Jason, right here in this moment. They'd been circling each other forever.

Zoe was ready to dance.

She slid her hands up his chest as he brought his arms around her. Her lips parted instantly when their mouths met, and when he swept his tongue inside to taste her, Zoe's senses flooded. He tasted faintly of chocolate, sweet and decadent. She sighed into his mouth, picking up the rhythm of his kiss, tongue tangling with his until she was breathless. She slipped her fingers into his hair, finding thick, dark silk coiling over her hand.

He moaned softly, one hand pressing into her back, one cupping the back of her head. A thumb trailed down her jaw, gentle even as the heat between them built. He made her feel cherished and bold at the same time—enough that she found herself breathing out words, punctuating them with kisses along his cheeks, his nose, his jaw.

"I want you," she told him. "So much."

He nodded, a ragged breath escaping his lips before his mouth was on hers again, his hands roving restlessly over her back. Zoe curled her legs beneath her and leaned into him, trying to press closer, but the angle was awkward. She ended up half sprawled across him, propped up on one arm and with a nagging pain in her side. When Jason's hand roughly cupped her breast, his thumb abrading the tight bud of her nipple, she arched into him and immediately lost her balance. Her moan became a yelp as she flopped over his legs, then lay there for a moment, overheated and muzzy headed, before she could collect herself enough to speak. Jason twisted to one side to loom over her, his cheeks flushed and his breath uneven. Then he smiled at her, a mischievous grin that put her in mind of a naughty schoolboy, and Zoe found herself giggling.

"We are not smooth together," she said. "I thought it was just you who was klutzy."

"Blame my busted leg," he said. "I blame it for everything. I don't mind sharing."

"Hmm," she said, reaching up to brush his hair out of his eyes. She'd been waiting to do it all week—longer—and to be able to touch him so easily now made her feel as though her entire body sighed. "I can try that."

"Good. I know what else we can try."

"Oh?" She quirked an eyebrow at him. "Do tell."

He looked down at her, his smile softening into something she'd seen flickers of all week. She didn't want to think about what that look meant—she didn't want to be wrong. But there was so much more of him beneath the surface than he let on, she thought. He was as complicated and interesting a man as she'd ever known. He just hid it. *Purposely* hid it. She understood his introversion, his preference for quiet and peace—she had plenty of that going on herself, though she had an easier time being outgoing when it was called for—but she didn't understand why he only let most people scratch the surface, if that.

He was more than he let people see. It was the one thing about which his mother was just a tiny bit right . . . just not in the way she thought.

"We could go kick Rosie out of bed," he said. There was a thread of longing in his voice that made her chest tighten, but she knew he wouldn't push her. It was one of the many reasons why it was so easy to say yes.

"I'll move Her Highness. You just . . . hurry."

She unwound herself from him and stood, her legs feeling wobbly beneath her. Still, Zoe managed to make it from the couch to the bedroom without running into a wall or falling, which in her current state she considered an achievement. She heard Jason get up and glanced back once. He was sexily disheveled, his hair tousled, cheeks pink, and when she caught his eye the look in it sent her nearly running down the hall. If he could have chased her, she knew, he would have.

One day he will, she thought, but tried to silence that little voice as soon as it appeared. She couldn't count on that. She wanted, just for once, to be fully present in the moment. She wanted tonight.

Zoe scooped Rosie up from the bed, cradling the little dog as she hurried back out to the great room and off-loaded her gently onto the couch. The Peke looked at her irritably through half-opened eyes, but she didn't seem inclined to come bounding after her, so Zoe headed quickly back to the bedroom. She started to shut the door but paused when she saw Jason sitting on the edge of the bed, stripping his shirt off.

She knew her mouth dropped open. She couldn't help it. His chest was all lean, rippling muscle, the kind a man got when he was faithful about working out without being obsessed with it. Zoe had always thought he was built well—you only had to watch him walk around in a pair of jeans to see that—but this was more than she'd expected. He glanced up at her, and whatever he saw made him smirk.

"Bet you thought I sit on my couch all the time, huh?"

"No," she said, shaking her head. "No, not at—okay, maybe."

"Well, I don't."

"I can see that."

He tossed the shirt on the floor and then, with another amused look at her, stripped off his shorts. He dropped those on the floor, too, tipped his chin down, and said, "Your turn."

She sucked in her lower lip and looked away, suddenly shy. She wanted desperately to be against him, skin to skin. But being completely exposed to him, removing every barrier she'd had to keep between them, felt like a bigger step than just going to bed with Jason. She more than enjoyed him . . . she actually cared about him. And once a person mattered to her, she was vulnerable to that person in ways she was with very few people.

Zoe was careful not to allow people to hurt her. After tonight, she knew Jason would be capable of causing her pain. This would be her last chance to mitigate the damage, if things didn't work out down the line.

She told herself that . . . but a part of her knew it was already too late.

"Hey," he said, drawing her attention back to him. His gruff voice had gone silken, even a single word from him skimming over her skin as though she'd been stroked. She had wrapped her arms around herself without realizing, a defensive posture he couldn't have missed. "Are you okay? If you don't want to do this, Zoe—"

"I do," she said, making herself let her arms drop back to her sides. "I just . . ." She couldn't finish the thought, finally just giving a flustered smile and shaking her head. "I do," she repeated. It was all she had for truth tonight.

"Then come here," he said.

She shut the door, plunging them into darkness for a few seconds until the small lamp on the nightstand went on, casting a pool of warm light around the bed. Jason held out a hand to her, a simple gesture she found impossible to resist when coupled with the desire that darkened his eyes. He spread his legs and pulled her between them when she took his hands, then placed his hands on her hips and, in a gesture that shocked her with its sweetness, dropped his head to press it against her stomach. He breathed in deeply, breathed her in.

"Zoe," he said softly, turning her name into a prayer. She lifted her hands, hesitated, and then sank them into his hair. She stroked his head, feeling him respond by leaning into her touch while his breath warmed her through her shirt. His thumbs traced small circles around her hipbones in a rhythm she picked up with her hands, threading her fingers through silken hair and then letting it fall, feeling that delicious tightness return in her lower belly. Her breaths grew shallower as Jason's hands began to wander, stroking up her hips and then down, thumbs following the vee that led to the heat at the apex of her thighs, his touch almost, but not quite, brushing against the place that had begun to pulse and throb for him.

She removed her hands from his hair, pulling her scarf over her head, then dragging up the long, thin sweater she wore and removing it, too. This time when he looked up at her, she felt no embarrassment. The naked longing in his expression left her shaken, even as power coursed through her like molten heat. He pulled back and ran his hands up her bare torso, and a soft sound escaped her.

"You're so beautiful," he said, his voice scraping over her nerves with a friction her body immediately demanded more of. He slid his hands around her back to unfasten the simple black bra she wore, unhooking it with a deftness that surprised her.

"You're good," she breathed, and meant it in a thousand different ways.

"I've only practiced that a million or so times in my head," he replied, pulling the straps down her arms, freeing breasts that felt full and heavy, aching for his touch.

He cupped them, filled his hands with them. Zoe leaned into his touch, eyes closing. She would have let him have her on the couch, fumbling in a rush of long-deferred need, and it would have been good—but this, having Jason drink her down slowly, was so much better.

He muttered a guttural oath, and then his mouth was on her, hot and wet, closing over the taut bud of one nipple to suckle. She gasped at the sudden flood of sensation, how it arrowed right to her core. She began to move against him with every pull of his mouth, every scrape of his teeth. Jason lavished attention on one breast before moving to the other. A gentle tug, and Zoe sank onto the bed beside him, stretching beneath his touch while he propped himself on one hip and continued the sweet torment with his mouth. When Jason took one of his hands and slipped it beneath the waistband of her leggings, Zoe spread her legs instinctively, allowing him the access he sought, and was rewarded as his fingers parted her slick folds and began to stroke her.

Zoe's mouth opened on a silent cry, her hands latching onto his shoulders as he toyed with her, his big hands deftly playing her body like an instrument. Zoe's head went back, even the light sensation of her hair brushing against her bare shoulders making her shiver. She was lost in a haze of lips and teeth and hands, her hips pumping restlessly in time to Jason's every rub and stoke as her body wound tighter, tighter, until she was shaking with her need for release.

Jason pulled his mouth away from her breast and rained kisses across her chest, her stomach. His breathing grew harsh as he rubbed her harder, faster.

"Come for me," he panted. "I want to see you. So beautiful, Zoe, God."

The world narrowed to a pinpoint, then burst in an explosion of sweet sensation. Zoe surged against his clever hand, throwing her head back and crying out, bucking against him. He cupped her hard while she rode her climax out, extending it with every light flicker of his finger. Then she was melting, barely able to keep her feet as he withdrew his hand and pushed himself back further on the bed.

When she opened her eyes, watching him through her sexual haze, he looked more animal than man, a barely tamed wolf at the end of its tether. "Now," he said, pulling off his boxers so roughly it was a wonder he didn't rip them. She gave herself a moment just to admire him, perfect without a scrap of clothing on, lean and muscled and hungry . . . for her. He was rock hard, his cock as big and perfect as the rest of him, and as Zoe watched as he maneuvered himself back against the headboard and spread his legs. "Now," he said again, and it was a plea.

She managed to strip off her leggings, along with the damp, silken scrap that passed for underwear, and crawled to him on all fours. Then Zoe leaned over him for a long, drugging kiss that was all hot tongues and nips and scraping teeth. She wanted to explore him the way he had her, to push him to the edge of his endurance with her mouth, but his eyes were wild, his muscles so tense every time she brushed against him that she felt as though he might snap from the tension.

He needed her. She'd forgotten what it was to be needed like this, if she'd ever known. It felt different, *more*. And because she needed him, too, Zoe was helpless to do anything but give him what he craved. She pushed up on her knees, hooked a leg over Jason, and straddled him, bracing her hands on his shoulders. He immediately gripped her hips and guided her down onto his cock, a slow, tortuous glide that filled the still air of the room with their gasps and moans. Zoe dug her fingers into his skin as he filled her, stretched her until she felt she could take no more of him. Then he was fully inside her, creating a low and rhythmic throb between her legs that she savored for a moment before beginning to move.

She lifted up, then sank down slowly, opening her eyes to watch Jason. His eyes squeezed shut, mouth opening on a harsh groan. He cursed, and on his lips the words were hot, sensual. The power between them shifted, and Zoe began to move on him, riding him with long, fluid pulses of her hips, grinding into him at the apex of every thrust. Watching him was a pleasure all its own, though Zoe soon found her breaths coming in time to his, her hips moving more quickly as he urged her on with his hands.

He opened his eyes, warm brown dusted with gold, and watched her watching him. She felt him move one of his hands between her legs, pressing hard against the swollen nub of her sex so that every thrust produced sparks of rapidly intensifying pleasure. She skimmed her hands down his chest, watching the muscles in his lower belly begin to flex and jump as he thrust up into her. Zoe tightened around him, crying out, her thrusts growing wild as she hurtled toward another climax.

Jason squeezed his eyes shut, arching beneath her with a shout as he came, shuddering, losing himself in her. Seeing him that way was all it took to push Zoe over the edge, her pleasure imploding, crashing through her with wave after wave of sensation. She could do nothing but ride them out, moving until she collapsed on top of him, utterly spent.

She was dimly aware of his strong arms encircling her, holding her close while she shivered with the tiny aftershocks of her climax. He nuzzled her hair, pressed a lingering kiss to the top of her head, and then tucked her face against his neck as he dragged the comforter over the two of them. A slight shift in position, a click, and the room went dark. Zoe snuggled more tightly against him, wanting nothing more than to wrap herself in his warmth and stay there, possibly forever.

"Zoe," he murmured, and then pressed a soft kiss to her ear.

"Mmm." She couldn't talk. She didn't care about talking. All she cared about was staying right where she was. Fortunately, Jason seemed to be on the same page, sighing her name one more time as though it meant something wonderful before his breathing grew deep and even.

Zoe rested her hand against his chest, lips curving into a soft smile, before drifting to sleep to the steady, comforting beat of his heart.

Chapter Sixteen

Jason woke up in a rumpled mess of bedsheets, on his back with one arm thrown over his eyes and his good leg bent at the knee, unsure whether he'd been asleep or dead. He hadn't slept so deeply in ages, the kind of sleep that restored every worn-down bit of a person, and he felt good, really good, for the first time in a very long time. Apart from the stupid cast, he was loose and limber, his entire body relaxed from having been used very, very well during the night. They'd slept wrapped around each other, surfacing twice to make love with the kind of intensity that produced even more amazing sleep. He lay there with his eyes closed, letting his mind drift back over his hands on heated skin, gasps of pleasure, whispers in the dark that demanded more, now, *please.*

That really happened. She was really here. He'd imagined it for so long that it hardly seemed possible, but last night had been better than any daydream. It was going to change things—but things between them had already changed so rapidly that it was hard to worry. All that mattered to him right this second was that Zoe wanted him as much as he wanted her, and the resulting explosion had been one for the ages.

The rest would work itself out. For once, he felt too damn good to worry.

Jason breathed in deeply and turned his head to the side, breathing in the light vanilla scent that was Zoe. When he opened his eyes, though, there was no one there but Rosie. As he stared at her, she snorted in his face, licked her nose, and then sighed in her sleep.

He sat up and looked around, confused. Her clothes were gone from the floor, and the door was shut. The alarm clock said it was eight a.m., late for him but hardly oversleeping. His euphoric haze faded as he maneuvered himself out of bed, pulling on his boxers and then grabbing his crutches. *She took off. She left and didn't even bother waking me up.* No matter how he tried to stop it, by the time he opened the door his mind had already conjured dozens of reasons why she might have vanished, each worse than the last.

He was so determined that she'd left that it took him a few seconds of staring to process that Zoe was perched, fully dressed, on a stool at the kitchen island. She was reading the paper, her curls piled on top of her head in a way that was both messy and inexplicably sexy. While he watched, she lifted a steaming mug to her lips, had a sip, and then realized she was no longer alone. Her eyes shifted from the paper spread in front of her to connect with his, and the shy pleasure in her expression banished all his dark thoughts like so much smoke.

"Hey," she said. "You're up." Her eyes dropped to his boxers. "Well, kind of."

"I thought you left," he said.

Her brows lifted, stormy gray gaze turning cool. "That's not very flattering."

"Bed was empty, house was quiet," he said, making his way toward her. As irritated as she might be, he noted the way she looked him over while he moved. He couldn't say he minded, though his boxers weren't going to disguise the direction of his thoughts if he didn't get his brain out of the gutter. "I didn't mean I wanted you to leave."

She set the mug down, swung her legs off the stool, and met him at the entrance to the kitchen. She rose on her toes, hands lightly placed on his bare chest, and pressed her lips to his for a kiss that was initially sweet. *Initially.* Jason's entire thought process short-circuited as she deepened the kiss, turning it into a slow, thorough, and extremely arousing good morning. By the time she pulled back, she could have no question about whether he wanted her here.

Zoe gave him a slow smile, her eyes hazed with plea-sure. "Let's get something straight. I wouldn't leave without saying good-bye, okay?"

"Okay," he replied. He would have been perfectly happy to demonstrate how glad he was to hear that, but Zoe stepped away, though she looked just a little regretful.

"I'm going to have to get home and change for work," she said. "And you probably want to sort things out with your mother."

He screwed up his mouth. "I do?"

She rolled her eyes and sighed. "How about *you ought to*? She's still your mother. You should be able to talk, at least, before she rolls out of town in a cloud of righteous indignation."

"That's a picture." Knowing she was right didn't make the idea any more palatable. Jason blew out a breath. "I guess. She can't stay away forever. Her stuff is here."

"Well, maybe she'll leave sooner, now that she hates me," Zoe said, settling herself back on the stool and picking up her mug. "So, there's that." She neatly folded the paper and put it aside. Jason watched her, unsure whether he should feel strange about the fact that even the way she was constantly tidying up after herself was charming to him.

"She doesn't hate you," he said. "She just doesn't like you." He quirked a smile at her when she gave him a look over the rim of her coffee mug, then slowly put it down.

"Is there some nuance there I'm going to catch the next time I run into her, or are we just talking about the difference between her being extremely unpleasant and, say, trying to stab me? Because if so, I'm not sure the distinction matters." She looked away. "I probably shouldn't have gotten into it with her. I was worn-out and I unloaded. That's on me."

He shrugged. "Like I told you yesterday, you're not the only person who has a hard time dealing with her. She tends to push people until they snap. It's like her special gift."

"You ever snap?"

"Occasionally. But I have a long fuse. That's *my* special gift, I guess."

She blushed prettily and laughed. "One of them."

Jason grinned. He couldn't help it. He wasn't particularly vain, and he'd never been into bragging about his sexual prowess, but it was good to know he hadn't gotten too rusty. He hopped over to the counter and set about getting his morning coffee, feeling her watching him. The kitchen was warm and cozy, but there was a new tension that blossomed as soon as they stopped talking. There were plenty of unspoken things hanging in the air between them, Jason thought, invisible but weighty. And most of them had to do with where they went from here.

"So," she finally said, "speaking of last night . . ."

Jason felt himself tensing and had to force his shoulders to relax. Every misgiving he'd had, every hard-earned shred of experience, surfaced and began pummeling him with reasons why she was getting ready to let him down easy. *It was great but it'll never work. It's not you; it's me.*

"I think," she said slowly, "it would be nice if you and I really gave this dating thing a shot. Now that we've put the cart before the horse and all that." When he turned to look at her curiously, she smiled at him. "Not that I'm not glad we're so, ah, compatible. In some ways, at least. But this . . . all of this . . . hasn't been the best way to get to know each other. So maybe we could try doing it the traditional way? Start over."

"Fancy dinners and artsy movies?" he finally asked, only half-joking. He didn't see why they should have to start over when things seemed to be clicking along just fine. Besides . . . she was bound to want to do things outside his wheelhouse, and he didn't know how concerned he should be.

Zoe narrowed her eyes at him. "Try burgers at Beltane Blues and renting an action flick. See, this is why we need to hit the reset button. You still think I'm secretly a snob."

"No, I don't." *Bull. You just like her anyway.* It was the unflattering truth. He still couldn't imagine her in jeans and a T-shirt, out at the spring barbecue on the beach. In fact, he thought the sight of such a thing might rip a hole in the fabric of space-time.

She pressed her lips together and leaned back on her stool, watching him skeptically. "Mmmhmm. Tell you what, then. Let me take you out. I'll pick something I like to do. You get to be surprised and apologize for making the face you're making right now. If it works out, you pick the next spot. If I don't run screaming, my turn again. Deal?"

He shifted uncomfortably and took a swig of his coffee. Apart from the presence of his mother, which was never a welcome addition, he didn't see what the problem with this past week had been. They'd eaten. Hung around the house. If he could have walked around the square, that would have been fine, too. He hadn't realized just how nervous the thought of moving from fake relationship fraught with sexual tension to actual relationship with a boatload of potential problems made him.

He hadn't been with anybody serious since Sara, and he knew damn well Zoe was no fling. She wasn't built for it.

He didn't think he was, either. That, more than anything, was what had the hair at the back of his neck prickling to attention. The way he was already so attuned to her presence, hungry for it, had alarms going off in the back of his mind. He'd jumped too quickly once, and he'd never really stopped paying for it. Letting that happen again was out of the question.

"Okay," he said slowly. "Any reason why the setup needs to be so, you know, formal?" That worried him, too. It sounded like each of them ought to hold up a scorecard at the end of the evening. It was practical, he guessed. And very Zoe, from what he'd seen.

"Yes," she said, and crossed her legs primly, threading her fingers together over one knee. In an instant, she'd morphed from Tousled Morning Zoe to All-Business Zoe. He would have laughed, if that hawkish gaze hadn't been fixed on him. "Tell me something, Jason. Where am I from?"

He groaned inwardly. It was too early for a pop quiz. "Georgia."

"No, *where* in Georgia?"

He opened his mouth to answer, then realized he had no idea. She seemed to understand this and pressed on.

"Okay, how many brothers do I have?"

"Um. Some?"

"What was my daddy's business? Where did I live before I came here? *Why* did I come here?"

"You . . . like New England?"

The gaze sharpened to a glare. "Let's try something else. What kinds of things do I like *besides* New England? Name anything. I'll wait." She bobbed her leg up and down, and Jason could almost hear the *Jeopardy!* music playing in the background while he tried to come up with some facts. He knew plenty of things . . . more than he'd be able to articulate to her . . . but he'd sound like he'd been pining for her. Which he hadn't. He just happened to think about her often enough, and pay enough attention, that he'd figured some things out. But rather than explain that, he scrambled.

"Jesus, Zoe. You, ah, like dogs. And art. And Chinese food. And me."

"Count yourself lucky on that last one." She sighed. "Jason, I get that this has not been the best week for you to pick up on all of this stuff, but we've known each other for more than two years. We share friends. I have tussled with you over price, hunted up pieces for you, and fussed at you for your dirty shoes more times than I can count. We've spent a lot of time together this week. And then last night . . ." She trailed off, stopped.

"You wish we'd waited," he said. Maybe they should have, though he would never actually believe it. What was between them had been simmering a long time. Prolonging the agony wouldn't have made much sense. Unless they'd finally killed each other over, say, Zoe's vacuum breaking due to some twigs snapping the beater bar, they were always going to end up right here.

She was shaking her head. "No, I don't wish that. Maybe it's because I've known you so long now. It was less 'too soon' and more 'finally,' if that makes sense." She was blushing again, and he found it impossible to stay irritated with her for trying to prove this particular point.

"What I'm trying to say is," Zoe continued, "if we're going to try to do this, to be together for real, then I think it's high time you and I really got to know each other. Taking turns planning dates is a good way to start."

He wasn't as sure about that—it sounded a little organized for him. But the look on her face, lips set in a line that indicated she was willing to argue but eyes pleading with him to just *agree*, for once, pushed him into an answer.

"Fine," he said. Then he grumbled, "Maybe I should get a notebook."

Her pleasure, at least, alleviated some bright burst of anxiety he felt at the idea of being dragged along on any number of the things he'd once had to do. Antiquing, for instance. Or some kind of coffeehouse thing involving poetry. Overpriced martini bars. Movies in which one of the leads died at the end, complete with a tear-jerking monologue. What would she pick?

He had no idea. And what would *he* pick? He actually had some thoughts on that . . . but there was a big difference between imagining taking someone someplace and actually doing it.

He knew that well enough.

She got up and came to him, interrupting his thoughts, slipping her arms around his waist and surprising him with a bear hug strong enough to make him grunt, then chuckle. Cool and standoffish Zoe liked to be touched, he thought. That was one thing he'd learned about her this week, from the moment she'd held his hand that first day at lunch. She'd sought him in little ways from the start, whether with the brush of her shoulder against his or reassuring pats or the kisses that had undone him last night. Little surprises, but good ones. Maybe that boded well.

Jason relaxed into her embrace, stroking a hand over her curls, down her back. Zoe leaned her head against his chest and sighed with what sounded like contentment, and he looked down at the top of her head, his brow furrowed even as his lips curved into a half smile. All this time, he'd seen a beautiful, sensuous woman with an attitude like a storm trooper. As it happened, there was a lot more waiting underneath. He felt the aching pull deep in his chest that he'd almost forgotten, a warning that he still had things to lose.

"What's the matter?" she asked, frowning up at him. "You've got that look on your face."

"What look?"

"Like you want to bite somebody," she said. "Were you always mad at the world, or is it just me that puts you in a mood?"

"I'm not mad at the world," he replied. "Well, maybe a little since my adventure in the woods with Rosie the wonder dog. But it's just the way I look when I'm thinking."

"You must think a lot, then," Zoe said, and he chuckled. He couldn't help it. She was the only woman he knew who would fight with him, and the only one unafraid to tease him. He knew he was intimidating. It kept people from bothering him unless he wanted to be bothered. The thing with Zoe was that she didn't seem to care—she bothered him whether he was ready or not.

"That's better," she said, and stepped back. "You should try smiling more often. It's a good one."

"We'll see," he said, and she heaved an exaggerated sigh. "You really want to do this, you're going to be making that noise a lot," he warned her.

"I already do," she said. "Okay, I've got to get going. You need anything, call me." She leveled a look at him. "I mean it. It's easier for me to get away than it is for Jake."

He bristled despite himself. "I think I can handle it, Zo."

"Well, your mother is MIA and she has your car," Zoe replied evenly. "So how about you consider me your backup plan in case things go awry."

He snorted despite his determination to thwart her. Wanting her and needing her were not the same thing, and he wasn't about to blend them together so quickly. "Things tend not to go awry around here, Dr. Watson."

She made a face. "Funny."

"Do you also use the words 'hullaballoo' and 'squiffy'?"

"I'll be using a number of things in conjunction with your posterior, most of them sharp objects, if you aren't nice. There's nothing wrong with having an extensive vocabulary, *Treebeard*."

"No," he replied. "You just sounds very . . . proper. Dr. Watson." He gave himself a nice, mental pat on the back for having found an irritating nickname for her. If she was going to keep calling him a talking tree, turnabout was fair play. Especially because he was almost positive that all of their mutual friends knew exactly what she called him.

"I double majored in art history and English literature at Emory. I thought I owed it to my parents to load up on the fifty-cent words, considering they thought that was all I'd be getting out of my education."

That gave him pause. She noticed, and her smirk had an air of victory. "Told you that you didn't know much about me." She cocked her head. "What about you? Where'd you go? University of Isengard?"

"Hey."

"You started it."

Yes, he had, and now he regretted teasing her for her vocabulary. A double major at Emory. *Jesus*. "You probably had a full ride, right? Academic scholarships?"

"You say that like it's a bad thing."

"No," he replied. "I just think it's a very Zoe thing. I can't believe you were less driven then than you are now."

She made a sound that was a lot like an elderly man's harrumph. "I did have scholarships, yes. Ones I worked my butt off for. There were six of us, and I'm the baby. The money wasn't there, though Mama and Daddy helped with what they could. And you didn't answer my question."

"UMass," he said. "Environmental science."

Her eyebrow arched. "And?"

"And what?"

"I don't know . . . you made a face. The grumpy face. I'm used to it, but I don't know why you're wearing it to tell me where you want to college. I just wondered. I don't know how you get to be a park ranger. For all I know you could have to run one of those crazy obstacle courses, like on the Japanese game shows, to graduate."

"I . . . really?" He tried to picture that. "I would have *loved* to do that instead of Geology 101. We used to take bets on which puffy vest the professor would wear. He had three. I was a pretty good guesser . . . I had a lot of extra money for the vending machines that semester."

She leaned against the island, and Jason found he wanted her to stay. Staring at these four walls all day— again—was even less appealing than it already had been. Zoe made him forget where he was. Or at least that where he was currently kind of sucked. Maybe if he was entertaining enough she'd blow off work.

Since that was an impossibility, he aimed for just sending her off later than she'd planned.

"Well, even if it wasn't as interesting as my game-show idea, did you like it?"

He shrugged. "Sure. UMass is a good school, but up here it gets a lot of crap for not being Harvard, Wellesley, a pricey private. It has a good program for what I wanted, though, and it was affordable. I actually did community college for two years. Good grades, but not scholarship-level grades. I worked to pay for the first two. Parents paid for the last two. So that was helpful."

"That *was* helpful," she agreed. "Sounds like we both got lucky. Even though I got an earful about not going into medicine."

"Oh yeah?" He had a hard time picturing anyone giving Zoe a rough time about anything she was determined to do. Her laugh, though, was rueful enough that he had to believe her.

"Oh yeah," she echocd him. "The fact that I pass out at both blood and big needles didn't seem to register. I was the flighty one in my family, according to everyone. Never mind that I didn't even have a social life all four years so I could keep those scholarships and . . . hmm . . . you don't need to hear me complain about that." She looked slightly embarrassed. "It worked out."

"Because you're stubborn," Jason said. "See? I know a few things about you."

Zoe looked amused. "I don't think either of us gets points for noticing the other one is stubborn."

"Okay, how about this? Your favorite color," he announced, "is purple."

That startled her, and Jason felt like kind of an ass for throwing that out there. He hadn't even been positive he was right until just now. But some part of him, frustrated by her perception that he didn't know her, had dug up and tossed out the information before he could help himself.

"How did you know that?" she asked.

"I hide in your closet," he said, and when she balled up a fist, he added, "or I might just have noticed that you have a lot of pieces of clothing that are shades of purple and guessed."

"You look at my clothes?" she asked, clearly pleased.

"I look at what's in the clothes. The color registers eventually." And the fact that the color was beautiful against her skin helped, he thought. Then she was moving toward him as though she might let him get a taste of her again . . . until the doorbell rang, cracking his cozy morning right down the middle. Zoe froze. Rosie began barking furiously in the bedroom, and he heard her paws hit the floor just before she scrambled out and went flying toward the front door.

He cursed softly. They both knew who it was. He'd just been hoping to postpone this discussion for another few hours. Days. Months, if possible.

"Great," he said.

"I think that's my cue," Zoe said. She walked into the dining room, picked up her purse, and headed for the front door. Jason followed, impressed with how she carried herself knowing who was on the other side of the door. He didn't get there quickly enough to open it, instead watching as Zoe very cordially addressed the woman staring at her from the porch.

"Good morning, Molly. He's right in here." She turned her head and gave him a sweet smile, though he recognized the wicked edge to it and had to bite back a smile of his own. Jake had been right. Zoe could handle his mother. "Give me a call later . . . sugar." She drawled the last word, and he couldn't help the laughter, which he had to cough to cover. Zoe held the door open for Molly and walked right on by, and he gave himself just a moment to admire the view before returning his attention to the matter at hand.

It was the strangest thing. He'd started to tense up, but watching Zoe glide through what could have been a very awkward greeting calmed him. Especially because he knew it was an act . . . She'd felt badly about making things harder for him. Not that she actually had. She couldn't know, but his threshold for tense and unpleasant when it came to his family was pretty high to start with.

The door shut, and Molly marched in, ready to do battle. He recognized the stance, the set of her jaw, the look in her eyes. And he discovered he just really wasn't in the mood to indulge her. In fact, he had a sudden urge to find some decent clothes and maybe go get a haircut. He felt cooped up and grubby, two things that weren't like him but which had become a way of life in the three weeks since he'd been in the cast and out of work.

As much as he loved his house, he felt claustrophobic. He missed his park, his woods. The Cove.

"You know what I'm going to say."

"It's going to be either that you hate my girlfriend, that you're disappointed in me and are going home, or that you think I should put Rosie out," he replied, and saw that he'd hit closer to the truth than she appreciated.

"That's a nice way to talk to me," she said. "Jason, she ruined the bonfire. You *let* her."

"She gets migraines. She needed me. I wasn't going to throw a party while she was like that. Actually, I wasn't going to throw a party anyway."

"She was completely disrespectful to me. She made it sound like I don't pay attention to you, even though I'm not sure how that can possibly be since I'm right here." She gave an angry, incredulous laugh. "Like I don't know my own son."

He gave her a long look, debating about whether he wanted to do this now or put it off again, and decided that as long as he'd started the day making changes he might as well make this one. It wasn't a new conversation, but maybe this time it would sink in. He told himself that every time, and probably always would. But it was the kind of gentle denial that wasn't hurting anyone, and a lot better than anger. His mother thrived on anger. He wouldn't ever understand it . . . all he could do was keep it in mind and stand clear when the situation arose.

"You do," he said, "and you don't."

"What the hell is that supposed to mean?" There was hurt mixed in with the anger, but he'd seen it often enough that he'd gotten a little hardened about it. It was her defense mechanism—she was always the injured party, always the victim. He considered his words, careful not to get worked up enough to give her the satisfaction of correcting him: *Now, Jason, slow down and try again.*

"Mom, you came up here as much to see your friends as you did to see me. That's not exactly a problem, except that you treat my house like your own and conveniently forget that I have to live here, too. You never ask; you just *do*."

"I asked—"

"No," he said firmly. "You didn't. On top of that, you never tried to make friends with Zoe. You just tried to compete with her. It makes everything that much harder."

"I did not! If anybody was competitive, it was her. Honestly, Jason, she's an out-of-towner gallery owner with delusions of grandeur." She threw up her arms. "It's Sara all over again! You defend her, you change yourself for her . . . I mean, an art collection? Really? I knew what was going on the second she said it. That's not you, Jason. That's you trying to be what she wants. In six months you'll be living together in some museum of a house and you'll be wearing a smoking jacket and growing a mustache."

He might have gotten a chuckle out of that, except her words had gotten just where she'd intended—under his skin. She hadn't liked his ex-wife, and he'd known it. Not everything she'd flung at him had been off the mark, either, though it wasn't as stark as she'd painted it. Things never were.

"Enough," Jason said flatly. "I'm sorry you don't like her. I do. And the art collection, for your information, is mine. If you took an actual look around here, you'd notice I've been picking up things for a while."

Her eyes darted to several points in the room, though she didn't appear to actually be looking. "I'm sorry, but that just doesn't sound like you, Jason."

"And that's what I mean about you knowing and not knowing me. I'm not a ten-year-old kid anymore, Mom. Do you remember when I brought you out to see the park I work at? Couple years ago?"

She seemed flustered, restless. Being confronted head-on never settled well with her. For all that she could be loud and demanding, she tended to be more insidious when she wanted things. It was why he pressed on. The only way he got through, even if it was only for a brief period of time, was to push her outside of her comfort zone.

"I don't really remember, Jason; that was a while ago."

"Exactly," he replied, and the dismissal stung despite the thick armor he'd developed over the years. "Well, you spent the whole time complaining about bugs, Dad was so busy trying to refocus you that he missed everything, and Tommy kept looking at his watch. It was great."

"Why are you doing this? To try to make me feel bad?

Well, I do, Jason. I feel bad that I came up here when you so obviously don't want me."

Her eyes filled with angry tears, and he bit back a sigh. It was all about her. It would always be all about her. She was wrong . . . he did want her. She just wasn't capable of giving him the part of herself he needed. He'd repeated that pattern once.

This ought to serve as a reminder to be very careful not to do it again.

"I do want you here, Mom. But I think we both need a break. Small house, limited mobility on my part, lots of stress. And I know you don't like my dog."

The tears vanished from her eyes as though they'd never been there, blue turning hard and hot. "You can have whatever kind of dog you want. You can collect whatever kind of art you want, though I don't see anything that looks like it qualifies—I don't care *what* she said. I obviously don't fit in your life here, so until you can make some room for me again, I'll just get out of your hair. I already made my plane reservation a couple of days ago. I could see the way this was going to go. I'm always last with you."

She walked stiffly past him, hurrying up the stairs to pack. He watched her go with a mixture of despair and resignation. "Mom, you know that's not true," he said, but it was a halfhearted denial at best. It fell on deaf ears, because it always did. She would punish him with silence for a while, because she always did. And eventually, his father would place a quiet phone call, asking him to reach out, to make things right. And he would, because that was the way things worked in his house. Then all would be quiet until the cycle started again.

He couldn't fix it. Unbeknownst to her, he'd seen a

therapist for a time at UMass to deal with some of his anxiety issues, and "you can't fix her" had been a recurring theme. He'd made as much peace with that as he was apt to. He just wished he had someone to stand beside him, maybe fill up some of the holes that had been left in him. Didn't seem like too much to ask.

He just wished he knew whether inviting another person in would leave him more alone than he'd started.

Chapter Seventeen

Switching off date planning to get to know each other had seemed like a much cleverer idea before she actually had to come up with something. Now, as Zoe slumped at her desk and pored over her options, all she could do was come up with reasons why Jason might not like any of them.

She could tell herself her fears were unfounded, that it was stupid to worry about it, and that Jason had never acted like he hated being anywhere she was. There was still pressure. From herself. Because she was fun that way.

"Ugh," she groaned, dropping her head to rub at the back of her neck, where tension was beginning to form a knot. It felt good enough to dig her fingers into the spot that she didn't bother to look up when Aaron's voice filled her office.

"Hey, did you want me to run that deposit over to the bank when I go or—Zoe Michaelina Watson, what are you obsessing about in here?"

She looked up at him, surprisingly professional in slim pinstriped slacks and an oxford shirt. Not even a week on the job, and he still seemed to be enjoying himself at the gallery. She was hopeful, despite the mischief he got up to, that he'd decide to stay on. So far, he was working out even better than she'd expected—and she'd never really had any doubt he'd be great. People loved him.

Well, except Marlis Pritchard, but the woman still bought his work.

"I'm not obsessing about anything. And my middle name is *not* Michaelina. Where do you even get this stuff?"

"It ought to be Michaelina," Aaron replied, inviting himself in. "Place is locked up, everything's neat and tidy, and oh my God, why are you looking at that cheesy travel brochure for Harvest Cove?" His brow furrowed as he strode over to the desk, then leaned over to rummage through her small, sad stack of date possibilities.

"My personal space, Aaron. You're in it."

"My sensibilities, Zoe. You've offended them," he returned, then looked at her with one brow arched. "What is all this about? Is your family finally coming to visit?"

"I wish," she sighed, flinging the small, laminated brochure she'd been staring at back onto the pile. Aaron picked it up, frowned at it, and then dropped it. After studying her a moment, his bright blue eyes narrowed.

"Hmm," he said. "Do I need to go kick his ass?"

She laughed, still trying to work on her knotted muscle. "No. You might need to kick mine, though."

That made him grin. "Yours? Never." He moved behind her, swatted her hand away, and began to knead at her shoulders far better than she could manage herself. "Well, you're obviously a bundle of nerves. So why are you trying to find the dullest possible place you could take a date in the Cove?"

Zoe tried to keep her eyes from rolling back in her head. "Aaron, don't take this wrong, but I think I want to marry you. Just for your hands."

"A Cole Porter/Linda Lee Thomas arrangement? We could make that work. Though you'll have to fight for me first. A sculptor's hands are in high demand," he teased her.

"With good reason." As her muscles loosened, she felt like her head might actually roll off her shoulders. She doubted it would bother her, if she even noticed. "Ryan Weston is a lucky man. You make sure he knows that."

"Oh, believe me, I remind him regularly. Hey, I'm not giving you this massage for free, you know, no matter how much I love you. Information, please?"

"Mmm. Sorry." She tried to focus her thoughts at least enough that he wouldn't stop rubbing her shoulders. "Jason and I are taking turns planning dates. Kind of an extension of our crash course in getting to know each other, since we mutually decided to keep each other around. I'm up first, and I'm failing miserably. I mean, it's not like I can surprise him. He's *from* here. Not to mention he has this not-so-secret fear that I'm going to drag him to something, whether it's food or film, that requires subtitles."

"So he thinks you're frighteningly classy, is what you're telling me," Aaron said.

"It's almost flattering. Almost. But not quite." She sighed and winced as Aaron found a hidden knot and went after it. "It isn't that I feel like I have all these mysteries about myself to unveil or anything. I just wanted to do something kind of special. Something me. But I'm so boring that's turned out to be kind of a problem."

Aaron clucked at her. "You stop that. Your love of movies just means you have a rich inner life."

Zoe smiled. "Ah, flattery. Please continue."

"No, because you're missing what's right in front of your face, so along with being many lovely things you're also being kind of an idiot."

"Hey."

"Zoe." Aaron's hands left her, and she made a small sound of unhappiness. He leaned on the side of the desk and looked down his nose at her with the same mixture of affection and impatience as a parent dealing with a child who was slow to catch on. "Think about it. Where is the most obvious place for you to . . . hit the reset button? I was going to say 'start things off with a bang' but the way you sashayed into work last Saturday says you already took care of that."

She laughed, eyes wide. "Aaron!"

"Is that a denial?"

"I . . . well . . ." She hated to let him win this, but she knew the truth was written all over her face. And so, of course, did Aaron.

"Moving on," he said. "You already know the answer to this, Zoe. And it isn't at"— he picked up a brochure— "the Old Mill Apple Farm and Gift Shoppe. Which is a rip-off, by the way. You want good kitsch, you go three miles farther down the road to Jameson's. Charming with out being insipid. And they make better cider doughnuts."

"I'll keep that in mind," Zoe replied. He hadn't been here that much longer than she had, but the man obviously had his bearings better than she did. Of course, that was one of the benefits of being an extrovert, she supposed.

"Do, because now I feel like we should get doughnuts there this weekend. Saturday, maybe. We need to make this happen."

She exhaled loudly. "If you do more than drop hints about this supposedly obvious thing that I'm missing, it's a date." When all he did was stare at her, though, she assumed it had to be very obvious. Which was when the pieces clicked together. "Oh. *Oh*. That's an interesting thought."

"You're welcome," Aaron said. "So, did you want me to stop at the bank before I go and spread joy to the rest of the world?"

"Yes, that'd be great," Zoe said. Then she laughed, shaking her head. "I knew there was a reason I hired you."

"Well, I do make a hell of an ornament, but plenty of skill lurks beneath the beauty." He smirked at her. "Now, toss the brochures and relax. I don't know Jason very well, but he doesn't strike me as the kind of person who'd be anywhere he didn't want to be. You think you don't know each other very well, but I bet you end up surprised at how much you *do* know."

"Anything is possible," Zoe replied, rolling her loosened shoulders. Maybe Aaron was right. The details were new, but Jason had been a constant in her life for so long that she hadn't even realized how much she'd come to count on his presence. Even, yes, to enjoy it, as purposely antagonistic as it had been. Maybe making this shift with him felt so natural because she'd always known that what had come before was just a game.

Just as she knew that both of them had stopped playing.

No pressure, though. Just planning an easy night out with a man I might want to keep around for a while. Like, forever.

Admitting it to herself—what some part of her had sensed the very first time she'd set eyes on him . . . or maybe not until she'd first opened her mouth to bicker with him—brought on a fresh wave of anxiety that threatened to undo all the work Aaron had just done. He noticed before he made it out the door. In an instant she felt herself enveloped in her friend's arms.

"Zoe Michaelina," he admonished her, making her laugh, "you don't need me to tell you that he should spend every day just basking in his luck that you descended from on high to notice him. He should do that even if you took him to the Old Mill and made him look at overpriced knickknacks and eat stale strudel. Do you know they don't even make their own? They buy it frozen. I got suckered once, and never again. Anyway," he continued, waving his hand dismissively, "stop worrying. You're perfect."

"And what's he?"

"Treebeard."

He was so perfectly deadpan that Zoe lasted all of three seconds before bursting into laughter. Aaron grinned, gave her a squeeze, and pulled away.

"There. That's the *right* way to end the day. I'll leave you to plot the details of . . . tomorrow night, I'm guessing? This sounds like a Friday night kind of thing."

Zoe nodded. "That's what we picked. I haven't seen him much this week. I thought maybe, you know—" She didn't say it, knowing she didn't have to. Aaron snorted and rolled his eyes.

"Things that move too fast are always the most fun. Quit trying to put on the brakes and just enjoy it. It's not like avoiding him is going to make you any less crazy about him."

She didn't bother to deny it. "No," she said, glad for the understanding, even if she still had no idea where things with Jason were heading. This gallery was the biggest risk she'd ever taken, and she'd done a full year of research before she'd even begun looking at property here. This thing with Jason felt like taking a risk on a similar scale, but with no research, and no safety net. And she was free-falling.

It wasn't in her nature to enjoy a ride like that—but if the choice was between trying to find some pleasure in the wind rushing through her hair as she hurtled downward or walking around with the kind of stress that would eventually manifest in a migraine, she guessed she might need to start making more of an effort to achieve the former.

There were far better ways to end up in Jason's bed, as she'd learned. Maybe she'd even discover a few new ones. The thought put a smile on her face.

"My work here is done," Aaron announced. Then he winked at her and headed out the door. "Call you about Saturday. And to get the scoop."

"I'll be waiting for it," she replied. Then she gathered up the brochures and dumped them in the wastebasket. There was nothing she could show Jason in the Cove that he hadn't seen . . . but she could show him those things in a new way, the way she saw them.

She thought of him here, giving her that slow smile, and she finally allowed herself the feelings that she'd been pushing away all week. She missed him terribly. She wanted him near her, solid and real and comforting. So she did what any intelligent, confident, independent, scared-to-death-she-was-falling-in-love woman would do.

She put in a call, turned out the lights, and headed out to sweep her man off his feet.

*   *   *

Jason was sitting in a camp chair in the backyard, leg propped up while he watched Rosie wander around and sniff the grass, when he heard his name being called.

"Out back," he said, and heard the slider open.

"There you are. Enjoying the peace and quiet?"

"You know it."

There was a pause, then the quiet sound of Jake's footsteps on the grass as he approached. "Ooh, new sweatpants? Sexy."

"Nice to see you, too. Jackass." Jason turned his head to smirk at his cousin, watching him squat down to greet Rosie when she bounced over to say hello. He wouldn't say so, but he was glad for some company this afternoon. The peace in the wake of his mother's angry exit had quickly turned into something more like oppressive silence. These past few years he'd savored the quiet at home. But just lately, all it did was rub his nerves raw. Worse, every day that passed without Zoe appearing to give him a hard time—hopefully with her arms wrapped around him while they sparred—made him less certain she was going to. Their phone conversations had seemed normal enough, but . . . maybe he'd been wrong.

Worse, maybe she'd decided she had been.

He took a sip of his soda and tried not to be morose. It was an unfamiliar effort for him, but this time it seemed worthwhile.

Jake dragged another camp chair over and situated it across from him. He seemed to be in a great mood, as usual . . . but Jake would openly admit he had a lot in common with his dog, who never met a day he wasn't excited about.

"You look comfortable," Jake said. "I helped myself to a soda."

"You always do. And yeah, as comfortable as it gets with the cast. Doc said yesterday I'm healing well, at least. Should come off right on time."

"Good. Bet they miss you at work. Manda Rudecker brought Horace in today, and she said Pete complains about you being gone so much that she's starting to wonder if she should be jealous."

Jason chuckled. "Yeah? Maybe I shouldn't have invited him to stay and play some *Battlefield* with me and Kato last night, then. I don't want to be called a home wrecker."

Pete had driven him to his doctor's appointment and stuck around, which had led to Kato being called, steaks being grilled, beer being consumed, and Kato rolling off his couch this morning to slink home and nurse his hangover—which would probably take no time at all. Sometimes Jason missed being in his twenties. He'd also been missing his friends. He might be picky about his people, but that didn't mean he didn't have any. Getting together with them once a week to do something stupid was part of his routine and had become a lifeline after the broken leg. Last week hadn't worked out, for obvious reasons, so it was nice to get back to normal. Well, what passed for normal.

"I think you're clear as long as you do eventually go back to work so Pete quits complaining. It's the unrequited longing that's getting to her."

Jason snorted. "Didn't realize I was so in demand."

"Hey, this is going to be the decade of Jason Evans. By the time you're thirty-five, you'll be Brad Pitt and there'll be paparazzi in the bushes."

That, coupled with Jake's grin, made him laugh. They'd never had much in common, at least outwardly—

Jake was average height, with a build that had made him a natural athlete and a face that screamed "boy next door" so loud that the girls had always come running if he aimed his sunny smile in their direction. Jason had always been too tall, too skinny, too quiet, and too acerbic, running cross-country because it kept him in shape and dating only rarely because his bony physique hadn't exactly been the kind of draw that would have induced girls to look past his defensive shyness. The skinny had gone, but not before graduation. His personality hadn't changed nearly as much. And yet, he'd always been closer to his cousin than most. He liked it better now that Jake had ditched the worst of his insulated little circle of immature high school buddies, though.

Jake's hazel eyes fixed on him like lasers as soon as he sat down. "So," he said. "Better week?"

"Yes," Jason said, nodding slowly after a moment of consideration. "Quieter."

Jake chuckled. "Bet the silence coming out of Florida is deafening."

Jason tipped down his chin to give Jake the most baleful look he could muster. "You know damn well that isn't the good kind of quiet. That's horror-movie quiet. The kind that happens right before someone gets brutally dismembered. I'm ignoring it while I can."

"I don't blame you. Aunt Molly was really on a roll this time."

"No kidding," Jason said, turning his head to watch a cardinal land on one of the bird feeders. "She seemed a little off the whole time. Even for her."

"Yeah, well, that would be a subtle difference. Did she say anything?" Jake asked.

Jason twisted his mouth up. "Sure, lots of things. Not

about anything wrong at home, though. I feel like that's got to be it, but what? Dad would never leave; she's got his number. Would he have an affair? Maybe. Or," he continued, lifting his soda to his lips, "it's Tommy." Voicing his suspicion only made it stronger. His parents' marriage was weird and dysfunctional, but stable. Tommy, though, had never been as perfect as their mother had made him out to be. It made him wonder what kind of trouble his brother might have gotten into, but he couldn't come up with anything.

Tommy would have invented some newer, better, more amazing way to screw up, he guessed. Maybe if they talked more often . . . but Jason had long ago come to terms with the fact that blood was the only tie they were ever going to share.

Jake's eyes glittered with mischief. "The golden child? Descending into imperfection? No way."

"Could happen," Jason replied, and he managed a rueful chuckle about it. "Maybe Mom found him someone just like her and he's tied up in a basement somewhere being forced to watch the Design Network until his mind breaks."

"I'm going to tell Fitz that," Jake said, grinning. "He'll like that one. Can add it to his little mental stash of revenge fantasies."

"I don't think he needs them, considering," Jason said. "If he wanted to brag, he would win so hard that my entire family would end up embedded in the pavement, like Loki after Hulk smashes him." Very few people knew about Fitz's line of work or financial situation, and their friend seemed intent upon keeping it that way. Jason thought he understood. It wasn't fun to have the eyes of the entire town trained on you. His divorce had gotten him more attention than he'd ever wanted, but it had faded quickly enough once all was said and done.

Fitz, though, was a different case. It wouldn't be so easy for him.

He relaxed in his chair, enjoying the afternoon as he watched Rosie start to roll happily in the grass. With his luck, she'd found something dead. Or something that had come out the wrong end of a much larger creature. "If she stinks, you get to bathe her," he informed Jake. "You owe me for all the pink accessories she keeps turning up with."

"You shouldn't be trying to suppress her femininity."

"She yacks up food on my rugs and lifts her leg when she pees. I don't think femininity is real high on Rosie's priority list."

"Still," Jake said with a snort. "Maybe you should call Zoe to come help you out with it." Jake cast him a sly grin. "Since, you know, she's *actually* your girlfriend now. Couldn't have seen that one coming a mile away."

Jason tensed immediately, even though he knew it was ridiculous. What did he care what people thought? His love life, such as it was, was his business. Except that wasn't how things worked in the Cove, or anywhere else. He and Zoe were interesting because they were an odd match. People, their friends included, would be watching with interest.

Just like the last time.

"Everything's okay with you two, right?" Jake asked, pulling Jason's attention back to him. His cousin was frowning, and Jason knew he must have had a look on his face.

"Yeah, fine. I think. I dunno."

Jake's eyebrows raised. "That's encouraging."

"No, it's fine. We talk. Been a busy week for her. That thing she's doing for Aaron is eating a lot of her time."

"Oh," Jake said. The word itself was innocuous. The way he said it was profoundly irritating.

"Oh nothing," Jason grumbled. "And don't try to give me advice. You got lucky because Sam has weird taste in men, not because you're some kind of love expert."

"Love, huh?" Jake asked with interest. "Is that—"

The panic that flooded him was immediate. "No! Jesus, I was just giving you a hard time! I'm not having this conversation. Zoe's fine. I'm fine. Things are—"

"Fine. Got it."

"Good."

Jason slouched back into his chair. Jake was silent across from him and seemed to have found something interesting to study off in the back of the yard. Jason felt a twinge of guilt for snapping. But he wasn't ready to examine his feelings for Zoe yet, much less have a discussion about them. All thinking about it did was tie him up in knots, which was useless . . . and he had no way to clear his head, being laid up the way he was. He was stuck with the company of his own thoughts way too often. And he would be again before too long if he kept being so sunshiny with his cousin. Knowing Jake's intentions, at least, were good, he sighed and relented a little.

"We're going out tomorrow night. She's picking the spot. So seriously, things are fine."

Jake regarded him with slightly wary interest. Finally he said, "Okay. You're pretty prickly about it, but okay. I didn't come over so we could fight about Zoe. She can deal with you."

"Sorry," Jason said, and shoved a hand through his hair. He really did need to do something about the length. He was going to go the full mountain man before he went back to work at this rate, though at least he could handle shaving his face himself. Zoe had inspired him to make shaving a regular part of his routine again . . . just in case. He wanted her to enjoy his kisses, not wince in pain. "I haven't seen her this week and I've been cooped up," he continued. "I really need to get this cast off."

That earned him a chuckle. "Yeah. You do. It's like watching a wounded bear in a cage."

"I want to start running again," Jason said. "When the leg is healed. I miss being able to blow off steam just by getting outside."

"We can do that. I can handle a few days of poking along so you can keep up," Jake said. "And quit worrying about Zoe. I can see the smoke coming out of your ears, and it's pointless. She likes you." He smirked. "Even if her reasoning remains a mystery, she likes you. Be grateful."

Jason snorted, though the ribbing did make him feel a little better. "I guess," he said.

"You *guess.*" Jake stretched his legs in front of him. "Zoe's beautiful, smart, driven, classy . . . and she seems pretty settled here." Jake looked at him pointedly. "That's a big plus."

Settled. Not like Sara was. Satisfied with her life here. Not like Sara was. At least Jake wouldn't say it out loud, though. He knew how tired Jason had gotten tired of hearing her name, of hearing it invoked as an excuse for the state of his personal life. So things hadn't worked out between them. That kind of thing happened every day. If he'd taken anything away from the divorce besides some hard feelings, it had been that some differences were just too big to work around. He knew who he was. In the future, he'd sworn, he would be more careful about finding women who understood and wanted what they were getting.

Which was, he supposed, why he was still single and living with a dog.

"Anyway, she's exactly your type," Jake continued. "I don't think you two getting together surprised anybody but . . . well, you two."

His type—what was that, exactly? He still didn't have it figured out, and it rankled that Jake seemed to. He and Zoe certainly created sparks when they were together, even now. This week, he'd discovered just how much he craved them, craved *her* when she wasn't around.

It was dangerous and shifting ground he was on.

"I don't think I have a type," Jason said. "Rosie's my type." At the sound of her name, she looked up curiously from where she was peacefully grazing on some grass and then, unimpressed, went back to munching.

"Pretty sure that's illegal," Jake said. "And that's uncalled for," he added when Jason responded with a gesture instead of words.

"So was the love advice, which I got anyway."

"Hey, don't knock good, free advice. Well, free advice, anyway. Okay," he said, getting to his feet. "I guess I've brought enough sunshine into your day. You want me to take fluffy butt here for a few hours? My lazy cat probably needs the exercise."

"No, that's okay. I appreciate it. She's good company, though. And she'd probably just puke up the grass at your house."

"I've seen so much worse," Jake replied. "A little grass puke doesn't faze me. You're just worried about the next pink thing, I bet." He grinned. "You should be."

They both turned their heads at the sound of a car pulling into the driveway. Jason immediately felt his stomach begin to dance and tried to mask it with polite interest.

"Expecting somebody?" Jake asked.

"Nope. Guess it's just my day for visitors," Jason replied. He heard the car door shut, and the familiar sound of bootheels on pavement. *Zoe.* He'd been waiting for her, hoping for her to just swing by when he wasn't expecting it. Not because he'd asked, but because she wanted to see him.

Some part of him hadn't really expected it, despite the night they'd spent together. She was busy, he reasoned. The novelty would wear off. They'd slowly go back to being . . . whatever. Incompatible. Which was better, right? Because then there'd be less heartache.

At the sound of Zoe's voice inside the house, that defeatist voice finally shut the hell up.

"Jason? Jake? You two out back?"

"We're out here, Zoe," Jason called to her. Then he noticed Jake's smug smile. "What?"

"I was right, see? You should quit worrying. I'm always right."

Jason groaned. "Jesus. Go home, Jake. Go inflict yourself on your pretty wife, whose taste I will never understand."

"She has superior taste," Jake said. Then his smile faded. "Hey, take this in the spirit in which it's intended, okay? But . . . be good to Zoe."

Jason blinked, startled by the earnestness of the request. And after a moment, he was more than slightly offended. "Of course I'll be good to her. What the hell is that supposed to mean? You know me."

"I do," Jake replied, and there was a look in his eyes that reminded Jason that his cousin knew more about him than almost anyone ... certainly more than he would have preferred. "I also know how hard you try not to let anyone get under your skin. She does. You might want to try and let that be a good thing and just go with it."

"I know," Jason interjected. "I've been around the block before, remember? Beautiful, artsy, classy, likes me for inexplicable reasons ..." He didn't know why he'd said it. It shouldn't have any bearing here, and from the look on Jake's face, his cousin agreed.

"Yeah, I remember. And if you think Zoe has anything in common with Sara, then you don't know her at all."

"I know," Jason said again. And he did, at least intellectually. He was just a lot more screwed up when it came to the emotional part of relationships. That was neither Zoe's fault nor her problem, though, and he needed to keep that in mind.

"I hope so, because you'd be missing out on a lot otherwise," Jake replied, just an instant before the woman in question stepped out the door and onto the deck. Her hair was down, an explosion of curls that framed her face and, coupled with the skinny jeans she wore, left her looking less businesslike—and more fun—than she normally allowed herself to appear. Plus, she was completely adorable. Jason heard a soft sigh, then realized it had come from him. Zoe wouldn't have heard it, but the snort beside him told him Jake had.

"You two playing nice out here?" Zoe asked, sliding the door shut behind her and heading toward them. Jason drank in the light in her eyes, along with her casual, sensual grace, and suddenly he wanted Jake to go very, very far away. To his credit, Jake seemed to think that was a good idea without being told.

"As nice as we ever do. I'm just heading out. Have fun, you two. Make good decisions."

Zoe laughed as Jake walked past her, watching him head back through the house. Then she turned her attention on Jason, stooping for a moment to greet Rosie even though she barely took her eyes from him. What he saw there made his heartbeat quicken, his breath grow shallow. Every worry about her absence this week vanished. He'd hoped for her to come to him because he was what she wanted.

The way she looked at him left no doubt that—at least for now—he was.

"Hey, stranger," she said, rising to stroll over to where he sat. "You busy?"

Jason's mouth curved up as he swept his arm to indicate his yard. "Just watching over my domain. Pretty intense stuff."

She laughed, the sound as rich and warm as cream. "I bet. You must be exhausted."

He willed her to close the rest of the distance between them, but she stopped just shy of him, nudging his sandaled foot with the toe of her boot.

"You want to get out of here for a little while?" she asked. It was a surprise—sometimes he thought everything about Zoe was a surprise—but a welcome one.

"Sure," he said. "What did you have in mind?"

All it took was a simple, suggestive quirk of her eyebrow to shift his day from "decent" to "awesome." He knew Zoe loved her fictional superheroes, but he doubted she was aware that she possessed one hell of a super-power herself. That was okay, though. She could still use it on him anytime she liked.

"Something you'll like," she said. She leaned over to tug at his hands. "Come on. Upsy-daisy."

"Sure. In a second. I just need one thing first," he said, capturing her hands with his and pulling her down to him. She laughed softly, her smile bright, and it was everything.

I'm crazy about her, he thought. Though he'd fought it for years, there was no denial left in him now. Just acceptance of the truth. So before he could worry about it, Jason threaded his fingers through her wild curls and brought her mouth to his, saying hello the way he'd imagined a thousand times before—with a long, hot, lingering kiss that said everything he couldn't. Not yet.

Not never . . . but not yet.

Chapter Eighteen

He'd almost flustered her enough to make her forget her plans.

"The gallery?" Jason asked, frowning a little as they pulled in. The sun was setting, and the lights on the wrought-iron lampposts that dotted the square were starting to come on. There was a warm glow coming through the windows of Two Roads, the inside lights dimmed the way she did for events they held here.

Zoe had set everything up before leaving. She'd run home to change. And she'd damn near crawled into Jason's lap and gotten frisky right in his backyard. Not like she was averse to plans changing—well, yes, she was— but this was supposed to be special. Something she'd arranged, instead of the two of them just being thrown together in a variety of odd or difficult or just plain annoying situations.

She guessed those worked for bonding after all, but they weren't much on romance. Jason might be big and grumbly, but the man looked like he'd been made to sweep a woman off her feet. Since he was physically incapable of getting the ball rolling on that right now,

Zoe really wanted to see what might happen if she started it.

"The gallery," Zoe agreed, turning her head to look at him after she killed the engine. "I figured that this is kind of our spot, so . . . maybe we could find something to do here instead of fight over my floors."

"Oh yeah?" He had what he was thinking written all over his face, and Zoe felt her cheeks flush as she laughed.

"Easy there, tiger. All in good time. Come on."

"Do I get to be tiger now instead of Treebeard?"

"No."

He wrinkled his nose in feigned irritation. "There'd better be something good in there, then."

She got out and held Jason's crutches while he maneuvered himself into a standing position, then walked with him to the door. Even before she unlocked it, she could hear the soft blues playing on the stereo system and smiled. When she opened the door, Jason didn't look inside, instead watching her.

"What have you been up to?" he asked, looking confused in the sweetest way she could imagine. There was a funny little half smile on his face.

"I told you. This is our spot, but since all we usually do here is argue, I thought it might be nice to give it . . . other associations."

"I could be persuaded to do that. Though I hope you know that even though we were arguing, I don't have any bad associations with this place. I like it in here," he said.

"You do?"

"I wouldn't come in so often if I didn't like looking at what was here," he replied, his gaze full of golden heat. Zoe couldn't help her own silly smile.

"Then I guess you should like tonight," Zoe said, slipping past him. She was just a little bit grateful that his hands were occupied with his crutches, because he looked like he wanted to grab her. And she knew she would have let him.

"Hey, what's this?" he asked behind her. She heard the smile in his voice before she turned back around, and this time his attention was focused on his surroundings instead of her.

"A picnic," Zoe said. "Two Roads style. I would have dragged you out to the park, but it's supposed to get cold tonight. In here it's warm and—"

"This is great," he said, heading toward the little area she'd arranged while the distinctive *creak-thump* of his crutches kept time with the music.

She cast a critical eye on what she'd created and decided it passed muster well enough. A couple of big square floor pillows from home to sit on, her nice chenille blanket, and on it, a bottle of crisp white wine chilling in a bucket of ice, two glasses, a couple of plates, forks, and the pièce de résistance—

"Is that Larkin's lemon meringue pie?" he asked, his deep voice full of wonder. He looked at her as though he couldn't quite believe what he was seeing. Zoe hadn't expected to feel embarrassed, but she did . . . though not in a bad way. She just didn't get to do this kind of thing for people. Or for herself. But it felt a little like sharing a closely held fantasy with Jason, and there was definitely risk in that.

Of all the things Jason could do to hurt her, laughing at her was near the top of the list.

He didn't, though. Instead, he hobbled over to her and gently tucked a few curls behind her ear. The tenderness in his expression wasn't what she was used to seeing, but somehow it seemed more right—more *him*—than all the frowns he'd put on in her presence since she'd known him. *I think he's shy,* Larkin had said. Zoe thought the baker had it right after all. And that made the way he'd started to open up around her all the sweeter.

"This is great," he said. "How'd you know lemon meringue pie was my favorite?"

"A little bird told me."

He smiled, and her breath caught in her throat. Her fingers itched to touch him, but she forced herself to back up. She wasn't going to sabotage something she'd planned herself. A flicker of amusement flashed across his face that said he knew exactly what she was thinking, but Jason didn't try to pull her back. Instead, he looked at the little nest she'd created on the floor.

"I might need some help getting down there."

"Not a problem," Zoe replied. She took one of his hands so he could keep his balance as he lowered himself to the floor, then set his crutches aside while he situated himself on the floor pillow. *So far, so good.* She sat on her own pillow, grinning over her triumph, and set about opening the bottle of wine. Once their glasses were poured, she cut two wedges out of the pie, handed one to Jason, and dug into her own. It was, as expected, heavenly.

"Mmm," Zoe said, rolling her eyes. "I'm so glad she'd already made this. I was going to bring it to you tomorrow. I didn't know if it would be ready early, but Larkin's on top of things."

"She does good work," Jason agreed. He frowned at his wineglass, sniffed the liquid, shrugged, and took a sip.

"Well?"

"Not bad. For being wine. It's, ah, citrusy?" he said.

"It is. To go with the lemon pie," Zoe replied. "Don't knock it yet."

"Not knocking it," he replied. "Just more of a beer guy. That doesn't mean I can't appreciate wine."

There was a slightly defensive note in his voice that she sought to quash immediately. There would be no bickering in her gallery tonight. Casually, Zoe leaned back, braced herself on one hand, and took a long sip of her wine. Jason's eyes traveled the length of her, and she allowed it—allowed herself to enjoy it, too.

"Well, maybe you'll have to school me on the finer points of beer appreciation one of these days," Zoe said. "I can learn to like new things, too. See how that works?"

"Mmm." Jason's response was a noncommittal noise, and she wasn't entirely sure he was listening to her. Not that she could complain about being admired. But he surprised her when he continued speaking, after a moment of what must have been collecting his thoughts. "I keep expecting you to look down your nose at the things I like, but you just have your own taste. You never make it a competition. It's a nice change from, ah, past experience. I'll try harder to keep that in mind."

She tilted her head to watch him, fascinated. He really was a much deeper pool than she'd once thought. It wasn't the first time she'd wanted to smack the woman who'd hurt him, but it was the first time she'd gotten a good look at some of the scars she'd left.

"Thanks," she said. Then Zoe laughed softly and looked down at her plate, unexpectedly flustered. "You aren't what I expected, either, if that helps."

"Maybe. Am I good different or bad different?"

"After last weekend, I'm surprised you have to ask."

He hesitated. "That . . . didn't have to mean anything. I mean, it doesn't always. I wasn't sure."

Jason was saved from her wrath simply because he seemed so genuinely uncertain. It was a strange paradox, to have a big, gorgeous man like him unsure whether she'd just used him for sex. Zoe prided herself on being a take-charge kind of woman, but this wasn't the kind of power people normally attributed to her. Nor was it one she'd ever tried to cultivate. That Jason found her that compelling, though . . . the knowledge was heady stuff.

"Jason. I wouldn't have gone there unless it meant something. I mean," she continued, sweeping her hand around the spread she'd put out, "I'd think that would be obvious by now."

He offered her a slightly sheepish smile, tipping his chin down and looking up at her with an expression that threatened to melt her into a puddle of goo right there. "Yeah. That did occur to me when I walked in."

Zoe rolled her eyes. "That's one thing I haven't changed my opinion on. You *are* hardheaded."

"You won't hear me denying it, but I'm going to go out on a limb here and say I think that's one of the things we actually have in common."

"Maybe," Zoe said. "That, and a love of Larkin's baked goods."

They ate in silence for a few minutes, and Zoe let herself relax into it. Jason was quiet in a companionable sort of way, and he never made her feel like she needed to fill the void. So she enjoyed the music—a little Chet Baker now—and looked around, just glad they were here. She wasn't one to slow down often, but she was glad she'd decided to tonight. As though he sensed the direction of her thoughts, Jason spoke into the warm quiet.

"This place really is something, especially considering how long it just sat here empty. How *did* you get here, anyway? You never said."

"You didn't ask the right questions," she replied, but relented when he gave her a long-suffering look. "Okay. Well, I told you about my academic background. The one that thrilled my parents with its earning potential."

He chuckled. "Yeah."

"I was determined, though. I'll never be more than a mediocre artist, but that was never really an issue. I would rather study art, be around it, soak up all the different forms and styles and mediums. And with a gallery, I knew I'd be around art all the time. With a *successful* gallery, I'd be helping get art out into the world. It seemed like the perfect job."

"Is it?"

"I love it," Zoe said firmly. "But . . . it *is* a job. I'm never going to love all of it. Paperwork, for instance. The occasional customer who needs to be drop-kicked into outer space. Little tedious things that keep the place running but aren't much fun. That said, this is my passion. The parts that are fun—seeing new work come in, helping a new artist get some exposure, the shows, just introducing people to art when they were always too intimidated to discover what they liked before—that's what makes this worth it. That's why I'll never do anything else if I can help it."

The flecks in his eyes seemed almost to glow in the dim light, like embers. "Why here, though? That's what I can't figure out. Did you come here as a kid or something?"

"No. I just . . . had my ideas about what I wanted. So I did research. Visited a few places. This is what clicked."

But she could see he wasn't satisfied with that, and prepared herself for the inevitable teasing when she had to give up the truth.

"Ideas about what you wanted?"

"Fine. I used to watch reruns of *Murder, She Wrote* on TV with my mama when I was growing up. Loved that show. This clever, classy writer showing up everyone and solving all the murders in Cabot Cove while she wrote her books . . . not that it probably would have been great to live there, since Jessica Fletcher seemed to inspire a body count wherever she went. But still, I loved the idea of a little coastal New England town. Picture-perfect, quaint, all that sea air. Actual seasons." She stared at him, daring him to make fun. "Every kid dreams of someplace else. That was mine. So I went out and found it."

Jason looked as though he didn't quite believe her, but the longer she stared, the more understanding seemed to sink in. Finally, he gave a soft chuckle. "Anything I would have guessed wouldn't have even been close to that."

"It's not stupid," she said. Lord knew the kids at school had given her a rough time when she'd told a friend, who'd told a friend, who'd told everyone who would listen.

Jason held up his free hand. "I would never say it was. No more assumptions, remember? I think it's cute." She made a face, so he qualified it. "Okay, I think it's interesting. Unique. And also cute."

The man had the gall to laugh when she made a disgusted noise.

"You can't mind it too much here. You stuck around."

"I did. It's home. Might not be perfect, but it's my kind of imperfect. It's also beautiful."

"Would you have stayed if—" Zoe stopped herself before she finished the question, then tried to come up with something reasonable to substitute. She didn't want to poke at him too much about his family. Jason answered before she could try to cover her original intent.

He didn't look angry, at least. Just resigned. She hated the way his smile faded and would have kicked herself if she could.

"You mean if my family had stayed? I don't know. I would have hated to go, but I might have had to, just to keep my sanity." One corner of his mouth curved up. "I probably have them to thank for my love of the outdoors, at least. All that avoidance had some benefit after all."

"Sorry," Zoe said, and meant it.

"Don't be." He lifted one shoulder, a half shrug. "It was okay. I had my grandparents. Some friends. Jake and Aunt Moira. I belonged here in the Cove, even if I never exactly fit into my family. Lots of people have it worse. I got to keep the good parts, and I get to do what I love for a living."

"It's true," Zoe agreed, letting it go because she sensed he wanted to, and because her heart already ached on his behalf. "You even got a fancy dog."

Jason chuckled, and she was glad to see the crinkles at the corners of his eyes return. "Yeah, she's something. I don't know about fancy, though. She's really not very ladylike."

"It's because you've provided her a safe, relaxed environment, Mr. Sweatpants Man. I have no idea where she would have gotten the idea it was okay to let it all hang out at your house."

"Hey. I'm expanding the wardrobe. It's Mr. Cargo

Shorts Man today," he said. Then he looked down at them and sighed. "You have no idea how much I miss my jeans."

"Me, too," Zoe said, and then laughed at his expression. "What? They look good on you. So does your uniform."

His brows lifted. "I don't think I've ever come in here with my uniform on."

"I've seen you around," she said. "It's not my fault you're oblivious to being stared at."

He looked surprised . . . and pleased. "I'm going to have to work on that."

"You really don't. It'll ruin my fun."

Jason smiled, then set his empty plate down beside his half-finished glass of wine. Zoe felt the muscles in her lower belly tighten immediately. It was crazy, how little it took for her to want him. But then, she kind of always wanted him. It was just a matter of suppressing it enough to go on about her daily business most days. When he looked at her again, heat suffused her from head to toe.

"I think we managed it," Jason said.

"Managed what?"

"An actual date. No crazy family members, no bribery . . ."

Zoe grinned at him. "That reminds me. You still owe me for my selfless gesture, Jason Evans. I aided you in your time of need. We had a deal."

He groaned softly, but it was good-natured. "I'm not off the hook? What are you going to make me buy? Nothing weird. Please. I don't know where I'd hide it."

"Actually," Zoe said, "I've been thinking. I'm willing to renegotiate your method of payment." She'd been thinking about it since early last week, though it had started as nothing but a lark at first, a silly idea to toy with. Now, though, it was something she actively wanted.

Jason's slow, lazy smile would have given her plenty of ideas if she hadn't already had something in mind. "Oh yeah?" he asked.

She had to jump in before she ended up just taking his clothes off. "Well, Aaron's show is the biggest one I've done here, and the one thing I don't seem to have for it is a good-looking man on my arm. So I thought, since we're sort of, ah . . ." She trailed off, not sure what she ought to call it yet. "Boyfriend" always made her feel about sixteen. "Lover" was cringeworthy. "Mine" was how she felt, but that might not go over as well as it did in her head. Finally, she avoided a term altogether. "Why don't you come to Aaron's show as my date?"

His reaction wasn't quite what she'd hoped. A little of the heat in his eyes died, replaced by wariness she'd hoped not to see again. "An art show?"

Zoe nodded. "It'll be dressy, full of critics and artists, and to be honest . . . completely terrifying." She saw the uncertainty on his face and pushed on. "For me, I mean. Not for you. But I could use the moral support. Somebody there just to lean on if I need it." Zoe hesitated, then finished, "You. It would mean a lot to me."

"So . . . critics and artists and buyers will be there. From New York?"

She didn't understand why it mattered. "Yes, quite a few. Why?"

He frowned, looked away, and Zoe got the distinct impression he wasn't telling her the whole truth.

"I'm just not sure . . . I respect what you do, Zoe. But I'm not an art-show guy. I'd stick out like a sore thumb and end up being more work you don't need."

Zoe stared at him, utterly puzzled. "You're not work. And you'd fit in fine anywhere. Give yourself some credit; you know plenty about—"

"I don't, though," Jason said. "I know about the things I like, but even then it's pretty basic. I can't talk art with those people."

"Those people? Meaning my people? Art people? You do just fine around Sam and Aaron."

"It's a different type and you know it," Jason said. "I've been around it, and it's not something I planned to do again."

His ex must have dragged him to shows, Zoe decided. Still, there was something in his expression, almost panicky, that suggested there was more to the story. She wished he would just tell her, but that didn't seem to be Jason's strong suit. He'd tell her in his time. Or not. The latter possibility didn't sit well with her.

His trusting process was very Ent-like, she thought. Slow, steady, and often infuriating. She'd nicknamed him well. And she still wanted to kick him.

"It would mean a lot to me to have you there," she said. But his posture, the sudden tensing of his shoulders, the way he couldn't quite look her in the eye, said she hadn't come close to convincing him. She'd get to the bottom of this . . . later, Zoe decided. Somehow, she didn't think this was about her. That didn't make it any less important to fix—she wanted him to be involved in this part of her life if they were going to make a go of this—but it didn't seem worth ruining the evening over.

Not tonight.

"I'm sure you'll be great," he said. When he met her eyes again, he offered a small, rueful smile, as though he had managed to frustrate even himself. "I don't contribute much but debris to the art world. You know that."

Zoe considered him and was swamped by a rush of affection she was helpless in the face of. The man didn't seem to know his own appeal. She supposed that was her good fortune. Otherwise, he would have been snapped up long ago. It pushed her to offer something she might otherwise have kept to herself.

"You'd be contributing to my enjoyment of the evening, debris and all, though I suspect you clean up well. I like to share things that are important to me with people I care about," she said.

His eyes darkened with some strong emotion she hadn't seen before, but his voice remained low and steady. "Then . . . I'll think about it."

"Okay." It was the best she'd get for now, but it was better than nothing, Zoe decided. And the way he was watching her, the unsteady beat of her heart as the heat that was always between them suffused her, pulled her toward him.

Am I really going to do this in the middle of my gallery? She considered it for all of two seconds. *Yes. Yes, I am.*

She set aside her plate and glass, drew her legs up under her, and crawled across the blanket to where Jason was comfortably sprawled on his pillow. He watched her steadily, like the wolf he often reminded her of.

"That still doesn't solve the matter of your debt to me," Zoe said. He chuckled, and she knew the tense moment had safely passed. For now.

"What did you have in mind?"

"Well," she said, rising on her knees in front of him, "I

did have some work out back I suppose you could do. Moving pavers around. Hauling dirt. That sort of thing."

One eyebrow curved. "But then you'd have to wait until my cast was off." He hooked a finger in one of her belt loops and tugged her forward, into his lap. Zoe went willingly, straddling him as he leaned back on his elbows. The feel of him, the memories of riding him until he bucked beneath her, made it difficult to keep up her end of the conversation.

She could no longer remember why she'd stayed away all week and vowed never to do it again. Diving in was scary . . . but not diving in would be so much worse.

"Do you have a better idea?" Zoe asked, her hips pressing into him when he glided one hand up her thigh to her waist. His soft laugh was slightly breathless. And oh, was he ever hard. She bit her lip to keep from moaning, wanting to keep the upper hand while she could. He might have a sweet side, but when he wanted her under him, she'd be begging him to do whatever he wanted as long as he didn't stop.

"I might," he said, and now he pushed his hips up beneath her, just enough to create hot little sparks of friction at the juncture of her thighs. This time Zoe heard her own ragged gasp. "I thought about having you like this all week," he said, his voice dropping to a rough growl that scraped pleasurably across her nerve endings.

"Just like this?" She slid her hands up beneath his shirt, over hard, lean muscle that jumped at her touch.

"No, I think I probably covered the entire *Kama Sutra*. But this . . . this is good." He pulled the shirt off over his head. Zoe did the same with her sweater, and he immediately filled his hands with her breasts. She rocked forward again, back arching to allow him better access.

He toyed with her nipples through the silk of her bra, the thin barrier sweet torment.

"This is better than good," she sighed. She lifted her hands from his chest to unhook her bra, then tossed it to the side. Her hips moved in a slow rhythm, teasing him, stoking the fire between them. Jason's cheeks were flushed, his breathing shallow as she ground into him. He dropped one hand to her hip and pulled her closer, quickening her pace.

"Christ," he groaned. She leaned forward to claim his mouth in a kiss that began as nips and licks, and quickly became a hot tangle of tongues. He tasted of sugar and lemons and wine, and kissed like pure, unadulterated alpha male. She felt her control slipping away as he took the lead, and Zoe gladly let him have it.

He moved like a cat, getting her on her back in a quick, fluid movement that Zoe barely registered before he was over her, nestled between her legs, his bare chest against hers. She could feel his pounding heart against her skin and knew her own matched its beat.

"Jason," she murmured, hands skimming down the muscles of his back as they tightened and released in time with the relentless pulse of his hips. Zoe arched beneath him, restless and aching. Everywhere he touched shimmered with sensation; everywhere he didn't cried out for his attention. He dropped his head into the curve of her neck, breath hot against her skin. When he licked the sensitive spot beneath her ear, then nipped it lightly, what was left of rational thought completely deserted her. So did her powers of speech. All she could manage was a broken moan and vague, insistent thoughts of *yes, more, now*.

"Hang on," he growled. He rose, shifted into a sitting

position at her feet, and stripped off his shorts in a few fumbling motions that told Zoe his thoughts were no less urgent than hers. She followed suit, stripping off her boots and jeans, the dampened scrap of silk that was her underwear. It was wonderfully decadent, being with him like this in the gallery with the lights low and the music winding sensuously through the air, nothing against her skin but the soft chenille of her blanket. She doubted she'd ever look at this place quite the same, and that was all right. She didn't want to.

She no longer wanted to imagine a life without Jason in it. Mistake or not, it was the truth. Zoe knew what it meant, couldn't dwell on it now. All that mattered was the way Jason felt when he covered her body with his, when he filled her with a single, hard thrust that sent pleasure crashing through her. He made a low, guttural sound that had Zoe tightening around him. She liked knowing he felt as good as she did. That his need matched her own.

Zoe drew up her knees to take him in more deeply as he began to move in long, hard thrusts that left her quivering every time he withdrew. Her fingers dug into his shoulders as he kept up the exquisitely slow pace. Every inch of her skin grew highly sensitized, until even the brush of an errant curl against her shoulder made her gasp with pleasure. Jason kept the pace steady, the seeming ease of his control belied by the occasional ragged breath he took when he drove deep.

Zoe could take only so much. Every minute that passed seemed to leave her hotter, tighter, wetter, until her body began to beg for release.

"Jason," she said again, a plea this time. He had to be able to feel her shaking against him, but he was relent-

less, quickening his pace only a little. With each thrust he brushed against the swollen nub of her sex, but never enough to free her. Instead, all that seemed to happen was more pressure, more pleasure, until Zoe began to lose herself in the haze of it. She writhed beneath him, finally reaching between them in desperation to stroke herself. Jason cursed softly—she'd never heard obscenities sound quite so hot as when he was growling them while he was inside her—and pulled back to look at her. His hair was in his eyes, sexily mussed, and his skin was flushed. Zoe removed her hand from between her legs, suddenly embarrassed, but Jason moved quickly to catch it and put it back. When his eyes met hers, there was a question in them she would never have entertained for any man before. Until him.

"Please," he said, "don't stop. I love to watch you get off, Zoe. Let me watch. Like this." He slid onto his knees, careful of his cast, and then sank down low before pulling Zoe's hips up onto his lap. He spread her legs wide, then caught her knees beneath his arms before thrusting into her again.

She thought she saw stars before her eyes closed, her mouth opening on a cry that caught in her throat. The change in angle took him even deeper, creating new points of friction that rippled over her skin, pooling between her legs with increasing intensity. She was completely exposed to him this way, but Zoe no longer had it in her to play shy. Her eyes opened, and the way he looked at her, as though she were the most beautiful thing he'd ever seen, torched any remaining inhibitions she might have had.

She watched his gaze follow her hand as she slid it slowly down her stomach, then parted the slick folds. Jason gave a broken moan as he began to move again, faster this time, harder, until her body rocked back with each thrust of his hips. The sight of him before her, lips parted, eyes burning, the muscles of his lower belly flexing as he drove into her, did as much to push Zoe toward climax as the rhythmic flickering of her finger. Her breath began to catch, her body quivering as she neared the tipping point. Jason hissed out her name, his pace growing wild, though he never took his eyes from her even as he came. His body went taut, hands gripping her knees hard as he gave a rough cry. The sight of him like that, losing himself in her, was what finally pushed Zoe over the edge.

Zoe arched as the world narrowed to a single, tiny point . . . and then burst, sending her flying into a shimmering abyss. She clenched around him, heard him moan, and then there was nothing but wave after wave of the kind of intense pleasure she'd never expected to feel—because she hadn't imagined it could actually exist until now. Jason covered her body with his own, hips still moving, prolonging the sweet agony of her release until she could do nothing but lie beneath him, shivering a little as the waves subsided. Jason slowed, then stilled. For a few long moments, there was nothing but the plaintive wail of a saxophone and the sound of their own breathing.

Jason rose just a little on his elbows to look down at her, taking a moment to brush her curls away from her face with a tenderness that Zoe felt take root deep in her chest, only enhancing what already grew there. Then, without a word, he pressed his lips softly to her forehead, the tip of her nose, her cheek . . . her lips.

Zoe threaded her fingers through his waves, drinking

in the sight of his face, which was at once familiar and wonderfully new. Words formed on the tip of her tongue, and she had to swallow them back. It wasn't right yet. She wasn't ready. But that didn't make them any less true.

I love you, she thought, and felt it resonate in every corner of her soul. *I love you. And I feel like I've been waiting to do just that for a very long time.*

If Jason sensed the direction of her thoughts, he gave no sign. He said nothing at all except her name, whispered like a prayer. It might mean nothing . . . or it might mean everything.

"Zoe." Then he kissed her again and pulled her against him, wrapping himself around her until Zoe felt as though there was nothing in the world but him, and her, and the hope that while she quietly loved him, Jason might be quietly loving her right back.

Chapter Nineteen

"So, when do I get to meet him?"

"I don't know, Mama. How about you come visit and you can meet him then?" Zoe held the phone between her shoulder and her ear while she poured herself a cup of tea. She talked to her mother several times a week, filling her in on the details she couldn't quite get her to come witness firsthand. They'd always been close, and Zoe loved sharing all the little things with her, both the triumphs and the complaints. But lately she'd been asking about Jason with increasing interest and Zoe didn't have any fresh answers for her.

Yes, she was finally dating someone. Yes, he was gainfully employed. No, he wasn't a serial killer. And was it serious? Well . . . maybe. Hopefully. Things were good. Really good, actually. Which was what made her nervous and left her wanting to say as little as possible so she wouldn't jinx it. Fortunately, her mother decided to make her usual excuses instead of prying further.

"Honey, we just can't travel right now, and Harvest Cove is far. James is coming to visit us this week. Why don't you come down, too? I'd love to have two of my kids under one roof again for a few days."

"I wish I could." Zoe sighed. "I have that big show coming up next weekend for Aaron."

"Oh, I'll have to call him and wish him luck! You give him a hug for me!" her mother said, and Zoe smiled. Aaron had video chatted with her parents before, and Miriam Watson had adored him at first sight. The feeling was mutual . . . Aaron didn't have much of a relationship with his own parents, so Zoe thought he liked having a surrogate mama he could call up if he needed one.

"You know what would be even better? If you came here to give him that hug yourself!" Zoe replied. Her mother simply tsked, and Zoe knew this round would go much the same as the hundreds of others had. Her parents hated to travel. Their kids were all over the place. Hence, they sat tight and waited for people to come to them. So far, the strategy had worked beautifully. For *them.* As proud as she knew her parents were of her, Zoe wished they would come see what she'd built in person.

Someday, she told herself, and hoped it was true.

"You need to get him on video chat if you're thinking about keeping him," Miriam said. "I want to be able to weigh in."

"Interrogate him, you mean." Zoe laughed. "I remember."

"It isn't my fault if you never liked to date boys who were any good at answering questions. Is this one better at it?"

Zoe thought about Jason, whom she was taking to Sereni-Tea in an hour—much against his better judgment—and tried to imagine his response to being peppered with personal questions. "I doubt it. He's not much of a talker until you get to know him."

"Then bring him *down*. I'll ply him with my famous peach pie, and he'll tell me everything before an hour's up."

"Mama. I've only been seeing him for three weeks. Give it some time."

"Hmm. You've been talking about this one for a lot longer than that. You've had plenty of time. And since you didn't deny it . . . you *are* thinking about keeping him. I know you."

Zoe gave a soft hmph, but the denial would be pointless. Her mother knew her too well, and there was no reason to lie about it. Keeping Jason . . . yeah, she thought about it. Far more than she should. Falling this hard and fast was like something she'd see in one of her movies and nothing she really believed happened in real life. It made her suspicious. But that didn't seem to matter . . . Her heart was in the driver's seat, for once, and it scared the hell out of her.

Especially because Jason had done nothing to indicate he was anywhere near declaring his undying devotion to her. Or even agreeing to come to Aaron's show with her, which rankled far more than she ought to let it.

Her mother seemed to be waiting for an answer. "Yes," Zoe finally said. "I think about it sometimes. We'll see."

"So, what's the problem?" her mother asked. "You still fighting over silly things like his shoes?"

"No. We argued about his getting a haircut, which I don't think I'm going to get him to do until that cast comes off this Friday and he can start working again. We also argued about him trying sushi, which is a battle I won because he liked the things that are fried. But the shoes haven't come up."

A soft chuckle. "Stubborn, sounds like."

"Mmmhmm."

"Is his mother talking to him yet?"

"No." She always asked—they'd hashed over that situation more times than Zoe could count—but the answer stayed the same. As far as she knew, there was nothing but silence from Florida. Maybe that was for the best, though she knew it bothered him sometimes, even if he never said much.

Reading Jason, she'd discovered, was something of an art. One she was still learning.

"Well, that's a shame," her mother said. "It sounds like she's missing out on a very nice young man."

Hearing Jason described that way made Zoe smile, but she supposed it was true enough. Jason was a very nice young man. When he wanted to be. And . . . sometimes she enjoyed it when he wasn't. Zoe cleared her throat.

"Yes. It's a wonder he turned out so well. He's not perfect, Mama." If by some miracle they ever met, she didn't want her mother to be expecting Prince Charming. Not that Zoe would want him if he was.

"As long as he's good to you, that's all that matters. I hope you found him a suit for Aaron's show. He can't go in those sweatpants you keep complaining about."

"W—ah, yeah. He's got a suit," Zoe said. She thought. She assumed. Not that she had any idea whether he'd be wearing it to the show, or attending the show at all. She'd broached the topic several times now, but all she got was evasion. He didn't seem to get the fact that not only did she want to show him off; she wanted him to be a part of things that were important to her. The gallery, her artists, this show, were very important.

It wasn't just his shyness, reserve . . . whatever she might call it. There was more, but she didn't know what. And as much progress as they'd made, there were still barriers he wasn't ready to let her broach. It was frustrating. But when had that ever sped him up?

"You got awfully quiet. Is everything okay, honey? If he's not treating you well—"

"Oh no, he is," Zoe said. "It's nothing like that. I've just got a lot on my plate with this show, like I said, and Jason is Jason. We'll figure it out."

"You will," her mother said gently. "You know your father still drives me crazy, and I love him dearly."

The memories of the two of them teasing each other, bickering, and laughing flooded Zoe with the homesickness she'd been fending off for the past month. "I miss you, Mama."

"I miss you, too, baby. Come home when James is here. After your show. You'll need some rest, and we can complain about these men we let give us fits."

Zoe laughed. "Maybe. If you promise to at least think about coming to see me here at Christmas, if I can get my brothers together. We could have it here." It was just a passing thought, but once she'd articulated it, Zoe found she wanted it very badly. Having her big, noisy family here would be a gift. And then they could meet Jason . . . if he didn't suddenly find a bunch of excuses to disappear on her.

She wished she had more faith that he wouldn't. But the one time she'd brought it up in passing, he'd changed the subject. *Not ready*. That was the message she was getting loud and clear. Not ready, and she couldn't push him to be. So as hard as it was, she was trying to let him move at his own glacially slow pace. Or maybe it just seemed glacial because she was already so certain of what she wanted.

Love is patient, she told herself. *Love is kind.*

Love is really damn annoying.

"Well, if you made that happen we would have to think about it," her mother conceded. "But it would take a miracle for those boys to all be in the same place at the same time these days. At least Theo is moving back to New York."

"I know! I'll be so glad to be able to call him without worrying about the time difference." Theo had been working for an architectural firm in Paris for the past few years, but his job had finally brought him back to the States. It wasn't a bad drive from the Cove, and Zoe was looking forward to teasing him about whatever European affects he'd picked up. Because it was Theo, and he *definitely* had.

Zoe looked at the clock on the stove. "I've got to go pick him up. The cast comes off Friday, and I think he might just pull a Forrest Gump and run off across the country."

"Okay, baby. Love you."

"Love you, too, Mama."

She hung up, flooded with the same bittersweet jumble of emotions she had been feeling more and more frequently lately. She ought to be happy. She had so much goodness in her life. But something was missing, some integral piece. Her parents . . . she missed them so much, but that wasn't all. She wanted what they had together. It was so simple and so complicated, all at the same time. Because she'd fallen in love with Treebeard, and he couldn't do simple if he tried.

Maybe today would be the day she found a way to

make Jason understand how much it would mean to her if he let her get just a little closer, so she could pull him not just into her bed, but all the way into her life.

The phone started ringing while he was waiting for Zoe to arrive and looking longingly at his truck.

Just a few more days, he thought. *A few more days, and I can drive anywhere I want. California. Texas. The gas station.*

He was enjoying the simple fantasy of parking at the Fresh Pride to get his own groceries when the buzzing of his cell interrupted his thoughts. Jason frowned, and the frown only deepened when he saw who it was. He debated answering it for a few seconds, but ultimately, he accepted it with a sigh.

"Tommy. Been a while. How are things?"

"Like you don't know. All Mom does is complain about her trip up there. Couldn't you have just sucked it up and been nice to her for a few weeks? It would have gotten her off my ass."

The self-centered complaining was normal. The bite in his brother's voice over their mother, though . . . that was new.

"I'd be nice if she could be nice back," Jason said. "But if she hasn't figured that out by now, she isn't going to. All it does is make you look better, so why are you complaining?"

Tommy snorted. "I'm complaining because for once, you and I have the same problem. Things are getting serious with Angela."

"Angela . . ." Jason tried to remember the last picture Tommy had texted him of whomever he was dating. They all blended into a sea of bleached hair and bikinis, but he had some vague recollection of the current flame. He just hadn't realized she was still current. "Okay. You're still with her?"

"Yeah, and Mom has suddenly discovered a million things that are wrong with her. Angela needs to cover up a little better. Angela needs to learn to cook for you. Angela ought to wear less makeup. People will think you're marrying a tramp."

"You're getting married?" Jason asked. He tried not to take any satisfaction in the fact that his brother was getting a taste of what Jason had put up with for years, but he couldn't manage it. The golden boy finally wanted to settle down. And Molly was having none of the idea that she'd be relegated to second place.

"Probably. If I can get the hell away from Mom long enough to do it. Angela and I were going to take a cruise. Who do you think booked herself a ticket?"

Jason winced. "Uh, sorry?"

"Yeah, me, too. This is bullshit."

"I'm familiar with it. I did have a wife once." His jaw tightened. "I'm sure you remember that."

Tommy was typically blasé. "Yeah, well, she's long gone, and I'm the one with the problem. It's not like you're getting married again anytime soon. Mom said this new chick is a cold fish."

Jason began to flex his fist. "You just got done telling me that she called your soon-to-be-fiancée a tramp, but you'll take her word on Zoe. You're not seeing the disconnect there at all."

"She was right about Sara, though."

Jason took a deep breath. This shit was old news, and it could still manage to ruin his day. "No. No, she wasn't, no matter how hard she tried to make it look like she was. I'm pretty sure Mom was part of why Sara left, actually. You might want to think about that." She hadn't been the whole reason, or even the biggest reason. But Jason had always known it was there, and he had never been able to stop resenting the hell out of it.

And he couldn't resist adding, because it still rankled, "You didn't hate her too much. Or do you not remember the split lip I gave you when she told me you'd called her at work?"

Tommy's voice hardened. "Because apparently I wasn't allowed to make friends with my sister-in-law. I was looking for lunch, not a hotel room. And you wonder why I don't call. You're still a goddamn Neanderthal."

"She was beautiful and smart, and you couldn't have her. It pissed you off. Just like everything you can't have. Noticing that doesn't make me a Neanderthal; it just means I've got eyes in my head."

"You're so fucking bitter. You always were."

Jason drew in a slow breath. He wanted to erase this conversation from his life and go on about his day like it had never happened. But he couldn't, because he couldn't erase his family. Finally, he said, "I can be bitter, sure. But I get to live my own life. You get cruises with Mom. In the end, I think I got the better deal."

"Bullshit," Tommy spat. "I don't deserve this shit." And in that moment he sounded like the snotty fourteen-year-old kid who'd rubbed it in Henry FitzRoy's face every chance he got that Fitz would never be a starter as long as Tommy was on the team. After all, hadn't the coach heard a rumor that Fitz was kind of a pothead? That he talked smack about the other players? That he was a lousy sport? Where did he think that had come from, if not Coach's new buddy Molly Evans? And there was more where that came from if Fitz thought about fighting back . . . There was always more.

Jason had watched it go down all the way back then with a sick feeling in the pit of his stomach. On the one hand, he'd been grateful that his mother hadn't felt like he merited that kind of intervention. On the other, who would ever want to put up with his family? He worried he would never get far enough away.

Even at arm's length, they could still cause trouble.

"Why did you call, Tommy? I can't fix this for you." He wanted to be done with the conversation, to say no to whatever this was and hang up.

"Yeah, you can. Angela and I are going to come visit you. Do the Cove, see some people. I figure I'll propose, maybe we can roll a quick thing with a justice of the peace all within a week or so. She'll be game; we've talked about it. Mom won't go anywhere near you until you apologize, so we're safe. And I could use a place to stay . . . a week at a hotel is steep and I'm trying to save for a honeymoon."

It was a sales pitch, and it was transparent bullshit, neither of which was a surprise. Tommy had always lived beyond his means. Jason assumed he was still in some hefty debt. Once, long ago, there had been a few requests for money, each of them turned down with only a little regret—and that only because Jason wished he looked like more than an opportune mark to his brother.

"No," Jason said, and there was no regret this time. Just the same weariness he always felt when it came to his immediate family. "You're going to have to work this out some other way, Tommy. I'm just getting back to work and everything else, and I don't want to be involved in this."

"You won't help me." Flat, angry.

"No."

"You won't help your brother get married. Your only brother."

"Maybe if you called when you didn't need things I would. As it stands, though, no. You'll have to deal with Mom or run away someplace else."

"What is this about, Jay?" Tommy asked, and Jason could hear him winding up, just like their mother did. The apple hadn't fallen too far from the tree. "You're jealous. Still. Jesus, you need to get a life. It isn't my fault I was the favorite. I didn't ask for it."

This was true, Jason thought. But any time he'd reached out, his younger brother had slapped his hand away ... or grabbed it and demanded something he didn't want to give. That had been a choice Tommy had made and continued to make. He blew out a breath, looked out the window, and saw Zoe's little Mini headed toward the house. There was instant relief ... and quick on its heels was doubt, seeping through every crack in his well-constructed armor.

She isn't going to want to deal with all this baggage. I don't even want to deal with it.

"I'm not competing with you," Jason said, not quite managing to keep the bite out of his voice. "I never was. We're not the same at all, but it never bothered me like it does you."

"Please," Tommy snapped. "You were always competing. You were always jealous of all the attention I got. But you can never make it work, right? Wife didn't work, stuck in the Cove, some girlfriend who won't last, busted leg. But instead of growing the hell up, I get this petty bullshit where you won't help me because of stuff that happened years ago. You just don't want me to be happy, right? You love it that Mom's screwing up my life."

"I don't, actually. And that's not what I want," Jason said. Tommy's entire worldview was constructed around the premise that people who gave him things were all right, and people who said no were jealous haters. It would never change.

"Then what? What do you want? An apology? Because I'm not—"

"No," Jason interjected smoothly, watching Zoe pull into the driveway. She wouldn't be getting the best of him today, not after this, but he'd try. Even if moving forward after so many years treading water was a lot harder than he'd thought, he would try.

"I just wanted a brother," Jason said. And into the stunned silence that followed, he added, "Good-bye, Tommy. Believe it or not, I hope it all works out for you."

Then he hung up the phone.

Chapter Twenty

He leaned over the teacup and sniffed suspiciously. "I don't know, Zoe."

Zoe watched him with exasperated affection. "Jason, tea is my thing. If you're going to be with me, you're going to be with my tea."

He looked up at her, brown eyes warming with mischief. "That sounds dirty."

She smacked him. "I'll show you dirty. Now, give it a taste—it won't kill you. You picked that one out, remember?"

They sat next to each other at her little kitchen table, teacups in front of them. She'd gotten out the cream and sugar, in case the only way she could coax him into what she'd tried to convince him was a fun new experience was to let him wreck the flavor of the tea by dumping a bunch of things in it. The trip to Sereni-Tea, where she spent so much time she had both an account and a friendship with the owners, had gone about as well as expected. Jason had hobbled uncertainly among the canisters of loose tea, sniffing things and looking as though he would rather be anywhere else, smelling anything else, up to and including the offerings at the nearest landfill.

There was hope for him, though. He'd chosen the Fireside Oolong she'd been meaning to pick up, and she'd taken him home and brewed it just about bubbling over with anticipation. The faces he was pulling were just par for the course. If she could make it through their afternoon looking at fancy fishing rods at Camping World, he could drink a damn cup of tea.

Besides, he seemed like he could use a little comfort today, though she wasn't sure what was wrong. He'd been off since she'd picked him up. Not bad, just not . . . *right*. And in typical Jason fashion, he was keeping it to himself. So she plied him with tea and hoped for the best, wishing that he'd just give up the fight and *trust* her. Maybe she couldn't fix his problems . . . but she couldn't even try if she didn't know what they were.

"It smells good, doesn't it?" she asked him.

"It smells . . . fine," Jason replied. His hair fell in sexy tousled waves, flopping over into his face. She knew that at this point, he was just leaving it to tweak her—and she had no intention of telling him that it was as sexy as hell, even if it made her crazy when it fell into his eyes. He also needed to shave. *Again*.

He sighed, picked up his cup, gave her one more reproachful look, and took a sip. Zoe leaned forward, eyes wide and trying not to bounce in her chair. "Well?"

Jason frowned a little, pulled the cup away, looked at the liquid remaining as though it were a great mystery, and then shrugged. "Tastes like tea."

She made a strangled sound and threw up her hands. "What am I supposed to do with you? I can't kill you. It's illegal!" Then he was laughing, and he flashed the grin that still made her breath catch in her chest. *Finally,* she thought. *Progress.* She wadded up a napkin and threw it at him. "You're yanking my chain!"

"It's so easy," Jason said. He picked up the cup and took another sip. "It's pretty good. And I like the way it smells. I'm not going to replace my coffee with it, but I'd drink it again. Happy?"

She rolled her eyes. "You sound like Sam. Cretins, all of you. Uncivilized cretins." She picked up her own cup and took a sip, savoring the toasted sweetness as it slipped over her tongue. "Mmm." She opened her eyes, and Jason was watching her with the singularly intense look he got when she'd piqued his interest, a hunter watching its prey. Heat quickly spread from her cheeks to points south. This was one area they had no problem connecting in. When Jason was inside her, there seemed to be nothing in the world but the two of them. He made it easy to lose herself, wrapped up in him until she wasn't sure where he ended and she began.

Zoe cleared her throat. If they kept up like this, he'd manage to distract her from her purpose, and this couldn't be put off any longer. Her conversation with her mother had lit a fire under her. It was time to get this sorted out.

"So, Aaron's show. You're coming, right? Because I'm finalizing everything and I really, really want you to be there with me."

She saw it, just a flash of the deer-caught-in-the-headlights look he got whenever she raised this subject, and had to stop herself from balling her hand into a fist on the table. She breathed deeply. *I've dealt with much more difficult customers than Jason and convinced them they needed what I wanted them to have. Why can't I get him to be my date for one night? What is it about this that's so terrible?*

"I'm not sure, Zo. I'll be fresh out of my cast; I might need to sit if the leg muscle gets sore or tired. . . ."

"I know. That's why there are these marvelous inventions called chairs." She leaned toward him, her hand brushing over his, seeking a reassuring touch. "Jason, this is my life. My business. And this is a really important show. I want you there with me. What about that is hard? I'll find you a suit if you don't have one."

Now he was irritated. "I can handle getting a suit myself, thanks."

"Oh, so you just don't *want* to. Okay, I get it." She could hear her accent thickening as her temper rose, but she couldn't stop it. The show had become a sticking point between them that she simply didn't understand. It was one night, just a dressy event that would be focused on Aaron and his work. All Jason needed to do was be there for her.

It was upsetting to realize just how much she wanted that, and how reluctant he was to give it.

"What is the big deal about this with you?" she asked.

"It isn't. I just . . . I don't know why you want me there. I'm not part of that whole scene. I'd just end up knocking something over or offending an art critic. I'm not going to add anything to the experience for you, Zoe. I can't talk art with these people."

She widened her eyes. "Are you kidding me? You've gotten pretty good at talking about what you like at the gallery, Jason. Aaron's work might not be your thing, but it doesn't have to be for you to be able to talk about it.

And you don't even *have* to talk about it. You can chill out by the canapés and give people the death glare so they leave you alone. I really don't care!"

"If you don't care, then why do you want me to come in the first place?"

"Because you're my boyfriend and this is what couples do. They go out of their way for each other. They don't hide just because something is out of their wheelhouse. I had no idea *I want you to be with me* was such an offensive thing to say!"

He glowered and began turning the teacup in a circle. "I just think it would be better if I steered clear. I don't belong at those things. I'll stick out like a sore thumb."

"The only thing that will stick out is your bad attitude. You know what? Forget it," she snapped. She smacked her hands down on the table, filled with the kind of helpless anger only Jason seemed to be able to produce in her. "I'll go on my own. You just stay right in your comfy house, sitting on your butt, happy because you don't have to go out of your way for anyone or anything that you don't want to."

"That's what you think?" his voice had taken on a hard edge, the kind that happened when there would be no budging him. All of Zoe's pleasure at taking him to do something she enjoyed evaporated, replaced by the same odd emptiness and frustration that she felt every time he shied away.

"I don't know what else to think," she said. "So yes. This sounds boring to you, you hate dressing up, and so you won't come. Not for me, or for anyone. I'm glad you're so happy with your own company that that's your preference most of the time, but not all of us are built that way."

"What the hell are you talking about? I'm with you

every day. What part of that do you think I'm not enjoying? If I didn't want to be with you, I wouldn't."

"I think you don't enjoy the parts that aren't on your terms," she said flatly, rising from the table to rinse out her cup. Leave it to Jason to spoil her damn tea. "If it makes you uncomfortable, you shut down. If I get too close, you shut down. If it gets too personal, you shut down. See a pattern there?"

"Bull." His voice was a rough growl, but his bluster had never scared her.

"No, truth," she said. "You like it light and casual. We have beer down by the harbor, which for the record I liked. We go eat, hang out. Mostly just the two of us. And that's all right; I can't complain. If I didn't like being with you, I wouldn't. But this is bigger, and you know it. This is an important part of my life, a *major happening in my life*, and this is when you start to get weird. I only get so far with you and you put on the brakes. When we decided to try and make this work, I didn't realize we'd hit your limits so fast."

He shoved a hand through his hair, his mouth a tense, thin line. "It's not like that. I thought we were just enjoying each other. If you had a problem I wish you would have said something instead of assuming . . ." He trailed off, tried again. "This gallery thing . . . I didn't . . . it's n-n-n-*fuck*." Jason gave her a furious look and shoved himself away from the table, grabbing his crutches and leaving the room as swiftly as she'd ever seen him do it. Zoe heard the front door slam a moment later, and the guilt landed on her like a ton of bricks. She had a knack for pushing his buttons, and she'd just purposely slammed her hand down on all of them. Though maybe she could have avoided that if he would just *talk* to her.

She put her face in her hands and closed her eyes, trying to get a handle on her feelings. It had always been like this with her. When she decided she wanted something, that was just it. She worked for it, focused on it, poured heart and soul into it until it became her reality.

Jason was different, difficult, and impossible to pin down. And she wanted him more than anything, because she'd been half in love with the man for years. It was no surprise that a few weeks had taken care of the rest. She loved him. It was the simple, inescapable truth. And while Jason might enjoy her company, she wasn't sure his heart was available. But bludgeoning him with words and wants wasn't going to get her where she wanted with him, no matter how well that worked for just about everything else in her universe. He might just need time.

Or this might be all he had to give her. It was going to be up to her to decide whether she could handle it if that was the case . . . if she could make it be enough. Except she already knew, with a sinking feeling deep in the pit of her stomach, that if things stayed as they were, it wasn't enough. Not for her.

Zoe rubbed her face, stood, and followed the path he'd taken. She headed out the front door and found him only halfway down the flagstone path through the front yard. She looked at him, the broad, strong back, the slightly lowered head as he stared at the ground, and felt a pang of longing so deep it seemed to echo in her very soul. *He's been awfully alone for a really long time.* If only she could get him to understand that he didn't have to be anymore.

She came up behind him. She wanted to wrap her arms around him but wasn't sure that would be welcome just now.

"I'm sorry," she said softly. "The show is just important to me, and I thought . . . it's something I just wanted to share with you. But if you're not comfortable being there, I'm not going to try to make you go."

He turned his head to look at her, and the weariness she saw etched on his face surprised her. "It's not that," he said.

"Then what? You can talk to me. I wish you would." She hated to fight. Bickering was an art she'd learned at her parents' knees, but real fighting . . . no. She didn't like to hurt. Not herself or anyone else.

"It's complicated," he said.

Zoe pressed her lips together and looked at him. "I don't think so," she said. "I really don't."

That seemed to take him aback. "No?"

"No. I think it's very simple. Somewhere in that handsome, thick head of yours, you're still comparing me to her. And you're scared to death that if you look too close, this is going to look like the same mistake all over again."

"It's . . . it's not . . ."

She put up a hand, resigned to having this conversation she'd wanted desperately not to have. Even if she'd known it was always going to happen. "Maybe that's an oversimplification, but that's what I see. You got stuck with a bad family and lucked into a bad marriage. The first one probably had something to do with the second, but that's not my area."

A faint, sad smile that nearly broke her heart curved the corners of his mouth. "What is your area, then?"

"Me. And my being good for you, because I'm nothing like her. Not in any way that would count."

He seemed to mull that over, turning his face a little

into the cool breeze that lifted his hair away from his face. Zoe could only watch him, finally sensing how fragile this all was. She couldn't let it slip through her fingers. She couldn't let it break.

"You don't know, though," Jason said. "You couldn't know that for sure."

"You're wrong."

One of his eyebrows arched as he looked at her again. "Because . . ."

"Because I know who you are, and I'm standing here trying to keep you instead of running away."

Jason drew in a deep breath and watched her silently for a long moment. Zoe grappled with the knots she was quietly tying herself into. If knocking some sense into him—maybe pounding on his chest while yelling at him that she loved him, so he really ought to just accept it, embrace it, and move on—would have worked, she would have balled up her fists in a heartbeat. But Jason had baggage. She was only just beginning to realize how much. And he was going to have to come to this himself, or not at all.

Jason was the only one who could decide whether to take another big risk. And whether he could take it with her.

Since it wasn't in her not to fight, though, Zoe tried one more time.

"I asked you to be with me on Saturday night because I'm happy with where I am, not because I'm unhappy. I have everything I want in this little town. I dreamed of a place like this. I know we're different people, Jason. I never thought that was a bad thing. But I'm not interested in spending all my time worrying that everything I do or say is going to get me compared to some woman

I've never met who hurt you in ways that are, frankly, not my style."

"I know," he said. "And I know you're not her, Zo. That's one of the only things I'm positive about right now. I just need to make sure I'm not setting us both up for something that's not going to make either one of us happy in the end."

She thought about it, nodded, and resigned herself to the facts. She wanted him. And he didn't know what he wanted much past the overwhelming desire to not get hurt again. All she could do was give him the space to figure it out.

"Come on," she said. "I'll take you home. I need to get at a few last-minute things for Saturday, and you . . . well, you let me know what you decide. I'll be here."

So would he, she realized as Jason gave a nod and headed for her car. The Cove was home for them both. He would never be very far away. The question was whether he would remain as he always had been— stubbornly, eternally just out of her reach.

Chapter Twenty-one

Saturday was a madhouse, and Zoe had never been so glad for the distraction.

"Why is this here? This isn't supposed to be here! Aaron, you don't get to change everything at the last minute. We worked this out weeks ago. And would you . . . oh my Lord, come here." She clicked across the floor in her mile-high heels, loving the way they looked and already regretting the state of her feet in the morning. Aaron rolled his eyes skyward and allowed her to straighten his bow tie, which he was rocking with an electric blue vest that matched the streak in his hair. He looked fantastic.

"I'm going to throw up," he announced. "Do you mind if I just do it in one of the potted plants? I won't bother anybody."

"No," Zoe said. "Meaning no, not in the potted plants, and not anywhere else. I've got medicine in the office if you want something to settle your stomach. I drank about half of it, but you're welcome to the rest."

Aaron grabbed her face and planted a noisy kiss on her lips. "Thank God. I may live after all. Where's Ryan? He was supposed to be here early. . . ."

Zoe looked around and saw his boyfriend dashing in the door looking slightly panicked. The man looked good in a suit, she thought, watching as the two of them came together in a quick embrace. Ryan looked too worried about Aaron to be shy, for once, his suit jacket stretching across his broad shoulders as he looked him over. "Are you okay? You sounded like you were going to pass out on the phone. Do you need to sit down?" He turned his head to fix Zoe with a reproachful glare. "Why is he standing up?"

"Because it's harder for him to tell everyone how close he is to death if he's sitting down," Zoe said. She patted Ryan's shoulder and fixed her gaze on Aaron. "It's on my desk. Take it or I'll make you take it."

"Yes, *ma'am.*"

She clicked away, scanning the shifting crowd for any sign of a tall, dark-haired figure possibly sporting a slight limp. It was stupid to get herself worked up this way when she seemed destined for disappointment. He hadn't said much on the way home the other day, and Jake had taken him to get his cast off yesterday. She'd had so much to do at the gallery that Zoe suspected that was more out of concern for her, but it had still hurt. That he hadn't called to give her a report afterward hurt more.

Should have told him how I felt, she thought for the hundredth time. But would that really have done any-thing? She'd said plenty. If that hadn't been enough, nothing would be. And he needed to figure this one out for himself. Besides . . . those were words she'd never said in a relationship. Maybe it was old-fashioned, or just plain chicken, but she didn't really want to say them un-less she was pretty sure she was going to hear them back.

Wherever he was with things, she didn't think Jason had quite made it there yet.

She looked at her watch and then around at the gallery. This was one dream that had come true for her, at least. The lighting was perfect, dim and intimate, and Aaron's sculptures were displayed on pedestals she'd had brought in for the occasion. A couple of the guys who played in a band that often performed at Beltane Blues were set up in a corner, and there was a bartender and an hors d'oeuvres selection that, thanks to the pink liquid she'd been chugging, made her stomach growl just thinking about it. Emma Henry, whose organizational skills had been behind most of this, was speaking to the handful of cocktail staff who stood ready to circulate. She caught Zoe's eye and gave her a thumbs-up—and the seal of approval from Emma was about the highest praise Zoe could think of. They really were ready. The rest of her friends stood in a group, ready to enjoy Aaron's success with him.

It was perfect . . . except for one thing. And that, she was just going to have to do without. Zoe looked at her watch, heard voices coming up the path. Burying her hurt, she hurried back over to Aaron and gave him a brief, tight hug. He returned it, whispering in her ear, "Thanks for all of this, Zo."

She blinked, eyes becoming suspiciously watery, and sniffed the tears back. Aaron could have shown at a much fancier venue than this, but he'd insisted. This was home, and no gallery but Two Roads would do.

"Oh, stop. You deserve all the good things headed your way," she said, and gave him a brilliant smile before she hurried away to get things started.

Almost perfect, she thought, letting herself believe that maybe he'd show up late. *Almost.*

*   *   *

Jason tugged at his tie for the umpteenth time and pushed open the door to Two Roads. The music and chatter hit him like a wave, bright and cheerful, ready to wrap around him and pull him out of the chilly night air. He wanted to just let himself go and enjoy it, but he'd been tense since this morning.

I should have told her.

The thought had occurred to him with increasing frequency over the last couple of weeks, ever since she'd asked him to come to Aaron's show. At first, he'd just wanted to put off the decision. If he pretended it wasn't happening, it was easier to ignore. That wasn't his usual tactic for dealing with things, but this was a special case. Still, there was no ignoring something that was such a big part of Zoe's life. That she wanted him involved in it was a big deal, and Jason knew it. He'd been stubbornly clinging to the idea that he was taking this slow, that he could walk away if he needed to, ever since she'd walked into his house with a pot of oregano and decided to stick around. Actually, even longer than that if he was being honest with himself.

So here he was, with a fresh haircut, the suit he dragged out for the occasional wedding, and a boatload of anxiety. He hadn't been to one of these things in years. He'd had no reason, and even less interest. Still, if it had just been a local thing, he would have pulled out the go-to suit and come along happily enough.

This, though . . . it had the potential to be messy, and he wasn't sure he was ready to find out whether he'd come far enough to handle it. He figured he had a fifty-fifty chance at getting through the night unscathed. Maybe it would be fine. Maybe Vane Duvall would have no interest in an artist like Aaron. Maybe he'd come alone.

Or maybe Jason would have to find out firsthand just how much he'd changed in the last few years . . . if at all.

Despite the crowd, it took him no time at all to spot Zoe. The woman had a magnetic pull he seemed uniquely sensitive to. She stood in a small group, her back to him, wearing a little black dress and mile-high heels. Her curls were pinned up, though a few had been allowed to fall and kiss the nape of her neck. She was beautiful, with an added sheen of glamour that made her seem even more untouchable than he'd found her the first time he'd ever walked into the gallery. She'd probably laugh if she knew just how awestruck she left him sometimes. And here, she was clearly in her element.

Nervously, he flexed his hands and reminded himself that yanking on his tie again wasn't going to do anything but mess up the tie. It wouldn't make him any more comfortable.

Of course, if you'd told her you might feel like you had an ally in here. Dumbass.

But what was he supposed to say? *Hey, my ex-wife's affair started at an art show, and so things might get weird if I show up. Is that okay?*

Except knowing Zoe, she would have said yes, then figured out a way to make it so. They would have been a unit in the face of whatever he might have to deal with. Instead, he felt very much on his own. He told himself that Zoe didn't need to be dragged into the smoking wreckage of his past. His baggage was no one's business but his own, and that was better for everyone.

Except it felt like self-serving bullshit, which he didn't have a lot of patience for.

"I knew you'd clean up well."

He turned his head to find the man of the evening,

Aaron Maclean, passing by with a small group of admirers in tow. The streak in his hair matched his vest, a look he somehow managed to make work for him.

"Yeah, showering occasionally does wonders," Jason said with a grin. "Congrats on your big . . . thing." He moved his hand around to indicate the room, but Aaron decided to take it the wrong way and started laughing.

"That's my compliment of the evening," he said. "Thanks. I'm going to tuck that one away. It's a keeper."

Jason shook his head. "You're welcome."

Aaron left him with a quick pat on the arm. "I'm glad you came. Now, go show Zoe what you did for her, big guy. She's been watching that door like a hawk."

It didn't make him feel any better about how he'd dealt with tonight. She'd worried . . . and why wouldn't she? He'd avoided her and generally been a pain in the ass without telling her why. Probably because he hadn't wanted to take a good hard look at why, either.

His weaker leg ached, but in a way that reassured him because he was actually using it again. Jason moved through the people, casting a few glances at the sculptures on display. People stood around them, admiring, discussing, sipping their drinks, and eating tiny hors d'oeuvres. It wasn't his scene—he'd been honest with Zoe about that. But it wasn't as pretentious as he'd expected.

That seemed to be a trend lately.

He came up behind her and slipped an arm around her waist, ignoring the rest of the group she was with. They were no one he recognized and no one he cared to know. He'd come here for Zoe, and the instant she responded to him, melting into his touch before she even turned, he knew he'd made the right choice tonight. He spoke softly into her ear.

"The place looks amazing. Not as good as you, though."

Her smile could have lit the entirety of the Cove. "Hey," she said. "You came." And in front of everyone, she slipped her arms around his waist and gave him a long, lingering hug that could leave no doubt in anyone's minds about what the nature of their relationship was. He tried to relax into it, but his nerves were practically crackling. She must have felt his tension, because when she pulled back to look up at him, there was a crease between her brows.

"What's wrong?" she asked quietly.

"It can wait," he replied, and hoped the hand he brushed down her back was reassuring enough. She didn't look convinced, and her expression said they'd be discussing this later—but for the first time, he wanted to talk about it. Words weren't his strong suit, though, and the ones he needed to say didn't belong here. Not in the middle of something she'd worked so hard on, on a night she deserved to enjoy. Zoe turned back to the group she'd been speaking with to introduce him. She left her arm around his waist, a small but protective gesture that gave Jason his first real smile of the night. They'd come a long way in a short time, and Zoe had no problem clearly staking out her territory. In this case, it was him.

Who would have thought?

"Everyone, this is Jason Evans. He's a park ranger here in the Cove, and he's also a patron of the gallery."

There was a flurry of interested commentary that Jason had to struggle not to find patronizing. He knew people didn't see him and think "art," but he didn't really enjoy being a novelty item. Still, he answered people's questions until the conversation turned and he was allowed to lapse back into silence.

Slowly, the tension he'd been carrying around began to leave him. The music was good, people seemed happy— the gallery was fairly thrumming with good vibes, and the crowd was dotted with locals, several of his friends among them. Jake and Sam were here, and Shane had somehow finagled himself an invite. He always did. Jason even caught a glimpse of Big Al Piche, wearing parachute pants and an REO Speedwagon shirt, holding an entire tray of miniature quiches and having an animated conversation with a tall, thin man in sunglasses as he popped them, one by one, into his mouth. They looked like they were talking about one of the paintings on the wall, but given that it was Big Al, they could just as easily have been discussing the relative merits of sweaters made out of pet hair. Or the finer points of nuclear physics.

One could never be sure. But at least he was wearing pants.

Zoe was warm where her body touched his, and the contact between them was more of a comfort than he'd expected. She didn't seem to want anything from him— no attempts at conversing about artists or styles he was unfamiliar with, no being pressed to make friends with people who couldn't have been less interested in him if they'd tried, and vice versa. No pressure to be someone he wasn't for the benefit of the crowd.

All she seemed to want was him.

Zoe had tried to tell him that, but Jason hadn't really understood that she'd meant it. Not until now. It was humbling. It was wonderful. And it made him feel even worse about holding back, making her worry.

He was a grown man. It shouldn't be so hard to wrap his head around the fact that he was finally enough for someone, just as he was.

"I'm going to go grab a drink. Do you want anything?" He kept his voice low, breathing in the warm, spicy vanilla of her perfume after he asked. She shivered just a little at his breath on her skin, and he gave her waist a gentle squeeze. He had plans for getting her out of that little black dress later on.

"No, I'm good," she said. Her hand brushed his as he pulled away, then turned to head for the small bar that had been set up.

He was waiting for the bartender to fix his water and lemon—he wasn't interested in drinking tonight—when a soft, familiar voice spoke behind him.

"Jason?"

He froze. The bartender set down the glass, offered him a smile, and turned his attention to another guest. He could feel her there, waiting, so Jason forced himself to turn around.

"Hi, Sara. How've you been?"

Zoe waited, glass in hand and half listening to Evan Marcel tell one of his rambling stories that usually ended in egregious name-dropping. She liked Evan, really . . . she liked almost everyone who was here tonight, some of whom she hadn't seen since her Atlanta days. But the show wouldn't have been the same without Jason, without his solid, comforting presence beside her. Whatever had been wrong the last few days seemed to have lifted, and she could see him beginning to relax and enjoy himself.

That was good, because between the fresh haircut and the suit, not to mention the absence of a cast or crutches, she was quite interested in continuing the celebration of the night back at her house. And he'd be so much easier to spirit away now.

She just wished she knew what had been his problem in the first place. She started to turn her head and scan the room during a lull in Evan's story when she was pulled into someone's arms, lifted off her feet, and spun around.

Zoe yelped, then laughed when she saw who it was.

"Vane! Put me down!"

He obliged, but not before she received a noisy kiss on the cheek. She feigned irritation and wiped her cheek. "I see you haven't changed." He hadn't, either. Tall and attractive, with short hair shaded silver and steel, Vane Duvall looked as though he'd just stepped out of an ad for designer suits. He was lightly tanned, the lines at the corners of his eyes the only indication that he wasn't simply a thirty-year-old who'd gone prematurely gray. She'd known him since she'd interned with his art brokerage over a summer in college, when she'd thought that might be the right direction for her. She'd decided against that particular career path but gained both a friend and an invaluable contact.

Zoe was glad to see him not just because she enjoyed him, but also because his presence was a very good omen for Aaron. Vane worked with buyers whose names would have made even Evan Marcel's jaw drop.

"I *have* changed. I've improved with age. So have you, over the last . . . what's it been, three years? That's right, because you didn't make it to the wedding. You missed a hell of a party."

"I know I did. I was trying to get this place ready to open, and going anywhere, much less St. Maarten, was pretty well out of the question." The man did tend to forget that not all of his friends had quite the same means he did. Vane looked around, blue-gray eyes taking in the gallery. Zoe watched him closely, curious about what he'd make of what she'd built. He smiled.

"You still have a great eye. I'll have to—" He stopped and frowned, his eyes anchored to a spot somewhere behind her. Zoe began to turn, puzzled.

"What's the matter?"

"Ah, it looks like it's fine. Just a little awkward. Sara's ex," he explained. It didn't register for a moment, but when it did, Zoe's eyes widened. She scanned the room with purpose this time, and when she saw Jason's tall, broad-shouldered figure over by the bar, this time she noted the small blond woman speaking with him, nearly obscured because of the way they were turned.

"Oh," Zoe said, and it was more of an exhalation than a word. Of all the things she might have expected tonight, Jason's ex-wife showing up was somewhere near the bottom, well under "Big Al removes pants, ruins evening." And his ex was married to her old friend....

It was as though all the tension Jason seemed to have let go of materialized just to sink into her own muscles. *This couldn't have been why he's been so tense about the show. He would have mentioned something this big if he'd known. He ... wouldn't he?* Suddenly, she wasn't sure.

"Hell. He's the last person I would have expected to see here. When I met Sara he seemed like he'd rather be anywhere than in a gallery. Like out chopping down trees, maybe."

Vane's voice took a moment to register. All Zoe could see was the pretty blonde, the way she looked up at Jason tentatively, then offered a smile when he said something. Jason ran a hand through his hair and dropped his head, a sweet, self-conscious gesture she'd come to find very endearing. Right this second, though, most of what she felt was ugly, ugly jealousy with a twist of righteous fury and a dash of deeply hurt feelings. If he'd known, or even suspected, that Sara would be here, why couldn't he have warned her? Why couldn't he have said *something* to her about it, instead of letting it land on her like a ton of bricks?

Zoe wanted to give him the benefit of the doubt. But looking back, it was almost impossible. *No. He knew. It's why he was going to stay away.*

The only spark of positivity she could find was that for some reason, Jason had decided to come anyway. She wanted to think he'd come for her. She thought he had. But all her pleasure drained away as she watched the two of them and the sort of questions she'd kept at bay until now began to poke at her insistently. *What if he's still carrying a torch? What if she burned him so badly he'll never get married again? What if he didn't tell me because he thought either of those things was a possibility? . . . What if . . .*

"Do you know him?" Vane asked, pulling Zoe back into the conversation. He didn't seem particularly concerned anymore, though he was keeping an eye on things, she noted. "Jason, his name is. Jason—"

"Evans. I know," Zoe interjected.

Vane snorted. "Big patron of the arts, is he? Or is he just here for the free bar? Sara said the locals around here are pretty . . . local."

She just stared at him. "Vane. He's here for me."

She saw the truth sink in, slowly at first, then all at

once. To his credit, his cheeks turned several shades of red. "Oh. *Oh.*" He looked beyond her again and winced. "Oh. I'm sorry, Zoe, I didn't know. I . . ." He laughed nervously, a sound she wasn't used to from him. "What are the chances, right? God, I bet you've gotten an earful about me."

Zoe shook her head slowly. "No. He hasn't mentioned you at all, actually. He's barely mentioned her. I didn't even realize the connection until just now."

Vane's brows lifted. "Really? Huh. That's . . . unnecessarily awkward."

"No kidding."

He looked in his wife's direction again. "That looks pretty awkward, too. Should we butt in?"

Zoe shrugged, and Vane sighed. "Yeah, maybe not. I don't want to get punched."

"He's not like that," she said quickly, and she could hear the hard edge to her voice. Even angry at Jason— and she knew she had not yet begun to explore just how angry she was about this—she was ready to bare her teeth over him.

Vane blew out a breath and rocked on his heels. "Well, I guess we can safely say I know nothing about him. So . . ." He shook his head. "I'm sorry, Zoe. I can leave if this is going to be an issue."

"Absolutely not," Zoe said quickly. She stepped closer to Vane, took his hand, and gave it a reassuring squeeze. "You didn't know. I didn't know. And even if I had, I still would have wanted you to come. If no punches were thrown in the past, I'm sure none will be tonight. Jason looks tough, but he's pretty civilized. Besides, this was all years ago. He mentioned it wasn't an ugly divorce."

"No." Vane appeared to think that over, maybe remembering. "No," he said again, "it was quick and easy, really. I didn't get the impression either of them was very happy. Not that I helped fix that." His smile was rueful. "Sara and I both fell hard. He was collateral damage. I could apologize, but it wouldn't be entirely honest. And I doubt he wants it, anyway. Besides, he's clearly doing just fine. Impeccable taste in women—I'll say that for him."

"Well. Obviously," Zoe said, and Vane chuckled. She wished she felt like laughing, too, but she was afraid if she tried that it would just come out as a scream. *Of all the nights . . .*

"Oh, here she comes," Vane said, brightening further. There was more than a hint of uncertainty in his eyes, though, when he refocused on Zoe. "Would you, ah, like to meet my wife?"

She hated that it was even a question. The divorce seemed to have been slightly messier than she'd thought, but Jason hadn't exactly been forthcoming, either. And Vane, for any faults he might have, had always been a friend. Right now, she had to separate out the pieces of her life and deal with them individually. If she didn't, the rest of the night would turn into the kind of howling mess she'd had nightmares about for weeks. She hadn't had time to process any of this. *Thanks, Jason, for trusting me with this very important info. I might have enjoyed having it before it was hitting me in the head.*

"Of course I want to meet her," Zoe said. "You're as happy as I've seen you, Vane. I'm guessing she's responsible."

"She is," Vane said, smiling.

The petite blonde joined them, and Zoe got her first good look at the woman who'd once been married to the man she loved. She wasn't much bigger than Zoe, with honey-colored hair that fell in a chic bob, big blue eyes, and china-doll features. She was everything Zoe had hoped she wouldn't be, and though she knew it was ridiculous to be jealous, she couldn't quite help the knot that formed in the pit of her stomach.

"Sara, this is Zoe Watson." He winked at Zoe. "I've told her all about you," he said.

"Oh Lord," Zoe replied, and hoped she looked at least a little amused.

"Hi. I've heard about nothing but you for two days. Vane was so excited to come," Sara said. The tentative way she spoke, her eyes flickering between her and her husband, told Zoe that this woman already knew about her and Jason. What had he said? She wanted to stalk off, grab him by the collar, and ask, but if anything would kill the party, it was that.

"Anything bad or illegal he told you isn't true," Zoe said. "Mostly."

That earned her a more earnest smile, and Zoe sighed inwardly at the fact that the woman was lovely. Because of course she was. Not that it really mattered, she reminded herself. *Obsessed with toile,* she thought. And though it was unkind, it made her feel a little better. She would bet that Vane had . . . developed . . . her taste since then. She couldn't picture the man's big, modern apartment done up in pastoral prints. Zoe turned her head to see where Jason had gone, but he'd vanished from where he'd been standing. She had to fight the urge to stomp her foot.

"He, um, said to tell you he'd call you afterward," Sara said, and her tone was apologetic. "I'm really sorry. I never expected to see him at something like—"

"Something like this, yes, I know," Zoe interrupted, irritated. "Being underestimated is one of his special talents, seems like." *Right along with being evasive.*

"That's true," Sara replied, surprising her. Zoe looked at her sharply, but the woman seemed to be dead serious. Vane looped his arm around his wife's waist, and in that instant they were a unit, a matched set. Zoe couldn't picture this woman with Jason . . . and that was just as well.

"He seems a lot happier," Sara said. She looked quickly at her husband, but Vane looked unfazed. He would be, Zoe knew. The man was hard to ruffle, and if he was to Sara's taste, then no wonder Jason hadn't been. The two were like night and day. "I hope it's all right to say, but I'm glad he seems so much happier. He's a good guy. He deserves some happiness."

Zoe knew immediately that Sara was talking about his family, and oh, how she would have loved to compare notes on that. But this was neither the time nor the place, and she had wanted to try to catch him before he pulled a Batman and vanished into the shadows.

So all she said was, "It's definitely all right. I think so, too. It's wonderful to meet you, Sara. If you two can just excuse me for a second, I need to—"

"Understood," Vane said. "Good luck. We'll be here. Still proud of you, Zoe. This is really something."

Touched, she tucked the compliment away to take out and cherish later. "Thanks," she said, and hurried off, dodging guests and hurrying out the front door into the cold air. It was a shock against her bare legs and arms, but the shock lasted only a moment. She saw Jason's rapidly retreating figure heading down the sidewalk, no doubt to where his truck was parked farther down on the square.

The door shut behind her.

"Jason," she said, not a shout but loud enough for him to hear. He wasn't moving fast yet, fortunately. He stopped short, not turning around to look at her, and she gritted her teeth. Her heels clicked on the pavers as she headed up the walk and out the little gate. Just being this close finally brought the anger on, mixed with hurt into a toxic brew of emotion. She only really had one question.

"Why?"

He did turn then, slowly, and she could see he was battling some anger of his own. "I knew it would have been better if I didn't come tonight. And I see you know Vane Duvall."

Zoe's mouth dropped open. "Are you kidding me? Vane's been a friend for years."

"Sure. He's a popular guy."

Jason's voice had taken on the low, growly quality it did when he was angry, and Zoe found herself taking up the old stance—arms crossed, legs slightly apart, chin up—that she'd used so many times with Jason in the gallery. He responded in kind, stiffening and glaring down at her.

"No," Zoe said. "You don't get to be mad. I'm not the one who didn't trust you enough to tell you that my ex-wife was going to be at your biggest event *ever*. Do you know how much easier this would have been if you'd just *told* me?"

"I wasn't sure she'd be here," Jason hedged, glowering at her. "Why would I make a big deal out of something I wasn't even sure about?"

"Oh, you had a pretty good idea," Zoe said, "or you wouldn't have been acting so weird about this. So much for *those just aren't my people, I won't fit in—*"

"I don't," he snapped. "I'm no Aaron Maclean or Vane Duvall. I'm just a guy who likes to clear brush and drag dirt around on his boots. You knew that going in. Trying to make me into something I'm not—"

Zoe's eyes widened. "I'm what, now?" She threw up her hands, utterly exasperated. He had the mulish glint in his eye he got when he was digging into a position, and she had neither the time nor the energy to wade through this right now. Not on what was supposed to be a good night. "Let me get this straight. You've made the leap from not giving me a heads-up on your ex-wife situation to me wanting to change you. Well, you know what, Jason? That's not you coming out of your mouth. That's your mother."

"The hell it is."

"The hell it isn't." She could feel her temperature rising. "You've moved past all that in some ways, but in others, not even a little. You hate being stuffed in that 'big, woodsy ranger man' box, but you're scared to death to get outside of it. You're afraid life outside of the box is going to be some kind of enormous failure. That's what your biggest problem is," Zoe continued. "You're scared that people like your mom and Sara . . . you're afraid they're right about you. So you reinforce the walls of that box and sit in it, and people like me get to try to pull you out. Well, you know what? I'm done."

His eyes were impossible to read in the dark. He stared silently at her, and Zoe felt sick to her stomach. This wasn't a fight she wanted to have tonight. Or ever, actually. But some part of her knew it would always have happened. It was just a matter of when.

Every frustration she'd had with him welled up and spilled over. He was so much more than what he'd been told. But she couldn't force him to see it, much less to embrace it.

"That's it?" he asked quietly. "'I'm done'? I know I should have told you she might be here. It was a dumb move. But I figured that my divorce, the affair, all of it was years ago, and it's nothing you need to deal with. We were all grown-ups about it."

"Damn it, Jason, it's not about needing to deal with it. It's about *wanting* to." She would have cuffed him upside the head to knock some sense into him if she'd thought for one second it would have helped get that stubborn expression off his face. "When are you going to get that I care about how you feel? I'm not just here for the good stuff. I'm here for the bad things, too, or I would be."

"It's nothi—"

"Don't tell me it's nothing one more time," she snapped. She pointed at him, a habit she'd picked up from her mother when she was at the end of her rope. "And don't ever tell me I've tried to change you. That pressure? Not coming from me. I didn't want you here to laugh at, or because I wanted to show you off like a shiny new toy. I invited you because I . . ." And even now, she couldn't say it. Jason wasn't the only one who was afraid of something. Zoe was desperately afraid she would say the words in her heart only to have them rejected . . . or worse, thrown back in her face. "Because I care about you," she finished. Then she shook her head, looking around at the night lit by lamps and stars and a low-hung moon. She needed to get back inside, tend to her party, necessary even if all her interest in it had fled. She locked eyes with him in the dim light cast by the streetlights. "You go run off and tell yourself whatever you like, if it helps," Zoe said. "But I only ever wanted one thing from you, and it wasn't turning you into somebody you aren't." He stared stonily back at her, and Zoe felt her heart sinking into her toes.

He's really walking away, she thought, and she felt the hot sting of angry tears prickling at her eyes. She couldn't do this right now, even if she never got another chance. She just didn't have any more fight in her tonight.

Jason's voice was slightly hoarse when he spoke again. They weren't words she wanted to hear. "I don't know what you want, Zoe."

She sighed, dropped her head forward for a moment, and then shifted her weight from foot to foot. She was tired, right down to the bone, and she had a long night ahead of her yet. She thought wistfully of the tea her mama made her when she was feeling low, and of the big blankets on the featherbeds in her parents' house, and of the creek this time of year, and the still-sultry air.

"I just want *you,*" Zoe said. "The guy who was laughing and having a good time earlier. The one who belongs at this show because he belongs in Harvest Cove. Because he belongs with me." It ought to be the simplest thing in the world, she thought sadly. And yet here they were.

"Damn it, Zoe, you have me," he growled.

"No. I don't think I really do." The air between them still crackled with anger, but Zoe took a step back, lowering her arms to disengage. Jason simply watched her, his wolf's eyes telling her nothing. She needed some time to sort all of this out. And, she suspected, so did he.

"Go home, Jason," she said. "That's what I'm doing after all this."

He looked past her, to the gallery stuffed with people having a much better time than the two of them were, and his jaw tensed. When he spoke, it was careful, slow. He was more upset than he was letting on. That, she thought, made two of them.

"Damn it, Zoe, we're not done talking about this. You don't understand."

"Then *help me* understand."

Jason's jaw flexed. "I don't . . . even know how to start."

Neither did she, but she was so tired from trying to puzzle him out. When she spoke, Zoe tried to sound cool, so much cooler than she felt. "Then we've talked enough for one night. I have to get back. You want me, I just told you where to find me." She looked at him a moment longer, willing him to say the one, simple thing that would heal every crack in what they'd been building together. But there was only silence, and then a sigh.

"Fine. Whatever you want," he said. "I'll see you." He turned and stalked away without another word, and Zoe had a single, wistful thought before she did the same.

If only.

Chapter Twenty-two

He needed air.

Jason walked down his road, shoulders hunched into his coat. The air was brisk, the sky a shade of gray that perfectly matched his mood. His leg was tired and sore, but just feeling it working again was more than enough to keep him from complaining. Rosie pranced ahead of him, nose up to sniff the breeze, panting as though she hadn't a care in the world. He was glad one of them felt that way.

He hadn't been able to sleep, tossing and turning and finally managing to doze at about four a.m. It hadn't lasted, and he had enough coffee in his system this morning that slicing open a vein would probably smell like Brewbaker's, the coffee shop downtown. It hadn't perked him up any. Though Zoe would probably tell him that Ents just weren't hardwired for perky.

Zoe. He shouldn't have left last night. He knew it now, and he'd known it almost as soon as he'd walked through his door. He'd gone there because he wanted her. He'd left because he was . . . in the way, he told himself. Or because he didn't want to have to socialize anywhere near Vane Duvall.

He told himself these things, but by three a.m., he was too tired to do anything but cut through his own bullshit. He didn't give a damn about Vane or Sara or the divorce anymore. She was right.

As soon as Sara had found him last night, it had been like stepping into the past. Not in what he'd once felt for her, but in how it had felt to lose her. To know that nothing he might do would ever be enough to have what he most wanted—a love that lasted, a family, a real home. In those moments, all he'd been able to see was Zoe. And instead of putting that ugly rush of nostalgia where it belonged, he'd panicked. He'd let his own fear convince him that nothing had changed.

But everything had changed. And right after he got Rosie home he was heading over to her place to tell her that. He just had to figure out how to do it without getting the door shut in his face.

His steps slowed as Jason finally let himself think the words that had been hovering at the back of his mind since around the time she'd pulled out that damn notebook and given him a pop quiz about his life over enough Chinese food to feed an army.

I love her.

And right on the heels of that: *Shit*. He had really screwed things up.

His phone went off in his pocket, startling him. It was early on a Sunday for anybody to be trying to get ahold of him. He had a brief, wild hope that it was Zoe . . . but the number, while familiar, wasn't hers.

"Jake?"

"What are you *doing*?"

His cousin's voice was grim, annoyed, and about as unsunny as it ever got. It wasn't hard to guess what he was calling about. But the possibility of a lecture made Jason far less interested in acknowledging it.

"Walking Rosie. You?"

"Reassuring my wife that you're not going to stomp Zoe's heart into a million pieces because then she'll have to kick your ass. That's a direct quote."

Jason thought about slim, not particularly tall Sam and had to try not to smile, despite everything. "I'd like to see her try, just for the laughs, but no."

"Then I repeat, what are you *doing*? Is this about Sara?"

"No. It's about me being a stubborn jackass. I'm . . . working through it," Jason replied.

"You want to define that for me?" Jake asked.

"No. I just want to head to Zoe's after this and try to fix what I broke. I panicked. The stupidity snowballed." He wished it sounded a little funnier, but he couldn't find a lot of humor in it. This was the first time he hadn't had some sense of where he stood with Zoe. The relief that came from finally just accepting how he felt vanished in the face of the knowledge that he might have done irreparable damage.

"You're not going to find her there," Jake said.

"Work, then?" But there was something in his cousin's voice that said the situation had changed. In his weird, twisted quest to prove to himself that he and Zoe couldn't possibly work, he had finally made headway. With her. "Where is she, Jake?"

"She went home. *Home* home. Sam and Aaron are running things while she's gone. That's what I called to tell you. That's why I wanted to know what you were trying to do. She left early this morning."

Jason stopped walking, closed his eyes. "Shit."

"Yeah, exactly."

"How long is she gone for?" he asked.

"I don't know, and I'm not sure she does, either. Sam said she seemed tired and sad, neither of which is like Zoe. You did a number on her. You know I love you, man, but—"

"I know. Believe me, I know." Jason took a breath. When he exhaled, a small vapor cloud appeared in the cold air. "I love her."

He couldn't tell whether the sound Jake made was a groan, a relieved sigh, or some combination of the two. "Finally. You finally figured that out. Well then, will you get off your ass and go tell her that?"

"I'm not sure that's going to be enough."

"You dumbass," Jake said, but there was affection in it now. "What makes you think she wants anything else?"

All at once, Jason remembered the conversation he'd had with Tommy the other day. How his brother didn't seem to be capable of understanding how simple Jason's needs actually were when it came to the two of them. Tommy just never really listened. All he'd wanted was a brother.

All Zoe wanted was him. How many times had she told him that?

It wasn't a great feeling to realize he might have inherited a little of the pigheadedness floating around his branch of the family tree, but recognizing it was the first step to fixing it, he guessed.

"You're right," Jason said. Jake had the audacity to laugh.

"Can you say that again so I can get a recording of it?"

"Not a chance."

"Then do something about this big revelation. Sam

can tell you where to find her if you let her yell at you first."

"That seems fair." But what he really wanted was to get home, throw some crap in a bag, and head out immediately so he could find Zoe and let her yell at him. Maybe if he called her . . .

No, that wasn't good enough. Not this time. She needed to understand exactly how much he wanted her in his life. Words wouldn't do it.

"Good. Then get your butt in gear. I'll see you soon." He paused before hanging up. "She's good for you, you know. You can make a better family than the one you got."

Jason smiled, even as his adrenaline kicked in, demanding he do something, find her, *now*. "It wasn't all bad," he said. "I kept the good parts."

"I'm blushing a manly blush right now."

"Jackass." Jason snorted. "I'll be over soon. And . . . thanks."

"Anytime."

Jason ended the call, then looked at the little dog who was very engrossed in sniffing a pile of soggy leaves. "Let's go get Zoe, girl," he said. It was as though he'd lit a fire under her. At the sound of the name of one of her favorite people, the little dog wagged her tail furiously, barked, and tried to run farther down the road . . . in the wrong direction. With a soft huff of laughter, Jason got her turned around and set off at a brisk pace, long legs eating up the distance.

All he had to give her was everything. And this time, if he could just find her, tell her, Jason knew it would be enough.

*   *   *

Zoe leaned against the base of a tree, face turned up to the sun. A pair of mockingbirds tried to outdo each other with original songs somewhere overhead, and the cicadas buzzed lazily, the sound blending with the occasional croak of a frog. It might be fall back in New England, but here in Georgia even late September was full of long, sultry days and muggy nights.

She was in cutoff shorts and a tank top, her feet in some ancient flip-flops she kept here to bang around in. This was home, where she had nowhere to be and nobody to impress, and Zoe had felt it wrap around her like a warm blanket as soon as she'd stepped off the plane and into her parents' arms. That was when she'd finally let the tears go, all the tension she'd built up inside leaking out until she was blissfully empty.

He hadn't called. Her phone was currently stuffed in the bottom of a dresser drawer, and Sam had the house phone number in case anything big came up, but Zoe had still snuck a few peeks to see whether Jason had tried to get in touch yesterday.

Nothing. So she decided to take a break from her little electronic nightmare, at least for today, and just try to decompress. Maybe Jason was thinking. Lord knew he did enough of that. Too much, usually. And he would think through all of this as deliberately as he did everything else . . . because the man was Treebeard, and he wouldn't be hurried. Not for anything or anyone.

She sighed softly, willing all this tension away. James had dragged her out to the creek to go fishing, like they had when they were kids. About an hour into it, though, he'd gone back up to the house to get food and hadn't returned, which was also the same as when they were kids. But Zoe found the silence and the sunshine soothing, even if her thoughts traced a familiar path hundreds of miles away.

She heard footsteps, the snap of a twig, and didn't bother to open her eyes. "I hope you brought enough for both of us," she warned him. "I'm not above tattling."

"Your mom handed me a picnic basket. I think there's a whole pie in there. If that's not enough, I'm not sure what to tell you."

Her eyes flew open. "Jason?" She whipped her head around to find him standing there in some of his ratty old cargo shorts and a Beltane Blues T-shirt, carrying a picnic basket and looking about as good as anything she'd ever seen. She blinked, wondering whether she'd fallen asleep, but he stayed stubbornly solid.

"I would have been here yesterday, but I figured flying was a better idea than trying to drive that many hours with my leg just out of the cast. Your brother came and got me from the airport," Jason said. His eyes, glinting gold in the light, searched her face. "I hope that's okay."

"He said he went to get lunch!" It was all she could manage to say. She couldn't quite believe that she was looking at Jason, *here*—that he'd come all this way. And that her family had known.

"I'm going to kill James," she said. Jason winced.

"Zoe. I know you're angry with me, and you have every right to be, but please hear me out. I need to tell you that I love you—*oof!*"

She jumped at him, wrapping her arms and legs around him with a high-pitched cry and hanging on tight. She felt his arms come around her, felt him squeeze her tighter as he buried his face in her neck. This was all she'd wanted. This right here.

"I panicked," he said. "I was an idiot."

"I know you're an idiot," she said, pressing kisses to his hair, his temples, his cheeks. "It's part of the reason I love you. I can't believe you came all this way! And so *fast*!"

"What are you trying to say?" he asked, pulling his head back to look at her. "That I'm slow? Ent-like, maybe?"

"No. Maybe. I kind of thought you'd *call* if you did anything." She smiled and shook her head. "But this is so much better. How . . . ? Sam."

"She loves you. And she knows I do, too. Or maybe she just got tired of Rosie barking at her while I tried to explain how much I love you. Either way, she told me how to get in touch with your parents. When I called that first time, I got James." He smirked. "I like your brother."

"I like him, too, when he's not sneaking around planning things behind my back. I might have to forgive him for this, though." She kissed him again, on the tip of his nose. "Did you bring Rosie, too?"

"I almost did. She wanted to see you. She doesn't handle disappointment very well."

"Like owner, like canine?"

"Something like that." He kissed her chin, then her lips, lightly at first and then more deeply, drawing her into a slow and thorough kiss that had heat curling through her from head to toe. When he finally pulled back, her heart was pounding in her chest. It was the look in his eyes, though, that made the moment complete.

"Zoe," Jason said, his voice the gentle rumble she heard even in her dreams, "I love you."

She smiled, the words going straight to her heart. "You said that. I don't think I'm ever going to get tired of hearing it."

"Good," he said. "Because if it's okay with you, I'd like to keep saying it for, say, the rest of my life."

She stilled, searching his face for some clue about whether he was saying what she thought he was. "You . . . would?"

"I think I've loved you since you threatened to chase me out of the gallery with your vacuum cleaner. You're beautiful and perfect and everything I ever wanted. Stay with me. Argue with me. Make me drink tea and let me hold you when you sleep. If not for me, do it for poor Rosie. She'd be lost without you."

Zoe laughed, laying a hand on the side of his face. "For Rosie, huh?"

"Yeah. Though I'd prefer if you did it for me. I'll probably track in dirt and earn my nickname on a regular basis. I didn't get much of a family. It's hard for me to let people in. But when you left . . . well, I figured out that the only thing I'm really scared of is having to live the rest of my life without you. What we can make together is better than anything I ever left behind. Marry me, Zoe Watson." Then he grinned. "Your mama promised she'd come for Christmas if you did."

Zoe burst out laughing. "What is this, blackmail? How dare you offer me everything I ever wanted. Ganging up on me . . . I'm going to have to think about this. *Marry you* . . . Hang on, now." She kissed him long and hard, love filling her up, making her complete in a way she hadn't realized she needed until she met Jason. The life she'd been building in the Cove was a wonderful one, but it had felt unfinished. She knew there was so much more to come now that she had him to share it with.

"I will," Zoe said, her mouth a breath away from his, and saw her future in his eyes. She smiled. "I will."

Read on for a preview
of the next book in the Harvest Cove Series,

COME ON CLOSER

Available from Signet Eclipse in March 2016

"You have frosting on your nose."

Larkin O'Neill rubbed her forearm across her face without looking up. The fluffy clouds she was piping onto the top of the three-layer cake had to look *just so*, and a little food on her face was the least of her concerns. "Better?"

"Well . . . it's at least more evenly distributed."

Larkin grinned and squeezed the piping bag, finishing the second cloud. "Cool. I like symmetry." There had been a time not long ago when Larkin would have found being observed by the perfectly put together half of the Henry sisters a little unnerving—and she didn't fluster easily. Now, though, Emma was a friend, which made her a welcome distraction. Larkin loved to talk while she baked. Or decorated. Or . . . Well, mostly she just loved to talk, provided the company was good.

One of her favorite things about Petite Treats, her little bakery on Harvest Cove's main square, was the ready availability of good company.

Larkin stepped back, planted her hands on her hips, and studied her creation.

"Is it done?" Emma asked, tilting her head as she gave the cake a thorough once-over. "I haven't seen you make one like this before."

Larkin glanced at her and smiled. Even in the cold, miserable depths of February, Emma Henry managed to look as fresh and bright as a spring daisy. Her dark brown hair was pulled up into a bun, and she wore a dress—which in this weather demonstrated a level of commitment to style that Larkin knew she would never be able to muster—of white wool, with a thin black belt, black tights, and a pair of cute little snow boots that Larkin suspected would be neither little nor cute if she bought them in her own size. The entire effect was charming. It also required, in her opinion, entirely too much work to pull off.

Larkin feared she was doomed to wear ripped jeans forever. *Oh well. I'd rather be comfortable and smell like a cookie.*

"Almost done. Can't forget the most important part." Larkin returned to the table, opened a small plastic package, and set about bending a sweet-and-sour rainbow to arch between the whipped cream clouds. When it was done, she made a fist. "*Yessss.* Rainbow cake achieved! I do good work."

Emma laughed. "It *is* adorable."

Larkin admired the tall, cylindrical cake. The design was simple: three layers, with pale yellow buttercream frosting setting off the sugar confetti scattered about the bottom third of the cake and a cheerful rainbow at the top. Once it got where it was going, the cake would sit on a short pastel pink pedestal with scalloped edges, a nod to the gender of Brynn's soon-to-be-niece. And, of course, there would be more sugar confetti. There was always room for more sugar confetti.

"I love it," she said with a nod. "I've only done this cake a couple of times before, but it's so cute for a baby shower. I'm just glad Brynn agreed with me."

"Brynn has good taste," Emma said. "And she really wants to make this a nice shower for her cousin. I still think she's crazy for having it at her house, but—"

"Oh, it'll be fine," Larkin said, waving her hand. "Her house is super cute, and there are only, what, ten people going? Little party, little house, little cake, big pile of presents . . . awesome. I just have to get this over there before she starts to worry." She popped the top onto her cake carrier, gathered the few items she'd need to finish up at Brynn's, and pulled her apron off over her head. "Want to come with? We can probably talk her into a mimosa in the kitchen before we have to clear out."

Brynn Parker was Emma's assistant at her event-planning company, Occasions by Emma, and Larkin had worked with the bubbly redhead often enough that they'd been friendly long before they'd gotten around to actually hanging out. Brynn and her employer were two peas in a pod in a lot of ways, Larkin thought with a smile—bright, beautiful, driven, and weirdly addicted to uncomfortable shoes. Though, as she'd discovered these past few months, Emma was substantially better at karaoke than her counterpart.

"Can't. Wish I could," Emma replied. "I've got the setup for an evening wedding to deal with, and Seth is making us a late dinner and renting movies."

"He's cooking? Seth doesn't cook." Emma's fiancé had some fine qualities—and he was a sexy thing to boot—but Larkin had never seen the man do anything in the kitchen that required more than the use of the microwave.

Emma frowned lightly, looking perturbed. "He bought a cookbook. And groceries. And then when I tried to look in the bags, he *physically removed* me from the kitchen."

Larkin smiled. "Aw. He wants to make food for you."

"He swears he knows how. I just hope he doesn't make a fire for me instead. I don't think we can handle another man who burns water in this family."

"Poor Jake," Larkin laughed. Emma's sister, Sam, was married to Jake Smith, the local vet. Nice guy. Legendarily bad cooking skills. He did keep trying, but the jury was out on whether that was a good thing. "So that's why you came to see me today," she said, arching an eyebrow. "You got kicked out."

"That's not the *only* reason," Emma said. "I also heard you had cookies. Big, chocolaty chocolate chip cookies"—she grinned—"and I had to get a couple of things from the apartment."

"Oh, I see how it is. I'm being used for witty repartee and baked goods. Mostly baked goods." Larkin heaved an exaggerated sigh. "I assume you saw the cookies on your way in."

"I may or may not have bought a bag of them for myself, which may or may not be sitting behind the counter with Aimee as we speak."

"Hmm." Larkin brushed her hands absently down her shirt. "The weeks I have chocolaty chocolate chip cookies are the weeks I wonder why I ever bother to make any other flavors. This is a town of chocoholics."

"This is a world of chocoholics. Don't act like you're

immune. I've seen you get into the batter while you're working."

Larkin snorted. "I'm powered by cake batter and cookie dough. I deny nothing. So, have you decided what you're going to do with the apartment yet? I can ask around if you're looking for a renter."

"I might be." Emma huffed a stray lock of hair out of her face. "I don't want to sell it. That's definite. It's right above the shop, and I'm attached."

"You also want to keep some control over who's banging around up there. I would, too," Larkin said.

Emma had moved in with Seth just before Christmas, leaving her cozy apartment mostly furnished but generally unoccupied. It was so convenient to work that Larkin might have been tempted to relocate, but the kitchen was way too small. Even though she did most of her baking right here in the shop, she still liked to have space for it at home. Her own little house might not be a palace, but it had enough room for her to spread out the way she liked.

It was more than she'd had growing up. And that was more than enough.

"I feel funny thinking of anyone else up there," Emma admitted. "But I'm going to have to get used to it." She offered Larkin a small, self-deprecating smile. "We all know how good I am at change."

"You've got all kinds of change going on. You're great with change. This is just a really big one." Larkin walked around the corner of the stainless-steel table and wrapped her arms around Emma, propping her chin on the shorter woman's head. "Do you need a song?"

"Oh God." Emma's voice was muffled. "No."

"I think you need a song."

"Please. Please no." But the "no" ended in a desperate giggle, so Larkin began to rock Emma back and forth. She heard a groan.

"Don' worry," she crooned, "'bout a thing. You know why, Emma?"

"Um—"

"'Cause every little thing! Is gonna be all right!" Larkin sang, increasing her volume to make up for the fact that she wasn't exactly on key.

"Larkin, Bob Marley is rolling in his grave right now," Emma mumbled into Larkin's arm.

Larkin continued signing as if she couldn't hear a word Emma said.

"You are totally losing customers right now." Emma was laughing again, allowing herself to be rocked from side to side.

Larkin stumbled sideways, and the two of them yelped as she crashed them, as gently as possible, into the counter. A stack of measuring cups tipped over, clattering to the floor. Larkin got one look at Emma's mussed hair and amused, disgruntled expression before throwing back her head and laughing. It was only a second or two before Emma joined her.

They were noisy enough that the male voice they heard was less of a shock than it might have been.

"Why don't I ever get invited to these things?"

Larkin took a split second to brace herself before she turned her head. Even then, it was hard not to make some sort of stupid yummy noise. It didn't seem to matter how many times she was exposed to him—and that was plenty, since being underfoot was one of his natural talents—the man only seemed to get better looking. He loomed in the doorway, his big athletic frame seeming just a little too large for his surroundings. His stance was relaxed, thumbs hooked in the pockets of his jeans, and he wore a classic, stylish wool coat open over a plain T-shirt. Melting snow puddled around his boots. Larkin forced herself to meet his gaze, pretending she hadn't taken yet another mental snapshot of his square jaw, the dusting of freckles across the bridge of his nose, the short crop of dark red hair that spiked up, just a little, and probably on purpose. Somewhere in the recesses of her mind, there was a gallery dedicated entirely to Shane Sullivan, God of Inappropriate Hotness and General Bad Idea, and that was where the snapshot went, to be savored later when no one could ask her why she was staring off into space and smiling like an idiot.

His deep-set eyes crinkled at the corners as he grinned at her, and Larkin offered what she hoped was a cheeky smile to him. Even though she was surrounded by baked goods, there was nothing in the shop she would rather take a bite out of than Shane. That was a problem. *He* was a problem. And because Shane liked being a problem more than just about anything, he would continue to plague her until the day she cracked, threw herself at him, and demanded he take her right here among the pastries.

Not that she had any fantasies about that sort of thing. Or an entire collection of them with only slight variations. No sir, she did not.

"You don't get invited because you do such a good job inviting yourself," Larkin said, releasing Emma from her clutches and laughing as her friend tried to smooth down her hair. "I didn't realize I was having a party back here. Did somebody kick you out of your house, too?"

"Not recently." He eyed Emma. "Trouble in paradise?"

"No. I was kicked out with love, and the promise of a gourmet meal later." Emma straightened her dress and turned her attention back to Larkin. "I'll call you tomorrow and tell you if the house burned down. Thanks for the, ah ... whatever that was."

"They were good vibes, and you're welcome. Don't eat all the cookies at once."

"No promises," Emma replied with a laugh. "Bye, Shane." He moved aside to let Emma pass, then took a few steps farther into the kitchen. He glanced behind him, through the doorway to the front of the shop.

"She still doesn't like me," he said.

"Emma? Sure she does." Actually, Larkin was pretty sure that Emma's feelings about Shane fell more into the benign ambivalence category these days, but it was at least an improvement over active dislike. And it wasn't like Emma was alone in being less than warm and fuzzy on the subject of Shane. His mouth tended to be as big as he was, and he had a reputation among the female population of Harvest Cove, and the surrounding towns, for being ... well, kind of a jerk. Kind of a *complete* jerk.

It made his appeal to her that much more mysterious.

Larkin had plenty of experience with the big mouth and zero personal evidence of his tendency to go through a string of women, but she had to believe there was some basis in fact there. The guy couldn't get a date to save his life these days. He seemed to have stopped trying.

The man was trouble, the spoiled only child of one of the town's founding families, in line to inherit daddy's law firm when the elder Sullivan decided he would rather play golf all year instead of just half. Shane had been handed everything he'd ever wanted, and he could buy most of the rest. He was a brat, and she didn't like brats.

ALSO AVAILABLE FROM

KENDRA LEIGH CASTLE

FOR THE LONGEST TIME

The Harvest Cove Series

After a perfect storm of events leaves Sam high, dry, and jobless, she has to head home to Harvest Cove to regroup. Growing up, she was the town misfit, and a brief high school romance that resulted in heartbreak made her realize she was never going to fit in.

Life's been good to Jake Smith, but Sam's homecoming makes him question his choices. The sharp-tongued beauty was never a good fit for the small community, but he's never forgotten her—or how good they were together. While she makes it clear she's not about to repeat the past, Jake's determined to convince her to give him—and Harvest Cove—a second chance.

"Harvest Cove will wrap around your heart like a snuggly blanket on a chilly autumn day."
—*USA Today* bestselling author Katie Lane

Available wherever books are sold or at
penguin.com

S0572

This was now a mantra she repeated to herself multiple times a day, but it hadn't worked yet . . . because no matter what she did, she couldn't seem to help liking Shane. Worse, he knew it. Otherwise he wouldn't darken her doorway as often as he did and beg for food like a big, obnoxious puppy.

A puppy she continued to feed. And hang out with. And occasionally grab a burger with when neither of them were doing anything.

Larkin sighed.

"Got any spare cupcakes?" he asked, as though he knew what she was thinking about. "If you're testing out anything new, my taste buds are available."

She gave him a look, and hated herself just a little when she turned to pick up a small cupcake box from the counter. It was Saturday. He always came in on Saturday. And when she'd been baking this morning, she'd done a test batch of a new recipe and put a few aside for him. His smile when he realized what she'd done instantly turned her insides to mush.